P9-CFE-057

CLOSE ENCOUNTER OF THE WORST KIND

Tess had just crossed Park Avenue when she noticed a long, salmon-colored car with dark brown trim make a sudden U-turn on the one-way street, fishtail to a stop with a great squealing of brakes, then make another U and head back in the right direction. Well, downtown Baltimore, with its warren of one-way streets, often had that effect on out-of-town drivers.

Two blocks later, as Tess turned north on St. Paul, the same car passed her, heading south. Again, the brakes whined and the car almost spun out on the slick road. She had a sinking sensation. Although she walked very quickly, she hadn't covered an entire block before the car reappeared, stopping short of where Tess stood.

The front passenger window rolled down slowly and a pair of oversize sunglasses studied Tess. Then the rear passenger door opened, creaking horribly.

"Miss Monaghan?" The voice, thin and reedy, came from the back seat. "Spike Orrick's niece? We saw him before he went into the hospital." A low, rusty chuckle. "*Just* before. Miss Monaghan, your uncle has something that belongs to us. It is ours, and we want it back. Do you know where we can find this thing?"

The man on the passenger side smiled and held up a gun.

Books by
Laura Lippman

ATTENTION: ORGANIZATIONS AND CORPORATIONS
Most Avon Books paperbacks are available at special quantity discounts for bulk purchases for sales promotions, premiums, or fund-raising. For information, please call or write:

Special Markets Department, HarperCollins Publishers, 10 East 53rd Street, New York, New York 10022-5299. Telephone: (212) 207-7528.   Fax: (212) 207-7222.

LAURA LIPPMAN

CHARM CITY

AVON BOOKS

An Imprint of HarperCollinsPublishers

Permissions appear on page 293, which serves as an extension of this copyright page.

This is a work of fiction. Names, characters, places, and incidents are products of the author's imagination or are used fictitiously and are not to be construed as real. Any resemblance to actual events, locales, organizations, or persons, living or dead, is entirely coincidental.

AVON BOOKS
An Imprint of HarperCollins*Publishers*
10 East 53rd Street
New York, New York 10022-5299

Copyright © 1997 by Laura Lippman
Front cover photograph by Greg Pease Photography
Library of Congress Catalog Card Number: 97-93019
ISBN: 0-380-78876-4
www.avonmystery.com

All rights reserved. No part of this book may be reproduced in any manner whatsoever without written permission, except in the case of brief quotations embodied in critical articles and reviews For information address Avon Books, an Imprint of HarperCollins Publishers.

First Avon Books paperback printing: October 1997

Avon Trademark Reg. U.S. Pat. Off. and in Other Countries, Marca Registrada, Hecho en U.S.A.
HarperCollins® is a trademark of HarperCollins Publishers Inc.

Printed in the U.S.A.

20 19 18 17 16 15 14 13

If you purchased this book without a cover, you should be aware that this book is stolen property. It was reported as "unsold and destroyed" to the publisher, and neither the author nor the publisher has received any payment for this "stripped book."

For John

I am fortunate to work at a place where my generous colleagues and conscientious editors bear little resemblance to the workers at the oh-so-fictional newspaper in this book. In particular, I am indebted to the following co-workers for their help and technical advice: Joan Jacobson, Mike James, Peter Hermann, Arthur Hirsch, Jon Morgan, Mike Littwin, Dan Rodricks, Kate Shatzkin, and William F. Zorzi. Any errors, deliberate and otherwise, are mine. Special thanks to Johnny Ketchum, king of the Baltimore malaprops.

I also want to thank Spike and Dulcie for their expert contributions.

1 ordinary man + 1 ordinary life = 0

1 ordinary man + 1 extraordinary adventure = News

1 ordinary husband + 1 ordinary wife = 0

1 husband + 3 wives = News

1 bank cashier + 1 wife + 7 children = 0

1 bank cashier − $10,000 = News

1 chorus girl + 1 bank president − $100,000 = News

1 man + 1 auto + 1 gun + 1 quart = News

1 ordinary man + 1 ordinary life of 79 years = 0

1 ordinary man + 1 ordinary life of 100 years = News

—George C. Bastian
"Editing the Day's News," 1922

By choosing to share your life with a Greyhound, you are participating in an act nearly as old as civilization itself. These are the same dogs that slept alongside the pharaohs, hunted with the noblemen of the Middle Ages, and have inspired artists and poets for thousands of years. Without a doubt they are worthy of us. The question is, Are we worthy of them?

—Cynthia A. Branigan
"Adopting the Racing Greyhound"

Drive-bys are out. Executions are in.

—Baltimore Police Commissioner
Thomas C. Frazier
in a 1997 interview on
local crime statistics

Chapter 1

Nothing wet was falling out of the sky. No snow, no ice, no hail, no rain changing to sleet, no sleet changing to rain. And that was reason enough, Tess Monaghan decided, to feel celebratory. She would walk home from work instead of taking her usual bus, maybe stop at Bertha's and squinch up her nose at the tourists eating mussels, or nurse something warm and alcoholic at Henniger's. A March Monday night in Baltimore would never be Mardi Gras, or even Lundi Gras, but it could have its moments, for savvy natives inclined to seek them out. Tess was inclined. For the first time in more than two years, she had a full-time job and a full-time boyfriend. Her life might not have the party-all-the-time euphoria of a beer commercial, but it was definitely edging into International Coffee territory.

The first few blocks of her walk home were deserted. Downtown tended to empty out early. But as Tess approached the Inner Harbor, she suddenly found herself in the thick of a jazzed-up, happy crowd. *Were those klieg lights up ahead?* Tess might have left newspaper reporting behind, but her instincts could still be juiced. Besides, she had caught a whiff of food—hot dogs, popcorn, pretzels, something sweet and scorched. Cotton candy, one of those seductive foods that smelled so much better than it tasted.

"It's all free, hon," a vendor said, holding out a hot dog slathered with mustard and relish. "Courtesy of the Keys."

1

Tess had no idea what he was talking about, but she took the hot dog anyway.

What would draw so many people to the harbor on a usually dead Monday evening, she wondered, finishing off the free dog in three bites. Businessmen types, coming from work. Young men in athletic gear and polished-looking women in gabardine raincoats, high heels striking sidewalks only recently liberated from the last ice storm. Then there were the suburban moms, in leggings, oversize sweaters, and fluffy jackets, holding tight to the hands of small children, who held even tighter to small black-and-violet flags.

Carried along by the crowd and its feverish anticipation, Tess found herself at the small outdoor amphitheater between Harborplace's two pavilions. Hundreds of people were already there, massed in front of the small stage. A man with a bullhorn, a local television anchor, was leading a chant. It took Tess a moment to understand the blurred, electronically amplified words.

"Slam dunk! Jam one! Slam dunk! Jam one!"

Other men filed out, a ragtag basketball team in black-and-violet warm-up outfits. Some wore shorts, their legs all purple gooseflesh in the brisk evening. Who would be crazy enough to come out like that on a night like this? Tess recognized the governor. That figured; he had never met a costume he didn't like. But the mayor, not known for his sense of whimsy, was there as well in a black warm-up suit, his trademark Kente cloth tie peeking over the zipper. Tess spotted another television type, two state senators, and a few pituitary cases from the old Baltimore Bullets, now the Washington Wizards, renamed in deference to that city's homicide rate. Surprisingly, the name change hadn't done much to quell the capital's violence.

"Slam dunk! Jam one! Slam dunk! Jam one!"

Beneath the crowd's chant, Tess picked out a tinny recording, the city's onetime public service jingle, which had encouraged people to keep the streets clean by playing "trash ball." She remembered it vaguely. The city's orange-and-white wastebaskets had been decorated with slogans such as *Jam One!* or *Dunk One!* Then they'd ended the campaign and collectors of Baltimorebilia had stolen the trash cans before they could be taken off the streets and repainted.

Another man limped out on stage, an aging athlete whose cane gave his garish warm-up suit a strangely aristocratic look. "Toooooooooooch. Toooooooooooch," men yodeled and a few women actually screamed when he acknowledged the cheer with a thumb's-up. Yes, Paul Tucci still had his Loyola boy good looks and the build of the star athlete he had once been, although he was fleshier since his much-publicized knee replacement surgery earlier in the winter. Tess suspected the women were swooning not for the Tucci physique, but for the Tucci fortune, which had started in olive oil, then oozed into virtually every aspect of Baltimore life, from food importing to waste disposal. "The Tuccis get you coming and going," it was commonly said.

The music on the P.A. system changed to the sprightly, whistling version of "Sweet Georgia Brown" associated with the Harlem Globetrotters. The governor, inexpertly dribbling a basketball, broke from the group, jigged forward, then passed the ball to the mayor, throwing it over his head. They had never worked together very well. The mayor recovered nicely, retrieving the ball and passing it beneath his legs to a state delegate with a quite new, quite bad hair transplant. The crowd roared its approval. *For the pass or the plugs?* Tess wondered. Tucci caught the ball and spun it on the tip of his cane, prompting a few more female screams. Then the real basketball players came forward, upstaging the pols with their perfunctorily perfect passes and moves.

After a few minutes, the television anchor—*At least he's not dumb enough to come out here bare-legged,* Tess noted—seized the floor again.

"Hellooooo, Baltimore." The crowd caroled the greeting back. "As you know, the city has been without basketball since 1972 and has only recently seen the return of football, despite the initial reluctance of the National Football League—''

"Kill the commissioner!" screamed one frenzied fan, straight into Tess's right eardrum. "Kill Tagliabue! Damn Bob Irsay! Fuck the rotting corpse of Bob Irsay!" Irsay had taken the Baltimore Colts away on a snowy night in 1984, and although the city had a new football team and Irsay was dead, he was still anathema. Baltimore sometimes forgot, but it never forgave.

The television anchor continued smoothly over the outburst. "But one man never said die. And now that man is going to bring basketball back to Baltimore. Within days, he expects to sign a letter of intent with a pro franchise that wants to relocate to Charm City. In return, the city has agreed to build a beautiful new facility, and you fans turned out tonight to show the NBA we can support a team here. Now, that's teamwork!"

And a great use of tax dollars, Tess thought sourly. Then again, the state had already done the same for the Orioles and the Ravens. If ever a city needed a self-help book, it was Baltimore: *Towns That Love Sports Too Much, and the Greedy Team Owners Who Use Them.*

"So please welcome the team captain, the guy who's brought us this far, the guy who 'winked' at everyone who told him it couldn't be done, our very own Gerard 'Wink' Wynkowski."

A slender, not quite tall man bounded onstage. He had bypassed the warm-ups in favor of a violet polo shirt, black jeans, and a black leather bikers' jacket. Gray-and-white cowboy boots of some exotic and politically dubious skin— ostrich, maybe snake—added a few inches to his height, so he appeared lanky alongside the governor and mayor. Shrewdly, he kept his distance from the former pros, who would have dwarfed him.

"Are you ready for some basketball?" he drawled, in an unmistakably Baltimore accent.

His face, angular and sharp, was deeply tanned, his brown curls worn in a white boy's Afro. Tess recalled a caricature of that sharp face and wild hair as the logo for one of his businesses, but which one? In the past decade, Wink's company, Montrose Enterprises, had created a half-dozen businesses, each more successful than the last.

"Wink! Wink! Wink! Wink!" the crowd yelled to their sports savior, much as they had yelled it on high school basketball courts twenty-five years ago, when the idea of a 5'11" Polish kid going on to a pro career had not seemed quite so ridiculous. His last name had provided the nickname, of course—his last name and, it was rumored, a tendency to hoodwink anyone he could.

"You guys are the greatest," he told the crowd. "You came out on a night like this, not even knowing which team I'm negotiating with. Imagine how many people will be here in a week's time, when I expect to make an official announcement about our new team, the Baltimore Keys."

The crowd chanted back eagerly: *"Jam one! Slam dunk! Jam one! Slam dunk! Jam one! Slam dunk!"*

Tess moved forward through the cheering crowd, curious enough to want a better look at this local hero. Wink's life story was straight out of some old thirties movie: a fatherless young hood who was actually rehabilitated in the system after a string of petty crimes had landed him in the infamous Montrose facility for juveniles. She had known he was rich, but hadn't realized his restaurants and health clubs had made him enough money to consider buying a sports team.

When the crowd became too dense to let her advance through the center, she cut left, zigzagging until she was down front, but far to the side. This close up, Wink's flat blue eyes were not the merry or dancing lights she would have expected above such a broad grin. Large and grave in his small face, they took everything in and gave nothing back.

Suddenly, someone shoved Tess roughly from behind, with the sense of entitlement found only in popes, royalty, and television news crews. Given that the Pope wasn't expected back for a while, and native daughter Wallis Warfield Simpson was the closest Baltimore had come to the throne in this century, Tess knew she would be face to lens with a cameraman when she turned around. She had wandered into the media clot, where the television reporters were taping segments for the 11 o'clock news.

"You're in my shot," the cameraman hissed at her.

"How inconsiderate of me." She didn't move—at least, not right away.

Nearby, two print reporters, a man and woman, stood with notebooks in hand. The woman scribbled madly, while the man just stared at Wink as if he couldn't quite believe what he was seeing. For a moment, Tess felt as if she should be with them, as if she, too, should have a notebook. Then she recognized the man—not by his face, which was turned away from her, but by his ankles, always bare, even on a night like this.

"Feeney!" she yelled. He looked up warily from beneath the bill of his battered wool baseball cap, smiling when he saw it was Tess who had called his name.

"Darlin' Tess!" Kevin Feeney called back, beckoning to her. "Come over here. We're just gathering atmosphere."

The young woman at his side surveyed Tess in one quick, lethal glance. Tess could almost hear her brain clicking away on the sort of points system that some women used: *Taller—1 point for her. Hippy—1 point against. Big breasts, long hair—2 points for. Hair, unstyled, worn in a braid down her back—2 points against. Older than me—3 points against. Face, okay. Clothes, not stylish, not embarrassing.* Tess wasn't sure of her final score, but apparently it was just a little too high. The woman gave her a terrifyingly fake smile, one that suggested she had little experience with real ones, and held out her hand.

"Rosita Ruiz." Ouch—a bad case of NPR disease. The Rs rolled off her tongue like ball bearings and the T was an aural machete. Rosita seized Tess by the hand, pinching the flesh between thumb and index finger the way a crab pinches one's toes in the surf. Tess, who often did gripstrenthening exercises with an old tennis ball as she spoke on the phone, took pleasure in squeezing Rosita's hand back, taking her own inventory as she did.

Short, but most women looked short to Tess. Built like a gymnast—slender above the waist, stocky and firmly rooted below. With her even features and glossy black hair, she should have been striking, even beautiful, but something had soured her looks.

"Tess Monaghan," she said, dropping Rosita's hand and turning back to Feeney. "I can't believe you're covering this. Don't they have interns to do this kind of crap? Or sportswriters? You belong in the courthouse, covering real news."

"I told you. We're here for color. Sparkling details."

"For what?"

"Can't say, darling, can't say."

"When Feeney says color, he doesn't mean it literally," Rosita explained earnestly. "You see, in newspapers, color means—"

"Tess used to be one of us," Feeney interrupted gently, although Tess sensed no interruption was ever gentle enough for Rosita. "Now she's a private investigator."

"Well, sort of. I still have to get my license. But I'm definitely no longer a member of the fourth estate." Funny, it didn't hurt to say that anymore. The *Star* was dead, life had gone on, Baltimore was a one-newspaper town, and the one paper, for better or worse, was the *Beacon-Light*—the *Blight,* as it was known by its often less-than-satisfied customers.

"Well, let us know when you do. Maybe Rosita can write a little feature about you when you crack a big case. Tess Monaghan, the rowing P.I."

"No rowing this time of year," Tess reminded him. "That's for the real diehards. I'll go back on the water on April Fool's Day, not a day sooner."

Feeney didn't hear her. He was practically glowing, lighted from within by his secret story. It could be about politics, Tess guessed, given the cast of characters onstage.

A new profile of the governor would require a fresh an-
ecdote about his propensity to make himself ridiculous. Or
the Tucci family might be using its considerable clout to
ensure another concession for its trash disposal business,
which found fewer and fewer neighborhoods wanted an in-
cinerator down the street. Like most rich families, they
were quick to cry poverty whenever a state regulation or a
new fee got in their way.

No, it was more likely that Feeney was writing about the
main event, about Wink and this basketball deal. But what
did any of this have to do with the courthouse? And why
assign a feature writer to help?

"Let's have a drink, soon," Tess said, lowering her
voice so Rosita wouldn't think the invitation was being
extended to her as well. "It's been too long."

He laughed. "You just want to pump me for details."

"Fair enough. But what's it to you if I interrogate you
over a round of drinks at the Brass Elephant? You'll get a
free drink out of it, and probably won't answer my questions anyway. Tomorrow night? Seven-thirty?"

"Make it eight. Who knows—it may be time to celebrate
by then."

"Okay. 'Til then." She squeezed his hand, then lied to
Rosita. "Nice meeting you."

The young woman smiled, a tight-lipped little V that
dropped the temperature ten degrees. *Okay, I wasn't exactly
warm, either.* But Tess figured she had only been respond-
ing to the little reporter's bitchiness, smashing it back the
way one returned a tough first serve in tennis. Rosita wore
her ambition the way oldtime reporters wore trench coats.
On her young frame, it wasn't particularly becoming.

Tess grabbed another free hot dog and tried to make it
last for the rest of the walk home. Out of eighteen blocks,
she ended up only sixteen short. Still, she was happy and
full when she arrived at her apartment. She decided to stop
in her aunt's bookstore on the ground level and rehash the
rally for her. Kitty had a fine appreciation of the absurd, as
evidenced by her store's name, Women and Children First.

"Oh, Tesser, where have you been?" Kitty cried out, before she could even begin to act out the governor's spastic dribbling, the mayor's pseudo-cool manuvers, Tucci's gimpy plays. "Tommy's been calling and calling. He just missed you at your office, and he's been phoning here every five minutes since then—"

"Tommy, Spike's hysterical busboy? What, did someone steal the lifts from his shoes? Take an extra handful of pretzels, or walk a seven-dollar check? Trust me, Kitty, Tommy's calls are never the emergencies he thinks they are."

Kitty's blue eyes were bright with tears. "It's your Uncle Spike, Tess. He's at St. Agnes Hospital. Someone tried to rob The Point and the crazy old goat tried to stop them— and he almost did."

"Only almost?"

"Only almost."

Chapter 2

〰〰〰

"The years, I saw the years," Spike muttered, his brown eyes glazed and unfocused, incapable of seeing anything. "Years."

"I know, Uncle Spike, I know," Tess said, patting his hand. But she didn't know. The years must be his life, fifty-some years in all, passing before his eyes. The cliché was a good sign, she decided. Surely, if death were near, one could be allowed a little originality.

"The years."

Spike's face was mottled and crisscrossed with tiny cuts, the liver spots that gave him a slight resemblance to a springer spaniel overwhelmed by vivid purple-red bruises. Only his pointy bald head, rising above the fringe of brown hair, was still white and unblemished.

"Years," he muttered.

"I found him?" said Tommy, the dishwasher from Spike's bar, who framed almost every thought as if it were a question. This wishy-washy tendency, combined with his thick Baltimore accent and talent for malaprops, made him virtually incomprehensible to anyone but Spike. "About two hours ago? I came by to get ready for the Monday night crowd? I was going to peel some hard-berled eggs because the new cook didn't show up, being so lacks-a-daisy as he is?"

"A robbery?" Tess had not meant this as a question, but Tommy's inflections were contagious.

"Yeah, a robbery, but we don't have much money on Mondays, not once pro football is over? That's why they got their dandruff up? They beat him to a pulp?"

Tommy was right: Uncle Spike looked like a plum gone bad, or a skinned, mashed tomato. Who did this to an old man? But Tess knew. Amateurs. Kids. Idiots, the kind of crooks who were giving crime a bad name. They didn't know from hold-up etiquette, which said you didn't kill a guy in a tavern robbery, and you certainly didn't try to beat him to death. You didn't rob taverns at all, in fact, for the owner usually had a sawed-off shotgun under the bar, especially if he had a flourishing side business as a bookie. Spike had the side business, Spike had the shotgun. Why hadn't he been able to get to it in time?

"Numbers," he cried weakly, as if he, too, were thinking of his bets, which produced far more income than the bar. And then he said nothing, eyes fluttering closed.

They remained frozen in this tableau—Tess holding Spike's hand, Tommy on the other side of the bed, rocking nervously, arms wrapped around his body—until a young doctor came in and asked them to leave.

Tommy, all ninety-five pounds of him, insisted on walking Tess to her car for her protection. There were frozen puddles in the lot and the promise Tess had sensed earlier in the evening was gone. March, with its morning rains and wintry nights, suddenly seemed as bitter as baking chocolate.

"He has something for you?" Tommy began, tentative even by his standards. "Back at the bar? Before the paramedics took him, he said to make sure to get it to you?"

"He doesn't expect me to run the bar, does he?"

Tommy cackled and cackled, bent over double at the thought of Tess running The Point, Spike's bar. Between sputtering laughs, he even managed a whole string of declarative sentences.

"No, not the bar. But it's *at* the bar. C'mon now, and

I'll give it to you. But follow me, okay? I got a special shortcut?''

They left St. Agnes Hospital and drove through Southwest Baltimore to her uncle's place, using back streets. Highways were seldom the fastest way to get anywhere in Baltimore, at least not east to west, but Tommy's shortcut seemed to be an unusually circuitous route, approaching The Point through the winding roads of Leakin Park.

The Point was dark, shuttered for the night, shuttered forever, perhaps. Tommy took Tess in the back way, through the kitchen—the kitchen where she had eaten her first french fry, her first onion ring, her first mozzarella stick, even her first stuffed jalapeño. Those had been the base of Spike's food pyramid, and who was Tess to disagree?

Tommy unlocked a storeroom and stood on the threshold, peering into the darkness.

''There,'' he said finally, pointing to what appeared to be a black bag.

''What?'' Tess said. Alarmingly, the bag began to move, rising on four sticks and walking toward her, into the light. ''What the hell is it?''

It was a dog, a bony, ugly dog with dull black fur and raw patches on its hindquarters. The brown eyes were as vague and glazed as Spike's, the shoulders hunched in an uncanny impersonation of Richard M. Nixon.

''It's a greyhound? Spike just got it this weekend?''

''But it's *black*.''

''Most greyhounds ain't gray, and you call 'em blue when they are.'' Tommy spoke confidently, sure of himself on this particular subject. ''Some are kinda beige, and some are spotted, and some are black. They say gray ones don't run so good, but that's just a super-supposition.''

''Was Spike going to race this dog?''

''No, this dog is *retired*. And she wasn't ever much good? Spike got her from some guy?''

''What guy?''

''The guy he knows from the place he goes sometimes?''

The dog looked up at Tess and her droopy tail moved ever so slightly, as if she had some vague memory of wagging it a long time ago. Tess looked back. She was not a dog person. She was not a cat person, fish person, or horse person. On bad days, she was barely a people person. She ate meat, wore leather, and secretly coveted her mother's old mink. Fur was warm and Baltimore's winters seemed to be getting worse, global warming be damned.

"Why can't you take her, Tommy?"

"Can't keep a dog in the bar, health department will close us down? Name's S. K.?"

"What do the initials stand for, S. K.?"

"No, *Esskay*. Like the sausage?"

"As in 'Taste the difference ka-wality makes?' and Cal Ripken, Jr., touting the role of bacon in his athletic endeavors?"

"Yeah, it's her favorite food, but she only gets it for special treats. Rest of the time, she eats this special kibble Spike got her."

Five minutes later, Tess was in her twelve-year-old Toyota, the kibble was in the trunk, and Esskay was standing stiff-legged in the backseat, sliding back and forth with every turn and whimpering at every pothole, which came roughly every fifteen feet. Baltimore's streets, never in the best repair, had suffered as much this winter as anyone. It didn't help that the car behind her, which had its brights on, seemed intent on tailgating her all the way to Fells Point. She ended up running a red light on Edmondson Avenue, just to get away from that inconsiderate driver.

"Sit! Sit down!" Tess hissed at the dog, but Esskay just stared back at her forlornly and resumed skidding along the vinyl covered backseat, hitting her head on one window, then slipping back and smacking her rump on the other. But she never barked, Tess noticed, never really made any sound at all, except that almost imperceptible whine from the back of her throat.

* * *

The sun had just come up, weak and feeble, when Tess opened her eyes the next morning. Strange, she usually didn't wake this early in the winter, her one season to sleep in. Spring through fall, when she rowed, she was up with the birds. "And now you're down with Crow," her friend Whitney had joked frequently, a little too frequently, over the past few months. It wasn't clear if Whitney resented the presence of a boyfriend in Tess's life, or simply found the boyfriend in question somewhat ridiculous. A little of both, Tess suspected.

But it was not Crow's long, warm body next to her this morning. She rolled toward the middle of the too-soft bed and found herself staring into the faintly cross-eyed gaze of Esskay, the dog's untrimmed toenails digging into her arm, her hind legs twitching spasmodically.

Tess propped herself up on one elbow and glared, and the dog shrank back, averting her mournful gaze.

"Don't take this personally, but you are the ugliest dog I've ever seen."

The snout was reminiscent of a dinosaur's, the long-jawed velociraptor, to be precise. The legs were skinny, the hair thin and mussed in parts. There were red sores on the rump and tail, and the watery eyes could not hold one's gaze. The total effect was not unlike Tess at thirteen—body too long, legs too thin, skin red and splotchy, manner socially inept. But the dog's teeth were bad, too, judging from the fishy, hot breath Esskay pushed out in quick, panting gasps.

Muttering to herself, Tess pulled on sweats and hiking boots to take the dog for a quick walk. The dog jumped up at the sight of her makeshift leash, a long, heavy piece of metal that Spike had probably been using to padlock his parking lot gate. But once at the top of the stairs, Esskay balked, refusing to start down. Last night the greyhound had declined to go up the stairs to Tess's apartment, so she had carried her up two flights of stairs, assuming the dog was too weak to climb. Now it appeared the greyhound was opposed to staircases on general principle.

"C'mon, you silly bitch," Tess said, grabbing the dog's collar, but Esskay wouldn't budge, no matter how hard she tugged. She crouched behind and tried to nudge her down, but the dog resisted, her scrawny limbs surprisingly strong.

"Move, dammit! I'm not going to ferry you up and down these steps every day."

Tess's words had no effect on the dog, but they did bring her aunt out onto the second-floor landing. Kitty was normally the kind of landlady one wanted on the premises, with few rules and a high tolerance for noise and rowdy companions. But she couldn't abide anything unpleasant looking, and Esskay was clearly in trouble on that score.

"How's Spike?" she asked, wrapping a teal-colored chenille robe tightly around her. Her pale face was flushed, her red curls rumpled. "I'm sorry I was out when you got in last night, but I had to go to that meeting for local business owners. We're still fighting the city over those megabars. And what is *that*? The world's largest rat?"

"It's a gigantic pain in my ass, that's what it is, courtesy of Spike."

A short, muscular man appeared behind Kitty, dressed in a plaid robe Tess had seen on many men in the two years she had lived above her aunt. She knew this one only by sight—a bartender at a new place on Thames, one of the so-called megabars that had the Fells Point neighborhood in an uproar. But Kitty had always been remarkably open-minded, capable of opposing a business while still feeling kindly toward its employees.

"That's one of those racing greyhounds," the bartender diagnosed smugly. "How long you had him?"

Funny, how some men project their own gender on everything, as if all living creatures must be male until proven otherwise.

"I've had *her* about twelve hours, give or take."

"Well, that's your trouble, then. An ex-racer like this has never seen stairs, so you gotta teach 'em. One foot, other foot. One foot, other foot. My cousin had one once.

You help 'em up and down until they get it. They don't know about mirrors, either.''

"All women should be so lucky," Kitty murmured. "This is Steve, by the way. Steve, this is my niece, Tess."

"Niece?"

Some women might have quickly told him that Tess's father was years older, which he was. Tess's aunt was the afterthought in a family of four boys, not even fifteen years older than the twenty-nine-year-old Tess. But confident Kitty merely smiled and nodded.

Tess squatted in front of Esskay and coaxed the dog's forelegs down one step. The dog was amazingly malleable, allowing her to pick up each foot, then set it down. But she still wouldn't move forward on her own. One-two, forelegs down, three-four, hind legs. Repeat. In this fashion, it took Tess only a few minutes to get the dog to the landing, where she paused to catch her breath. She was in good shape, but apparently nothing in her various workout routines had developed the necessary muscles for this greyhound walk-and-hobble. And the crouching position was hell on her back and knees.

"What else don't they know how to do?" Tess called back to Steve the bartender, as she and Esskay started down their second flight.

"Well, they're kennel trained, but not housebroken. You gotta crate 'em at first, if you don't want accidents. Also, don't yell at her if she loses control. They're real, real sensitive.''

"Aren't we all?"

Tess was worn out by the time they reached the first floor, but the dog was suddenly ecstatic, wiggling her snout and pulling her lips back over her front teeth in a serviceable James Cagney impression. Tess took her on a tour of Fells Point's vacant lots, which Esskay found olfactorily fascinating. Tess dimly recalled the city had an ordinance about cleaning up after dogs, but she figured dog waste was the least of the indignities visited on these sites, scoured by chemicals and toxins over the last five decades.

Intriguing aromas were drifting out of Kitty's first-floor kitchen by the time they returned home. Tess lurked in the hallway, fiddling with Esskay's leash, hoping to be asked in, if only to forestall the long climb back to her apartment. Kitty, like all Monaghans, assumed Spike came from the Weinstein side of the family, but she had always had a soft spot for him. She'd want to know more about his condition. Sure enough, generous Kitty cracked open the door and beckoned them in.

Kitty's kitchen was an odd room for someone who needed heels to top five feet. Everything was oversized, so Kitty seemed doll-like by comparison. Tess had long ago decided the effect was not incidental, as Kitty's latest beau usually ended up preparing all the food. The beau also tended to be at least fifteen years younger than forty-something Kitty, a clever redhead who had avoided the sun while other women of her generation were basting themselves with baby oil.

Today's menu was French toast, courtesy of Steve the bartender. He had a tight, hard look that Tess despised. Small men who spent so much time developing their muscles tended to neglect other vital parts. Then again, she hadn't liked any of her aunt's boyfriends since Thaddeus Freudenberg had left to attend the FBI academy down at Quantico. That had been in January—two months by the regular calendar, four boyfriends ago on the Kitty calendar.

"So, did Tommy provide any more details about what happened last night?" Kitty asked, as Tess helped herself to coffee. "And how's Spike doing?"

"Not so good. He lost consciousness while we were there. Someone—several someones—really worked him over. Probably got all of thirty dollars for their trouble."

Steve, uninterested in such mundane family matters as the robbery and near-death of a relative, yanked the conversation back to a subject he could dominate.

"So, did you get your dog from one of the local rescue groups?" he asked, serving Tess two slices of French toast, then sprinkling powdered sugar on top. Tess would have preferred something a little less sticky on a Tuesday morning, a bagel or a bowl of cereal, but she wasn't about to complain.

"I got her from my Uncle Spike."

"Well, he must've just got her, if she didn't know how to do steps. Those raw patches on her butt, that's kennel burn."

Esskay whimpered, as if aware of being the center of a less-than-flattering discussion. Kitty broke off a piece of toast and offered it to the dog, who wolfed it down with amazing speed.

"You should call one of those rescue groups, get the drill," Steve continued. "There are all sorts of things you need to know."

"Like what?" Kitty wouldn't be able to put up with this one for long, Tess decided, no matter what talents he possessed in the kitchen and boudoir. She liked quiet breakfasts.

"Diet. Exercise," he said vaguely, waving his fork in the air. Something in the gesture told Tess he had exhausted his little storehouse of greyhound facts.

As Steve held his fork aloft, a chunk of French toast still on its tines, Esskay leaped up and snatched the syrupy bite. The dog's eyes were bright for the first time and she no longer hung her head in that "don't-hurt-me" droop. Esskay looked ready for a fight to the death over the rest of the French toast, and Tess thought she had a chance of taking Steve. Esskay was hungrier.

"I've got an idea," she said, cutting the rest of her toast into small pieces. "Kitty, come out into the hall for a second."

At the foot of the stairs, Tess handed Kitty the plate and sent her halfway up the first flight. She then positioned herself behind the dog, arms braced on the dog's hind legs.

"Hold out one of the toast chunks," she told her aunt. Kitty proffered one of the smaller pieces between forefinger and thumb, as Tess moved the dog's legs up the steps.

Foreleg, foreleg, hind leg, hind leg. Right, left, right, left. She could feel the tension in the poor beast as she craned her neck forward, trying to get closer to the morsel of French toast only inches from her mouth.

"Back up a few steps." Kitty retreated. Foreleg, foreleg, hind leg, hind leg. Again, the dog was almost in reach of the toast.

"Okay, let her have that bite, then go up to the landing and hold out one of the larger pieces."

The small taste, drenched with syrup and powdered sugar, almost drove the dog wild. Whimpering now, Esskay strained toward Kitty, out of reach on the landing. Tess crouched behind the dog, feeling like a mother who was about to let go of her kid's two-wheeler. A slight nudge and Esskay surged forward, taking the rest of the steps in one bound. Kitty fed her another French toast chunk, then pranced up four more steps. The dog followed on her own, Tess crawling behind her. Within seconds, they were at the top of the stairs outside Tess's apartment and the plate looked dishwasher clean.

Steve, who had watched this impromptu lesson from the bottom of the stairs, was not impressed.

"You better call that greyhound rescue group," he yelled upstairs. "I doubt French toast is going to agree with her stomach. You'll be lucky if she doesn't have diarrhea all over your apartment."

Kitty scratched the dog behind the ears. The dog looked up lovingly. It was more than toast. As Crow had once told Tess, falling in love with Kitty was a rite of passage for anyone who spent time at the corner of Bond and Shakespeare streets. He should know: a clerk at Women and Children First, Crow had nursed his own impossible crush on Kitty before suddenly, unpredictably switching his affections to Tess five months ago.

"Even dogs," Tess marveled. "Is there anyone immune to your charms?"

"Thousands. I just don't waste time on those lost causes, the way most women do." Kitty called downstairs. "Steve, you can go ahead and wash up now. I'm going to change and get ready to open the store.''

Steve turned back to the kitchen, whistling as if it were a privilege to clean up after the meal he had prepared. Kitty floated to the landing and slipped inside her second-floor bedroom suite. Tess had to hold onto Esskay's collar to keep the dog from trotting after her.

Familiar with athletes and their needs, Tess poured the dog a huge bowl of water, placing it on a copy of the *Beacon-Light*. She then found an old blanket and arranged it into a bed on the floor of her bedroom. Puzzled, Esskay stood over it, staring at the blue plaid wool as if waiting for it to do something. When Tess came out of the shower, the dog was still standing over the blanket, growling faintly in the back of her throat.

Once dressed and ready for work, Tess stood in the bedroom's doorway and looked at the dog awkwardly. What was expected in a person-pet relationship? She had never understood people who talked to animals and babied them, but it seemed odd to walk away from a warm-blooded creature without some acknowledgment. Besides, this dog meant something to Spike, so she had to treat her well. Esskay was not unlike Tommy—not exactly human, but a part of Spike's life, and therefore deserving of common courtesy.

''I'm going out tonight,'' Tess said at last, ''so I won't be home until late. I'll tell Kitty to check on you.''

Esskay looked up briefly, then went back to staring at the blanket. *Great,* Tess thought. *I'm talking to a dog, and it's not even paying attention.* And she ran down the stairs, late for work. That was the one drawback of the office being only ten minutes away. You couldn't make up lost time on the commute.

Chapter 3

~~~~~~

Tyner Gray's law office was in an old town house on Mount Vernon Square, a pretty neighborhood clustered at the feet of George Washington, who kept watch from the top of a modest monument. "But it's older than the one in DC," some local was always quick to point out. Tess didn't care much about the monument, but she liked the pretty park outside her office window, the strains of classical music that drifted over from Peabody Conservatory, and the good restaurants in the neighborhood. Last fall, fate and circumstances had brought her here, in what was to be a temporary job. Tess had ended up staying on, although Tyner reminded her every day that her goal should be to obtain a private investigator's license and open her own office.

As she came through the heavy front door at 9:15, she could hear the whine of the old-fashioned elevator only Tyner used. Tess darted up the broad marble steps between the first and second floors, then took the narrower staircase to the third floor, confident she could beat the wheezing lift. They had timed it once with Tyner's stopwatch, the one he used when putting novice rowers through drills. It took exactly one minute and thirty-two seconds for the elevator to make the trip from first to third. By the time Tyner arrived, she was at her desk in the front room, which she shared with Alison the receptionist, making notes on an interview she had conducted last week, some woman who hoped to sue her neighbor in a boundary dispute.

"I'm not fooled, you know," Tyner said, rolling past her in his wheelchair.

"Really, Mr. Gray, she's been here all along," volunteered Alison. A preppy beauty, as overbred as a golden retriever, Alison was a good egg. She couldn't lie to save her life, though.

"I heard you on the stairs," he called back to Tess. "You have a very heavy tread. I never remember—do you pronate or supinate?"

"Pronate," she said, following him into his office, a spare, uncluttered room. In a wheelchair for almost forty years, Tyner hadn't waited for anyone to make the world accessible to him. Although his office was in a nineteenth-century town house better suited to antiques, he had chosen sleek, modern furnishings, which took up less floor space. His desk was a large, flat table, custom made so he could roll right up to it. The chairs facing it were tall and slender, expensive maple pieces with narrow strips of leather for seats. They also were wretchedly uncomfortable, and, not incidentally, reminiscent of the sliding seats in a racing shell. Rowing was Tyner's true passion, even if his years as a rower had ended up being only a fraction of his life.

"My uncle got robbed last night," Tess told him, perching on one of the chairs. "Someone worked him over pretty bad."

"Jesus. Which one? Which side?" Unavoidable questions, and difficult ones, for Tess had nine other uncles— her father's five younger brothers, her mother's four older ones. Spike was actually a cousin, and to complicate things further, no one had ever agreed to which side of the family he belonged. His last name was Orrick. *Changed from O'Rourke*, Tess's mother always said. *Could be one of those Eastern European Jew names,* her father inevitably countered, *screwed up the immigration officials*.

"The one who owns The Point, that bar on Franklintown Road. It was a robbery, and they were pissed because he didn't have anything."

"This city is becoming unlivable."

"You say that every other day. You're just looking for a reason to buy that house in Ruxton." This green, sheltered suburb, no more than five miles outside the city limits, was a kind of code between them, symbolizing the ultimate surrender.

Tyner smiled ruefully. "The city doesn't make it easy for a taxpayer to stay here, Tess. Especially after this winter. My street wasn't plowed or salted even once. Every time it snowed, I was stranded."

"You don't have to tell me. Remember, I was the one who drove out there five times, using cross-country skis to get up your street. You always acted as if it were a terrible imposition, having me show up with groceries."

"I wanted brandy, not food. You'll never make it as a St. Bernard, Tess."

St. Bernard. Tess's mind jumped from the past to the present, free-associating. Dog. She should call that greyhound rescue group Steve had been blathering about.

Leaving Tyner to his usual grumpy funk, she went back to her desk and flipped through the phone book until she found a listing for Greyhound Pets of Maryland.

"Greyhound Pets." The breathless person on the other end was a woman with a sweet, throaty voice. Dogs barked frantically in the background. Tess had an instant image of someone in blue jeans, covered in dog hair. *Yech.*

"Hi. I seem to have inherited a greyhound from my uncle and I'm trying to find out what I need to do for it. Food, exercise, routine, that stuff."

"How long has your uncle had the dog? I mean, is he a recent adoptee, or has he had him some time? How's he doing?"

Tess became confused, thinking "he" must be her uncle. Then she realized the woman was referring to the dog. "Um, pretty recent, I guess. She didn't know how to go up stairs."

"Is he from here?"

"The dog? I don't know."

"Your uncle. What's his name?"

"Spike Orrick."

"That name doesn't ring a bell, and we do most of the placements in the Baltimore area." The woman's voice suddenly sounded much less pleasant. "Are you sure he adopted this dog through proper channels? Has he gotten her fixed? You have to get them spayed or neutered, you know. It's part of the agreement. Is the dog with you now? We do have an identification system, and if you'll just . . ."

Tess placed the receiver back in its cradle. Who was she kidding? Spike had never gone through proper channels for anything. If only Esskay could talk. If only *Spike* could talk.

But a call to St. Agnes dashed those hopes: Spike was in a coma now, prognosis uncertain.

"What is so rare as a day in spring? What is so rare as a Baltimore day in March when the sun actually shines?" Tess muttered to herself, climbing the stairs to the Brass Elephant bar that evening, her mood a strange muddle of anxiety and anticipation—worry over Spike, delight at spending time in her favorite bar, with one of her favorite drinking companions.

The Brass Elephant bar was a well-kept secret and the regulars conspired to keep it that way. An inexpensive hide-away above an expensive restaurant, it had been an essential place to Tess when she was unemployed, a refuge where she could feel civilized, pampered, and well fed for as little as fifteen dollars. The lights were low, as was the volume on the stereo, with Chet Baker, Johnny Hartman, and Antonio Carlos Jobim murmuring their songs of love so quietly that one caught only an occasional rhyming whisper of love/above, art/heart, or sky/thigh. There had been an ugly scare a few years back, when a new bartender had begun playing a jazz version of the hit ballad from the latest Disney cartoon musical, but someone had quickly set her straight. The Brass Elephant survived good and bad fortune, from Maryland's peripatetic economy to those best-of-Baltimore ratings that stumbled on its martinis, creating a brief flurry of interest among people who didn't necessarily like martinis, but liked to say they had tried the best.

Good, her favorite bartender was here. So was Feeney, settled deep in the corner banquette, fingers pinching the stem of his martini glass, a telltale mound of toothpick-skewered olives on the white tablecloth in front of him. Tess pointed to Feeney's glass, signaling she wanted the same, and slipped into the chair across the table from Feeney's slumped body. But he didn't acknowledge her, unless one considered a few muttered lines of Auden a suitable greeting.

"I sit in one of the dives / On Fifty-Second Street / Uncertain and afraid / As the clever hopes expire / Of a low dishonest decade."

Tess sighed. Richard Burton couldn't have done it much better, or much drunker. Auden was a particularly ominous sign, reserved for all-time lows. Only Yeats or Housman was worse.

"You're on Charles Street and the Brass Elephant is hardly a dive, although I won't debate you on the merits of this particular decade."

"All I have is a voice," Feeney countered, his voice slipping into a singsong cadence as he notched up the volume. *"To undo the folded lie, / The romantic lie in the brain / Of the sensual man-in-the-street . . ."*

"Is that what they did to you today? A man in the streets?" A minor complaint, one Feeney could be jollied out of. Tess knew the real folded lie was the media's never-flagging belief that ordinary people knew anything about current events. Whenever anything big happened far away, the editors sent reporters into the street to sample the common sense of the common man.

The bartender appeared at the table with her drink. The ritual was part of the pleasure—his wrist action with the shaker, the way he poured the martini with a nice bit of showmanship. Tess took a sip and immediately felt better, stronger, smarter, ready for Feeney *in extremis.*

"So what was today's question? Something about

NATO? NATO is always good for a man-in-the-street. I remember back in my *Star* days, when someone in Pigtown thought NATO was an indoor swimming pool the mayor wanted to build in Patterson Park.''

"You disappoint me, Tess," Feeney said balefully, gnawing on one of the toothpicks from the pile in front of him. "You're as literal minded as my dumb-fuck editors.''

Tess took a second, more generous sip from her glass, relishing its chill and the tiny tongue of heat behind it. Truly a lovely drink.

"It's nice to see you, too, Feeney.''

"Nice to see me? You can't even bear to look at me.''

Lost in his own private pity party, Feeney had spoken an unwitting truth. Tess was avoiding his eyes, squinted tight from bitterness, and his turned-down smirk. Feeney had always been gray—gray-blue eyes, gray-blond hair, even a grayish-pink pallor, only a few shades lighter than the undercooked hot dogs he bought from the sidewalk vendors outside the courthouse. But tonight, everything looked a little ashier than usual, as if he wasn't getting enough oxygen. Against his drained face, the broken blood vessels on his cheeks were stark blue road maps leading nowhere. Gin blossoms, the one flower you could count on finding year-round in sodden Baltimore.

"What's wrong, Feeney?''

"My career is over.''

"You make that announcement once a month.''

"Yeah, but usually it's only free-floating paranoia. Tonight, I got the word officially. I don't belong. Not a team player.'' The last sentence came out so slurry it sounded more like "Knotty template.''

"They couldn't have *fired* you.'' The *Beacon-Light* was a union paper, which made it difficult for them to dismiss employees, although far from impossible. But Feeney was good, a pro. They'd have a hard time building a case against him. Unless he had done it for them, by ignoring an editor's orders. Insubordination was grounds for immediate termination.

"Suppose you had written the story of your life, Tess?" he asked, leaning toward her, his face so close to hers that she could smell the gin on his breath, along with the undertones of tobacco. Strange—Feeney had given up smoking years ago. "The best story you could ever imagine. Suppose it had everything you could ask for in a story, and everything had at least two sources? And suppose those goddamn rat bastard cowardly pointy-head incompetents wouldn't publish it?"

"This has something to do with that basketball rally, doesn't it? The story you wouldn't tell me about last night."

Feeney picked up his fork and began stabbing the happy hour ravioli, until little spurts of tomato sauce and cheese freckled the tablecloth. "Well, I can tell you now. In fact, the only way anyone is ever going to hear this story is if I tell it to 'em. Maybe I could stand on a street corner with a sign, offering to read it at a buck a pop."

"How good is it? How big?"

He slipped back into his singsong poetry voice. "Wink Wynkowski, Baltimore's best hope for luring a basketball team back to Baltimore, has many things in his past he prefers no one know about, especially the NBA. His business is a house of cards, perhaps on the brink of bankruptcy, beset by lawsuits, from ambulances to zippers. He may be able to get up the scratch for a team, but he isn't liquid enough to keep it going."

"Then why buy it if it's going to make him broke?"

"Good question. Two answers. He's a fool—doubtful. Or he plans to unload the team pretty quickly, as soon as the city builds him that brand-new arena, which will double the team's value overnight."

"That seems a little far-fetched."

"Hey, remember Eli Jacobs? He bought the Orioles for $70 million in the 1980s. When his business collapsed in the recession, he sold them for almost $175 million and it was Camden Yards, paid for by the state, that made the team so valuable. If Wink can keep all his spinning plates aloft for a couple of years and sell the team before his creditors come calling, he stands to see a huge profit.''

''Is there more?'' Feeney scowled. ''Not that there has to be,'' she added hastily. ''You connected the dots, and I can see the picture.''

''But there *is* more. Much more. Dark secrets. A rancorous first marriage. Bad habits, the kind professional sports can't abide. How much would you pay for this story? $39.95? $49.95? $59.95? Wait, don't answer—what if we throw in a set of ginsu knives?'' He began to laugh a little hysterically, then caught himself. ''Trust me, Tess. It's solid. I wish my house had been built on a foundation half as good.''

''Then why won't the paper print it?''

''All sorts of reasons. They say we don't have it nailed. They say it's racist to cover an NBA deal so aggressively when we let football, which appeals to a white fan base, slip into town without a whimper. They say we used too many unidentified sources, but some of the people who talked to me still work for Wink, Tess. They have damn good reasons to want to be anonymous. One guy in particular. The top editors told us this afternoon we had to turn over the names of all our sources before they ran the story. They knew I couldn't do that, I'd see my story spiked first. Which was the point. They want an excuse to kill the story because they don't trust us.''

''Us?''

''Me and Rosie. You met her. She's good, for a rookie. You ought to see the stuff she dug up on Wink's first marriage.''

''It's probably her they don't trust, then. Because she's new, and young.''

Feeney shook his head. ''New and young is better than old and old at the *Beacon-Light* these days. Her. Me. Both of us. I don't know and I don't care anymore. I'm tired, Tess. I'm so tired, and it's such a good story, and all I want to do is go to sleep right here on the table, wake up, and find out they're going to print it after all.''

"Feeney, I'm sure they'll do right by you, and you'll have your big scoop," she said, pushing his water glass closer to him, hoping to distract him. *He seems to be settling down*, she thought. *Maybe the evening can be salvaged.*

Feeney lurched to his feet, martini glass still firmly in hand. "This isn't about me, or my big scoop!" he shouted. The other people in the bar looked up, startled and apprehensive.

"Okay, it *is* about me," he hissed, bending down so only Tess could hear him. He had drunk so much that gin seemed to be coming through his pores. "It's about my career, or what's left of it. But it's also about all that important stuff newspapers are suppose to be about. You know—truth, justice, the first amendment, the fourth estate. We're not suppose to be cheerleaders, going 'Rah-rah-rah, give us the ball.' We're the goddamn watchdogs, the only ones who care if the city is getting a good deal, or being used by some scumbag."

He swayed a little as he spoke, and his words were soft, virtually without consonants, but he wasn't as drunk as she would have been on five martinis. His melancholy had a stronger grip on him than the liquor.

"Feeney, what do you want *me* to do about it?" Tess wasn't the best audience for a speech on the glories of journalism.

"Why, drink to the end of my career!" he roared, toasting the room with his now empty glass. The crowd, mostly regulars, raised their glasses back in fond relief. This was the Feeney they knew, acting up for an audience.

"What are you so happy about?" a white-haired man called out from the bar.

"Am I happy? Am I free? The question is absurd! For it is a far, far better thing I do now than I have ever done before!"

Feeney smashed his ratty cap onto his head and swept out of the bar, the tasseled ends of his plaid muffler flying behind him, martini glass still in hand. Tess was left behind with a half-finished martini, Feeney's tab, and no company for the tortellini she had planned to order. Feeney knew how to make an exit, credit him that. Only the *Tale of Two Cities* allusion was the slightest bit off—too recognizable for Feeney's taste. He preferred more obscure lines, like his penultimate one, *Am I happy? Am I free?* It was tauntingly familiar, but she couldn't place the source.

It wasn't even eight o'clock and she was now alone, as well as ravenously hungry. And Tess loathed eating alone in restaurants. A character flaw, she knew, and a reproach to feminists everywhere, but there it was. She finished her drink, took care of Feeney's staggering bill, along with her own, then left. She could stop at the Eddie's on Eager, grab a frozen dinner for herself, maybe a stupid magazine to read in the bathtub. Damn Feeney. Her big night out had been reduced to no company, one gulped drink, and a frozen low-fat lasagna.

But when she reached her apartment thirty minutes later, the fragrant smells in the hallway came from her own kitchen, not Kitty's. Her nose identified lamb, hot bread, baking apples. She took the steps two at a time, leaping as wildly as Esskay had that morning.

Crow met her at the door, wrapping his lanky frame around her before she could take off her coat or put down the grocery bag.

"I didn't expect to see you here," she muttered into his scratchy wool sweater, hoping he couldn't see how pleased she was. "I left a message on your machine that I was going out with Feeney tonight."

"I closed for Kitty tonight, so I figured I'd let myself in and make some dinner. Worst case scenario, you'd come home from your drinking date all giggly and fun, I'd tuck you in, then eat lamb stew and apple pie for lunch tomorrow."

"Trust me, Feeney was neither giggly nor fun tonight."

Crow wasn't really listening. He was kissing her brow and her ears, patting her all over, always a little surprised to see her again, even in her own apartment.

"Your face is cold, Tesser," he said, using the childhood nickname she had given herself, a blending of her two names, Theresa Esther. A name reserved for family and very old friends. Crow was neither of those things, not in five months' time. He was twenty-three to her twenty-nine, a happy, careless twenty-three, with glossy black hair almost as long as hers, although usually with a green or red stripe, and a bounce in his walk. It still surprised her that she had to look up to see his thin, angular face, as if their age difference meant he must be shorter, too.

"What do you think of the new addition?" she asked, pointing with her chin toward Esskay, who was staring at Tess as if trying to place her.

"She's cool. Kitty and I took her out for a walk earlier, then made her some rice and steamed vegetables. She's a very old soul, our new dog."

Tess frowned. "Our" was a word to be avoided at all costs. Their rules of engagement—more precisely, their rules of disengagement—said no shared books or CDs, dutch treat for all meals out, and no joint purchases of any kind.

But all she said was: "I don't know why you made it rice and vegetables. I have a twenty-pound bag of kibble."

"I like to cook for my women," he said, pulling out her chair at the mission table that did double duty as a dining room table and Tess's desk. "Hey, did I tell you Poe White Trash has a gig Saturday?"

"Where?"

"The Floating Opera."

"I guess this means I can't request any Rodgers and Hart," she said, trying not to make a face. The Floating Opera was an ongoing rave with no fixed location, hopscotching across the city—or, at least, its more fashionably decadent neighborhoods—according to a pattern understood only by its denizens. As a result, the F.O. had none of the amenities of a real club, such as alcohol, food, or bathrooms, and all the drawbacks: cigarette smoke, too-loud music, too-young crowd.

"Rodgers and Hart," Crow groaned. "We don't go in for that retro crap."

"Elvis Costello sang 'My Funny Valentine.' "

"Tesser, Elvis Costello is old enough to be my father."

"But not old enough to be mine, right?"

He smiled, disarming her. "Was Feeney's mood contagious? Or are you itching for a fight tonight?"

"A little of both," she confessed, and, embarrassed by her crankiness, scooped up her stew meekly and quietly.

With dinner done, she put the bowls in the sink, only to have Crow snatch them back for Esskay, who made quick work of their leftovers. Crow patted the dog and thumped her sides. For a skinny dog, she had a lot of muscle tone: Crow's affectionate smacks sounded solid, drumlike.

"Is stew good for her, after all that rice and vegetables?" Tess asked, remembering Steve's dire predictions from the morning.

"Kitty had this book, in the 'Women and Hobbies' section, on greyhounds," Crow said, rubbing Esskay's belly. The dog had a glazed look in her eyes, as if she might faint from pleasure. "It said they usually need to gain weight after they leave the track, so I don't think a little stew will hurt, although the woman who wrote the book recommended making your own dog food, from rice and vegetables. She also said you're suppose to put ointment on these raw patches, like for diaper rash."

The dog shoved her nose under Crow's armpit and began rooting around as if there might be truffles hidden in the crevices of his fraying thrift shop sweater. Crow laughed and gave the dog another round of smacks, then sang, in a wordless falsetto, *"Rou-rou-rou."*

Esskay answered back, in a higher key, the vowel sounds slightly more compact, *"Ru-ru-ru."*

"I'm not really a Jeanette MacDonald and Nelson Eddy fan," Tess said, turning on the stereo. Sarah Vaughan's voice filled the room, drowning out the Crow-and-canine duet. "And I'm beginning to feel like three's a crowd. Would you two like to be alone?"

Crow walked over to her and gave Tess's backside the same affectionate thump he had given the greyhound. Tess was solid, too, but meatier, so her tone was deeper, mellower.

"I'd put ointment on your raw patches if you had any," he whispered. "Do you have anything that burns, Tesser?"

Through her clothes, his hands sought out the places where bones could be felt—the ribs below the heavy breasts, the pelvis bones sharp in her round hips, the knobby elbows. He pulled her blouse out of her long, straight skirt and stuck one hand under the waistband, rubbing her belly as he had rubbed Esskay's. With the other hand, he traced the lines of her jawbone and her mouth, then moved to her throat and the base of her neck, where he freed the strands of her long braid.

"Do you like this, Tess?" She could only nod.

Sarah was running through the list of the things she didn't need for romance: Spanish castles, haunting dances, full moons, blue lagoons. The greyhound moaned to herself, softly now, almost in tune. *"Ru-ru-ru."* Tess's breath caught and she reached for Crow's face. Sex would seem almost less intimate than this, and therefore much safer.

"Tesser?" Crow held her wrists, forcing her to meet his gaze.

She waited, apprehensive about what he might say next. Afraid he would start lobbying to move in again. Afraid he would say he loved her. Afraid he would say he didn't.

Sarah sang that her heart stood still. Tess's was beating faster and faster.

"Let's go to bed," Crow said.

Chapter 4

∽∾∽∾∽

The Maryland Motor Vehicle Administration, like most bureaucracies, ran inefficiently. Unless, of course, one was *trying* to stay away from work. Then it was suddenly a model of speed and productivity. On Wednesday morning, Tess, desperate for five minutes to herself, didn't even have a chance to take her *Beacon-Light* out of the plastic yellow wrapper before a cheerful clerk brought out the batch of driving records Tyner had requested. Oh well, there was no law against lingering here on a bright blue bench, drinking scorched take-out coffee and watching the frustrated drivers and driving aspirants. They, unlike her, were in a hurry and therefore must be thwarted at every turn. It was MVA policy.

"I'll pay you ten bucks if you've got a number lower than mine," a harried businessman whispered to Tess. She knew the type, someone who was Much Too Important, who rushed through every chore as if he were the Secretary of State and needed to jump ahead of you at the dry cleaners, or cut you off in traffic, because he was en route to board Air Force One for some summit in the Middle East.

"I don't have a number at all," she said complacently, smiling at the way he edged away from her. Yes, only a real sicko would hang out at the MVA on her recognizance, as Tommy would say. But Tess had been on the run all morning, since the alarm failed to go off, putting her thirty minutes behind. She had lost another thirty minutes when Esskay had decided to throw up on the living room rug. Tyner, to punish her for her tardiness, had sent Tess on his version of a scavenger hunt, with a list of documents that required visiting five government offices in two jurisdictions. Now it was almost eleven, her first chance to sip a cup of coffee instead of dumping it on her lap in the car. It was also the only time she had to call the hospital for an update on Spike.

"Still stable," said a cheerful nurse, whose uncle presumably was not lying in a coma.

"*Still* stable. Isn't that a redundancy?" Tess snapped, banging the pay phone down. She gulped her coffee, hot and strong enough to provide a stinging pain behind the breastbone, then skimmed the front page. Nothing of interest above the fold. Her eyes worked down to the bottom of the page, the part usually reserved for features and boring-but-necessary stories. Tidal wetlands, budget votes, welfare reform. "Duty fucks," as one of her old editors had put it so elegantly.

But Feeney's byline was anchoring this particular piece of front-page real estate. And there was nothing boring here, except for the headline.

RECORDS, SOURCES INDICATE
WYNKOWSKI HAS PROBLEMS
by Rosita Ruiz
and Kevin V. Feeney,
Beacon Light staff writers

Gerard S. "Wink" Wynkowski, the self-made millionaire who has promised to bring professional basketball back to his hometown, may never realize his dream, given the precarious condition of his financial empire and his own checkered past, which includes domestic violence and a compulsive gambling problem, the *Beacon-Light* has learned.

" 'Checkered past'?" Tess said out loud, prompting the vibrating businessman to take a seat even farther away. "Oh, Feeney, tell me you didn't write that line."

Otherwise, it was Feeney's story, exactly as he had described it to her. How could he not have known it was to run today? Was he that far gone? No, even drunk, he'd have a sense if his story was going into the paper. Something or someone had changed the editors' minds late last night. Maybe one of the TV stations was close to breaking a piece of it, improbable as that seemed.

Wynkowski's business, Montrose Enterprises, is a veritable house of cards, in which money is moved from one subsidiary to another in an attempt to maintain cash flow and obscure shortages. His creditors literally run the gamut from A to Z—from AAA Ambulance Services to Zippy Printing Services, which printed up the fliers for his Inner Harbor rally.

Wynkowski always manages to pay his biggest suppliers, but small-time creditors often are forced to sue to collect on old debts, a situation that raises doubts about whether Wynkowski has the cash on hand—an estimated $95 million—to bring a team to town.

Even if Wynkowski can put the deal together financially and cover the monthly costs of owning a team, a background check may prove to be his undoing with the NBA, when the league discovers:

• Wynkowski is an inveterate gambler, according to friends and associates, who has dropped large sums on sporting events.

• He had a tempestuous first marriage, in which police were frequently summoned on complaints of domestic violence, according to sources close to the couple at the time. He pays his first wife generous alimony because the damage inflicted by her years with him makes it impossible for her to hold a job.

• Wink's activities as a juvenile delinquent, which he has portrayed as harmless boyhood pranks, included a string of armed robberies while he was still in junior high.

It was then that Wynkowski ended up at the Montrose School, the notorious and now closed juvenile facility whose name he took for his business. A source confirmed he remained at Montrose for almost three years, an unusually long sentence.

Yet it was at Montrose that Wynkowski discovered his talent for basketball. When he returned to the community as an apparently reformed high school youth, his heroics for Southwestern High School in his junior and senior years helped erase memories of his unsavory past. Since becoming a wealthy man, he also has given generously to local charities. (See Basketball, 5A)

"Well, you did it, Feeney." Tess spoke out loud again. "Good job." With a satisfied sigh, she read the rest of what could prove to be the obituary for Baltimore's dream of a basketball team. Feeney was right, it had everything—crime and money. And wife-beating as a bonus! Feeney and Rosita had hit the allegation trifecta.

Baltimore did not necessarily share Tess's pride in Feeney's work. As she went through the rest of her bureaucratic rounds that morning, she could feel the city humming and whispering about Wink Wynkowski in heated commiseration. Theirs was a unified lament: the basketball team might be lost to the city now, all because of that bad news *Blight*.

"I don't know why they gotta be so negative all the time," she heard a man grumbling on line at the Never on Sunday sandwich shop, as she waited for a turkey sub with

tomato, lettuce, and extra hots. "Be just like the NBA to
hold a little bad publicity against a guy."

"They're just looking for a reason to block the deal,
those bastards," the counterman agreed. "They hate Baltimore."

Everyone on line agreed to that, even those who had
missed the rest of the conversation. *They* hated Baltimore.
The NBA, Washington, DC, the suburbanites who had fled
years ago, taking their tax dollars with them. The Eastern
Shore, the Western counties, the lawmakers in Annapolis.
New York, Hollywood, big business, little business, God,
the universe. They were all in a league against poor little
Baltimore.

A woman's piercingly clear voice cut through the ca-
maraderie of victimhood.

"Oh, spare me another day on the grassy knoll, folks. I
am *not* in the mood. From there, it's always just a short
stroll to the Trilateral Commission and the worldwide Jewish banking conspiracy. Is it too much to ask for a moment
of silence while I wait for a grilled cheese with bacon—no
tomatoes, please, they're like dead tennis balls this time of
year."

The voice was familiar, the attitude more so.

"Whitney Talbot," Tess said, turning to inspect her old
friend. "What are you doing this far uptown?"

"Tess! I've been meaning to call you. Ever since you
took up with that little boy, you never have any time for
your old-maid friend." This piece of information sharpened
the crowd's interest in Tess for a moment, but all eyes
quickly returned to Whitney. Blushing and windblown,
Tess was no match for this fabulous creature who looked
like the patron goddess of field hockey.

Whitney Talbot was as tall as Tess, 5'9", but thinner. She
wore her thick blond hair in a girl's careless bob and spent
$60 every six weeks to keep it even with her jaw, the sharp-
est bone in a body of long, sharp bones. It was her one
flaw, if a Talbot could be said to have flaws. Rich and well
bred, they tended toward quirks. Tess knew Whitney's

quirks well: they had been college roommates, crew mates, and competitors, vying in the secret way so many female friends do.

Tess worked her way back through the line and threw her arms around her friend. *Was* she turning into one of those women who dropped friends when a steady man was around? But it had been such a wretched winter, a time for digging in, not going out.

"Crow's okay, but he's just a *boy,*" she said. "No one can replace you, Whitney. Bring your sandwich back to Tyner's office and eat lunch with me. We'll catch up."

Whitney shook her head. "I need to get back to the *Beacon-Light*. Things are a little crazy over there today."

"Because of Feeney's story? You know, my sources tell me—" strange how good that phrase felt, more than two years out of the business—"his story wasn't suppose to run."

Whitney wasn't impressed. She knew Tess had precisely two sources at the *Beacon-Light*, and she was the other one. "Did you hear it wasn't going to run *today,* or that it wasn't going to run at all?"

"You tell me."

"Really, Tess, you know editorial is separate from the news side. I wouldn't know anything about the Wynkowski story except that, as we like to say in my section, 'This bears watching.' " Whitney was one of the paper's youngest pundits, but she was well suited to the job, a born second-guesser.

"C'mon, Talbot. Don't stonewall me. I've got photographs of you from college in compromising positions with a cigar, a boy, and a fifth of Scotch."

"The old edict about never being caught with a dead girl or a live boy doesn't apply to our gender, dear." Whitney frowned. "Then again, given the double standards at the *Beacon-Light*, the cigar alone could kill my prospects. Girls aren't suppose to have fun."

"Is this the sound of one head banging on the glass ceiling?"

Whitney didn't smile. "Know where I was this morning? A soup kitchen on Twenty-Fifth Street. They start serving breakfast at seven-thirty A.M. and don't finish until almost eleven most mornings. And today was a slow day, only two hundred people served. By month's end, it'll be three hundred. Some women stop by every morning with their kids, in order to stretch out their food stamps."

"Well, I'm encouraged to hear the *Blight* is taking an interest. You usually only write about hungry people in sub-Saharan Africa."

"Forgive me, Tess, but I hate doing all this bleeding heart social services crap. I've covered city politics, I'm fluent in Japanese, I had a fellowship in economics down at College Park. But I don't get to write editorials about those things. You know why? *It's because I don't stand up when I go to the bathroom!*"

Whitney's outburst, while not particularly loud, filled one of those odd silences endemic to hectic public places. The men in line stirred uneasily. They might have wanted to envision Whitney in the bedroom, standing or sitting, but not in the bathroom. Tess had to admit the image didn't do much for her appetite, either.

"Turkey sub, extra hots," the counterman called. Tess took the greasy brown paper bag, plucked a bag of Utz cheese curls off the metal rack, and turned back to Whitney, who was focused on her grilled cheese's progress with bird dog intensity.

"Call me, hon." She had started using the local endearment ironically, only to find it a natural fit over time, Baltimore being an irony-free zone. Even its synthetic nickname, Charm City, had begun to take on a life of its own. "Crow doesn't take up all my time. In fact, he's so busy being a local rock hero, I have plenty of free weekends and evenings."

Whitney nodded absently. But as Tess began working her way out of the crowded carryout, Whitney reached out and caught the sleeve of her coat.

"Tesser?"

"What?"

"How's your job? The investigator thing? Tyner keeping you busy?"

"In spurts."

"Spurts." Whitney laughed. Even her laugh seemed better than most people's—rarer, richer, deeper. "I thought that was how Crow kept you busy. Are you licensed? Have you bought a gun? You know, if you want to go to a range with me sometimes——"

"I don't have a gun yet. You know how I feel about them." Whitney, who had hunted ducks and doves with her father most of her life, and always kept her rifle handy, had tried to interest Tess in the sport during their Washington College days, to no avail.

"I know, I know. But you should get a license to carry, since you're entitled to one by law. If you had been carrying a gun last fall—"

"I probably would have shot myself in the foot by accident." *And everyone who was dead would still be dead,* she reminded herself, as she did whenever someone alluded to that malevolent September, to what might have been, and who might still be among the living. The little movie, the one that seemed to have been booked into her dreams for eternity, rolled again in her head, a trailer for that evening's coming nightmares.

"If you say so." Whitney gave her a kiss on the cheek, not one of those fake, airy ones preferred by her class, but an exuberant smacker of a smooch that left a pink smear of lipstick on Tess's cheek. The crowd loved it. Quicksilver Whitney had already turned her attention back to her sandwich.

"It's getting too brown. Turn it, turn it, turn it!" she implored the short, swarthy man at the grill, who grinned goofily, as if her imperious orders were a declaration of undying love. "And would you be so kind as to cut off the crusts?"

Chapter 5

Never a cheery place, The Point was particularly bleak at twilight. Even the dusk's faint light illuminated too much, accentuating the bar's distinct charmlessness. Tess could see dust on the tables, the smeared glass in the jukebox, an odd assortment of stains on the floor. She couldn't blame this on Spike's absence. The truth was, the place looked marginally better under Tommy's care.

"So, Tommy," Tess tried again, fixing herself a watery Coke from the bar nozzle. "How did Spike end up with a greyhound?"

"That blond girl sure is pretty," he said, eyes fixed on the early news, on the television set bolted above the bar. "But I don't like the black guy. How come it's always a blond girl and a black guy? How come it's never a blond guy and a black girl? You ever think about that? And who do you think makes the more exuberant salary, the girl or the guy?"

"Exorbitant salary, Tommy. And I'm more interested in greyhounds right now. What was Spike's interest in dog racing?"

"We don't have no dog races in Maryland?" he protested.

"We don't have world champion prizefights, either, but Spike has been known to take a few bets on those. Look, did he buy an interest in Esskay? Is he a partner with some out-of-state trainer? Or is he mixed up in betting on grey-hounds?"

"He didn't want nothing to do with greyhounds," Tommy insisted. "He said they were spooky looking? It bothered him to look at them?"

"Look at them *where*? Where he got Esskay?"

Tommy turned back to the television. Reporters were camped out in front of Wink Wynkowski's mansion, a new house built in a pseudo-Tudor style out of place in a treeless subdivision. Apparently, Wink had not emerged all day, nor had he provided any response to the *Beacon-Light*'s allegations. The TV reporters' only hope to advance the story was to get a reaction. They couldn't duplicate the kind of reporting Feeney had done over the last several weeks. Besides, why look at some boring old court documents or chat up sources when you can chase someone across his own front lawn, screaming, "How do you feel?"

"Be too bad to lose the basketball team because of the newspaper," Tommy said to the TV screen. "Woulda helped our business?"

"You seem awfully proprietary about things around here, Tommy. Someone might think you didn't care if Spike never woke up."

Tommy plucked nervously at his lower lip. "You're treading on thin ground, Tess. I don't see where you get off, talking to me like that. I'm around more'n the rest of the fambly. More'n *you*."

"Where did the dog come from? Why was Spike beaten? How are the two things connected?"

He turned away and began fiddling with the beer tap. The regulars were drifting in, providing Tommy with enough distractions to ignore her for hours. Slowly, with great ceremony, he shook miniature pretzels into wooden bowls along the bar, then slapped down coasters, which no one in the history of The Point had ever used. Behind the bar, Tommy looked as fresh as the coasters, in his bright yellow shirt and black pants. He even looked taller. Tess peeked over the Formica top and saw he was sporting a pair of high-heeled caramel-colored ankle boots with side zippers, circa 1976.

"Spiffy shoes," Tess said.

"Oh, yeah, well, you know I can't wear loafers. Thin ankles."

"Don't those heels hurt after a day on your feet?"

"You know what they say—a hard man's day is never done." Tommy looked bewildered when everyone laughed, but Tess suspected he was playing to the crowd. It wasn't the first time she had heard this particular Tommyism.

Esskay had also put in a hard day, shredding paper towels and toilet paper, gnawing on the pieces, then spitting up clumps behind furniture and in corners. Tess found a particularly large, soggy chunk in the center of her pillow. Her pillow, not the one Crow used, which was actually closer to the door. Did Esskay know which side of the bed Tess preferred? And if so, was this fealty, or a veiled threat?

Later, after a hot bath, she was still plucking bits of paper from odd places when the phone rang.

"Tesser! You told me to call you, so here I am, calling you." Whitney, a little too hale and hearty. The rah-rah team captain persona was usually reserved for strangers, strangers Whitney wished to keep strangers.

"Here you are," Tess echoed, without much enthusiasm.

"Can you come out and play?"

"Now?"

"Why not? It's only eight-thirty, spring is coming, and I haven't been taking enough people out on my expense account. They'll lose respect for me if it's under three figures for the month. Come be my recalcitrant source. I'll make it worth your while."

Tess studied the wad of soggy paper towels in her hand. "I'm in my bathrobe and feeling kind of cranky. Can't you buy some bourbon, bring it over here, and put that on your expense account?"

She was counting on being refused. Tess couldn't give

Whitney a receipt or a credit card slip. She couldn't even validate parking.

"Okay, but be ready to throw a coat over your bathrobe. I want to sit out on your terrace, at least as long as we can take it. See you in twenty minutes."

Tess's apartment took up only half of the space of the two floors below. The rest belonged to a flat, unremarkable roof, reached through French doors off her bedroom. A more ambitious tenant might have filled this pseudo-patio with pots of geraniums, or splurged on wrought-iron café chairs and a matching table. Tess left two vinyl lawn chairs out year-round, sponging them off as necessary. The harbor view was so spectacular it seemed unnecessary to do more. Who needed fripperies like tiny white lights in ficus trees with the neon Domino Sugar sign across the water in Locust Point blazing red throughout the night?

Yet when Whitney arrived, she was in no hurry to go outside.

"Do you have any . . . ?" she asked, sniffing delicately. Esskay wandered over to see if Whitney was good for a few pats, or a morsel of food. She stroked the dog's head, never bothering to ask how or why Tess had acquired such an ugly beast. Incurious Whitney. Reporting had never come naturally to her.

"Have any what, Whitney?" Tess knew exactly what she meant, but loved to torture the answer out of her friend, force her to say what she wanted.

"You know." Her voice was now a stage whisper. "The little box under your bed."

"My sweaters? Dust balls?"

"Your pot. Your dope. Weed. Mary Jane. Ganja. The 1970s smokable herb now making a comeback, as they say in the *New York Times* every time they do one of those 'Whatever-happened-to-marijuana?' stories. Satisfied?"

"Oh, *that*. I stopped making purchases when I went to work for Tyner, given it's a crime. A condition of my employment." A half-truth. Tyner disapproved of marijuana only because it hampered the lungs' ability to maximize oxygen intake.

Whitney looked so blue that Tess took pity on her. "I still have a little left, though. I've been hoarding it."

"Well, dig it out. And let's order pizza from BOP or Al Pacino's. Do they deliver?"

"They do to Kitty's address."

Within an hour, Esskay was nosing through two grease-stained boxes in a corner of the terrace, searching out stray bits of pepperoni and Whitney's uneaten crusts. The night was not at all springlike, but Tess and Whitney, warmed by doses of bourbon and pizza, were inured to the temperature as they shared a second post-dinner joint. Time had collapsed. They could have been in Washington College again, smoking on the banks of the Chester River.

The joint almost gone, Whitney improvised a roach clip with a garnet stickpin from the lapel of her blazer. "I like your boy-toy Crow, but I'm not sorry he's away tonight," she said, coughing a little. "I wanted to have you to myself. It makes me feel like I'm nineteen again. That, and *this*." Another furtive puff.

"I was thinking the same thing. Except the nights were so black on the Eastern Shore and they're so bright here. Have you ever noticed the city looks faintly radioactive from here? It has this smudgy glow, from the anticrime streetlights and all the neon."

"What did we talk about back in college, all those nights we smoked and drank and talked?"

"Our classes, our love lives, our futures. I was going to be a street-smart columnist and you were going to be the *New York Times* Tokyo correspondent. You're still on track, at least. We also played Botticelli. Remember?"

"You called it Botticelli. My family called it 'Are You a Wily Austrian Diplomat?' And you picked the most incredibly obscure people."

"Jackie Mason is *not* obscure, Whitney."

Tess's turn to inhale. It wasn't very good pot. The mild buzz was giving her a mild headache right between the eyebrows. Ever the good hostess, she let her guest have the last toke. Whitney pulled hard on the stub of the joint, then tossed the remains off the roof, to the graveyard of vices in the alley below—broken bottles, limp condoms, Twinkie wrappers.

"So you had drinks with Feeney last night," she said suddenly. "Did he say anything of note?"

"You know Feeney. Sometimes you can't get a word out of him all night."

Whitney snorted. "The only thing you can't get out of Feeney's mouth is his foot." She started to bring her fingers to her lips, then realized the joint was gone and refastened the stickpin to her lapel instead. "He told you about his story, didn't he? That's why you asked me about it today."

"He told me it was on life support and not expected to make it through the week." Spike's face flashed in her mind, and she suddenly felt guilty for her glib metaphor. "It was."

"What happened?"

"Biggest resurrection this town has seen since Jesus or our last crooked governor, depending on your frame of reference. Spiked in the afternoon, it rose again that night for one edition only, the final. But one edition was enough. The Associated Press overnight guy moved it on the wire, which went to all the broadcast outlets, and there was no turning back. Everyone in town went with it, and everyone attributed it to the *Beacon-Light*."

"Why only one edition?"

"Good question. One of many being asked around the office today." Whitney's eyes locked on hers, steady and serious. "It wasn't suppose to be there, Tess. Not today. Maybe not ever. Someone decided otherwise."

"So what happened? You should know, you're a lock for a Pulitzer for in-house gossip."

"I'd rather have that Far East fellowship, the one in Hawaii, or one of those Alicia Patterson grants for young journalists," Whitney said, as if "Pulitzer" was the only word she had heard. For a moment she seemed lost in some private reverie, perhaps an image of herself striding through the Orient, literally head and shoulders above the populace. She blinked, returning to Baltimore, Tess, and the roof.

"As it turns out, I do know quite a bit about this. I got it all from the big boss, right after I saw you today. Editor in chief Lionel C. Mabry himself."

"Do I know him?"

"He came to the paper nine months ago, lured out of semiretirement at Northwestern University. Ran the *Chicago Democrat* in its glory days. Reporters call him the Lion King, because he has this mane of blond hair sweeping back from a high widow's peak. They also call him the Lyin' King, because he has a tendency to tell you nice things to your face, then go to the editors' meeting and stick knives in your back. Long, elegant, quite sharp knives."

"Not *your* bony back, Whitney. Bosses always love you."

"The old bosses did. But Mabry doesn't know my work as a reporter, and he's going to have a big say in who gets the Tokyo bureau when it opens up this summer. I'm on the short list, but I'm not a lock. Not even close."

Whitney frowned. She looked baffled, much in the same way she had the first time she'd attended a Passover dinner with Tess's mother's family. "That's not horseradish," she had insisted politely, poking the tuberous root with her spoon. "Horseradish comes in a jar." No one had dared contradict her.

Tess poured more bourbon into Whitney's glass. "You'll win him over."

"Or die trying. I even used the elevator technique on him today."

"What's that, some blow job tip from the pages of *Cosmo*?"

"Well, it's not fellatio, but it *is* a kind of oral sex." Whitney hoisted herself up on the ledge and sipped her drink, legs crossed demurely at the ankles. "There's a theory that the most important part of your career is the thirty seconds you spend on the elevator with the boss—or in the hallway, or the john, but that last outlet doesn't exactly work for me. It's prime exposure time, and you should prepare for it in advance, the way you prepare for orals in college, or the way you train for a race, so it's all second nature.''

"Prepare *what?*"

"Your tapes. Think of your brain as a mini tape recorder. You need two or three tapes at the ready, to drop in the slot at the first sight of the CEO. Editor in chief, in my case. Each tape features a timeless question or observation, demonstrating you are a motivated, loyal, dedicated, happy worker who's willing to do a hundred and ten percent to make your terrific place of work even more terrific.''

"I think I need a demonstration.''

Whitney threw her shoulders back and shook her hair away from her face, transforming herself into an eager acolyte. "Mr. Mabry,'' she began, a little breathlessly, her voice higher and sweeter than usual. "Mr. Mabry, I noticed our circulation numbers for the evening edition have stabilized. Do you think the redesign, and the attempt to market the evening paper as a street-driven product, have helped reverse the years-long trend of dwindling afternoon circulation?''

Bourbon burned when it came out through the nose. "That's the most fatuous thing I've ever heard,'' Tess said, snorting and laughing. "Does it really work?''

"Well, I got on an elevator three years ago as a reporter, chatted up the editorial editor about the wonders of an Ivy League education, and by the time I got off, I was well on my way to being an editorial writer.''

"And to think I thought you were crazy when you left Washington College for Yale,'' Tess said, shaking her head in wonder. It wasn't that she wouldn't do the same, given the chance. She just wouldn't do it *as well*. Perhaps there really were only two kinds of people in the world: suck-ups and failed suck-ups.

"Then today, right after I saw you, I ran into the Lion

King,'' Whitney continued boastfully, as proud of her talent for obsequiousness as if it were a sport she had mastered. ''I said, 'The Wynkowski story—it wasn't on the budget at yesterday's four o'clock, was it, sir?' The four o'clock is the last news meeting of the day. Some things break later—''

''I know, I know.''

''Right, I sometimes forget you're a defrocked journalist. Anyway, he said, very tersely, 'No, it wasn't.' So I said, 'Well, it's none of my business, but if you want to get to the bottom of it, and want someone you can trust—a discreet private investigator with a special knowledge of newspapers—I happen to know the perfect person.' We went back to his office and chatted for an hour, mainly about his impressions of Baltimore and his backhand. It turns out he really wants to get into the Baltimore Country Club. My uncle is on the membership committee, you know.''

Tess had not been distracted by Whitney's rambling details. ''Back up a little. Who's this discreet private investigator with the special knowledge of newspapers?''

Whitney smiled coyly. ''Let's play Botticelli, Tesser. My letter is 'M.' Ask me a yes-or-no question to figure out who I am.''

''Let's see. Are you a five-foot-nine Washington College grad whose former college roommate is apparently out of her fucking mind?''

''You guessed it right off the bat. I'm Theresa Esther Monaghan, the perfect woman for the job, don't you think? In fact, you've got a meeting with the editors at two o'clock tomorrow. Do you have something decent to wear?''

Tess tipped up the bourbon bottle and took a swallow, largely for effect. Actually, she was not staggered by the thought of Whitney, without consulting her, volunteering her for a job. Whitney was always pushing Tess forward, trying to make her more than she was. But she had overlooked a few key details here.

''I have a job, remember? I work for Tyner.''

''Who wants you to be more of a self-starter, by the way.

I ran this by him before I called you tonight, and he's all for it. Said he really doesn't have enough to keep you busy right now, and this sounds like a good opportunity."

Great, Tyner and Whitney, president and vice president of the Let's-Make-Tess-Apply-Herself Club, had been conspiring behind her back again. Tess was surprised they hadn't needed her mother, the club's founding member, for an official quorum.

"My Uncle Spike is in the hospital. If Tyner doesn't need me, I'd rather spend my time getting to the bottom of what happened to him."

"Then it couldn't hurt to have the *Beacon-Light*'s files at your disposal. Computerized court documents, the paper's morgue, Nexis-Lexis—all there at your fingertips, as long as you're on the payroll."

Tempting, but Tess saw one last, huge flaw in Whitney's plan.

"Look, you're saying this was deliberate, right? Hacking, pure and simple?"

"That's the scenario."

"So they're looking for someone with a motive?"

"Naturally."

"Well, wouldn't Feeney, along with this Rosita Taquita, be a prime suspect? I can't investigate one of my friends. What would I do if I found out he did it?"

"You're getting ahead of yourself. The reality is, you probably won't be able to figure out who did it, but Mabry wants to show the publisher he takes this sort of thing very seriously. I think Mabry's secretly delighted the story got in the paper. It's the biggest thing going, and the *Beacon-Light* had it first. Mabry only held it to begin with because of the unnamed sources. All he wanted was for Feeney and Rosita to go back and get people on the record first. Someone just accelerated the schedule, that's all."

"Still, what if Feeney—"

"Look, I'll let you in a secret, but don't let it cloud your judgment: the smart money's on Rosita. No one thinks Feeney is capable of something like this. He may bitch and moan more than most, but he wouldn't risk losing his job over one story. Besides, Feeney has an ironclad alibi.''

"He does?"

Giggling, Whitney punched her in the arm. Such physicality was a sure sign of drunkenness, better than any Breathalyzer test. A punch was about 0.08 on the Talbot scale, while arm-wrestling indicated she was well over the legal limit. It wouldn't be the first time Tess had made a bed on her couch, or put Whitney in a cab for the trip home to Worthington Valley, where she still lived with her parents. If living in a guest house on a twenty-acre estate could be properly described as living with one's parents.

"Very funny, Tesser," Whitney said, still giggling and jabbing. "Feeney told me today the two of you were out drinking past midnight. In fact, it's about all he can remember from last night. Now, that's not the sort of thing you want to tell the editors, given the circumstances, but he couldn't have a much better alibi, could he?"

Tess chewed on the inside of her cheek, a habit she thought she had outgrown. It hadn't even been eight o'clock when Feeney had lurched out of the Brass Elephant. Why had he told Whitney it was midnight?

"Tess?" Whitney tried to punch her again, but missed, sending her bourbon glass crashing to the alley below. "So what do you think?"

"I think as alibis go, that's a pretty good one."

Chapter 6

Tess had been to the *Beacon Light* on official business once before, for a job interview after the *Star* had folded. She had bought a suit she couldn't afford from Femme, borrowed Kitty's best pocketbook, and put on pantyhose that she had managed to avoid running until she got back into her car. The paper had granted interviews to every one of the *Star's* 383 newsroom employees. They offered jobs to fewer than ten. A new suit, a borrowed pocketbook, and intact pantyhose were not enough to make Tess one of them.

Luckily, the suit had stayed in style, even if the store that had sold it had gone out of business. Nothing went out of style in Baltimore, especially the simple clothes suited to Tess's unfashionable figure. Almost three years later, her interview suit was still smart, as her mother would say: navy blue, with a fitted jacket that didn't require a blouse, and a straight skirt to the knee. With her hair up and navy high heels, she was the picture of demure femininity, stretched out over six feet.

"A real lady," Tyner judged, inspecting her Thursday morning as she turned slowly in front of the full-length mirror inside his office's closet door.

"The neckline is kind of plunging," said Whitney, who had ended up spending the night on Tess's sofa. She had awakened with a headache that she refused to admit was a

53

hangover, and was now perched on Tyner's desk, lost inside a sweater and skirt borrowed from Tess. On Whitney, the too-big clothes looked chic and deliberate.

"Thanks, Whitney. You're a real pal."

"I'm not being rude. But if they were making a training film about sexual harassment, you'd be cast as the doe-eyed secretary. Someone could fall into your cleavage and never be seen again. It's too sexy. You lack authority. You need a scarf."

"Of course. I've noticed the President always wears one during the State of the Union address."

Ignoring her, Whitney dug through her Dooney & Burke bag until she produced an Hermès with a Western motif—lassos, spurs, and horseshoes in shades of copper and gold, against a navy-and-ivory background.

"Cool," Tess said. "Now can you make a quarter come out of my ear?"

"I've got better tricks than that." Whitney arranged the scarf so it filled in the expanse of flesh without making Tess look as if she were a cross-dressing Boy Scout. "There, that creates interest around the face, as they say."

"It does make the outfit," Tess admitted grudgingly. "But if they didn't want me as a reporter, why would they want to hire me as an investigator?

Whitney put her arm around her shoulders, joining her in the mirror. Cool Snow White and flushed Rose Red stared back. White bread and rye bread, baked potato and potato hash.

"Half the editors at the *Beacon Light* today weren't even there when the *Star* folded," Whitney reminded her. "The other half can barely remember what their wives look like, much less the hundreds of supplicants they've turned down over the years. You'll be a whole new person to them, someone with the power to turn *them* down. By the way, I hinted you might not be able to take the job, because you're so much in demand."

"Wives?" That was Tyner, who seemed to be enjoying his temporary membership in this girls' club. Tess expected him to start wielding a lipstick or mascara brush in her direction any moment. "I never thought I'd catch you being a sexist, Whitney. You mean spouses."

"No, I mean *wives*. Little women. Helpmates. There's only one woman in the upper ranks at the *Beacon-Light*, the managing editor, and she's got the biggest balls of all of them. She had a husband once, maybe two, but I think they went into the federal witness protection program. Now she makes do with a little slave boy at home, running around in nothing but a ruffled apron, with a Scotch and water at the ready when she comes clomping home at ten or eleven."

"It doesn't sound so bad to me," Tess said.

"Well, that's what you have, isn't it?"

The *Beacon-Light*'s founders, the Pfieffer family, had been savvy about many things. Real estate was not one of them. The family had calculated on the city's center moving west over time, beyond the great department stores along the Howard Street corridor. So after World War II, when the expanding paper needed a new building, Pfieffer III had built the plant on Saratoga Street, near the ten-story Hutzler's, the grandest of all the stores. The result was a marvel of blandness, a building of tan bricks with no discernible style. Its only charm had been its real beacon, a Bakelite lighthouse revolving on a small pedestal above the entrance. The lighthouse had been torn down in the '70s and was now the Holy Grail among local collectors. The City Life museum was dying to find it, but rumor had it that a former *Star* columnist had unearthed it at a flea market and kept it on the third floor of his Bolton Hill townhouse, where he performed quasi-voodoo rituals intended to make Baltimore the country's first no-newspaper town.

Tess glanced up at the empty pedestal as she climbed the low, broad steps, picking her way among windblown McDonald's wrappers and crumpled newspaper pages. The local department stores, the few that had survived the '80s, were long gone from downtown. A drunk was sleeping among the daffodil shoots in an ill-kept flower bed. Squeegee kids—really, squeegee adults, a few squeegee senior citizens—had staked out the intersection. As the Pfieffers had predicted, the city had moved. Only it was in the other direction, south and east, toward the water. The *Beacon-Light* was a lonely and inconvenient outpost on the edge of an urban wilderness. Reporters consoled themselves with its proximity to two of Baltimore's best dining experiences, the open stalls of Lexington Market, and the white tablecloths of Marconi's. The *Beacon-Light* also was convenient to St. Jude's shrine. According to newsroom lore, reporters made pilgrimages there after deadline, always uttering the same heartfelt prayer to the patron saint of lost causes: "Please, St. Jude, don't let the editors fuck up my story."

Feeney had told Tess about this ritual. And now she was facing the prospect that Feeney was the one who had fucked up. It seemed unlikely—certainly he had been too drunk to sneak into the building, perform a little computer hackery, and leave without a trace. But if the trail did lead back to him, Tess was determined to be there to protect him, even if she hadn't figured out how.

On the sixth floor, the publisher's secretary, one of those strangely proprietary women always found hovering at the elbows of powerful men, ushered Tess into an empty conference room adjacent to the publisher's office. It was a subtly opulent room, a place to wine and dine—well, coffee and croissant in these leaner, more abstemious times—the city's powerful. Mahogany table, Oriental rug, a silver tea set on a mahogany sideboard, the inevitable watercolors of nineteenth-century Baltimore. What must it be like for the top editors, the ones who traveled back and forth between this glossy dining room and the chaotic newsroom below, all the while trying to reconcile this realm of commerce with all those romantic ideas about journalism? How did they bridge these two worlds, the corporate and the cause?

Amnesia, Tess decided. Editors quickly forgot whatever they knew about reporting. If a man named Smith drove his truck into a local diner, killing five people, editors couldn't understand why you didn't call him up and ask for all the details. "Just look it up in the phone book," they would say, as if there were only one Smith, as if he weren't in jail, out of the reach of any phone. And if by some miracle you did find Smith and get the full story, the editors would say, "Well, that's what we pay you for." Or, "We're tight tomorrow, it might have to hold."

And now Tess had to face three of these amnesiacs at once, plus the publisher. The executive editor, the managing editor, and the deputy managing editor.

"Three editors," she said out loud, staring out the window to the north. "Well, Hercules slew the Hydra."

"And *it* had *nine* heads."

A man had slipped into the room behind her, a man with high color in his face and shiny brown hair falling in his eyes. In blue jeans and a T-shirt, he might have passed for 25. In his gray wool trousers, red tie, and blue-and-white striped Oxford cloth shirt, he looked closer to the 45 he probably was. But a cute 45, Tess decided, checking out his muscular forearms, the wide grin, the boyish way he kept pushing his hair out of his eyes.

"Jack Sterling," he said, holding out his hand. "Deputy managing editor."

"Tess Monaghan." Out of habit, she grasped his hand hard, the way she had pinched Rosita's when they'd met. But Jack Sterling just squeezed back even harder. Flustered, she broke the grip, feeling something she did not want to put a name to.

He sat on the edge of the gleaming table, openly appraising her, rotating the wrist of his right hand as he massaged it with his left.

"Baltimore mick," he pronounced, talking to himself as if she were on the other side of a one-way glass. "Something else blended in, though. Something solid, good peasant stock. About twenty-seven or twenty-eight. Athletic. Doesn't like pantyhose or diet soda. How am I doing?"

"Midwesterner," she replied. "Corn-fed Protestant, a onetime *wunderkind* who is still *wunder*, if no longer *kind*.

Probably plays racquetball—note how he flexes his wrist and rubs his forearm as he speaks, something an athlete might do. How am I doing?''

Sterling laughed. Good, he had a sense of humor about himself. ''Close enough. Only my game is squash, when my back isn't out, and my wrist hurts because twenty-two years in this business have bestowed on me a chronic case of carpal tunnel.''

He began to massage his wrist again, then dropped his hand abruptly, suddenly self-conscious about the gesture. ''Midwesterner? Well, I guess Oak Park, Illinois, is about as Midwestern as it gets. How'd you figure that out? I like to think I've acquired some East Coast polish over the last few years.''

Tess smiled noncommittally. Whitney had given her thumbnail sketches of everyone she would meet today, but she saw no reason to divulge her inside information. ''Baltimore isn't the best place to come if you're looking for polish. In fact, if you're not careful, your nice, bland accent will start adding Rs to words like water and wash.''

Jack Sterling leaned toward her. His eyes were even bluer than the stripe in his shirt. ''Then what *is* Baltimore the best place for?'' Before she could think of a clever reply, the other editors began filing into the room. A little guiltily, as if he had been caught consorting with the enemy, Sterling took his place among them.

They looked more alike than they knew, this quartet. All white. No one younger than 35, nor older than 60. Two suits—gray pinstripes on the shortest man, obviously the publisher, Randall Pfieffer IV, and a flashy turquoise one on the sole woman, managing editor Colleen Reganhart, who had the kind of dark hair–fair skin–light eyes combination that the Monaghan side of Tess's family would call black Irish.

The last man was dressed as Sterling was, but his blue-striped shirt was just a little better made, his red tie heavier and silkier.

''Lionel C. Mabry,'' he said, offering a limp hand to

Tess. The hair, of course. How could she miss the hair? It was thinner than Tess had imagined, and Whitney had been uncharacteristically tactful in describing it as blond, but it was definitely a mane. Mabry's hair was a dull gray-yellow, the color of diluted piss. Otherwise, he was well preserved, with a vaguely patrician air. But then, everything about him was vague—the mumbled greeting, the clouded brown eyes, the limp-wristed handshake.

"Take a seat, Lionel," Colleen Reganhart ordered. She gave his name an extra syllable and feminine lilt. *Li-o-nelle.* He smiled at her, as if thankful for direction, and slipped into one of the large leather chairs alongside the table, Colleen to his left and Jack to his right. That left Tess and the publisher at either end, creating a strangely lopsided table.

Pfieffer's chair, she noticed, was hiked up slightly higher than the others, perhaps to give him an advantage he didn't have on dry land. Behind his back, Randall Pfieffer IV was known as Five-Four by his employees. The nickname, while not affectionate, was generous, granting the publisher two inches above what nature had given him, maybe three. But the thronelike chair was a miscalculation: his feet swung above the floor, drawing attention to his diminutive stature. Fortunately, his high, hoarse voice had no problem filling a room. He had been a cheerleader at Dartmouth, according to Whitney's dossier. ("If it comes up, say yell leader.")

He began the meeting. "Miss Monaghan, we have asked you here today because we have a job that requires discretion, tact, and a certain sophistication about our business. We've been assured you have all these qualities."

Whitney had really laid it on thick. "I'd like to think so, Mr. Pfieffer."

"I want to stress to you that as far as we're concerned, no crime has been committed here, no errors of fact have been made. We're distressed because we planned to run the Wynkowski piece on Sunday. The . . . unscheduled publication has forced us to scramble for another page one story

on that date. It concerns us our procedures have been . . .
bypassed, creating this dilemma.''

Thirty seconds into the discussion, and the first lie had
already clocked in. ''Of course,'' Tess agreed, adding from
sheer perversity, ''Isn't computer tampering a federal
crime? If you really want to find out who did this, I think
the FBI is better equipped to solve your mystery.''

The editors exchanged glances. Jack Sterling began to
speak, only to be cut off by Reganhart.

''As Randy said, we stand by the story, although we
won't be surprised if that asshole Wynkowski files a lawsuit. Let me stress, he has no fucking grounds for a libel
suit. No errors have been brought to our attention to date,
and we think he meets the test for a public figure. He'd
have to prove actual malice. Still, we prefer the general
public not know the story ran by—ran early. It could erode
readers' confidence in our product.''

Product. Colleen Reganhart had definitely gone over to
the other side. When you were a reporter, it was a story,
an article, your life's blood on the page. The higher you
went in the organization, the more it resembled canned
ham.

''Of course, if you called the FBI, or even the Baltimore
police, you couldn't control what happened to the information they uncovered,'' Tess said innocently, as if thinking out loud. ''If it got out the story ran by mistake—
excuse me, that the story ran *early*—and there are any in-
accuracies in the story, Wink Wynkowski may be able to
prove actual malice, which is essential to a public figure
who wants to bring a libel suit. Certainly it would be an
interesting test case, probably the first of its kind.''

Reganhart raised her eyebrows, dark, straight lines that
made her look as if she were constantly frowning. ''Perhaps. Our lawyers tell us he could prove negligence in our
security system. But that's *all*. We stand by our story. In
fact, we're quite proud of having exposed this fucking char-
latan.'' With her raven black hair, bright blue suit, and salty
tongue, she brought to mind the infamous mynah bird who

had been removed from the Baltimore zoo for cursing out visitors.

"So why did you hold such a hot story to begin with?" Tess asked. "I know you don't have any real competition, but I think you would want to run this story before Wynkowski signed a letter of intent with an out-of-town basketball team. It would have been heartbreaking to report that the city was getting a team, then announce the owner was never going to survive the NBA's scrutiny. And what if the city had gone ahead and started on the new arena, only to find out Wink was already entertaining offers for his team?"

Mabry seemed to come into focus for a second, like an autistic child enjoying a moment of clarity. "News judgment is not a science, Miss Monaghan. Interests must be balanced. Men do outrun their pasts. It was not our role to judge Mr. Wynkowski's fitness as an NBA owner, or to shape the decision the league will make. We do not wish to be 'players' in that sense. We had to ask ourselves, what is relevant? What is fair? Is it really necessary to reveal Mr. Wynkowski's unpleasant but largely trivial past? In the event we do so, shouldn't he have the right to know who his accusers are? That, most of all, was the real issue here. It is *still* the issue that concerns me."

His piece said, Mabry retreated back into his private world. Pfieffer hadn't spoken since his opening remarks, but he was paying careful attention, watching the interplay among his top editors with great interest. Colleen glared at Lionel, while Jack Sterling doodled on a legal pad before him.

"So the story is fine and everyone lives happily after— except, obviously, Wink. What am I supposed to do?"

Again, Colleen Reganhart and Jack Sterling began speaking at the same time. Again she cut him off.

"Tomorrow, our assistant managing editors, Marvin Hailey and Guy Whitman, will walk you through the normal procedures here and give you a list of people to interview. We don't expect you to find the person responsible, but we assume you can eliminate the majority of the people who were in the building at the time.''

"Can't your security system at least narrow down who had left for the night?''

"Unfortunately, we put in a new security system last fall, after the old system was, um, breached. The new one breaks down all the time, and has been down for two weeks now, forcing us to prop open the doors with trash cans. But I'm sure you'll find most of our employees were home with their *families* the night this happened.'' Reganhart made ''families'' sound more profane than any of the expletives she had used. "All we ask is that you interview all relevant newsroom employees, tape the conversations, then turn the tapes and transcripts over to us. Anything you discover is the property of the *Beacon-Light.* Your contract also will have a confidentiality clause, forbidding you to discuss this matter with other news organizations—or anyone else. Your information belongs to us.''

Tess wanted to ask about the movie rights, but thought better of it. ''Do you want me to work out of this building, or my office in Mount Vernon?''

"We prefer you do everything on site,'' Jack Sterling said, finally beating Colleen Reganhart to the punch. ''You'll have a cubicle on the third floor, where the old presses used to be. For the duration of your contract, you'll also have a security card and a temporary ID, so you can come and go as you please.''

"What about the union? Won't it keep the employees from cooperating with me?

Colleen Reganhart stood. ''Let us worry about the union.''

Pfieffer jumped to his feet, hands on his hips as if ready to lead a cheer—make that a yell—while Sterling stretched, audibly cracking his lower back. Only Lionel Mabry continued to sit, staring out the window at a brown-breasted pigeon on the ledge. Even by a pigeon's standards, it was a mangy thing, vicious and cruel looking.

"What a pretty, pretty bird,'' Lionel cooed with pleasure. "Spring's first robin.''

Chapter 7

Sour and disoriented, Tess left the *Beacon-Light* feeling as if she had spent an hour trapped with a querulous family in some run-down boardwalk fun house. She made her way carefully down Saratoga Street, her usually quick stride slowed by the unfamiliar high heels.

"S'cuse me, miss. You know the way to the hospital?"

An old car had pulled alongside her, a bright blue AMC Hornet that had to be at least twenty years old, one of those lumpy little seventies cars like the Pacer, which had seemed good ideas at the time. The man calling out to her was in the passenger seat. Burly and bearded, he wore dark glasses that hid most of his face, despite the overcast skies.

"There's more than one," she said, taking care to make sure she wasn't within grabbing distance, a street-smart practice drilled into her years ago by a paranoid mother. "Is it an emergency, or are you looking for a particular one?"

The man twisted his head to confer with someone in the backseat, someone Tess couldn't see, then turned back to her.

"It's a Catholic one," he said. "That help?"

"You must mean Mercy. Go straight and you'll see it in about four blocks."

Again, a hushed conference with the backseat. "Naw,

that's not it. The one we want is named for some lady. Agatha, Annie, somethin' like that.''

"St. Agnes?''

"Yeah. We got a friend there. Got beat up real bad. Word is, he might not make it.''

"I'm sorry to hear that,'' Tess said, taking a step back and casing the street quickly. There were a couple of stores along this strip and a one-way alley she could dart down. She'd kick her shoes off if she had to, make a run for it in her stocking feet.

"Yeah, poor old Joe is at death's door, the doctors say.''
Then why was he grinning so broadly?

"Joe?''

"Joe Johnson. Real good guy. You know him? Small world and all, like they say.''

"No, but I can help you find St. Agnes. It's way out in the suburbs. Take the next right, go up about two blocks, and then make a left on Franklin, taking it out to the Beltway, then take the Beltway to I-95 South and get off at Jessup.'' If they followed her directions, they'd go wildly out of their way and end up either at the State Police barracks or one of the state prisons. She had a feeling either destination would be appropriate.

"Thanks. Hey, can we drop you off wherever you're going?'' The back door opened, but not wide enough for Tess to see anyone in the backseat.

"No! I mean—I wouldn't want to take you out of your way. I'm sure you're anxious to see . . . Joe.''

"Oh yeah, we're real anxious.'' The man smiled at her, and the car roared off. She watched them head north as she had instructed, then made her way to the closest pay phone. Spike was in intensive care, the nurse reminded her. No one but family was allowed to visit, and no one but Kitty and her parents had tried.

Tess wasn't reassured. A call to admitting told her what she suspected: no Joe Johnson had entered St. Agnes this week.

Adrenaline pumping, she quickly thought of someone

who could help her out. And best of all, she could work out while consulting him.

Durban Knox had owned his eponymous boxing gym in East Baltimore for almost forty years. When the neighborhood had been infiltrated by the upwardly mobile in the 1980s, he had tried to cash in by adding fancy weight machines, Lifecycles, Stairmasters, and Star-Track treadmills. The club had caught on, but not because of the new equipment. Instead, doctors, lawyers, and stockbrokers came to box alongside the regulars, usually within days of some newspaper article announcing that boxing was the newest workout for doctors, lawyers, and stockbrokers. The most recent version of the boxing-is-back story had professional women taking up the sweet science. Tess was not tempted. With everyone else in the ring, she enjoyed almost exclusive title to most of the non-boxing equipment. And as Spike's niece, she also enjoyed the almost exclusive protection of Durban, who made sure the male patrons left her alone. Even if she had wanted one to talk to her, he wouldn't have dared, not under Durban's watchful eye.

But now it was Spike who needed protection.

"Yeah, I know some guys who could keep an eye on him," Durban said, after hearing about Tess's encounter on Saratoga Street. "Better do it that way, instead of going to the cops. Spike wakes up and finds some cop outside his hospital room door, he ain't going to be very happy with you."

"I don't know how I'll pay them—"

Durban flapped his hand in front of his face as if he smelled something bad. "We'll talk about that when Spike wakes up. Now, stop wasting time and get cracking. Tyner told me you gotta lot of work to do to get ready for the rowing season. I'm suppose to make sure you don't dog it."

Although it was above freezing, warm enough to run outdoors, Tess opted for five miles on the treadmill, jogging until she had the sweet, rubbery feeling only an overheated

gym can provide. Imagining Colleen Reganhart's bright
blue body beneath her feet, she pounded out her last mile
in under 7:30, the treadmill's top speed.

"I'm watching you, Tess," Durban called across the
room, pointing to the clock. "Seventy-five minutes on aer-
obics, Tyner said. He also says you gotta do more weight
work."

"Fine, I'll do the bike. I've got *Don Quixote* to keep me
company."

"Yeah, well get him to spot you on some bench presses,
too. Tyner *said*."

Tess settled on the stationary bike with her book propped
on the control panel. After a few minutes, she barely noticed the gym's sounds around her—the throb of the speed
ball, the duller tones of the heavy bag, the muted thuds of
colliding bodies. In its own way, Durban's was a serene
place. She always felt safe here.

A sudden breeze swept through the room, changing the
pressure like a cold front coming through town. An entourage had arrived, and the bright white light of a television
camera was capturing its every movement. What was the
fuss? Durban had trained a few moderately successful boxers in his time, but no one who could generate this kind of
heat. Tess saw the silver-haired anchor from Monday
night's rally, unnaturally pink in his makeup, schmoozing
with Paul Tucci, still walking stiff-legged but no longer
using a cane. The Tucci money seemed to promote that
kind of reflexive brown-nosing. The rest of the group
looked like bankers and Chamber of Commerce types, blue
suited and bland.

The suits parted and Wink Wynkowski emerged, shock-
ingly scrawny in a gray wool singlet. *Interesting costume
for someone with legs the size of my forearms,* Tess
thought. Wink hadn't gained weight as he aged, but he also
hadn't put on any muscle, or bothered to expose his narrow
chest and stringy arms to the sun. With his tanned face and
pale body, he appeared to be wearing a white turtleneck
and stockings beneath the skimpy one-piece.

"I'm going to work out, get a little glow going," Wink told the anchorman. "I work out every day, I tell you that? Wait, here's a line for you: 'Wink Wynkowski might be sweating at the gym, but he's not sweating the bullshit charges against him in the *Beacon-Light*.' Pretty good, huh? I mean, I know you can't use the profanity, but I think that's got a nice feel to it."

"I write my own copy—" the anchor began. Wink cut him off with a flap of his hand.

"Go ahead and use it. I'm not going to sue *you*. Besides, you won't think of anything better. Now, what do you want to do, get some shots of me moving, maybe talking to the other guys here?" Wink was a natural boss, directing the television segment as if it were a subsidiary of Montrose Enterprises. "You know, these are just regular guys, black and white, working out together, the kind of people who really want to see a basketball team in their hometown. How's the light in here? A little harsh, don't you think? When I started my chain of workout places, the first thing we did was move away from this fluorescent crap. People want to look good when they're working out. I mean, that's the point, right? If you look good in the gym, maybe you won't have to go any farther to find someone to cozy up to, she'll be right there. But Durban and I go way back, so I wanted to drop by. I fought Golden Gloves when I was seventeen, I ever tell you that? Welterweight. Won, too. You can look it up."

Tess caught Durban's eye. He shook his head, mouthing "Glass jaw."

"You going to get in the ring today, Wink?" That was the oh-so-chummy cameraman.

Wink looked around the room. His eyes rested on Tess for no more than a second, then moved on quickly, taking in the rest of the equipment.

"The bike. I think I'll warm up on the bike." He hopped up on the Lifecycle next to Tess, only to find the seat was too high: his height, what there was of it, was in his torso.

Debonairly as possible, he set the seat three notches lower, and started pedaling.

"Which program you using?" he asked Tess, leaning over to see the readout on her machine, which happened to be covered by her book. His breathing sounded ragged, for he had started out much too quickly.

"Manual. Level six." She knew the drill: short, curt answers, no questions, no eye contact. This method was the best way to kill a conversation at the gym, or anywhere else, for that matter.

"I do the random program. Much more challenging."

Honor dictated a reply. "Not really. You have some tough intervals, but you also have a lot of downhill stretches. Manual is flat and constant. At this level, I'll burn about 750 calories in an hour. You'll be lucky to burn 450—assuming you can last an hour."

The cameraman, who had been creeping across the room, turned the light on full in Tess's eyes and began filming this exchange. Reflexively, she held up *Don Quixote*, shielding her face.

"Excuse me, but I'd prefer not to be on the evening news." Her voice, although somewhat muffled by Cervantes, was nevertheless distinct. "This is private property, and I didn't give you permission to photograph me."

"Oh, you're not in the shot," the cameraman lied smoothly. He probably assumed everyone secretly yearned to be on television. "I'm just shooting Mr. Wynkowski here for a story we're doing on him. It's a tight shot. No one will see you."

"What about sound? Don't you have a built-in microphone, which picks up everything I say?"

"Everyone has those now. Don't say anything, and you'll be okay."

Tess lowered the book to chin level, stared into the camera, and recited in a bored monotone, "Fuck. Shit. Bite me. Eat me. Piss on you, asshole." Then she smiled sweetly. "Did you get that?"

Wink laughed so hard he almost fell off the bike, while

the cameraman flushed with anger and turned his camera off.

"We could still use it, you know," he said. "We could use that part of the video as B-roll if we really wanted to, putting in a voice-over."

"You could," Tess agreed. "But when you look at the tape, you'll see I was giving you the finger the whole time, on both sides of my book." She demonstrated. "I don't think that would look very nice on the station that bills its six o'clock program as 'Good news for the whole family.'"

Irritated, she was cycling faster and faster without realizing it, while Wink had given up any pretense of working out. He leaned toward her again, as if they were co-conspirators. Just two private citizens, ambushed by the local television station. He waved his entourage away, Paul Tucci practically leering at them as he retreated. Wink then dropped his voice, so Tess had to move her head closer to his in order to hear.

"You're pretty ballsy. I find that attractive in a woman."

"I don't want to infer too much from what I'm sure is an innocent, heartfelt compliment, but aren't you married?"

"I *am* married," he confided, "but my wife lets me date."

"What do you let her do?"

"Have babies and buy things."

Although she was not belligerent by nature, Tess briefly considered punching him. She was sure one well-placed sock would knock him from his perch on the bike, maybe even knock out a few teeth if he fell against the pedals on the way down. There was a perverse fairness to hitting someone who hit on you. Wink Wynkowski, reared on the playgrounds of Southwest Baltimore, would understand a good solid thump to the jaw.

But hitting him was just a fantasy, and a stupid one at that. Tess opted to hide behind her book, rereading the scene in which the muleteers beat Sancho Panza.

"You'd rather read a book than talk to me?"

"I'd rather be set on fire than talk to you."

Wink dismounted, grabbing her left arm as if to balance himself, although his footing seemed sure enough. She tensed, hoping he could feel the clenched bicep, the long tricep beneath it.

"I guess you don't want to watch basketball games from the floor. It's a good way to meet good earners. Unfortunately, we tend to be married, us rich guys."

"From what I read in the papers, *you're* not so rich."

"Yeah, well, maybe I'll get richer, courtesy of the *Beacon-Light*. Maybe I'll have some of the Pfieffer family's millions before this is all over."

"Are you saying the newspaper libeled you? I'd like to hear more about that. I'm sure a lot of people would." The *Blight* editors hadn't asked her to probe Wynkowski's legal intentions, but it couldn't hurt.

"I'm saying they'll be sorry. Like you, honey." This time, he ran his index finger along the inside of her arm. "You listen to the Boss, or are you one of those younger kids who thinks you're too cool?"

"Actually, I like Springsteen." *I'm just not queer enough to call him the Boss.*

"Well, the Boss may have been from New Jersey, but he coulda been writing about Baltimore all these years. This is a town full of losers, baby, people who are so scared of the future, they end up talking about the past all the time. There's more to life than getting Barry Levinson to make some fucking movie about you. No one made a movie about me, but I'm going to be bigger than any of 'em. Don't believe everything you read in the papers."

A parting squeeze of her arm, then he returned to his satellites, who had been lost without him, bumping into each other and looking around. Relieved, they clapped him on the back, although a little gingerly, in case there was any moisture left over from his five minutes of activity. Paul Tucci glanced back at Tess curiously, then limped out after them.

* * *

That night, Tess and Crow tried to watch the 6 o'clock news from bed, while trying to protect the perimeter from Esskay, who circled them, intent on stealing their Chinese food or curling up on their pillows, maybe both.

"What a hedonist," Tess complained, rescuing a carton of General Tso's chicken from the nightstand just as Esskay tried to clamp down on it. Thwarted, the dog grabbed one of the pillows and carried it off into the corner, where she appeared to be making a nest. So far, she had kidnapped an old, stuffed bear of Tess's, placing it in the center of a pile made from one of Crow's T-shirts, tissue salvaged from the trash, and several pairs of Tess's underwear.

"Have a heart," Crow admonished. "You'd need pillows, too, if you were all bones."

"You're saying I'm not?" Tess asked in mock outrage. "Hey, turn up the sound. They're doing the piece on Wink."

The TV showed several television crews massed in front of Wink's fake Tudor mansion, an overdone confection of turrets and stained glass. Stock footage, Tess realized, shot the day before, when the *Blight*'s story had run and all the TV reporters had camped out in front of Wink's property, waiting in vain for him to comment.

"What's the point of a new house designed to look old?" Crow wondered.

"I guess it's for people who have to have wainscoting, ivy, *and* a subzero refrigerator. Louder, please. I still can't hear."

The anchor's voice, so deep and rich it vibrated on Tess's cheap set, filled the room: "Channel Eight has learned tonight that Wink Wynkowski plans a news conference Monday to respond to the charges against him in the local press." The footage changed to shots from the gym—Wink pedaling, Wink thumping the heavy bag, Wink flirting.

"That's your arm!" Crow exulted. "I recognize the mole on your elbow."

"And although he took time out to sweat at Durban's gym today, Wink assured me, in an exclusive interview, that he wasn't sweating the basketball deal.'' So the reporter had stolen the line after all.

Cut to a shot of Wink outside Durban's gym, breathing clouds of smoke in the wintry air as he spoke into a microphone. Tess was thankful he had put a jogging suit on over his singlet.

"All I want to tell my supporters—and I know I have a lot of them—is to rest easy. I always knew we'd have people fighting us on this. I just didn't expect they'd be right here in my hometown." He paused, as if he expected cheers or applause, then remembered he was being taped for television. "You know, maybe when I wrap this deal up, I ought to look at starting a new newspaper, or convince one of the big chains to buy the poor excuse for the one we got. You know what they say about Baltimore? It's the biggest city in the country without a daily newspaper."

"What about those charges in the *Beacon-Light*, Wink?" the anchor asked, puffed up with pride at his daring. "Any truth to them at all?"

Tess rolled her eyes. "He's going to hit this one farther than the home run Frank Robinson hit out of Memorial Stadium."

"I can't comment on that now, but I expect to have a detailed response by Monday after talking to my advisers. It's a complicated situation and I have to keep my priorities straight, not get distracted. The game plan is, number one, buy the team, number two, get it here, and then, number three, I'll worry about those little dogs nipping at my heels."

"But what about the information on your, uh, youthful transgressions? Can you elaborate on that? Some people have noted that three years is a long time to send a juvenile away on robbery charges."

To Tess's surprise, Wink's eyes began to tear up in what seemed to be a genuinely spontaneous show of emotion. He started to speak, stopped, cleared his throat, and continued, almost seething and crying at the same time.

"There's a reason they keep your name confidential

when you do things as a kid, you know. It gives you a chance to start over, get things right. And I did pretty well with the chance I got, better than most. Yet I get singled out. Is that fair? You gonna open up the records of every guy in town who went to Montrose? Because I'm not the only one, you know. I'm not the only guy in this town who needed a fresh start.''

Tess and Crow were so mesmerized by this performance that Esskay was able to make another lunge toward the Chinese food, snaring a gnawed sparerib from Crow's plate. Her victory was short-lived: she began retching, the bone lodged deep in her throat.

"Try the Heimlich maneuver," Tess cried, panicking. Unruffled, Crow reached his hand down the dog's throat and extracted the rib, gooey with drool and sauce. Esskay stared at the bone as if she had never seen it before, then tried to snatch it back from him.

"Pavlov, indeed," Tess snorted in disgust, but her heart was still beating a little fast. "This stupid mutt can't learn anything. She can't even remember she almost choked to death on that same damn bone ten seconds ago.''

"Oh, I don't know," Crow said, forgiving as always. "We all have things we desire even though we know they wouldn't be good for us. Don't you have a few spareribs in your life?''

A rhetorical question, one of Crow's flights of fancy, nothing more. To Tess's consternation, an image of Jack Sterling flashed through her mind—his blue eyes, the strange little sensation she had felt when they shook hands, as if he had caught a spark of static electricity from the carpet in the conference room and passed it on to her. Blushing, she hid her hot face in Esskay's hotter neck, stroking the dog until she was sure the telltale color had subsided.

Chapter 8

"I can think of five other things I should be doing right now. I really don't have time to be your tour guide."

It was Friday morning, and metro editor Marvin Hailey was leading Tess through the newsroom, which looked more like an insurance office gone to seed. Scurrying behind the reluctant Hailey, Tess tried to keep tabs on where she was going in this maze of cubicles, dented metal filing cabinets, and ancient computers rigged with various accessories to make them slightly less lethal to the users and their wrists. Cardboard file boxes were stacked around some desks, creating makeshift walls, while old newspapers rose toward the ceiling in shaky yellowing towers. Recycling was apparently too avant-garde for the staid *Beacon-Light*.

"It looks like you're running out of space," Tess said, trying to make conversation with the unsmiling editor.

"We are," Hailey said, glancing over his shoulder as if acknowledging even this obvious fact was fraught with risk.

"Any chance of the whole operation moving out to the 'burbs? I know you're already printing the paper out there."

"We had to have new presses, and it made sense for delivery purposes to be outside the Beltway. But the other departments will remain here until Five—uh, Pfieffer—can get a good price for the property.''

''Forever, in other words.''

Hailey grunted, a safely neutral noise.

It was 9 A.M., a rare quiet moment in the cycle of an all-day newspaper. Within an hour, the skeleton crew of over-night editors would put to bed the ''evening'' paper, a publication identical to the morning paper except in layout and the updates on predawn carnage provided by a lone police reporter. Most of the other reporters had yet to arrive, with the exception of a dark-haired woman with her feet propped on an open desk drawer, reading the morning pa-per while she listened to a police scanner. A phone rang on the city desk, but no one was there to answer it.

''So this is where you make the magic happen,'' Tess said.

Marvin Hailey lunged for the still ringing phone, suc-ceeding only in knocking over an old mug of coffee. Tess watched him try to stem the milky-brown spill with wad-ded-up newspapers, only to spread the puddle over more of the desk top. Such a dry husk of a man—shoulders speckled with dandruff, lips whitish and cracked from con-stant, nervous licking. He looked as if he might break up and blow away in a strong breeze.

''Oh, hell,'' he sighed. The newspaper had finally ab-sorbed the coffee, only to leave his hands black with ink. Resignedly, he tossed the crumpled sheets into a nearby trash can, wiped his palms on his pilled trousers, and sat down at his computer.

''We've got you all set up on our system. To sign on, you hit this button and type in MONAGHAN,'' he said, doing just that. Even his typing had a jumpy, paranoid rhythm, as if he expected someone to creep up behind him and find fault in whatever he did. ''Now the computer wants a six-letter password. You want me to pick some-thing out for you? It's not as if you'll need a secret one.''

''That's okay, I'll do it.'' Tess slid the keyboard away from Hailey and tapped in the first six-letter word that came to mind: E-S-S-K-A-Y, which showed up on the computer only as a series of asterisks. Who knew what secrets she might want to keep as this progressed? "Now what?"

"Well, I assume you're going to start interviewing people. I drew up a list of people we know were here that night. Editors, reporters, custodial staff, the printer who set the bogus—um, unofficial—story. You should be able to get to most of them today, except for Feeney and Ruiz. They flew to Georgia yesterday, aren't expected back until late tonight."

"Georgia? For the Wink story?"

"I guess so, but no one's informed me officially." Hailey allowed himself a small, bitter smile. "This is so hot only Colleen, Mabry, and Sterling are in the loop. I guess I'll find out when the Sunday paper comes out, like everyone else in Baltimore."

"Don't be so bitter, Marv. They haven't clued me in, either, and I'm the sports editor. The story came out of my department, don't forget that." A grinning, square-jawed man appeared out of the warren of desks and cubicles to offer his arm to Tess, which she declined to take. "Guy Whitman. I'm here to lead you to the system manager, who will explain what happened electronically Tuesday night. The computers are part of my province."

"What do computers have to do with the sports department?" Tess asked, as she began following him along a new path through the newsroom labyrinth.

"I'm also in charge of *Beacon-Light* 2000, a task force set up to examine the paper's information services, what we'll need to go into the twenty-first century."

"Aren't newspapers already in the information services business?"

Guy looked as if he wanted to pat her on the head. He was handsome, in a fluffy-hair kind of way rare in a newspaper editor. *And didn't he know it.* Too bad his taste in ties appeared to be terminally whimsical. Tess tried not to make a sour face at the dancing lacrosse sticks.

"You sound like everyone else around here, Theresa.

Haven't you noticed the times, they are a-changing? You can read virtually every major metropolitan newspaper on the World Wide Web. The *Washington Post* has its own on-line service. But the *Beacon-Light,* one of the last family-owned papers in the country, has only started beta-testing its Web site, and they're doing it on the cheap. They think they can continue to work primarily in paper.'' He spat out the last word as if it were something caught in his teeth.

"Well, paper is awfully handy for taking on a bus, or sharing at the breakfast table. By the way, my grandmother on my mother's side is the only person who gets away with calling me Theresa.''

"I hope you're not one of those types who's still hot for hot type, Theresa.'' Whitman didn't seem to be deliberately ignoring her, he had just lost the habit of listening to any voice other than his own. "Dreaming of pneumatic tubes—don't tell me that's not Freudian. But things do change, and usually for the better, I think, although that's not always a popular opinion these days. Do you think football should be played in leather helmets? Should we use carrier pigeons to cover breaking events? Would you have preferred to come here today via streetcar? You're young, you're suppose to embrace the future, while old farts like myself—'' he paused here, in case she wanted to object to his characterization of himself. "Anyway, you make a lovely Luddite.''

For someone who's so gung ho about the future, Guy Whitman was sure behind the times when it came to the current thinking on what constitutes sexual harassment. Tess thought about reprimanding him, but he had ducked through a narrow space between two plastic dividers covered with soiled, once-blue fabric—the systems manager's "office.''

Behind the dingy dividers, all was order—a severe, meticulous order. The metal cabinets shone, as did the desk, giving the alcove the high-tech, unused look of an office in an Ikea catalog. With the exception of a Georgia O'Keefe wall calendar and one Post-It note on the computer terminal, there was not a single scrap of paper in this office. Not even a newspaper, Tess noticed.

"So, where's the computer geek who presides over this electronic kingdom?" she asked Whitman.

A scratchy female voice came from somewhere around their ankles. "The geek is under her desk, unplugging a laptop whose batteries she was recharging because the prima donna reporter who had it last couldn't be bothered with such a mundane task."

A plump woman in her late thirties crawled out and stood up, brushing off her jeans. Of medium height, with flyaway brown hair that had long ago surrendered to a nest of cowlicks, she was as soft and disarrayed as her office was hard and sleek.

Tess held out her hand. "Tess Monaghan, vicious purveyor of stereotypes."

"Dorie Starnes. And I don't mind being called a geek. It's a promotion for someone who started in circulation. Who'da guessed I had a natural gift for computers? Not the teachers at Merganthaler Vo-Tech, that's for sure. They kept trying to steer me toward the commercial baking classes."

Dorie was not someone to do one thing when she could be doing two or three. As she spoke, she settled into her ergonomically perfect chair, complete with tie-on backrest, and rolled another chair to her side, patting it in invitation even as she began to type a series of mysterious codes into the computer.

"Move on, Mr. Whitman. You'll just be in the way. Go make a news decision, or convene a focus group on box scores. Aren't you going to run a reader's contest to name the new basketball team? Oh, I forgot, that was a promotion marketing worked out with Wynkowski. Guess that's no longer a go."

Whitman forced a hearty laugh. "That's a good one. Of course, Dorie doesn't even read the paper, do you, Dorie? Who's the prime minister of Israel, Dorie? Is the state legislature currently in session? Who's the President of the United States? What's NAFTA stand for?''

"I try to read the newspaper, Mr. Whitman, I really do. But all I see are the computer commands that make it possible to put black stuff on white stuff. Sometimes the arrangements turn into stories I want to read, but most of the time they just look like those crazy paintings in that new wing at the Baltimore Museum of Art. Black stuff on white stuff.''

Dorie stared at her computer monitor as she spoke, running her fingers rapidly across the keys like a pianist warming up. As far as Tess could tell, she wasn't really doing anything, but it looked impressive, blocks of copy appearing and disappearing on her screen.

"Very clever, Dorie. When you're through taking Ms. Monaghan through the system, ask my secretary to take her to the office we've set up for her. Jean also has a list of the workers you need to interview, Terry.'' *Terry! That was worse than Theresa.* "By the way, would you like to have lunch with me today? I find myself unexpectedly without plans.''

"What happened?" Dorie asked, all sweet innocence. "Was there a fire at your favorite motel?''

This time, Whitman's fake chuckle was not so robust. "Now, Dorie, Miss Monaghan will have the wrong impression of me if you keep this up.''

"I'm afraid I couldn't join you today, anyway. I have plans.'' Dorie might have been kidding about the motel room, but Whitney had warned her that the very married Whitman felt honor bound to make a pass at virtually every woman who passed through the office.

Dorie kept her eyes trained on the monitor, fingers tapping away. "NAFTA is the North American Free Trade Agreement,'' she said softly to herself. "The Maryland legislature convenes on the second Wednesday in January and meets for exactly ninety days. Is he gone?''

"Yes,'' Tess said, glancing over her shoulder. "Is he always such a jerk?''

"Actually, he's generally harmless, which is saying something around here. He was only trying to impress you. But I don't *love* him. And Whitman needs to be loved, and not just in the boy-girl way. He needs complete, unconditional adoration, something I reserve for Johnny Unitas."

"Hey, I grew up in a house where the Colts were the only theology my parents could agree on."

Dorie allowed a small, crooked smile at that. She was typing rapidly again, with some purpose now. A copy of Feeney and Rosita's Wink Wynkowski story appeared on the screen.

"Okay, this is a story, or a 'take,' which is stored in a directory. The Wynkowski piece was assigned to CITY HOLD, a directory for stories that have been edited, but are waiting clearance, sort of like jets ready to take off. Some are evergreens—stories that can run anytime there's space, but it's not urgent. Others are hot potatoes, designated WFP—Wait For Permission. The Wynkowski piece had an WFP on it—Wait For Permission. Only three people, Mabry, Reganhart, and Sterling, can move one of those."

"Does an WFP have limited access, then? I mean, can only those editors call it up?"

"Good question." Dorie's tone suggested she had not expected Tess to ask good questions. "WFP is a policy, not a program; the computer doesn't make any distinctions. Anyone could pull a story out of this directory and make changes, but they'd better not. The computer keeps a history, and if Colleen found someone messing with a WFP, that person would be history."

Tess studied the words on the screen. "Is this *the* story, or a copy?

"It's the original. The one in the paper was a copy of an earlier version, before Colleen had edited it last. But there's still a trail. The computer tells us someone sat down at computer number 637, the classical music critic's terminal, a little before eleven-fifteen P.M., the time the story was sent to composing. Everyone in the building knows the critic never remembers to shut his machine off. He's legendary for it."

"So you can use his sign-on, knowing you won't get caught."

"Yeah, but even with the guaranteed anonymity of working under the critic's user name, this person was real, real careful. Watch."

Dorie tapped another key and Tess saw a form, which showed when the story had been created—almost six weeks ago, by Rosita Ruiz—and who had made changes to the story since: Ruiz, Feeney, Sterling, Reganhart, Hailey, Whitman, Mabry. *Too many cooks*, she thought. No wonder Feeney's usually clean writing had broken down into clichés and chest-thumping hyperbole.

"Here's my working hypothesis." Dorie said the word as if it were two words, hypo thesis. "He/she called up the old version on 'Browse' and saved all of the text—" Nimbly, Dorie demonstrated how to define a large block of copy and store it with just three keystrokes. "Then he/she went into the set directory and picked out a Page One story already set into type. A tidal wetlands story in this case, which the paper probably could live without. You see, the coding is already there, so all our unofficial editor had to do was erase the wetlands text and put the Wink text in its place."

"What about the headline?"

"Wrote a new one—not a very good one, but it was the same number of characters as the tidal wetlands head, so it fit. Probably didn't want to take the time to make it good. Now watch this." Dorie hit one key, and the body of the Wink Wynkowski story appeared. "I hit justify—" she stroked another key "and the computer tells me I'm over by six lines. I cut from the bottom—" She deleted the last graph with two keystrokes. "I justify again. Perfect. Now all I have to do is change the bylines and I'm ready to roll.

"Last step." She hit another key and the type was now underlined as she wrote "SUB, SUB, SUB FOR TIDAL" at the top. "See, that's in a special format, the computer can't 'read' it, but the guys in the composing room can. A final command—Command X, in fact, and it's on its way. Vol-A.''

"What's Vol-A? Computer jargon for Volume A?''

"No, it's French. You know, like a magician might say. Vol-A!'' And she made a large, sweeping gesture with her hand, as if pulling a rabbit out of her computer.

"Oh, *voilà*,'' Tess said, hating herself for it when she saw Dorie's face.

"I saw it in some book. I didn't know you said it that way.''

"Hey, I'm the same way, phonics screwed me up for life. I can't pronounce half the words I see in print. But it's more important to know something than to know how to pronounce it.''

"Not around here,'' Dorie said, looking unhappily at her keyboard. "I read a lot—history, especially the Civil War, and I've been listening to all these books on tape—full-length, not abridged. It took me a month to get through *Great Expectations*. But it doesn't matter. Here, it's *how* you say things, not what you say. It's how you talk, it's how you dress, and whether you went to some fancy college. And if you're a woman, it's how you look, too.''

"But you have the real power, Dorie. You could bring this place to its knees. They couldn't put the paper out without you.''

"Yet I'm still just a computer geek, right?'' Apparently, she had not forgiven Tess's tactless opening line. "Lesson over. You're on your own now. Let me tell you one more thing—''

Tess looked up hopefully.

"If you spill soda or coffee on one of my keyboards, your life won't be worth living.''

Although barely in his thirties, classical music critic Leslie Brainerd wore voluminous khakis hiked up to his sternum, belted so tightly they suggested an Empire ball gown. This effect was heightened by his long-fallen pectoral muscles, bobbling like voluptuous breasts in his knit polo shirt. Alone at his desk, he appeared to be listening to music on his headphones, which looked like a strange growth on his shiny bald head. But when Tess tapped him on the shoulder, he jumped with a violent start, awakened from a covert catnap.

"Small details are for small minds," he sniffed, once he understood why this strange woman had disturbed his sleep. "I have more important things on my mind than turning off this machine every night."

"I'm sure you do," Tess assured him, determined to ingratiate herself after her rough start with Dorie.

"Tuesday night was very busy for me," Brainerd continued fretfully. "I had to write on *deadline*. A most exquisite concert, featuring a young violinist." The name he mentioned meant nothing to Tess, and her blank look must have given this away.

"But you must know her! She's *lovely!* To see her in a black velvet gown, slit to the femur, is to experience heaven. *'The curves of her body mirror the curves of the violin, creating an almost sexual tension between the performer and her instrument.'* That's from my review."

She couldn't stop herself. "When Pinchas Zukerman was in town, I don't remember any details about *his* body."

"Oh, yes, my Zukerman piece. Another exceptional piece of deadline writing. I received quite a few compliments on that."

Good, Brainerd's hide was too thick to pierce, armored as it was with self-importance. Tess would bet that perhaps 5,000 of the *Blight*'s 400,000 readers actually slogged through his reviews, but they were the right 5,000, the men and women likely to fraternize with the publisher and the top editors.

"So you left here about ten-thirty. Did you see anyone on your way out? Did you go straight home, or did you stop somewhere along the way?"

Brainerd looked confused. "Where would I go?"

"I don't know. A restaurant, a gas station, a bar. I'm

trying to figure out if you can *prove* the time you left here, or if someone else can establish the time frame. The computer tells us when you filed, but because you didn't turn it off and the security system was down, there's no record of when you left the building. And your boss edited the piece from home, so he doesn't know when you left, either.''

''I was *not* happy with Harold's changes. He never gives me enough space. Just slashes from the bottom, like some vandal, or that crazy Hungarian who hammered Michelangelo's *Pièta.* I asked him once if he thought Mozart could be edited, and he said, 'He could if he wrote for me.' ''

Tess mentally crossed Brainerd off the list of possible accomplices. It was obvious to her now that Leslie Brainerd was too egotistical to care about any story written by someone other than Leslie Brainerd. If he had stumbled into the Watergate burglary, he probably would have written about how sleek the Cubans looked in their black pants.

The others on Tess's list of those known to be in the building the evening of ''unscheduled publication'' were night-side workers who wouldn't arrive until 2 P.M. or later. She took a long lunch at Lexington Market, opting for an all-peanut meal: fresh roasted nuts for her main course, then brittle from Konstant Kandy for dessert. After a morning at the *Beacon-Light,* with its strange codes and conflicting agendas, the old market felt refreshingly real. *You want an apple? Some bananas, maybe?* Apple meant apple; banana meant banana. No more, no less.

Back at the *Blight* a little after 2, she found custodian Irwin Spangler taking a cigarette break on the loading dock. He shook his head mournfully at all her questions. ''The only thing I ever notice around Mr. Brainerd's desk is how many cups of coffee he's managed to spill in a day. Tuesday must have been a good day for him, because I don't remember needing too much time up there. I was off the floor by eleven.''

Following the story's journey through the paper, Tess went to the composing room, on the third floor. Howard

Nieman, the worker who had pasted the story in place and sent it on its way, was starting his shift. A stoop-shouldered man with thinning brown hair, he had a permanent squint from a lifetime of working with agate type.

"Didn't anything seem out of the ordinary to you that night?" Tess asked him, after introducing herself. "Wasn't there something about the story, or the way it arrived, that seemed unusual?"

"It fit and it didn't make the paper late. Those are the only things I really care about, miss."

It was a slow time for Nieman, the lull between the advance Sunday editions, which would be followed by the rest of the Sunday paper, and then the Saturday paper. He showed her how the copy came in, on shiny rolls of paper with gummy backs. The strips were sliced, then pasted on the pages. A camera shot a photograph of the page, and this photo was used to make the printing plate. Tess had known this once, albeit dimly.

"I'll tell you one funny thing," Nieman said. "This kind of trick would be difficult to pull off if the pagination system were in place. That's where they design all the pages by computer. They do some of them that way, but not page one, not yet. Ol' Five-Four is always slow to put out money for the new stuff."

"What are you going to do when they go to pagination company-wide? Would you take a buyout if they offered it, like they have at some other papers?"

He smiled with only half of his mouth. "Our contract calls for lifetime job security, so they'll retrain us for some monkey work around here. I'm fifty-two—too young to stop working, too old to learn another trade. I gotta stick it out."

Tess stopped next to an easel where the Real Estate section front was displayed. The standing "sig" across the top—the columnist's name, in this case—said Annie Heffner. The photograph showed someone with a full, glossy beard. She pointed this out to Nieman, who shrugged.

"We catch *most* of 'em. What's that thing about the forests and trees? Well, we're the tree guys."

Tess understood. Howard Nieman, like Dorie with her head full of computer commands, saw the paper differently than the average reader, or even the average reporter. His version was a modular collage, pieced together from strips of copy, photographs, and standing features. Tidal wetlands or basketball, what did he care? As long as he was off the floor on time and his paycheck came through for another week, he was a happy man.

And another unlikely accomplice.

The editors had given Tess a small, windowless office near the old, now unused presses. Tess consulted a list of *Beacon-Light* employees and sent an e-mail message to Lionel Mabry's secretary, asking to see the night rewrite, Chick Gorman, as soon as he arrived for work.

Tess had assumed Chick was a man, but the person who burst through her door minutes later was a small woman with close-cropped dark hair, the same reporter she had seen that morning. At first glance, the woman could have passed for a college intern. Then one noticed the fine lines at the corners of her eyes, the shadow of a worry line between her eyebrows. Her poise finally gave her age away: absolute self-confidence can't be faked at 22.

"I'm Emma Barry," the woman said politely. Tess offered her hand, but Emma ignored it. "We're shutting you down."

"We?"

"The union. The Newspaper Guild. I'm the shop steward for Metro." She folded her arms across her chest, as if delivering a rehearsed speech. "According to long established legal precedents, any procedure that may result in disciplinary action entitles guild members to representation. Since your findings may be used by management in dismissal actions, reprimands, or suspensions, we've notified management of our objections and instructed our members not to meet with you without a union rep. Until management agrees to this, no one under our jurisdiction is available to you.''

''As someone who used to belong to the Newspaper Guild, I think you're overreacting. I'll probably do more to clear people than I will to implicate anyone. What's the harm in that?''

''Where do I start? For all we know, the bosses are using the Wynkowski story as an excuse to pry all sorts of personal things out of employees. You asked Brainerd if he went to a bar Tuesday night—are you suggesting he's an alcoholic? If he had said yes, would that information have gone into his personnel file? And you asked Nieman if he would take a buyout, which is something that can be negotiated only by *his* union.''

''It wasn't exactly like that—''

''No more interviews with our members without union representation, and I believe everyone you need to interview is a guild member. See you Monday.''

''See you Monday?'' Tess muttered to herself, after Emma had gone. ''Who said I was taking the weekend off?''

Chapter 9

Tess began Saturday by visiting Spike at St. Agnes. Unfortunately, her parents had the same idea. Not that she had anything against her parents, but a little bit went a long way, and she had been over for dinner just three weeks ago. Now here they were, chairs drawn up to the foot of Spike's hospital bed as if it were a television set and he was the host on the old *Dialing for Dollars* show. *The amount is $35 and the count is 4 from the top.* They stared at him intently, not speaking. A stranger might have concluded that Patrick and Judith Monaghan were the kind of long-married couple comfortable with silence. Their daughter knew they were merely resting between bouts.

"Hi, Mom. Pop."

"The hair," her mother said.

"It's nice hair," her father said.

"I didn't say it wasn't nice. But she's too old to wear it hanging like that, in a tail."

"It's very neat."

"It's blah. And those pants. Tess, if one's pants have belt loops, one should wear a belt."

"These are blue jeans, Mom, and belts are for people who don't have hips to keep their pants up. Never been one of my problems. Besides, I dress differently when I'm working. Honest."

"How would I know? It's been *months* since we've seen

you.'' Judith was turned out with her usual monochromatic perfection, in a dark mustard sweater with matching tweed skirt and suede flats. Tess suspected her mother shopped with paint samples from the hardware store, so flawlessly did she match everything. Patrick wore his winter uniform: Sansabelt pants, long-sleeved white shirt, and a plain red tie. Come Memorial Day, he would vary the look by switching to a short-sleeved white shirt and pale blue tie.

"What does the doctor say about Spike?" Tess asked, hoping to divert her mother from such loaded topics as grooming, wardrobe, and lack of attentiveness.

Judith shrugged. "A lot, but all it means is they don't know why he's not doing better. Maybe he'll wake up, maybe he won't. Maybe there'll be permanent damage, maybe there won't."

"Weinsteins are slow to heal," her father observed slyly.

Although everyone agreed Spike was a relative, neither side would claim him. Legend had it that he'd appeared shortly after Tess's birth, working his way through a sesame seed bagel with lox at one of Momma Weinstein's Sunday brunches. But he seemed equally at home at the Monaghans' gatherings, eating Easter ham and neatly side-stepping any question attempting to pinpoint his origins.

Today, however, Tess's mother chose to ignore her husband's invitation to this familiar favorite argument. "You know, we saw him just two days before this happened. It always feels strange, when someone you don't see very often pops up, then the next thing you know, they're . . . different."

Different. Her mother was given to such euphemisms. Well, a coma sure was different, even for Spike.

"Did he say anything to either of you about a greyhound?"

"Greyhound? No, he brought us two cases of Old Milwaukee—he gets it for your father at cost. And he brought me ten bags of mulch, which I asked him for last fall. Ten bags! Two would have been plenty, I wanted them for the flower beds along the front. But he was being thoughtful, in his own way. I'll be able to use most of it when I put my vegetable garden in this spring." She smiled triumphantly at Patrick. "So maybe he *is* a Weinstein. The Monaghans are not given to thoughtfulness. I remember when your mother—"

Spike seemed to stir slightly, and everyone turned back to him expectantly. But it was nothing.

"I guess it doesn't do much good for us to sit here and stare at him," Tess said. "I think I'll go downtown and take advantage of the *Beacon-Light*'s database, see if there's been a string of tavern robberies, or anything about greyhounds in the news recently. It's a long shot, but it's all I've got."

"You're going into work dressed like that?" her mother murmured, as Tess bent down to kiss her cheek.

"I like the way she looks," her father insisted. And they started again, like some museum exhibit with a tape-recorded loop.

It was almost 4 before Tess stopped to meet Tyner for a late lunch at Roy Rogers, one of their shared guilty pleasures along with gangster films and fried green pepper rings dipped in powdered sugar. Tyner ordered what he insisted on calling the Trigger special, the quarter-pound cheeseburger with a side of macaroni salad, while Tess settled for the "holster" of french fries. That was their term, not hers.

"Happy trails," Tyner said, as he always did, lifting his twenty-ounce Coca-Cola, another shared vice.

"Same back at you. I'm surprised some do-gooder group hasn't targeted the fries packaging for extinction. Baltimore has always been good at symbols, even if it sucks at doing anything about real problems."

"You're so crabby you remind me of me. You know what you need?"

Tess gave him a dark look. "That is not an issue in my life right now, thank you very much."

"I'm talking about rowing. You need to get back on the water, the sooner the better. You know, you can go out this early if you dress properly. Rock told me—''

"Rock? I heard the Natural Resources police pulled him off the water in February and threatened him with charges if he didn't wait until it was safe." Tess dredged a fry through her own mixture of barbecue sauce, ketchup, and horseradish, another reason she loved Roy's. "But you're right, I *am* in a mildly rotten mood. I spent most of the afternoon with the *Blight*'s computer system, to no avail. It's a bitch to learn, and once I finally got it up and running, it wasn't much use."

"Did you find out anything you can link to Spike's beating?"

"I found out there have been several tavern robberies this winter, but no one was beaten in any of those. And the only mention of greyhounds was a two-year-old story on this annual picnic held by local people who had adopted the dogs. Totally goofy. They hold contests for the dog with the longest tail and best costume. Too bad there wasn't a halitosis prize, Esskay could win that in a walk."

Tyner rolled over to the "Fixin's bar" for a plate of free pickles and onions, which he sprinkled with pepper and ate raw. The girl behind the counter gave him a dark look— once one's sandwich was gone, these extras were presumably off-limits—but Tyner was a regular and the staff had learned long ago it was easier to let him do what he wanted. Tess knew she should learn the same lesson, but she couldn't help trying to match him for sheer orneriness.

"What about your paying job?" he asked, when he returned. "Made any progress on that?"

"I skimmed the *Blight*'s early Sunday edition. One of the sports columnists had an intriguing rumor, says Paul Tucci might be willing to put together a new ownership group if the NBA tried to block the basketball deal on the grounds Wink wasn't morally elevated enough to join the ranks of NBA owners."

"Tucci's probably floating that rumor," Tyner said.

"Yeah, I thought the same thing. You know what he said? 'We shouldn't lose sight of the fact that basketball would be good for the city under any local ownership plan.' Isn't it strange how quickly this has become the conventional wisdom, like an-apple-a-day, or early-to-bed-early-to-rise? A sports franchise will make you healthy, wealthy, and wise.''

Tyner pointed a long finger at her nose. ''I'm going to give you some advice—''

''Oh God, no, anything but that.'' Tess pretended to cower, even as she finished off her last fry.

''What did Deep Throat say in the garage? Follow the money? Well, I have much older, much more universal advice. *Cherchez la femme,* Tess. *Cherchez la femme.*''

''*La femme?*'' Tess needed a moment, then she smiled. ''Good idea, Tyner. I think I'll stop by the home of Rosita Ruiz on my way home tonight.''

''Giddyap,'' Tyner said, then made a whinnying sound so accurate that the other Roy diners looked around uneasily.

Nothing put Tess more in the mood to work than strict injunctions against it. If she had been Bluebeard's wife, she would have been in the secret room the first night. Pandora's box? Opened before it was across her doorstep. The editors had told her to conduct all interviews on-site, the union had told her to stop the interviews entirely. She was counting on Rosita, out of the newsroom for two days and on deadline for most of today, not to know either of these injunctions.

Rosita lived in a high-rise north of Johns Hopkins University's Homewood campus. The strip of apartment buildings along University Parkway catered to every taste: struggling students, well-to-do seniors, young professionals, even those rich enough to pay $1 million for a view of Hopkins' lacrosse field. Rosita's building fell in the lower part of the range. A stark modern tower, its dingy lobby had the feel of a graduate student dorm, while its balconies held the accessories of young adults in transition from school to career: expensive bicycles, cheap hibachis, plastic stacking chairs. There were two views: nostalgic residents could face south, toward the campus they had left so recently, while the strivers looked hopefully toward the stately homes of Baltimore's north side.

In the foyer, the mailbox showed an R. Ruiz, on the eighteenth floor. It was almost too easy for Tess to slip through the security door, disappearing among the people lugging home groceries and take-out food. No one seemed to know anyone here, nor wanted to, judging from the way everyone stared at the elevator's ceiling as it ascended.

A pink-cheeked Rosita answered the door in bicycle pants and a T-shirt with a picture of a bare-breasted mermaid, labeled *La Sirena.* Her hair was slick and wet, her toes separated by wads of cotton, apparently in preparation for the bottle of polish she held in her hand, a very girly pink. Tess would have expected something darker, bloodier.

"Feeney's friend," Rosita said. "Bess."

"Tess. And I'm here as a contractual employee of the *Beacon-Light,* part of the paper's preliminary investigation into what is being called the unscheduled publication of the article you wrote with Kevin Feeney."

"You're the investigator they hired?" Rosita asked incredulously. She had not dropped her arm from the door, so Tess was still in the hall.

"Yes. I work for a local attorney and have a little experience in the field." *Very little.*

"I thought you were suppose to conduct the interviews in the office, starting with the people who were there that night."

"There are no hard-and-fast rules. I happened to be in your neighborhood and thought I'd drop by. I guess I'm kind of a workaholic." She smiled at her lie, suspecting it might create a bond. "This isn't about guilt, you know. It's a fact-finding, cover-your-ass kind of thing, in case Wynkowski sues. That's all."

Rosita gave her terrible imitation of a smile. "Trust me, this is all about guilt. Luckily for me, I'm not guilty."

"So why don't we sit down and talk about this for a few minutes? Then I can put a little check by your name, and everyone will be happy." *Except the editors, the union, and you, when you realize you weren't supposed to talk to me at all.*

"Okay, but you can't stay long. I've got plans tonight and I just got home from work—we have an amazing story running tomorrow. It's going to blow the lid off this city."

"Blow the lid off this city?" If Tess hadn't been intent on charming Rosita, she might have reminded this newcomer that Baltimore had managed to keep its lid firmly in place through the great fire of 1904, the riots of 1968, the Orioles' 21-game losing streak in 1988, several crooked city officials, and a savings-and-loan scandal that had anticipated the national S&L crisis by several years.

Instead, she widened her eyes in a creditable imitation of amazement. "Wow, what's the latest?"

"A guy down in Georgia was at Montrose at the same time as Wink. He heard about our story from relatives up here and called the paper. It seems Wink liked to brag he was there because he killed a man."

"Maybe he was just a scrawny little kid trying to survive by manufacturing a tough-guy reputation."

"Maybe." Rosita smiled serenely. "You can read all about it in tomorrow's paper." She dropped her arm and let Tess into the apartment, walking on her heels to protect her pearly toe polish. Her legs were disproportionately short, with thick, curving calves. While not working twelve hours a day, she obviously found time to run or use a Stairmaster. *Probably with a newspaper propped in front of her and the all-news station on her Walkman.*

Rosita sat on a wooden chair that needed refinishing, leaving Tess the full run of an ancient corduroy sofa that looked as if it had been stolen from a state institution. The decor, at least here in the living room, was Early Dorm: ratty furniture, an orange crate full of CDs, a portable stereo. Rosita hadn't even bothered to build bookcases out of cinderblock and boards, piling her few books on the floor. The only grace note was a poster of a pale pastel cowboy, literally disappearing into the landscape, and the view, which was toward the north and its expensive homes.

"Let's start with an obvious question. Where were you Tuesday night?"

"I thought you used to be a reporter. You should know you don't cut to the chase like that. You're suppose to lull me into a warm, expansive mood with a little nonthreatening chitchat."

"This isn't a profile," Tess said. She couldn't help sounding a little sharp. "It's a report. If you don't want to talk to me, fine. I'll write that down and pass it on to your supervisors, who assured me everyone would cooperate. Let them worry why you don't want to answer the questions I ask in the order I ask them."

"Fine." Big dramatic sigh and a double eye-roll. "I was here."

"Alone? From what time on?"

"I left work at seven-thirty and stopped at the Giant for a salad, then bought some wine at the liquor store. I wasn't very happy. Remember, I thought the best story I had ever written had just been killed." Funny, Feeney had said almost the same thing—except in his case, it had been *his* story.

"Did you get any telephone calls? Did you make any calls or have any friends drop by?"

Rosita pressed her right hand to her forehead, as if the question required deep thought. "No. No calls at all. And no visitors."

"Then you don't really have an alibi. You have a *story.* I mean, you can't prove you were here. And the electronic security system at the paper was down, so it's impossible to prove you weren't there unless you can prove where you were. As a reporter, you should know one can't prove a negative."

When surprised, Rosita forgot her poses and mannerisms. Her eyebrows relaxed and she no longer held her chin so high it made Tess's neck ache to look at her. For a moment, she was as pretty as she should have been all the time. The moment passed.

"In that case, a lot of people aren't going to have alibis. Are you going to ask *Feeney* to prove where he was?"

"Feeney has a very satisfactory alibi, or else I wouldn't even be working on this. That would be totally unethical." Funny, how smoothly a lie could come, when it really had to. "And, yes, everyone will be held to the same standard."

"Don't be naive. There are more sets of standards at the *Beacon-Light* than you'll ever know."

Spare me, Tess thought. The last thing she wanted to hear was Rosita's list of grievances against her bosses. Perhaps she would do well to follow the reporter's advice after all, steering her into innocuous territory so she would be less hostile.

"You know, I don't pay attention to bylines as much as I should, so I'm not really sure when you started at the *Beacon-Light*, although I remember admiring your writing on several pieces. What has it been, a year or so?"

"Fourteen months, but I lost four months on the sports copy desk. I really wanted to cover baseball—I covered the minor league team in San Antonio, and Guy—Guy Whitman, the A.M.E. for sports and features—keeps promising me I'll have a shot at the number three slot covering the Orioles. Until then, he has me in the girl ghetto, features."

"What's wrong with features?"

"I want to be a *real* reporter. That's why I lobbied to get on the Wynkowski story. And I've done a good job. Feeney got the financial stuff, but I got the stuff about his marriage and his gambling problem. If you listen to what people are talking about around town, it's my part of the story."

Jesus, Tess thought, all roads led to Rosita, at least in her mind. The domestic violence was sweetly salacious, and the gambling could be a huge stumbling block, but that was nothing but hearsay. The financial angle was the real story.

"Are you from Texas?"

"Texas? Oh, because of San Antonio. God, no. I spent

one year and seven months in that godforsaken place and it seemed as if the temperature was above ninety for all but three days. I'm from New England. I like seasons, and I prefer cool ones to hot ones.''

''Baltimore's summers are pretty wicked.''

''Yeah, and the winters are wimpy, with people going crazy at the sight of the first snowflake. It's still an improvement, for now. I'll get to the *Globe* yet.''

''Just the *Globe*? Why not the *New York Times* or the *Washington Post?*'' Why not the Vatican?

For all her instructions on how to conduct an interview, Rosita wasn't a very good listener. ''What I really need to do is get back into sportswriting. It's still something of a novelty act, the woman in the locker room. Some 22-year-old in overalls won a Pulitzer this year for an umpire story, for Christ's sake. No, there aren't many more female sportswriters than there were ten years ago. The difference is, editors don't feel as guilt-ridden about it.

''You sound like one of those people with a five-year plan you update every December thirty-first.''

''I am. Two five-year plans, actually, one for work and one for my alleged personal life. Work is proving to be more manageable.'' Her smile this time wasn't her usual fake grin. It was tiny and rueful, fading away quickly, the Cheshire Cat in reverse. She glanced past Tess, who followed her eyes to the clock in the kitchen gallery. No wonder Tess had cats on the brain: the clock was one of those insanely grinning Kit-Kat Klock tchotchkes, sequined tail swinging back and forth in time with round eyes that cased the room.

''Look, I really don't have any more time for this,'' Rosita said abruptly.

''Sorry, you obviously have plans. Big date?''

''No, no, just dinner with a friend. You know, the usual unattached single woman's routine for a Saturday night. Are you married?''

''God, no,'' Tess said.

''Boyfriend?''

"Sort of. I mean yes, yes I do. In fact, his band is playing tonight, so I have to go do the band member's girlfriend thing. Stand in a crowd, stare adoringly at him."

"In my experience, it doesn't matter what your boyfriend does. Sooner or later, you're expected to stand in a crowd and stare at him adoringly." Rosita almost seemed likable to Tess now. She was sharp, she had a certain wit. Then she reverted to being merely sharp. "Of course in Baltimore, there are no available men, not if you have *standards*. I'd rather be dateless."

With someone else, it might have been mere tactlessness. In this case, there was no doubt the remark was deliberately waspish, an intentional implication that Tess did not have standards.

"Protect those toenails. I'll let myself out."

It was dark now along University Parkway and Tess, a born voyeur, glanced into lighted windows as she walked to her car. This stretch of buildings was older than Rosita's tower, with the elegant touches once common to the city's apartments—dark wood paneling, high ceilings, crown moldings. Why did people's lives, captured on the sly like this, look so enticing, like old photographs unearthed in an antique store? Tess caught glimpses of women her age, yet so much more polished looking in their real Saturday night date clothes. She saw their men, in jackets and ties. Grownups, headed to restaurants and Center Stage, perhaps the symphony. And where was she going to be on Saturday night? Lost in the funhouse of the Floating Opera until the wee small hours of the morning, keeping company with wee small minds.

Chapter 10

"How much do you weigh?"

The voice, thin and high, interrupted Tess's reverie. She was keeping herself awake by coming up with new nicknames for Baltimore neighborhoods. They were in an old ballroom in SoWeBo, Southwest Baltimore, once home to H. L. Mencken and Edgar Allan Poe, now home to restaurants like Mencken's Cultured Pearl and the Telltale Hearth. But how about SoO (South of Orioles Park at Camden Yard) or SoPoeBo, near where Poe was buried? So-SoBo, which could encompass the isolated south side neighborhoods. It was a mark of how tired she was that this seemed incredibly witty.

"What?" she asked groggily, stealing a look at her watch. Almost 3 A.M., up for twenty hours. She had caught a second wind about 11, over Afghan food followed by a round of Galliano liqueur. She was reasonably sure the Galliano was not authentically Afghani, but it had made a nice kicker. The licorice-like syrup reminded her of prescription cold medicines, the old-fashioned kind that really made the pain go away for a while. And it had kept her going through the first three bands, but it was wearing off now, just when she needed to radiate the kind of mindless devotion and appreciation expected of a Musician's Girlfriend. Not to mention a certain proprietary zeal. While her mouth smiled at Crow, her eyes were suppose to flash "no poaching" signals to all the females present. It took a lot of energy, this Musician's Girlfriend gig. But she really did care about Crow, who was possibly the nicest man she had ever known. And he would get over being twenty-three. After all, she had.

"I asked how much you weigh," the chirpy little voice repeated. It was Maisie, one of her two cohorts in the Poe White Trash Ladies' Auxiliary. She was sure it was Maisie, because Maisie had the pierced nose. Actually, the nose stud was a fake, a gold ball she attached to her nostril with a small magnet. Maisie's boyfriend, the bass player, had told Crow, who then shared this useful piece of intelligence with Tess. It allowed her to tell Maisie apart from Lorna, the one who wore those tight little necklaces that appeared to be choking her. But that was probably just wishful thinking on Tess's part.

"I don't know. I don't own a scale."

"She doesn't own a scale," Maisie told Lorna, who squealed in delight.

"What about at the doctor's office?" This was a familiar topic, but a favorite one, the tyranny of the tiny. *Their* weight barely registered in the three digits. Lorna could be particularly tiresome, talking about the high-protein shakes she had to drink because pounds just fell off her.

"I don't look."

"She doesn't look," Lorna informed Maisie, giggling.

"But, like, what if you had to tell someone your weight?" Maisie persisted. "What would you say? Like, if a cop stopped you and wanted to know if you fit the description of some crazy woman who was killing a bunch of people, and she was, like, two hundred pounds?"

"I'd tell him to lift me over his head and make his best guess."

Maisie and Lorna stared at Tess, unsure if this was a joke. With their curveless bodies and fluffy hair, they always reminded her of the not-quite-human girls in some Dr. Seuss stories, Cindy Lou Who carving the roast beast for the Grinch. Tess reminded *them* of their parents. Although she had done the math for them several times, they refused to believe she was only nine years older. To them, twenty-nine was Almost Thirty, which was Awfully Close to forty, which meant she was almost their parents' age, for God's sake.

Luckily, Poe White Trash crashed into its opening number just then, so Tess could pretend absolute absorption in the music and ignore Lorna and Maisie. It was not unlike exchanging nails on a chalkboard for longer nails on a chalkboard. Despite Crow's sweet, true tenor, or perhaps because of it, Poe White Trash was determinedly anti-melodic, chaotic, assaultive. They were *loud*. Maisie and Lorna couldn't quite make Tess feel old, but putting that adjective in front of music did the trick.

When she'd first started going with Crow, she had tried hard to pretend an interest in his musical ambitions, had even trotted out the little intelligence she had gleaned from the city's almost-progressive radio station, WHFS. Crow had laughed, convincing her she could never keep up, so she might as well fall behind. She wished he would sing just one standard, one ballad, for her. Sid Vicious had sung "My Way." No one did "So in Love" better than k. d. lang. Certainly Crow could assay "All the Things You Are." Or "My Heart Stood Still." Just once, just for her.

A stray lyric became audible, probably the result of a malfunctioning sound system, "tongue-kissing the black dog." Inspired by Esskay? At any rate, it was as close as she would get to a ballad tonight.

She leaned back against the wall, sending little flakes of lead paint into the air, and took a long drag on her drink. No alcohol was allowed at the Floating Opera, only LSD and various new synthetic potions, so Tess had settled on one of those ubiquitous iced teas that seemed more religion than beverage. Behind her closed eyes, she imagined young people running down a beach, hand in hand, deliriously happy because they had raspberry-flavored iced tea. The boy looked like Crow. The girl was skinny and short. Unlikely as it seemed, she dozed off. It was morning when she opened her eyes again, or some time of day that passed for morning, and Crow's band was taking a final bow. Time for breakfast.

Jimmy's had just opened its doors by the time they returned to Fells Point. Tess was feeling much older than the twenty-nine years Lorna and Maisie found so fascinating. For once, she was glad the waitresses at Jimmy's automatically served her the same thing, even when she didn't want it. Today, their presumption saved her from the effort of forming words. Her bagels were on the griddle the second she crossed the doorstep, along with toast for Crow's egg-and-hash browns plate. Her coffee reached the table before they did. Tess thought of asking for decaf, then decided against it. If she fell asleep now, it would only screw her body up more. Might as well push on through the day and go to bed a little early. Say, at 6 P.M.

Crow was quiet in the morning, especially after a gig. He chewed ice, drank tea with honey, and skimmed the soft sections of the *Beacon-Light* while Tess pretended to read the *New York Times*. Well-kept secret of the news business: Sunday papers were comfortingly soporific, devoid of any real news. The usual words swam before her groggy eyes, as familiar and sweet as lullabies, so familiar as to be meaningless. *Bosnia. Pact. GOP. Dow. Future. Remains to be seen.*

Crow crunched a large piece of ice, inhaled it by accident, and started choking. "Sweet shit Jesus," he said, after coughing it out.

Tess, who knew that many things could prompt such a response in Crow—an interesting fact about wool-gathering in China, for example—did not react immediately. The soothing gray of the *Times* had begun to resemble one of those hidden 3-D pictures. The copy swam in front of her eyes so she couldn't make out the words, only shapes. She was seeing the paper the way Dorie Starnes and Howard Nieman did. Computer coding. Black stuff on white stuff. Big boxes and little boxes.

"Jesus fuckin' Christ," Crow said, shoving the front

page of the *Blight* toward her. Tess had no problem making words from the bold black lines she saw there.

WINK WYNKOWSKI FOUND DEAD, APPARENT SUICIDE; BEACON-LIGHT HAD UNCOVERED SECRET PAST

By Kevin V. Feeney
and Rosita Ruiz
Beacon-Light staff writers

Gerald "Wink" Wynkowski was found dead last night, an apparent suicide victim discovered just hours after he had learned the *Beacon-Light* planned to publish a story about his role in the death of a West Side shopkeeper almost thirty-one years ago.

Wynkowski was discovered in his running '65 Mustang about 10:30 in his closed and locked garage. He was pronounced dead at the scene. No note was found, but a Bruce Springsteen song, "Thunder Road," was playing on the car stereo when police arrived.

Although Wynkowski had always acknowledged his time at the Montrose School for juvenile offenders, he had characterized his crimes as "one notch up from Andy Hardy—a little vandalism, a little larceny." Sealed juvenile records had made it impossible to contradict this account before now.

But a former Baltimore man now living in Georgia told the *Beacon-Light* this week that Wynkowski had bragged about causing a man's death while incarcerated at Montrose. The man—who passed a polygraph test, but asked that his name not be revealed because his own delinquency is not widely known among his associates in Georgia—said Wynkowski claimed to have beaten the man to death during a hold-up.

A source familiar with the state's juvenile justice system yesterday confirmed that Wynkowski was sent to Montrose on a manslaughter charge, although the circumstances were slightly different. Nathaniel

Paige, a shopkeeper on Gold Street, was pistol-whipped during a hold-up there in the summer of 1969, but the official cause of death was a heart attack. Under Maryland law, Wink, who had been involved in several minor crimes before this, was charged with manslaughter.

Contacted yesterday for comment, Wynkowski said he wanted to speak to his lawyer and would have no statement until Sunday morning. He was found dead 12 hours later, and his lawyer, Michael Ellenham, said he had not been in contact with his client all day.

Tess skimmed through the rest of the story, but most of its length was devoted to the Georgia interview and a re-hashing of what the paper had already reported. She tried to work out the timing in her mind. If police had been called at 10:30, Feeney couldn't have arrived at the scene before 11—just enough time to call in two paragraphs to the night rewrite, who had done a pretty good job blending the new information into the existing story. Under the circumstances, the *Beacon-Light* had been lucky to get the story at all.

"What would you want to be listening to as you die?" asked Crow, for whom all news tended to be abstract, impersonal. "I don't think I'd pick Springsteen. Yet it would be unseemly to die with Poe White Trash playing. Everyone would assume I did it because I was a failure at my music. The blues would be too obvious, opera too pretentious. Hey, maybe that Chet Baker album you're always playing. 'It Could Happen to You.' "

"Sounds good," Tess muttered absently, rereading the story in case she had missed anything. No suicide note. Blood alcohol 0.1—too drunk to drive, but not drunk enough to die. Cause of death pending toxicology reports, due in two weeks, but that was a pro forma check for drugs that the blood test would have missed. Mrs. Wynkowski and the children were at her mother's place in New Jersey, where they had been spending the weekend.

Tess and Crow sat in silence, except for the occasional cracking sound from his mouthful of ice. So one of the city's longest winning streaks had come to an end in a chugging Mustang, with a soundtrack by Bruce Springsteen. Tess knew she should be thinking deep thoughts about the past and personal responsibility, about what it was like for a beloved figure to face the loss of the public adoration he enjoyed.

But all she could wonder was if she still had a contract with the *Beacon-Light*.

Chapter 11

When Tess switched on her computer at the *Beacon-Light* Monday morning, she found three messages waiting: a perfunctory note from Dorie Starnes about basic computer commands she might need, another lunch invitation from Guy Whitman, and a polite, professional welcome from Jack Sterling. "Welcome aboard," he had written. "Let me know if I can do anything." Sent on Friday afternoon. Did the offer still stand? And was there anything personal to be gleaned from the impersonal words? Even as she was deconstructing his first message, another notice from him flashed across the top of her screen: "U there? 10:30 premeeting to daily 11 o'clock in Colleen's second office. BE THERE. But U didn't hear it from me."

Like all newspaper editors, the *Blight* bosses met constantly, in various sets and subsets. There were two news meetings a day, one feature meeting, two metro meetings, a Page One meeting, and a sports meeting. When the editors weren't in formal meetings, they were in informal ones, dashing into offices and shutting doors to whisper conspiratorially. The 11 o'clock was the first news meeting of the day, mandatory for all department heads. But what was a pre-meeting? And where was Colleen's second office? Jack Sterling gave her too much credit, Tess thought, dialing Whitney's extension.

"This is Whitney Talbot." Tess waited a second, unsure

if she had reached a real person. Whitney was one of those people who sounded exactly like her voice mail.

"Well, is someone there?" Whitney snapped impatiently.

"Hey, it's Tess. I'm here. But I'm not sure for how long. I've just been summoned to Colleen Reganhart's second office, whatever that is."

"Look, Reganhart might act as if she has the authority to dump you, but she doesn't. Only Lionel or Five-Four can terminate you. Don't let her bluff you." Whitney actually sounded concerned, as if Tess were still an underemployed bookstore clerk who needed the *Blight*'s fee to keep body and soul together.

"Don't worry, I have a little advantage where that's concerned. But I'm not sure what I can do for the *Blight,* with the union on my back and Wink dead. Obviously, he's not going to bring suit now, so what's the point?"

"You were hired to look into the computer sabotage, remember? Wink's death doesn't change the fact that someone, most likely Rosita, compromised the paper's integrity. What would the paper look like if every reporter greased the skids for her pet project?"

"Look, I'd better find this meeting. Where can I find Reganhart?"

"On the fourth floor, behind the door marked 'Ladies,' an irony that quickly becomes apparent in any prolonged discussion with Colleen Reganhart."

The fourth-floor women's bathroom was a suite with a large anteroom separated from the facilities by the kind of double doors usually associated with saloons. Tess, pushing her way into the sitting area at 10:25, reflected that the size, placement, and fixtures of such restrooms could give future archaeologists much to ponder about the late twentieth-century workplace.

Upstairs, where men had dominated the news pages throughout the *Blight*'s history, the women's bathroom was an afterthought, a cramped, windowless room carved from a corner of the original men's room, barely large enough for two stalls. But this bathroom near the former Woman's Page was a two-room suite suitable for an attack of the vapors. The lounge had a long sofa and two upholstered chairs. It even had a vending machine, stocked with sanitary napkins and pantyhose in formidably large sizes. The dispenser, dusty and dented, didn't look as if it had been restocked since the late 1960s, about the same time the *Blight* had stopped discriminating against black and Jewish brides on the wedding page. Tess took her place on a banana-yellow vinyl chair and waited.

At precisely 10:30, Colleen walked in, lighting a cigarette and taking a deep drag before the door swung shut behind her.

"It's against the law to smoke in Maryland offices," Tess said helpfully.

"If you have a problem with cigarette smoke you can leave. In fact, you can leave even if you don't have a problem with cigarette smoke."

Jack Sterling came through the swinging door and did a not-bad job of feigning surprise to see Tess there.

"Given that Miss Monaghan was to be the subject of our discussion here, don't you think she should stay?" he asked. *Very cool,* Tess thought.

"No, I don't. I think she should go to her desk, clean it out, and get the fuck out of here. We don't need her. We never needed her. This weekend's story makes the first one look like a goddamn puff piece. Who cares any more how it got in the paper? It led to the second story, which is even better."

"What if—and I'm just playing devil's advocate here—what if his widow still tries to sue?"

"Let her. You can't libel the dead. *Besides, we didn't libel anyone.* Wink's suicide proves we don't know how much shit he had to hide. This is a goddamn fucking purple orgasm of a story, and it gets better every day."

"A little self-examination won't keep us from nailing the story, Colleen," Sterling said.

"It won't get us jack shit."

"What are you so scared of? That Tess's investigation will lead us straight to your protégé, Rosita?"

Tess sat on the sofa, feeling as if she were watching her parents bicker. Jack Sterling and Colleen Reganhart had an odd chemistry. It wasn't sexual, not like one of those television romances where hate turns to a clinch in mid-quarrel. This tension was the kind one expected from romantic rivals or siblings. And the object of their affection was the *Beacon-Light*, as embodied by Lionel Mabry, dear old dad.

"We all have our *protégés*," Colleen told Sterling, exhaling smoke aggressively into his face. He didn't flinch or cough. "We hired Miss Monaghan because Lionel's would-be protégé, Whitney Talbot, talked him into it. But that was last week, when Wink was alive and Five-Four couldn't eat at the Center Club without someone waggling a finger in his face for screwing up the basketball deal. Now we look brilliant and Five-Four can pretend a great enthusiasm for the fourth estate. Everybody's happy."

"Lionel's not. And neither am I. We got lucky. It doesn't change the fact that tampering with Page One isn't something to be taken lightly, and the use of unnamed sources on this story has been far too liberal. Wink Wynkowski died without knowing the names of his accusers. Do you think that's right?"

"The bottom line is cash: this investigator's salary comes out of my budget—our budget, Sterling, the newsroom's budget—and it's a waste of money."

Tess was tired of being discussed in the third person. Sterling hadn't tipped her off about this meeting for her to sit here meekly.

"Paying me is not a waste of money, *Colleen*." The name felt strange in her mouth, but Miss Reganhart, for a woman not even ten years her senior, would have seemed stranger still. "Besides, it's not something you can renege on. This morning, I checked with my boss, Tyner Gray, and he confirmed he had inserted language to that effect into our contract. You can play me or trade me, but you still have to pay me. *Colleen.* For at least two weeks' work.''

Reganhart looked stunned, a poker player who had plopped down a straight only to be confronted with a flush. Spike always said arrogance was the worst thing you could bring to a wager. ''Math don't play favorites'' was how he put it.

''So you have a contract, too. And the union has its contract,'' Colleen said at last. ''Me, I can be fired at Lionel's whim. If he can't get the tee time he wants, or the counterman in the company cafeteria forgets to put his salad dressing on the side, I'm outta here. Whatever happened to the idea of a meritocracy? Whatever happened to people doing their jobs without counting on all these . . . gimmicks?''

''A contract's not a gimmick. And the problem with meritocracies is they assume one or two individuals have any clue about what merit is, uncolored by their own biases.''

Reganhart slumped on the orange plastic sofa. She was neither as tall nor as large-boned as Tess had first thought. Unlike most women, she dressed to maximize her size— four-inch heels, seriously big hair, oversized and out-of-fashion shoulder pads tucked into her pea-green wool jacket. On the losing side of a battle, she seemed to shrink, like a Persian cat caught in a rainstorm.

''Assuming that you're telling the truth about your contract—and you can bet your ass I will check—then you can go ahead as planned.'' She turned to Sterling. ''Now I'm actually going to use this room for its intended purpose. Could you give us girls a little privacy?''

As soon as he left, Colleen fixed a hard, blue stare on Tess.

''Your contract also stipulates thirty hours of work a week. I want you here six hours a day, Monday through Friday. And you're to check in and out with my secretary. If we pay you to work here, you work *here.*''

''No problem.''

''The problem will be how to fill your days. You see,

I've just decided I don't want union representatives sitting in on your interviews with staff. The union will, of course, file a grievance over my decision. I'll fight it. I'll take it to arbitration. I'll take it to the fucking Supreme Court. And we'll end up putting the whole investigation on hold until the matter can be resolved, which should be well after your contract expires. So go ahead, collect your paycheck. Doing nothing is the hardest work you'll ever do. If you don't believe me, I can refer you to some reporters I've put in the same position. In the end, they all quit.''

"This isn't about money," Tess said. "What's your problem with me?"

"I don't trust you. I don't trust any friend of Whitney Talbot's. Jack Sterling's gunning for my job and she thinks she'll get his job if he forces me out."

"Whitney doesn't want to be an editor. She wants to go to Tokyo."

"I'm sure Whitney would be willing to forgo three years in Japan if she could become a deputy managing editor before she turns thirty. You may know your friend; I know ambition. How do you think I went from city editor in Wilmington, Delaware, to managing editor here in just five years?"

Reganhart dropped her cigarette to the floor and crushed it beneath her pump. Deprived of a prop, her hands flopped nervously at her sides, and she quickly lit another Merit. Tess had a hunch the managing editor was a collection of barely controlled tics—a reformed fingernail biter, a hair twister, a scab picker, an earring fiddler. Chain smoking probably kept her from tearing herself to bits.

Before Tess could make her exit, an excited Marvin Hailey pushed his way into the room, followed by Jack Sterling.

"We've got a good murder in Northwest," Hailey panted. "Really juicy. Two carjackers tried to take a minivan from an Orthodox Jewish mother with seven kids. She put up a fight and they shot her, right in front of the kids. The kids were so freaked they wouldn't get out of the van, so the carjackers left on foot, heading over to a fast food place on Reisterstown Road for fried egg sandwiches. Cops arrested them while they were still on line. One of the photographers heard the call on the radio and managed to get to the scene before the police. *Great* stuff. Amazing. But we need to decide how to make it big, how to tell people something tomorrow they won't see on the television news tonight. TV is all over this.''

"There are no good murders." Sterling's voice was gentle in its reproof. "But Marv's right, we do need to throw a lot of bodies at this. Our readers will expect the definitive version from us, something more than what they'll get on TV tonight."

"I assume the art department is already working on a map—where it happened, where the guys were caught." Colleen dropped her fresh cigarette and rubbed her palms together, as if the story were a rich meal or a pile of money set before her. "I want Bunky Fontaine on the community angle, rounding up the usual rabbis. And isn't Northwest the police district where the community was bitching about the decision to suspend foot patrols?"

She rushed from the room, Hailey hard on her heels like a happy puppy. Sterling followed, moving more slowly, but still following. Whatever their personal differences, Colleen and Jack could work as a team when the situation demanded it.

"A good murder," Hailey had said, and to Tess's sorrow, she knew exactly what he meant. In her own newspaper days, she had done a brief rotation on the night rewrite desk. There, at a safe remove from victims and grieving relatives, one quickly learned that value system. Good murders, great murders, wonderful murders, all determined on a sliding scale of hometown, money, race, body count, and celebrity.

"We've got a good one." How many times had she said the same thing? How many times had her fingers flown with delight over the details of someone's final moments

on earth? It was small consolation to remind herself that Colleen was the one who had called Wink's death the ultimate orgasm, a climax powerful enough to bring an entire newsroom to a collective shudder.

Chapter 12

Whitney was waiting in Tess's bare bones office when she returned from the ladies' room. Sitting in Tess's chair, scrolling through files in Tess's computer. Tess had nothing to hide, but *still*.

"So did Reganheartless try to shut you down?" Whitney asked, without lifting her eyes from the computer screen.

"She *did* shut me down. I'm still getting paid, but she's arranged it so I won't be able to talk to anyone on staff. Yet if I don't put in my hours, she'll say I've breached the contract and stop payment. I'm fucked. I have to come in here every day and sit at this desk doing nothing."

Whitney tapped a few keys and Tess heard a modem's rasping beeps and gurgles. She hadn't known the *Blight*'s computer was equipped with one.

"Didn't Dorie tell you about the on-line capabilities built into the system here?"

"You mean the electronic library? I tried to use it over the weekend, but it's a fussy little program. Make one mistake and you have to start all over. The court files aren't much easier to use."

"Yeah, well, Marvin Hailey had a hand in designing our computer network, so that's to be expected. It's as jumpy as he is. But there are other things on the computer, too. Nexis, MVA records, Autotrack."

"I know about the first two. What's the last one?"

"A little program that allows you to find all sorts of stuff. Social Security numbers, past addresses, mortgage histories, current and former neighbors. Might be interesting to put Rosita through it."

"And Feeney."

"You know where Feeney has been the last twenty years of his life. And you know where he was that night." It was hard, to hear one friend's lie in another friend's mouth, as casual and uncontested as a passing comment on the weather. Why had Feeney told Whitney he and Tess were together that night? Now it was Tess's lie, too, and it was too late to disown it. "Rosita's the mystery woman."

"Not so mysterious. I talked to her over the weekend. Pretty routine résumé—last job was in San Antonio, she's from Boston, wants to move back there. No husband, no boyfriend."

Whitney picked up the receiver and held it out toward Tess. "You don't need Colleen's permission to dial long-distance. Just an access code and I'll give you that: five-four. Sheer coincidence, I assure you, nothing to do with our beloved publisher. What's the paper in San Antonio, the *Eagle*? No harm in checking out Rosita's reputation down there."

Tess took the phone and placed it back in its cradle. "You got me the job, Whitney. Now let me do it. My way."

Unlike most blunt people, who tend to be extremely tender about their own feelings, Whitney was nearly uninsultable "Okay. Just trying to be helpful. I'd ask you to lunch, but I have a squash date with Sterling, assuming it hasn't been overtaken by recent events."

Perhaps Colleen Reganhart wasn't so paranoid after all. Tess was surprised to feel a little stab of jealousy on her own behalf. "Lobbying for Japan? Or something bigger?"

"Japan *is* big enough. For now. And yes, I'm working all the angles. Luckily, Sterling is a better player than I am, when he isn't having problems with his back, or his carpal tunnel. It's hard to throw games without being too obvious about it.''

Tess waited about five seconds after Whitney left, then pulled out the phone book and looked up the area code for San Antonio.

Newspaper bureaucracies are as byzantine and hierarchical as any government office. It took Tess almost an hour to find a San Antonio editor who would talk to her about Rosita Ruiz. Rosita's supervisor, the sports editor, seemed the obvious choice, but he referred her to the managing editor's office, where she learned the assistant managing editor for administration handled all such queries. It turned out this editor had an assistant who oversaw the two-year intern program, in which Rosita had been employed, and only he could serve as her reference.

''Edward Saldivar.'' His was a soft, young-sounding voice with a slight accent, one Saldivar seemed to try and minimize, anglicizing his first name as much as possible. Quite the opposite of Rosita, hitting her consonants with hurricane force.

''My name is Tess Monaghan and I'm checking Rosita Ruiz's references. She listed you as the contact there.''

''Ah.'' When stalling for time, Saldivar made a singing sound, as if he were warming up his vocal cords for a chorale performance. ''Our policy is to confirm the position an individual held here, and verify dates of employment, no more, no less.''

''That's not exactly a reference.''

''Ah.'' A little higher this time. ''I see your point. But recent litigation by, uh, disgruntled workers, suggests companies should adopt uniform policies, lest they be accused of slander. Unfortunate, but that's the way everything is going today. Besides, Rosita left here more than six months ago, for a job at the paper up in Baltimore. Why don't you call them?''

''I'm calling *for* them, from their offices. Did you provide a reference then?''

"I don't recall being asked, and I don't know if someone else was contacted. But whoever was called would have given only the dates of employment. That's our—"

"Your policy. Yes, I understand, Mr. Saldivar. But Rosita has the job and she *knows* I'm calling you." A harmless lie. "Surely you should be able to speak freely about her work at the *Eagle.* She covered minor league baseball, right?"

"She worked here for nineteen months, leaving last October to join the Baltimore *Beacon-Light.*"

"I thought she had a two-year internship. Why did it end in nineteen months?"

"It's not unusual for our two-year interns to leave for permanent positions at other papers before their terms are up. Rosita Ruiz resigned on October first after securing a job at the *Beacon-Light,* a larger paper that could afford to pay her much more. We were very happy for her. Good day, Miss Monaghan." Saldivar was not the type who would slam a phone down to end a conversation. No, he slipped the receiver back into place, almost as if he regretted breaking the connection. That was something she could learn from Saldivar, Tess decided, without the benefit of a two-year internship: Good manners are a great way to be rude.

It was almost 7 when Tess left the *Blight,* a lonely time in that forsaken neighborhood, especially on a rainy March night. Her shoulders ached, as did her neck, and she had a splitting headache. Doing nothing was hard work, and she had done little more than play solitaire with the computer after running into the dead-end known as Ed Saldivar. Out of sheer perversity, Tess had stayed even later than Colleen Reganhart had specified, forgetting she would have to walk back to Tyner's to get her car. On top of everything else, the *Blight* had forgotten to provide her a parking place, and the Nazi who supervised the lot had told her the visitor spaces couldn't be used by an employee, even one as tenuous as she.

Head down against the wet wind, Tess shuffled along the sad, deserted blocks of Lexington, bricked in during the 1970s, when downtown "malls" were thought to be the secret to urban renewal. There were still stores here, discount chains and cheap clothing boutiques, but they closed along with the state offices at 5 P.M. Even the Nut House was shuttered, much to Tess's disappointment. A handful of pistachios would have made a big difference in the quality of her life just then.

She was crossing Park Avenue when she noticed a long, brown-colored car with bits of salmon paint peeking through. It made a sudden U-turn on the one-way street, fishtailed to a stop with a great squealing of brakes, then made another U and headed back in the right direction. Downtown Baltimore, with its warren of one-way streets, often had that effect on out-of-town drivers.

Two blocks later, as Tess turned north on St. Paul, the same car passed her again, heading south. Again the brakes whined and the car almost spun out on the slick road. But even at this hour, one-way St. Paul was too busy for the car to dare going the wrong way. She watched it turn left at the next side street, suddenly overtaken by a sinking sensation that these might be her hospital-bound buddies, in another untraceable vehicle.

"As long as I'm walking against the traffic, I should be okay," she told herself, speaking out loud from nervousness. She started up St. Paul, and although she walked quickly, she hadn't covered an entire block before the same car—an old Buick, she saw now—passed her again. She looked for a license plate, but there wasn't one, not on the front, and the back plate was thick with mud.

Tess stopped for a moment to think. She'd never make it to her car, not along these increasingly desolate blocks north of downtown. She could disappear into the Tremont Hotel just ahead, or turn around and go south, vanishing into the shops at the Gallery or Harborplace. Even on a Monday night, the restaurants would be busy enough to offer her some protection while she waited for Crow, or a taxi. But she had to be sure it was the same men. There had to be a way to confront them without putting herself at risk.

To the east, City Hall's gold dome shone in the misty dusk, all the inspiration she needed. She checked her wallet. Forty dollars in small bills. Should be enough. She sprinted for South Street, but not so quickly that her friends in the brown-and-salmon–mobile couldn't see her.

Because of the parking problem in downtown Baltimore, an underground economy of de facto valets had taken hold in the more congested areas near City Hall and the district court building. Homeless men earned money by feeding parking meters for people who "tipped" them. Even if one didn't plan to stay beyond the meter's time limits, it was smart to offer a dollar or two, if only to protect one's car against the men offering protection. Tess, who had patronized these attendants while on various errands for Tyner, knew they scorned the local shelters, preferring to sleep near their place of business. They should be settling down for the evening just about now, having scored some sandwiches from the nearby missions. The trick was getting them to emerge from the cubbyholes and doorways where they slept.

"Anybody want to make a few bucks?" she called. "Easiest five dollars you'll ever make in your life!" She heard a rustling noise, then three men appeared out of the shadows. Three *large* men, she noted happily. She pulled out her wallet, showed them the cash, then slipped the wallet back into her knapsack.

"All you have to do is stand around me and look mean. Think you can do that?" The three nodded, unfazed by the strange request. They huddled close to her and Tess caught the bitter scent of sweat dried on old wool, the too-sweet grape of bad wine.

"You do something wrong?" asked one man, a white man who was brown all over—brown hair, brown clothes, brown eyes, skin the color of a pecan from what must be years of living outdoors.

"Not that I'm aware of."

Within a few minutes, the brown-over-salmon car turned onto South Street, stopping short of where Tess stood. Even without a valid license plate, it would be an easy car to recognize. The windows were one-way mirrors, the job done so cheaply that strips of the reflective material were already peeling away. The paint job was new but cheap, a flat shade of dung-brown. The fenders were pitted with dents and scrapes, one headlight was cracked, and the muffler appeared to be loose. But these guys had a habit of changing cars—first a bright blue AMC Hornet, now this Buick. Or was the Hornet the first car, after all? She suddenly remembered the high beams of a car behind her on Franklintown Road, the car she had lost by running a red light the night she had acquired Esskay. The night Spike had been beaten.

The front passenger window rolled down slowly and a familiar pair of oversize sunglasses studied Tess. The concerned friend of Joe Johnson, the one who had wanted to give her a lift the other day. Then the rear passenger door opened, creaking horribly.

"Miss Monaghan?" The voice, thin and reedy, came from the backseat. Tess did not reply.

"It is Miss Monaghan, isn't it? Spike Orrick's niece? He has always spoken so highly of you. We saw him just the other day."

"Did you go see him when you visited your pal Joe?"

"For various reasons, we didn't have a chance to stop in and visit. But we did see Spike before he went into the hospital." A low, rusty chuckle. "*Just* before."

Her paid protectors drew closer, as if they understood the threat implicit in this exchange. Or perhaps they wanted to be sure to grab her knapsack if someone bolted from the car and dragged her away. In the space between the door and the car, Tess could see a leg, a beefy one in tight black denim. A brown leather jacket, styled like a blazer, hung over the jeans. But she couldn't see any faces. Somewhere deep inside the car, a small dog yapped.

"Hush, Charlton," the reedy voice admonished indulgently. The voice was colder, steelier, when it addressed her again. "Miss Monaghan, your uncle has something that belongs to a friend of ours. It has no real monetary value, but it is his, and he wants it back. Do you know where we could find this . . . item?"

Tess shook her head. "I have no idea what you're talking about."

"Are you sure?"

One of the homeless men, the nut-brown man, stepped forward. "She said no. Isn't that good enough?" There was just enough light to catch the short blade clenched in his right hand.

The man in the front passenger smiled and held up a gun. *Paper beats rock, rock beats scissors, scissors beat paper, gun beats knife,* Tess thought. But the rear car door slammed shut and the old Buick took off, accelerating so quickly it bounced off one curb and then the other. Her bodyguards stayed close to her until the car disappeared, and Tess was touched, until she remembered she owed them money. She doled out five dollars to each. The first two said nothing, but the third one, the one with the knife, was curious.

"You owe them money?"

"I don't, but my uncle might. He's a bookie."

"That's a bad business. Stay away from that." With those words of advice the brown man was gone, melting into the dusk. A taxi pulled up as he vanished, and Tess, who had already spent fifteen dollars on her trip home, decided to spend another five dollars to reach her car. Shifting her weight to avoid the bad springs in the cab's backseat, she thought of how Spike had always kept the family at arm's length from what he called "my little sideline." Until now, she had assumed he was being dramatic, indulging his proclivity for mystery and secrets. Until now.

Chapter 13

∾∾∾

"Reminder: when you want to destroy files, simply hit Command X. When private files are transferred to the Trash directory, it is recommended you erase them first, for the Trash directory can be ACCESSED BY ALL USERS. Many reporters and editors forget to delete their files, allowing prying eyes to skim them. Remember, each department—Metro, Features, Sports, etc.—has its own Trash directory. D. Starnes."

Puzzled, Tess stared at the computer screen. It was Tuesday, about 11 A.M., and she had just started her day at the *Beacon-Light,* after checking in with Colleen's secretary, as required. Funny, she had expected Colleen to have a male secretary, an unctuous himbo guarding her office, but the secretary was a pleasant moon-faced matron, who put a little smiley face next to Tess's name, along with a notation of the time—to the minute.

In her office, Tess had turned on the computer thinking she might fill her daily sentence of six hours by exchanging e-mail with Whitney, or reading the wires, only to see this message pop up. It was phrased as if it were a directive to all users, yet she knew enough about the system to realize the message was addressed only to her. Strange. Dorie wanted her to find something, but didn't want to make it too easy, or appear to be doing her any special favors.

With a quick glance at the cheat sheet posted next to the keyboard, Tess typed in the command instructing the computer to call up all items in "Trash Metro." The computer obliged, quickly and silently, and Tess soon found herself sifting through the electronic equivalents of cigarette butts, half-empty coffee cups, and tissues with lipstick traces. Here were memos as dull and plodding as any corporation's. Here were reporters' ill-crafted leads, the false starts they would have crumpled and tossed across the room in the typewriter era. Here were notes from telephone interviews. "Sez city mayor No can do/Constinal ish big. Pres. no agree. Wld req ref. More stdy requrd." Good fodder for a libel trial, Tess thought. It was doubtful the writer could reliably decode this Tarzanese. Fortunately, the notes would soon disappear: whatever was dumped in the trash expired in twenty-four hours.

Moving from Metro Trash to Features Trash and Sports Trash, then back to Metro Trash, Tess found daily staffing reports from each department's executive secretary and a log of overtime requests. Anyone filing for more than ten hours per week was flagged and expected to provide an explanation for daring to request what the contract guaranteed. Rosita, who had filed for twelve hours of overtime in the last pay period, had written an obsequious little note to Colleen, with copies to Mabry and Sterling, reminding them that the Wynkowski story was the reason.

> "Now that the story has appeared, I'm sure you can appreciate how much time it took. I would never take advantage of your generosity. In fact, I worked almost 20 hours of overtime, but deferred the rest to comp time."

Tess thought she detected a lot of attitude in that one word, "Now." Feeney had filed for eighteen hours of overtime without bothering to defend himself in writing. That, too, was in character.

Why would any reporter, especially a cagey type like Rosita, allow her craven brown-nosing to be on display? Tess couldn't be the first pair of "prying eyes" to pass through these directories. She checked the history field, the way Dorie had shown her. Of course: reporters created the files, but the *editors dumped them*. And the editors weren't concerned about safeguarding anyone's privacy except their own. Reganhart, in particular, never erased reporters' notes before trashing them, while Sterling was erratic. Only Lionel Mabry, who had seemed so vague and out of it, scrupulously expunged everything he discarded.

Digging deeper into the electronic trash, Tess found yesterday's news budget, which included ongoing projects at the bottom. Reporters assigned to the Wink story were to keep checking with county police, on the off chance the death would be classified as an accident or homicide when the toxicology reports came back from the medical examiner. The budget also indicated at least five other reporters had been deployed in case Wink had even nastier skeletons in his closet. So far, they had come up empty. Meanwhile, Feeney was responsible for tracking the basketball deal, which was expected to unravel unless Paul Tucci could find more backers, but there had been no developments on that front, either.

In fact, the only Wink-related story in today's editions was a thin piece on his wake by Rosita. As published, the piece had been flat and unremarkable. The original, sent to the trash by Reganhart, was inappropriately vicious, the kind of piece in which the writer mistook mere bitchery for wit. Tess was particularly struck by the description of Wink's high school basketball team members in "green-and-gold letter jackets that would never button again, not in this lifetime." At least Reganhart, whatever her weaknesses, understood how disastrous this would have been. Death demanded reverence not only for the deceased, but for his mourners.

"So what's moving on the wires this morning?"

Startled, Tess jumped and banged her right knee hard on

the lap drawer of the old metal desk, which caused her to swear under her breath. Jack Sterling was leaning against the door jamb, hands in his pockets, shirt sleeves rolled up. A solid blue shirt today, which made his eyes almost too blue.

"Not much," she lied automatically. Even if she wasn't actually hacking, she didn't want to admit she was digging through the *Blight*'s electronic trash. "Spring training stories."

"In March, it's hard to believe Opening Day will ever come. In August, when you're a Cubs fan like myself, you sometimes wish it never had."

As Tess casually cleared her screen of any incriminating files, Sterling came in and sat on a corner of the desk, inches from her right elbow.

"Do you like baseball, Tess?"

"I watch the World Series. Want to know my deepest, darkest secret?"

"I'm a journalist. I live to know secrets."

"I don't even know where the Orioles finish, most years."

He laughed, a sound so spontaneous and generous that Tess wished she could find other secrets to confide in him. *I didn't report all my income on my taxes last year. I think you're cute. I've been known to be something of a round-heels under the right circumstances.*

"Let me ask you something, Tess."

Yes.

"Did anything bother you about the first Wynkowski story? The, um, unofficial one?"

She knew she was suppose to say she had been bothered, and she hated to disappoint him. But what had been wrong? She wracked her brain.

"I know there were a lot of anonymous sources. Then again, you let the guy in Georgia cloak his identity, too."

"At least I know who he is this time, and what his motivation is. I don't know anything about the sources in the first story. I've got a bad feeling in my gut about this whole thing. What about you? What do your instincts tell you, Tess?''

It was an uncomfortable question for Tess, who had once watched as her best instincts had collapsed against the backdrop of three separate deaths. But it was foolhardy to tell the unvarnished truth to an employer, and Jack Sterling was still just that: her employer.

She settled for a partial truth. ''My gut tends to be opinionated, so it's not infallible.''

Her stomach picked this exact moment to groan with hunger. Tess wanted to crawl under the desk, or find some graceful way to inform Sterling she did not normally make such noises.

''Running on empty? Let me treat you to lunch at Marconi's.'' Tess grinned at him the same way Esskay the greyhound grinned at any offering of food.

They walked down Saratoga Street to the restaurant. It was a little cool, but the sun was out and the sky clear. A few brave crocuses peeked out among the stunted trees planted along the sidewalks. A horrible tease, Tess knew. Did spring have an equivalent term for Indian summer, a way to describe these March flirtations with nice weather?

''We'll probably have another snowstorm before the month is out,'' she said. How lame could she be, falling back on the weather to make conversation? She should have said something about politics, or today's front page. But that would have involved actually reading the front page. She had been having far too much fun wallowing in the electronic trash heap.

''Baltimore is lovely in the snow,'' Sterling said, ''even if Baltimoreans aren't.''

''Are you going to go into that usual out-of-towner rap, about how we can't drive in it, and we all act like idiots, rushing to the store for supplies?''

''It's the nature of the supplies I've never understood. Bread, milk, and toilet paper, hon.'' Sterling did a decent Baltimore accent for a newcomer. ''The holy trinity of Baltimore life. Can you explain it, hometown girl?''

"My parents always say it goes back to the Blizzard of '66, which seemed to come out of nowhere," Tess said, as they climbed the marble steps outside Marconi's. "Milk for the kids, bread for sandwiches. And I think the toilet paper was for women to wrap their beehives."

Good, she had made him laugh again. "And now people run to the Giant or the SuperFresh near Television Hill so they can be sure of making the evening news."

"Hey, don't knock it. Being identified as a 'panicky snow shopper' is how most locals earn their fifteen minutes of fame."

"Funny, how that phrase has been perverted over the years," Sterling mused, as they followed an ancient maître d' to a table in the rear dining room. "Warhol actually wrote in an exhibition catalog, 'In the future, everyone will be famous for fifteen minutes.' Now we talk about it as if it were an entitlement, or part of the Declaration of Independence. The right to life, liberty, and the pursuit of our fifteen minutes of fame. Have you had yours yet?"

Tess took her seat, thinking about the brief article the *Blight* had run last fall, when she had been attacked. If she was going to be famous for fifteen minutes, she hoped it wouldn't be for that. "I might have slept through mine."

"Well, then, you can have my fifteen minutes. Unless I'm on the masthead, the only time I ever want to appear in any newspaper is when I die."

It was Tess's turn to laugh. "How Junior League of you. What's the rule? A proper person's name appears only three times: at birth, marriage, and death."

"Exactly. So I have two more opportunities left."

She ducked her head, taking more care than necessary as she unfolded the linen napkin, hoping Sterling couldn't see the wide grin spreading across her face at the realization he had never married.

Marconi's was a dowdy *grande dame*. The dining room was too bright, the food too heavily sauced, the wallpaper faded and waterstained. Prices, while not steep, climbed quickly on the a la carte menu. And although the owners had finally agreed to a reservation system, the last seating for dinner was at 8 P.M., ensuring the regulars were at home in time for reruns of *Matlock* and *Murder, She Wrote.* But Baltimoreans cherished the place. Tess opened the menu with happy anticipation.

"I'll have the house salad—it's big, we can split it if you like—fried pork chops, and potatoes au gratin," she told the waiter, who was young by Marconi staff standards, not even sixty. "And please make sure the kitchen doesn't run out of fudge sauce. I know I'm going to want a sundae for dessert."

Sterling seemed slightly taken aback by Tess's appetite, but he tried gamely to keep up with her. His choices were healthier, however—broiled sole and a plain baked potato. And while he urged Tess to have a drink, he settled for club soda and lime. After hearing his abstemious order, Tess wished she could at least rescind her request for a glass of white wine. Bad enough to be such a pig, did she have to be a drunkard, too?

"Don't worry, you won't lose points for drinking in front of me," Sterling said, again guessing what she was thinking. "I'd love a drink myself, but my metabolism went south when I turned forty. Can't afford those empty calories."

"I guess I do have a pretty good metabolism. Of course, I exercise every day." Tess was aware she sounded boastful, yet she didn't stop. She wanted Jack Sterling to know how strong she was, how fast, how firm. "On a typical day, I bet I burn at least a thousand calories from my workouts—rowing in the warm weather months, running and weight lifting year round. That's five glasses of wine, or almost four packs of Peanut M&Ms."

"Well, you look very . . . healthy," Sterling said. His naturally pink cheeks turned a little pinker and a dry cough almost choked him. He gulped his club soda, spilling some on his shirt front. "I'm sorry, that was inappropriate."

Tess wanted to ease his embarrassment, the way he had eased her discomfort earlier. "You don't know from inappropriate. You should have heard what Wink Wynkowski said to me when I ran into him at the gym.''

''When was this?''

''Friday. The day before . . .'' she stopped, flustered.

''You can say it, Tess. The day before he killed himself, thanks to the *Beacon-Light*'s enterprising reporters. Maybe I will have a drink after all.''

The salad arrived, a welcome distraction. Tess watched the waiter as if she had never seen someone toss and cut greens before, then forked up several mouthfuls in a row to avoid saying anything. It seemed tactless to speak of Wink's death to Sterling, although she wasn't sure why.

But Sterling wouldn't let her off the hook.

''Did we do it, Tess? Did the paper, in its zeal for a story, kill a man?''

''Of course not. You didn't know—you couldn't have known what he would do when the story ran. It's no different than what happened with *Newsweek* and Admiral Boorda. Wink made himself out to be such a tough guy. Who knew it was all an act?''

''Who knows anything about anyone? I'm burning out on this business, and on the glib explanations we offer up for everything, as if we could ever really know a man's soul. I'm no longer so confident I know what's right and what's wrong. I'm not even sure Wink's crimes are relevant. Wink Wynkowski left behind a wife and three children under the age of five. How do I weigh their pain against the readers' 'right to know'?''

The entrees and side dishes arrived, along with a bourbon and water for Sterling. Although she knew from past experience how hot the potatoes were, Tess plucked a cube from the yellow-orange cheese sauce, which had tiny grease bubbles on the surface. Sure enough, it burned the roof of her mouth.

Sterling stared glumly at his food. ''I think about his widow a lot. I wonder if she spoke to him Saturday, if he told her what he was going to do. I wonder if she knew about the story before it was in the paper. Had Wink ever confided in her? Had he ever confided in anyone about his past?''

''Are Feeney and Rosita working on a Sunday story about how it . . . happened?''

''No—not if I have anything to say about it. I'm not worried about answering these questions for the *Beacon-Light*. I want to know for myself, for my conscience. But Mrs. Wynkowski's not talking to anyone. I'll never know how she feels or what she's thinking.''

Tess sliced off a piece of pork, chasing it with another potato cube. Still hot, but no longer lethal. ''What if someone intervened, asked her a few questions? Questions you wanted asked.''

''Who would do that?''

''I would, if it counted toward my six hours daily of indentured servitude. I can't take being on such a tight leash, Jack. I'm probably in trouble right now for not checking out with Colleen's secretary before I went to lunch. Maybe if you told Colleen I was talking to Mrs. Wynkowski on your behalf . . .''

''Why would Lea Wynkowski talk to you?''

''Because I'm not a reporter. Which means I can misrepresent myself, becoming someone she might like, someone she would want to confide in.''

When Sterling smiled, really smiled, his grin split his face like the crack in a cheap watermelon. ''I think I know now why Whitney is so devoted to you. I couldn't see it at first. The two of you seem so different, but you both have a devious side.''

Tess probed the roof of her burned mouth with her tongue. Comparisons to Whitney seared in a way no potato could. ''Are you saying you're surprised we're friends because she's gorgeous, rich, and successful, and I'm a plain, poor failure?''

''Don't beg for compliments,'' Sterling said, wagging his fork at her, still smiling broadly. The color in his cheeks was even higher than usual, perhaps because of his drink, and his hair was falling in his eyes again. Tess had a sudden desire to push it back. "You're both good-looking women, and I suspect you know that. Which is the main reason I find your friendship intriguing. Most attractive women pick plain friends."

"*Smart* women prefer beautiful friends: you meet more men that way, especially if you complement one another. I've met a lot of my boyfriends through Whitney."

"Including Jonathan Ross?"

The name, the too-casual way Sterling used it, made something catch in Tess's throat. Before his death, Jonathan Ross had been one of the *Blight*'s star reporters. Obviously, Sterling would know that. He also had once been Tess's boyfriend, and she wondered if Sterling had learned this as well. She saw Jonathan again, the way she saw him in her nightmares, in clumsy flight over Bond Street. He had saved her life, losing his in the process. *Not my fault,* she reminded herself. *Not my fault.*

"Jonathan and I worked together at the *Star* years ago, then he moved to the *Beacon-Light*. We were friends, Whitney, Jonathan, and I. Friends. Men and women can be, you know."

"Sometimes I think Whitney would like to be a man."

"Whitney would like all the opportunities open to men. There's a difference."

Sterling didn't pick up on her dig. "Whitney reminds me of a man in one of those English hunting prints. I always expect her to stride into my office one day, a riding crop in one hand and a dead fox in the other. I've never really liked those blueblood types. Something androgynous there. You're actually more feminine, even if you do spend a lot of time trying to hide it." He turned pink again. "Sorry. There I go again, being inappropriate."

"More bizarre than inappropriate. Whitney's not mannish at all."

"I've been known to hold minority opinions before. I didn't get where I am by embracing the conventional wisdom."

"Obviously. The conventional wisdom is that you should let the widow Wink alone."

"I know." He shook his head. "I know. But I have to find out how she's doing, Tess. Won't you talk to her for me? I'll get the okay from Lionel, so you don't have to worry about Cory any more. Whitney told me you're trying to figure out what happened to your uncle. Do this for me, and you have carte blanche to come and go as you please for the next two weeks."

Tess raised her glass. "To unconventional wisdom."

Chapter 14

It was almost 2 o'clock when Tess finished scraping the last bit of hot fudge from her ice cream bowl. Sterling, who had faded during the main course, watched with a slightly stunned look that might pass for admiration. Together they walked back to the paper, where her car was now safely parked in the visitors' lot behind the building.

"The shit-and-salmon gang," she said out loud, remembering the brown Buick's original color, outlandish enough so it might be possible to track the model and make through MVA. How many salmon-colored Buicks could there be in Maryland? Then again, they'd probably have a new car the next time she saw them.

"What?"

"Nothing. Just a stray thought. My brain sometimes doesn't process a piece of information for days, but it never lets go of anything."

She felt a little giddy, as if returning from an unusually good first date, and had to remind herself not to seize Sterling's arm or touch him in any way. Wine at midday, even one glass, made the world a dangerously warm and tender place.

They had agreed, somewhere over her dessert course, that she should start the new assignment immediately, going to call on the widow Wink this afternoon.

"Their house is in that new development out Reisterstown Road," Sterling told her when they reached the *Blight.* "The Cotswolds, I think. Or Tudor Village. *Something* English. He lives on Tea Rose Lane. I always remember that detail from the stories, because I thought it was funny, a tough guy who grew up in Violetville, then ended up on Tea Rose Lane. But I don't have the number. Come upstairs and I'll get it for you."

"No, I don't want to run the risk of entering Colleen's field of vision. She's like one of those big dinosaurs, the kind who can't attack unless she sees you moving. I've got a map in my car which should get me to Tea Rose. Then all I have to do is look for the place with a lawn trampled by all those camera crews. I may make one stop en route, pick up a little something I might have to put on my expense account. Is that okay?"

"Whatever you need," Sterling assured her.

Whatever?

The Cotswolds seemed to feature every kind of architecture except for the modest cottages found in the part of England from which it took its name. The lots were deep but narrow. Huge houses crowded up against one another, almost as close as the city rowhouses the residents had fled. After a few wrong turns, Tess found Tea Rose, a looping cul de sac off the main road, Cotswold Circle. Her joke about the camera crews had been prescient. Although all the lawns here were still winter-brown, the yard at number seven had a particularly hopeless look to it.

After several seconds of scrutiny through a fisheye in the huge oak door, Lea Wynkowski opened the door.

"Yes?" she asked, eyes and voice dull.

"Mrs. Wynkowski? I'm Sylvia Weinstein, from Weinstein's Jewelers in Pikesville." The lie almost made her lips pucker, as tight and unapproving as the lips of the real Sylvia Weinstein, widely believed to have been born with a lemon wedge in her mouth. Tess could think of few people she'd less like to be than her aunt. But she did exist, and she worked alongside Uncle Jules in his Pikesville store when the mood struck her, or when she wasn't in Boca Raton. Her story would check out, if anyone thought to check it out.

"Honestly, I don't have as much money as everyone thinks I do," Lea said. "Even if I did, I'm not exactly in the market for jewelry right now."

"But I'm here to bring you something, Mrs. Wynkowski, something Wink had been planning to give you. He stopped in the store last week and said he would pick it up after the weekend. It's paid in full, it's only right you have it."

She pulled out a box and showed Lea the simple gold bracelet inside. More than $100, even at cost, but she had told Uncle Jules to bill it directly to the *Blight*. She'd like to see Colleen Reganhart's face when that expense came through for authorization.

"Kinda plain, for Wink's taste," Lea said dubiously. "Did he say why he was buying it?"

"Just because—just because he loved you."

To Tess's horror, Lea burst into tears and embraced her.

"I'm sorry, it's only that it's exactly what I would have picked out for myself," Lea said, wiping her nose on the sleeve of a butter-yellow sweater, then grabbing Tess again. "I guess Wink finally noticed I didn't wear that fancy stuff he was always giving me. Good thing. I'll probably have to hock most of them now."

Money was certainly on her mind, Tess noticed. "Are you having, uh, financial difficulties?"

"We're having financial catastrophes. Wink had a five-million-dollar insurance policy, but it doesn't pay off in the event of suicide. By the time you figure closing costs on this place, I'll lose what little equity we have in it. I could sell the business. But the business isn't worth anything without the basketball team, and there's no guarantee there will be a basketball team, or I'll get a piece of it if there is."

"Shit."

"You can say that again. Hey, you want a cup of coffee or something?" Lea asked. "My mom took the kids out for the afternoon so I could be alone for a little while. Although it helps a little, being so busy with the kids. Between cookies and diaper changes, I don't have much time to feel sorry for myself.''

"How many children do you have?" Tess asked, as she followed Lea to the rear of the house.

"Three. Three kids in four years. What was I thinking? What was Wink thinking?"

A family room as large as a hotel lobby ran across the back of the house. Tess suppressed a smirk at the needle-point pillows along the sofa, adorned with Springsteen titles: "Born to Run," "Hungry Heart," and "She's the One."

Tess could see how Lea Wynkowski might inspire that last sentiment. Young and fresh looking, she had the kind of beauty that stood up to crying jags and insomnia. Large brown eyes, brown hair a shade lighter, with the shine and bounce of hair in a shampoo commercial. She wore blue jeans, a yellow cotton sweater over a white T-shirt, yellow socks, and no shoes, and she looked better than most women would in couture clothes. Tess had thought men who traded in their first wives went for high-maintenance types the second time around. Lea looked like a first wife, or someone's high school sweetheart. She could be the girl in an early Bruce Springsteen song, lured onto a motorcycle and out of town, knocked up and abandoned. Instead, she was living out the lyrics to "Hungry Heart"—the part about the wife and kids back in Baltimore, left by the guy who went out for a ride and never came back. In his own way, Wink had done just that.

"How are you holding up?" Tess asked. Her sympathy wasn't fake—if anything, the wretched success of her bracelet trick made her feel she owed Lea Wynkowski true compassion.

"I'm not," Lea said. She opened a wooden-and-copper box on the low, distressed pine table in front of her and took out a cigarette. She didn't light the cigarette but held it in her right hand, twirling it like a miniature baton. "I'm in a million little pieces—one for every dollar Wink didn't leave us.''

''Your doctor could write a prescription for a sedative.''

''I don't want to be sedated. I want to feel what I'm feeling.''

''What are you feeling?''

''Pissed.'' Lea smiled at Tess's surprise. ''I know it doesn't sound very elegant, and it's not in any of those grief books my mother keeps bringing me, but it's what I am. I'm *pissed*. Furious with Wink for what he did to us.''

She sniffed the cigarette she was holding, then placed it back in the box. ''I gave up smoking the first time I got pregnant, but I never stopped missing it.''

''Me, either,'' Tess said, willing to say anything to find common ground with this strange young woman. Lea's grief was sincere enough, but it was shot through with something darker, something disturbing.

''You have kids?''

''Uh, no, but I gave up cigarettes.'' Not even this was true. It was one of the few vices Tess had skipped along the way.

''Then you can't know how weird it is. Killing yourself, I mean, when you've got three kids. He loved our girls. He would have killed anyone who hurt them, but now he's hurt them more than anybody else could. I wish I could ask him why.''

''Where did you two meet?''

''In Atlantic City. Tooch—Paul Tucci, his best friend—introduced us. Tucci's the one who really likes to gamble, not Wink. But I was a blackjack dealer, so he played blackjack. Won a date with me on a bet. We got married six months later. We would have gotten married even sooner, but—''

''But?''

''But we didn't,'' she said flatly.

''When was the last time you talked to him?''

''Friday, in the afternoon. He called me at my mom's

house in Jersey. Whenever I went away, he called me every day. He was devoted to me.''

Yes, a devoted husband, checking in by phone when he wasn't making passes at other women.

''When did you hear about what was in the paper on Sunday?''

''Not until Sunday night, after I got back. I don't know why Wink killed himself over it. That guy who died—I mean, so he had a bad heart. He could have died if some kid jumped out of a closet and said 'Boo.' It wasn't Wink's fault.''

Tess picked her words carefully as possible. ''According to the account in the paper, Wink stood over the guy and pistol-whipped him, then bragged about it.''

''That's not true. Wink couldn't have done something like that. He's—he was—a pussycat. A sweetie. Anyone who ever knew him loved him.''

She stood up and walked over to a large pine armoire, which Tess knew would store the requisite electronic toys. Sure enough, the doors opened to reveal a large TV, stereo, VCR, laser disc player, and two shelves of videotapes. Lea reached behind the videos on the lowest shelf and pulled out a slim book bound in bright blue. Tess read the white lettering on the spine: *The Happy Wanderer.*

''This is Wink's yearbook from junior high. Before he . . . went away,'' Lea said. ''He never knew I had it. I found it in his stuff, and I liked to look at it sometimes. Sometimes I wish we were the same age, that we had started going together in sixth grade and been together forever. I would have been good for him.''

She handed Tess the book, and its well-worn spine opened automatically to a photograph of Wink, taken with the basketball team. He had been even scrawnier then, but his hair had been close-cropped, so you couldn't tell how curly it was. What an unfashionable hairdo, among the bushy locks and sideburns of the early '70s. Most of the boys looked like they were werewolves, caught in mid-transformation.

"And look here," Lea said, leaning over Tess and turning to the frontspiece. "Look at the things the kids wrote, boys and girls. They all loved him." She traced her fingers over the faded ink. *"Right back here and out of sight/I sign my name just for spite." "Make no friends/But keep the old/One is silver/but the other's gold. You're golden, Wink. RGJH 4-ever." "That means Rock Glen Junior High forever." "Love, Lynette."* Someone else, presumably a boy, had signed nearby, *"Silver and gold. Gag me. Ray-ray."*

Tess started to flip through the rest of the pages. Lea tried to snatch the book away from her. But Lea was timid, scared of damaging the precious memento. Curiosity sparking, Tess held it out of arm's length and scanned the pages. It took only a moment to find what Lea didn't want her to see: a classmate's photo had been crossed out with an emphatic black X, the legend "Cunt" written beneath it. Despite these additions, the name was still legible.

"Linda Stolley," Tess read out loud. "If I remember the *Beacon-Light*'s first story, she was Wink's first wife. I guess the divorce wasn't too amicable, if he had to go back and deface her junior high school yearbook picture."

Lea looked scared, but she didn't back down. "She was a . . . well, I don't like to say that word, but it's what she was. Wink left her years ago, but he never got divorced from her officially. So when he decided to marry me and finally wanted to get a divorce, she held him up for a fortune. Her alimony cost more than the mortgage on this place, but it was the one bill Wink never skipped, I can tell you. Oh no, Miss Linda always had to be paid first no matter what."

"You make it sound as if he had a habit of paying other bills late." Unwittingly, Lea was confirming the *Blight's* story, line by line. The violence, the rage against his ex-wife, the financial problems.

"I'm not—" Lea snatched the book back. "I wanted to show you how loved Wink was. I thought you were on *our* side."

Tess had forgotten her role. "Look, I've upset you. That

was the last thing I wanted to do. Please, wear your bracelet in good health. And if you do have to sell anything, call Jules Weinstein first. I'll make sure he does the appraisal for free. It's the least I can do.''

Lea looked at her skeptically. ''Was that the whole reason you came over here, to get dibs on my jewelry? Maybe you made up the whole story about this gold bracelet. Maybe you've never even met Wink.''

''I met him. I talked to him just last Friday.'' At least this was the truth.

''What did he say?''

''He said you were very good to him, that you had a good marriage.'' And this was sort of true.

Lea might have pressed her for more details, but a key was turning in the lock. Tess assumed it would be her mother and the children, but there was only one person, someone with a heavy, irregular tread. A tanned man in a navy windbreaker came into the room. It took Tess a second to place the familiar face in an unfamiliar place. Paul Tucci. Tooch.

''Oh, Tooch!'' Lea said. ''Wait until you hear, this woman is from Weinstein's Jewelers, where Wink bought me the most beautiful bracelet last week.'' She held up her arm so he could inspect it.

''Weinstein Jewelers? That a fact?'' Tucci stared at Tess, who hoped he would not be able to match her to the sweat-slick cyclist from Durban's. Certainly Wink's conquests and would-be conquests must blend together over the three decades he and Wink had known each other. ''When did you say Wink stopped by?''

''I didn't, but it was recently. Just last week.''

Tucci looked at Lea's face. You couldn't call it happy, but it was slightly more animated than the dull, flat countenance that had greeted Tess. Lea was looking at the bracelet, as pleased as a child. Over her head, Tess shot Tucci a pleading look. *Yes, I did something really shitty, but don't take this away from her. Let her believe her husband did something nice for her before he died.*

''Nice work,'' he said. ''Very classy. Maybe I'll stop by Weinstein's, pick up something for my mama's birthday.''

''Call first. I'll personally help you.''

''Oh, I'm counting on that,'' Tucci assured Tess.

Chapter 15

⋙⋘

Tess was just pulling out of the Cotswolds when she caught the latest traffic report on the radio. "An accident on the inner loop of the Beltway has traffic there backed up all the way from Providence to Security," announced a cheerful man who happened to be hovering above it all in a helicopter. "Better find an alternate route unless you have a lot of time to kill."

This day was just getting worse and worse. Sighing, Tess snapped off the radio and resigned herself to making her way home along secondary streets. But her mind was still back at the Wynkowskis'. Would Tucci tell Lea who she really was? How dear a friend did someone have to be to warrant his own house key?

Preoccupied, she didn't notice she was on Route 40, not even a mile from her parents' house, almost as if her car had a homing device. Perhaps the Toyota was looking out for her best interests: surprise visits were worth big, big points in her family. And her mother had sounded a little plaintive at the hospital. A drive-by schmoozing, if handled properly, might erase all Tess's other demerits.

The Monaghans lived in a too-big house in Ten Hills, a neighborhood that had run to huge Catholic families when Tess was growing up. Six kids, eight kids, ten, eleven, twelve. This was normal; it was Patrick and Judith Monaghan, with just one child, who had seemed freakish. Tess's classmates had assumed the Monaghans hadn't had more children because they eschewed sex, an abstinence adolescents found admirable in their parents. Tess had seen no reason to disabuse her friends of this notion. How much more embarrassing for them to find out her parents were certifiable voluptuaries. But now that she was grown, she was secretly proud her parents' marriage was still a passionate one.

Judith was sitting at the kitchen table, rubbing a foot just freed from an Italian pump, and reading the morning paper. For a second, Tess saw her as the rest of the world must see her—not as her maddening, monochromatic mother, but as a handsome woman, even a pretty one. She was both right now, her face smooth, without the frown lines her daughter so often provoked.

"Tess!" Judith cried when she sensed her standing there. Then, almost reflexively: "Your *hair*."

Tess put a hand up to her forehead, unsure what offense her hair had committed this time. It was loose, which her mother usually preferred to other styles—the long braid down the back, the ponytail low on the neck. Wait, here was the problem: she had used an old plastic headband to hold it back, one in a tortoiseshell pattern. Her mother did not approve of headbands for females over fourteen. Judith wore her glossy brown hair in a short, thick pageboy, which required exactly twenty-five minutes with a blow-dryer every morning. And today's outfit was perfect, as always, if not exactly fashionable. Navy shoes, now discarded, navy hose, navy skirt, white silk blouse, and navy jacket. Her earrings were lapis, dark enough to match the suit, and set in silver, which went with the silver beads at her neck.

"When a woman turns thirty, she shouldn't have a *mane*," Judith chided. "You need to shape it."

"I was in a hurry this morning. I've been working on special assignment."

"As an . . . investigator?" Her mother was lukewarm about the job with Tyner. When Tess was unemployed, she had insisted any job would do. Now she longed for Tess to be a professional, someone with regular hours, a fat salary, and a thin husband.

"Yes, as an investigator, although this is a contract job. But I think I'm suppose to keep things confidential. Like a lawyer."

The word "lawyer," even in passing, had a softening effect on her mother. If Tess worked at a law firm, perhaps she would go to law school and become someone Mrs. Monaghan could brag about, ever so casually. Better yet, maybe she'd meet a doctor on a malpractice case. Tess knew how her mother's mind worked.

"Would you like something to drink as long as you're here? A Coke? Tea?"

Although still full from her Marconi's lunch, Tess knew this was a cheap way to make her mother happy. "Tea would be nice. Let's have a cup together."

The kitchen had been redone three years ago, and it reflected Judith Monaghan's single-minded approach to color. Almost everything was white—walls, cabinets, appliances, the tile floor—with a few red and blue accents placed carefully throughout. As the water boiled in a bright blue teapot, Tess took down fire engine red mugs. The spoons, the everyday ones, had blue wooden handles. A bright red Le Creuset casserole sat on a back burner. When spring was further along, there would be red and blue flowers in a white vase on the whitewashed table. Perverse Tess sometimes longed to bring her mother pink tulips, or something yellow, to see if Judith could tolerate these unchosen, clashing colors.

"Forsythia," she said out loud, and her mother looked out the bay window in the front, to the row of ancient forsythia beginning to bud.

"I told your father to cut it back last fall, but I think he got carried away. It looks straggly, doesn't it?" Then, without transition, without any change in inflection, "That car again."

A brown car, with ever-larger portions of salmon showing through, was driving slowly down the street, the Buick that had trailed Tess the night before. *Damn, my car is in plain view*. But it seemed unlikely they could have followed her today, from downtown, through the maze of the Cotswolds and on her aimless journey. Were they keeping tabs on everyone close to Spike?

"Again. You said, 'That car *again*.' Have you seen it before?"

"It was here on Saturday, when we got home from the hospital. It drove up and down a couple of times, so I called the neighborhood patrol. That's one good thing about the mayor's people moving into this neighborhood. You get action when something is going on."

"The mayor's people" was her mother's code for professional blacks. Tess usually corrected Judith's euphemistic racism, but enlightenment could wait. The Buick was pulling over, parking at curbside.

Tess shrank back behind the kitchen island, trying to find a place where she could watch the car through the kitchen window without its occupants seeing her. The front passenger door opened and, after a few seconds, a man came up the walk. A short, chunky man in a leather blazer, with a face that defied any specific description. It was a generic face, a clean-shaven oval beneath bushy brown hair, dark glasses hiding the eyes. *A good face for a criminal*, Tess thought, as the doorbell pealed.

"Mother—" her voice was urgent enough to stop Judith, who was bending over and putting her shoes back on.

"He's probably selling something," she assured Tess. "I'll send him on his way and we'll have our tea."

"Don't let him know I'm here."

Judith could be distressingly obstinate and slow at times, but she picked up on Tess's tone. "Is this something to do with your work?"

"Yes." There was no point in letting her parents know that the unsavory side of Spike's life was in the ascendance. "This man is very angry with me. Don't let him in. Whatever he says, don't let him in. I'm going to stand by the phone, ready to call 911 if I have to. But I won't unless I absolutely have to.''

Her mother studied Tess. She was torn, Tess knew, between lecturing her daughter on her unorthodox life and enjoying this sense of mission between them. The bell rang again. She walked to the door with the brisk air known to quicken the pulses and words-per-minute of the clerk-typists in her division at the National Security Agency. Tess crouched down by the wall phone, eavesdropping on their conversation.

''Spike Orrick told me he was gonna leave something for me here,'' the man was telling Judith. ''You know anything about that?''

''I think you must have the wrong house,'' she replied. Tess could tell she tried to shut the door on him as firmly as possible without slamming it, but her swing ended prematurely with a dull thud. The man must have stuck his shoe between the door and the frame.

''Maybe you better let me come in and look.''

''I don't think so. In fact, I'm going to call the police if you don't leave Ten Hills right this minute.'' This time, Tess heard a sound she couldn't identify, followed by a quick exhalation and a muttered curse. The door slammed shut firmly and the deadbolt turned. As Judith marched back into the kitchen on her navy heels, Tess lunged for the kitchen door and locked it, just in case the men tried to come through that way. Outside, the Buick roared away from the curb. It sounded asthmatic, the way a car does when it's going to need a new muffler soon. Good, she'd be able to hear it coming.

''How did you get him to leave?'' Tess asked.

''Stepped on his foot with my high heel.'' Judith laughed, pleased with herself. ''He's not the first man to stick his foot in the door. But what does this have to do with your job? That man was asking for something from *Spike*. Is that why you didn't want to call the police, because Spike is mixed up in this?''

The teapot sang, momentarily sparing Tess a reply. She

poured the water over the tea bags—good old Lipton's, nothing flavored or new-fangled for Judith—wondering why the men would come here. Spike would never implicate her parents in any part of his gambling operation, given her father's job as a city liquor inspector. Yet this was the second time they had been here in four days.

"They tried to get into Dorothy's house on Saturday, but she didn't even take the chain off," her mother said. "They told *her* they were looking for a dog. You know what I think? I saw something on television about burglars who tell some story in order to get into your house, to see what you have worth stealing. Then they back up a truck as soon as you go to work and cart everything away."

Tess almost scalded herself with water as she swung around, still holding onto the teapot.

"They were looking for a *dog?*"

"That was the story they used Saturday, down at Dorothy's."

"Did they say what kind of dog?"

"They didn't have time to say much. Dorothy blew her police whistle in his face and slammed the door on him."

The greyhound—of course, they wanted the greyhound. But why? Why would anyone want that dog under any circumstances?

"Esskay," she said.

"You want a piece of sausage? Oh, honey, you know your father and I don't eat those fatty foods any more. But let me see what I have for a snack."

"I'm sorry," Tess said, putting her untouched mug of tea on the kitchen table. "I have to go."

"Why?" Her mother called after her. "What's going on?"

She searched for the only reason her mother would accept. "I just remembered, I left my iron on."

There was no brown-over-salmon car wheezing down Bond Street, or waiting in the alley outside her apartment. Inside, Esskay was in bed with Crow, napping. Tess stood over them, watching them, feeling an odd mix of tenderness and responsibility toward both. *I didn't ask for this*, she thought. *I can't handle this.*

Crow's breathing was slow and measured. The dog's inhalations were quick and sharp, her lip curling back over her teeth, her legs moving as if she were chasing rabbits in her dreams. Crow wrapped himself around the twitching dog, nurturing even in his sleep. Tess took off her clothes and took her place behind Crow, joining in their conga line. She began to fall asleep, only to jerk awake at the sound of a car moving slowly through the alley. She got up, looked out the window, snorted down a quick whiff of bourbon. Back in bed, she had barely surrendered to the not unpleasant mix of hot flesh and warm fur when the phone rang, waking everyone entwined there.

"Hello," Crow whispered dreamily to her, as she reached over him to pick up the phone. He squeezed her thigh in welcome.

"Hello?" Jack Sterling's voice came over the line, tentative and shy.

"Yeah," she said to both men, a little groggy from being right on the edge of sleep.

"I'm sorry to call you at home, but I admit I couldn't wait. Did you talk to Lea Wynkowski?" Crow rolled toward her and pushed his leg between hers, as if trying to warm himself.

"Yes, I did talk to her," Tess said, feeling a rush of shame as she recalled her heartless trick.

"Does she blame the paper? Does she think we killed her husband?"

What was it about Jack Sterling that made her want to say whatever he longed to hear? "Right now, the only person she really seems to blame is Wink."

"Did he call her before he . . . did what he did?"

She was fully awake now. "No, the last time she talked to him was Friday. And he was in a pretty good mood then. Said he thought the deal would still go through." She glanced at Crow, who was looking at her expectantly, the way Esskay sometimes stared at the kitchen table, even when there was no food on it. "She didn't even know about the story until Sunday night."

"I guess that's something. Although even if she absolves us, I'm not sure I can. Did she say anything else? Anything at all? Don't spare my feelings, Tess."

"Nothing, really. Did I do okay? Or does this mean I have to go back to sitting in that office six hours a day?"

Sterling laughed. "You do whatever you like. I told Colleen I've given you a special assignment." His voice changed, warming a shade. "Tess?"

"Hmmmm?"

"You sounded hoarse when I called, as if you were sleeping. Are you in bed?"

"Uh-huh."

He hesitated. "Are you alone?"

Again, she told him what she assumed he wanted to hear, what she wanted him to want to hear. "Uh-huh."

"Go back to sleep, Nancy Drew." He hung up the phone, as did Tess. But she did not go back to sleep. It was only 7 o'clock. She rolled into Crow, and they made love like an old married couple, quickly and silently, with small, efficient movements that barely rocked the bed. Esskay slept on, undisturbed by their rhythms, still chasing rabbits.

When they were finished, Crow put on his jeans and went whistling into the kitchen to prepare everyone's supper. Tess, who had never been a stare-at-the-ceiling sort, found herself studying the old-fashioned light fixture over her bed as if she had never seen it before. Something worrisome was skulking around the edges of her mind. Not one thing. Three things.

One: the men in the salmon-under-shit car wanted Esskay, whom Spike expected her to protect. She had to find a safe place for the dog, someplace with no connection to Spike. Then she had to make Tommy tell her whatever he knew.

Two: she and Crow, usually so conscientious, had forgotten the whole safe sex routine tonight.

And three: she hadn't thought about this until now, because she had been thinking about Jack Sterling all along.

Chapter 16

~~~~~~

"Did you get her blanket?" Tess asked Crow the next morning. "And the kibble? What about her Teddy bear?"

"I got everything," he assured her, slamming the trunk of his Volvo. "Even the Teddy bear. I know Esskay considers him her own personal boy toy."

"Everybody needs a little Crow. And it's toy boy. Girls *have* toy boys. Think about it."

Toy boys, smart ones, had their uses. Last night, after a skittish Tess had gone to the window a third time to check for the two-tone Buick in the empty alley below, Crow had demanded an explanation. It was Crow who had come up with the idea of asking one of Tess's friends, someone who considered himself forever in her debt. That was Plan One. Tess had figured out Plan Two, how to force Tommy to talk.

They drove south in silence, heading toward Annapolis, then veering down Route 2, into one of the old summer towns along the Chesapeake's western shore. These villages had once seemed remote, appropriate only for August-desperate escapes from Washington and Baltimore. Now the houses here were considered within commuting distance of both cities and tear-downs were common, as shacks made way for million-dollar mansions. A few rough cottages still stood along the South and West rivers, but only a hardy soul would consider them tolerable in the winter.

Darryl "Rock" Paxton, the nationally ranked sculler who Tyner always held up as a role model for Tess, was the very definition of a hardy soul.

Some people chose to live close to work; Rock had chosen to live close to his workout. He had found the cottage a few months ago and used his savings to buy it. The house needed much in repairs and updates—a new roof, siding, double-hung windows to keep out the drafts. The long, twisting driveway from the main road had lost most of its gravel and was little better than a dirt trail. Those things could wait. Rock's only improvement project so far had been to clear the overgrown path to his dock. It gave Tess a pang to realize she wouldn't see Rock on summer mornings along the Patapsco any more, now that he had this place.

Today's workout behind him, Rock was waiting for them in his kitchen, a homely room furnished with one table, two chairs, and an elaborate array of coffee-making accessories. Despite the coffee consumed on the way down, Tess and Crow quickly accepted Rock's offer of a fresh cup. Rock was famous for his coffee.

"Today's selection is Jamaican Blue Mountain, prepared in a French press," he said. If ever lost his job as a researcher at Johns Hopkins, he could always try Donna's, Baltimore's answer to Starbucks. The three stood with their steaming cups, watching Esskay amble from room to room. The cottage had only four rooms and there wasn't much for a dog to sniff, although Rock's futon provided some momentary interest. Inspection finished, Esskay came back to stand between Crow and Tess. *Simple but intriguing,* she seemed to be saying. *Now let's go.*

"She'll want to sleep with you," Tess told Rock. "She jumps into my bed, and that's a foot off the floor. There's no way to keep her out, unless you lock her in another room, and then she cries."

"No problem. She'll keep me warm."

"We never did get her a new leash to replace this chain. If you do, I'll pay you back. Did I tell you she tears up trash when she's lonely? And she needs ointment for those bare patches, at least for a little while longer.'' Tess felt a strange sensation in her throat, an itch at the back of her eyes. Crow took her hand.

''It's not forever,'' he said.

''I bet you'll be back to pick her up before the first race of the spring season,'' Rock said. In Rock-speak, this was the shortest time span imaginable.

Tess hugged her friend, marveling as she always did at the aptness of his nickname. In every sense, he was the most solid man she knew. He was so hard and competent that people often made the mistake of assuming he needed nothing from others: he was Rock, he was an island. Tess, who knew more than she wanted about the circumstances of his broken engagement last fall, thought Esskay might prove good company in the short term. And with the dog here, she would have incentive to visit him, something she had neglected to do since he had moved from the city.

Rock and Esskay stood on the back porch as Tess and Crow climbed into his Volvo. Tess tried not to turn her head, stealing a quick, final glance through her eyelashes and hair. The dog looked puzzled, glancing at Tess and Crow in the car, then back at Rock, who had placed his hand on her collar. Ever so slowly, in her ever so tiny brain, Esskay was realizing that something was amiss. They would be down the gravel driveway before she figured it out. By the time they reached Baltimore, she would have forgotten she had ever known anyone but Rock.

''He'll have to build a fence or keep her on a leash all the time,'' Tess muttered, more to herself than to Crow.

''She couldn't be in a better place, or a safer one. You know that.''

Esskay cocked her head to one side, as if saying ''What? What? What?''

Don't be a sap. You've never been stupid about animals. Don't start now.

Rock's hand rested on the dog's collar, but he hadn't curled his fingers around the fabric. So he wasn't ready for Esskay's quick surge as the Volvo started rolling down the driveway. Rock was strong and fit, but he wasn't a sprinter, and he wasn't as fast as Esskay, now trotting after the Volvo. The dog was moving at twenty mph, Tess judged. Maybe twenty-five. At any rate, she was right on their bumper.

"Greyhounds can reach speeds of up to thirty-seven miles per hour," Crow said.

"I'm more interested in what speeds you can reach right now."

"I can't go any faster on this driveway. But don't worry. Once we're on the highway, she'll give up."

The car's speed had notched up to thirty now. Esskay still kept pace. She did not seem angry or upset, just determined. Her tongue lolled out of her mouth, giving her an antic appearance. She was enjoying the chase. This was a game, the dog had decided. *They would never really leave me.* She looked a little like a kangaroo, the way her rear legs kicked up behind her as she ran. She took the driveway's twists and turns better than the Volvo did, cutting sharp on the corners.

"Stop the car, Crow."

"Don't worry, I see her, I won't clip her. We're almost to the highway."

"Stop the car *now.*"

The Volvo was still rolling when Tess threw open the passenger door and leaped out. Esskay jumped up, placing her paws on Tess's shoulders, ready to be congratulated for her effort. Crow braked and put the car in park, but Esskay ignored him, intent on licking Tess. Rock arrived a few seconds later, panting much harder than the dog.

"This gives me some ideas for cross-training," he said, when he caught his breath. "I'll take her back to the house and you can be on your way. I promise I'll hold tighter this time."

"She loves you," Crow said wonderingly, and Tess could hear a trace of bitterness in his voice. "She loves you."

The dog licked her from chin to eyebrow. Her breath

was nothing short of awful, but it was familiar to Tess now. She almost liked it.

"Look, if Esskay wants to stick it out with me, I guess I have to take her home. We can walk her after dark, turn the terrace into a dog run, get a bodyguard. We'll figure something out. If Spike wanted me to take care of this dog, there must be a reason."

Smugly now, the dog took her position in the backseat, insisting on standing, just as she had the first night Tess had taken her home. But this time, Esskay was more firmly rooted, holding her stance on the turns. A week ago, a day ago, even five minutes ago, Tess had firmly believed dogs could not smile. Yet this one was practically leering in her delight.

"So much for Plan One," she told Crow. "Still up for Plan Two?"

"Sure," he said, eyes on the road. "It doesn't seem fair, though."

"Plan Two?"

"The fact she loves you more than she loves me. You've hardly done anything for her, while I was reading books and making special meals and pulling bones out of her throat. She should love me best. But I guess that's how it works, sometimes."

"Sometimes," Tess admitted.

At the Point, Crow parked near the delivery door. While he rang the bell, Tess crouched out of sight behind the car. After a few minutes, Tommy came out, blinking in the morning sun. Although he wore what appeared to be sleep clothes—a dingy white T-shirt and Carolina blue sweatpants with a crotch that bagged to his knees—he had taken the time to put on his ankle boots, the zippered ones that wouldn't slip off his thin ankles.

"We don't start serving for a couple hours, buddy," he told Crow between yawns. Luckily, they had never met, although Spike had checked Crow out when he and Tess had first started seeing each other. "You and your collitch friends can come back at noon."

"But Mr. Orrick, you won the television set in our fraternity raffle," Crow said with sunny sincerity. Tess was impressed. She hadn't known he could lie as well as she could.

"I won a TV?"

"Big-screen," Crow said, gilding the lily. Tommy could be had for a Walkman, or an old transistor radio. "You are Spike Orrick, aren't you? I wasn't here the night you bought the raffle ticket, but my fraternity brother said I would find you here."

"Oh, sure, sure," Tommy said excitedly. "*Now* I remember."

"We've got it back at the frat house. I thought I'd take you over so you could get it today. Do you have time now?"

Tommy practically ran to the car, settling himself in the front passenger seat. Esskay, who had finally stretched out in back, stuck her head between the bucket seats and licked his neck.

"Hey, where'd ja get this dog—" Before Tommy finished, Tess had slipped into the passenger door and plunked herself in Tommy's lap, fastening the seat belt over both of them. Crow roared out of The Point's parking lot like an experienced getaway driver.

"What the fuck are you doin', Tess? This is kidnapping." Then, as an afterthought, "Damn, you're a big girl, ain'cha?"

"We're taking you down to my Aunt Kitty's place and we're going to keep you there until you tell us what happened to Spike and what Esskay has to do with it." She curled her hands over his, so he couldn't pinch or tickle her. Tommy was not above fighting dirty.

"I don't know anything," he whined, pulling his head to the side so he could breathe. Esskay licked his forehead with increasing interest, perhaps trying to decide if Tommy might be a good substitute for her Teddy bear, left behind at Rock's. Certainly, he was larger, with more surface area to lick.

"This is kidnapping," Tommy repeated. "That's a feral offense."

"Luckily, Kitty isn't dating anyone in law enforcement right now, so who's going to know? And with your only real friend in a coma, who's going to *care?* You remember, your good friend Spike, whose big-screen TV you were about to take for yourself."

"I just wanted it for the bar, to help business. By the way, I'm adding torture to those charges. This dog stinks."

"As you once said so memorably, Tommy, that's like the pot telling the kettle to get out of the kitchen if it can't stand the heat."

Chapter 17

∾∾∾

You couldn't call Tommy tough, but he had a stubborn streak, and that could be almost as good under the right circumstances. For most of the morning, he sat sullenly and silently in Kitty's kitchen. Tess sensed his dignity had been offended by her ploy, which had been predicated on Tommy not being a serious physical threat. To make him feel better, she tied him to his chair with a pair of Kitty's silk scarves, although she doubted he would try to run and knew she could catch him if he did. His zippered ankle boots would slow him down on the cobblestones of Fells Point.

"Would you like something to eat?" Crow, although fortified on doughnuts, had prepared a large breakfast of scrambled eggs and bacon, hopeful the smell of food would entice Tommy into talking. But food had never interested Tommy. He ate only enough to balance his beer intake.

"No, thank you, I'm maintaining just fine," he said, giving Tess a wounded look. Laurence Olivier couldn't have delivered the line with more gravitas.

"A coma's a serious thing," Crow told Tommy, pushing the plate of eggs a little closer.

"Uh-huh. Serious as a heart attack," said an unmoved Tommy.

"And what if Spike never comes to?" Crow asked. "These guys may not go away. They may hurt Tess, or her parents. They seem to be pretty dangerous guys."

"The dredges of society," Tommy agreed.

Tess leaned over and whispered in Crow's ear, "This is hopeless. We're going to have to pull out our big gun."

Crow left the room and Kitty returned in his place, red curls bouncing, bright red high heels dancing across the wooden floors. Just looking at her, Tommy flushed a shade even darker than her shoes. He had never actually spoken with Kitty—he had always been too tongue-tied to dare. But Tess knew he had noticed her. All men did.

"Good morning, Tommy," Kitty said, as if it were perfectly normal for him to be tied to a chair in her kitchen. "I hear you've been doing a great job running The Point in Spike's absence."

Tommy nodded curtly. Even with his pillow hair and baggy baby blue sweats, he had an odd dignity.

"He'll be so proud of you when he hears." Kitty leaned over Tommy, her mouth deliriously close to his ear, her long skirt brushing against his ankles like a friendly cat. "I really do think he'll wake up, that he'll be with us again. People do come out of comas, you know, sometimes with remarkably few ill effects. There's still so much we don't know about the brain."

"I have read that myself," Tommy said, his thoughtful tone suggesting he gleaned his medical news from the *New England Journal of Medicine,* instead of the *Weekly World News.*

"What worries me is how Spike is going to feel if he finds out you refused to tell Tess what she needs to know," Kitty said. "I'm sure you think you're protecting him by not sharing his secrets with Tess, but I can't imagine Spike wanted Tess endangered."

Tommy looked confused and troubled. Suddenly, this conversation was headed somewhere he didn't want it to go.

"But she kidnapped me!" he protested. "She used brute force!"

"Only because you wouldn't talk to her when she visited

you at The Point that last time. And now these guys are following her, because they think she has whatever it is they want. Maybe because you told them that.'' Kitty was at eye level with him now, her mouth so close to his it must have hurt a little. ''What if they hurt her as badly as they hurt Spike? Do you want to be the one to explain that to him? Do you want to be the one to tell *me* something has happened to my niece?''

Tommy looked at Kitty and licked his lips, helplessly enthralled. ''Okay,'' he said at last. ''But I'm gonna tell Spike how Tess tricked me. He wouldn'ta liked the way she squashed me like a bug. I almost smothercated.''

Kitty kissed him on his sweaty forehead, then went back to the store, as Tess untied the scarves at his wrists and ankles. Tommy made a big show of rubbing his wrists and forearms, as if his bonds had been tight ropes instead of loose, silken scarves.

''So where did Esskay come from?'' Tess asked.

''I swear on my mother, I don't know the answer to that. Two weeks back, Spike showed up with this dog, looking like Monday's meatloaf on Friday.''

''Come again?''

''You know. He was all gray and lumpy looking. Said he had met with this guy he knows, and the guy wanted him to have the dog?''

''What guy?''

''Jimmy Parlez. It's a French name? As in parlez the English, you know?''

''Why did Monsieur Parlez give him a greyhound?''

Tommy shook his head. ''Spike wouldn't tell me nothin'. He said ignorance was piss.''

''Bliss. Ignorance is bliss.''

''You sure?'' Tommy wrinkled his forehead as he thought about this. ''Anyways, the only thing he did tell me 'bout was the numbers.''

''Numbers? I *knew* this had to do with book-making.''

Tommy shook his head. ''Uh-uh. Spike don't run no street numbers no more. Can't compete, what with the state doing Pick 3, Pick 4, and all those gimmicky instant win games. He's down to a sports book now, a little action on Pimlico.''

"And on dog races?"

"Tess, there are guys who come into The Point and put money down on how much a bushel of crabs is gonna cost on July fourth, but nobody around here is gonna bet some greyhound race in Florida or New Hampshire when ya got stakes races right down the road. Now, tell that dog to come to me.''

He waggled his fingers, but Esskay ignored him until Tess placed a piece of the dog's namesake bacon in Tommy's hand. Gingerly, he held the crunchy bite out to the dog, who snatched it with such alacrity Tommy almost lost part of a finger. He clambered on top of the chair, but Esskay only became more agitated, leaping around him wildly until Tess gave her another piece of bacon.

"I'm a little scared of dogs?" Tommy confessed unnecessarily.

"Don't worry, she's harmless unless she thinks you're a piece of food,'' Tess assured him.

He climbed down from his chair and tentatively began scratching behind Esskay's ears. As the dog relaxed under his touch, he pulled the left ear back and turned it inside out, exposing the ghostly pale interior, the way one might turn a little leather glove.

"All racing dogs have tattoos here, like ID numbers. That way, the tracks can keep track of 'em. But the numbers also mean you can trace 'em back to their trainers.''

"Why would you want to do that?" Tess asked.

" 'Cuz a few bad trainers can't be bothered to do the right thing when the dogs can't race no more. They'd just as soon kill 'em and dump 'em. The ear tattoos make that hard to do.''

"So who was Esskay's trainer? How do we track her number?"

"You *can't*. That's what I'm tellin' ya." Tommy ran his finger over the smooth skin inside the dog's left ear.

"Someone put a new tattoo on this dog, a home-made job like you see in prison. See? Where this dog once had numbers, all she has now is these red Xs. It's like filing down the serial number on a car or a TV set. Untraceable."

Tess looked at the crude markings inside both ears. Although a vivid red, they would be easy to miss unless you knew to look for them, or spent a lot of time playing with a dog's ears, something Tess was not inclined to do. Esskay's breath had kept even Crow from going nose to nose with the dog. The marks still looked a little raw, and there were tiny scabs. It must have been painful, being on the receiving end of a tattoo gouged with penknife and filled in with ballpoint. No wonder Esskay had been so fearful at first.

"Okay, so you cover up the dog's tattoo and no one knows who it belongs to. Seems like a lot of work to dump some racing dog. And this dog is still alive. So what does it all mean?"

"That," Tommy sighed, "is what Spike and only Spike knows. Look where it got him. You know what? He *did* say ignorance is piss. Ignorance is piss, and knowledge ain't shit, that's exactly what he said the last time I talked to him."

Armed with Tommy's tissue-thin leads, Tess headed to the *Beacon Light,* figuring its computer databases could help narrow her search. But Tommy's scraps led nowhere fast. In the *Beacon-Light*'s Nexis account, Tess searched for "greyhound" and "ears" in various combinations, but found only a few stories from the country's major newspapers, most of which recounted successful rescue efforts. There was no Jim Parlez at all in the court files, no matter how she spelled it, and no possible explanation for why someone would go to so much trouble to change a greyhound's tattoo.

As for the MVA, its records claimed there were no salmon Buicks in all of Maryland, and there were too many brown ones to count. That didn't surprise her: the car had probably been stolen, then hastily painted so it was as untraceable as the greyhound its occupants sought. The only thing left to do was to go to the courthouse and feed Parlez's name through the computers there, just in case he had a record that predated the *Blight*'s system, which only went back to the late '80s. Spike's associates usually had had at least one brush with the city's criminal system, although Spike himself had never been caught doing anything illegal.

Baltimore's Clarence Mitchell courthouse is an unspeakably sad place, a limestone-and-marble reminder of how innocent the city had once been. Imagine the folly of a public building with entrances on four sides, as if people could be trusted to come and go at will, without passing through metal detectors and opening purses and briefcases in front of armed guards.

Tess surrendered her Swiss Army knife to the security guard. Now her only problem was to figure out where to go. Normally, she would have relied on Feeney to walk her through the circuit court computer files. But some newbie she didn't know was filling in for Feeney while he continued to chase basketballs and millionaires. Tess was on her own.

She fed Parlez into the criminal system. No dice. She then tried the civil system, but still came up snake eyes. Tommy had probably mangled the name beyond recognition. For all she knew, she was really looking for Hervé, St. Tropez, or Parsley.

"Ma'am? Ma'am?"

Unaccustomed to being ma'amed, Tess didn't respond to the earnest young voice until she felt a tentative tap on her shoulder. She turned to face a nervous young man with an amazing mane of bushy brown hair falling to his waist. Despite temperatures in the forties, he wore only a denim jacket over a faded black T-shirt.

"I don't work here," Tess snapped. Why did people always assume a woman was a clerk, ready to serve?

"Oh." He looked forlornly at the computer next to her.

"I just thought you might be able to tell me if you can find divorces here. I'm looking up my wife."

"Shouldn't you know if your wife has gotten a divorce?"

"Yeah, sure—if it was from me. I need to find out if she ever got one from her *first* husband. I'm her second husband. She's Mrs. Roger Hehnke now." He thumped his chest with his index finger. "I'm Mr. Roger Hehnke."

Disarmed by his pride in acquiring a wife, Tess showed Mr. Roger Hehnke how to look for the file. She was glad she did. It was gratifying to hear his relieved giggle when he found his wife had remembered to end the first union before starting a second—at least, in the legal sense.

"See, her first marriage ended on April second last year, and we got married on April fifth. Our baby wasn't born until May, so we're totally cool."

"Congratulations." Mr. Roger Hehnke didn't look old enough to drive, but you didn't need a driver's license or a high school diploma to be a father in Maryland. Unless you planned to marry, which required one be at least eighteen or sixteen with parental consent. By local standards, Mr. Roger Hehnke was quaintly old-fashioned.

"Thanks. Hey, you know how the first anniversary is paper? Would tickets count? I thought if Hammerjacks had a band that night, we could go there."

"That's good, but I think you should take her to dinner, too."

"Oh, of course. We're going to Chi-Chi's. And we're gonna have the *gold* margaritas, the ones they make with the good tequila. They cost five dollars!" Mr. Roger Hehnke held up his palm and Tess high-fived him, thinking: *I hope it lasts forever. But I give you three years at the outside.*

Who would she have married at age eighteen? Joel. Joel Goodwin. A neighborhood boy she had chosen precisely because he seemed so safe and pliable, someone with whom to practice sex and love before she left for college. Today, she probably wouldn't recognize him if he passed her on the street.

How long had Wink and his first wife lasted? It was of no concern to her; she had kept her bargain with Sterling and didn't have to worry about Wink any more. Still, Tess found herself tapping out Wynkowski's full name, if only because she longed to have something to show for her field trip to the courthouse. At least she knew Wink's name wouldn't disappoint.

Sure enough, dozens of files came up, most of them the civil suits Feeney had documented. Wink had sued and been sued, in that never-ending shell game some sleazy businessmen played. Tess had to go back almost fifteen years to find the case she wanted, *Wynkowski v. Wynkowski*. She wrote down the number, then asked the clerk for the complete file.

The file was thick with papers, but in the end it shed little light on the marriage or its dissolution. Linda had petitioned for the divorce on grounds of irreconcilable differences and mental cruelty, but made no mention of Wink's physical cruelty. Well, alimony was more common at the time; maybe Linda didn't need to drag Wink through the dirt to get the financial settlement she wanted. Although the two had no children, she was to receive $500 a month, as long as she lived. That wasn't so much. What had Lea been complaining about?

Tess paged through the file. There was a revised order from five years ago, upping the alimony order to $20,000 a month. And the revised order included a rider that stipulated that in the event of Wink's death, his estate would continue to support Linda through an irrevocable trust, an annuity independent of any life insurance policy. So the first Mrs. Wink was better off than the second, since Wink had killed himself.

She looked at the date again. Right around the time Wink had remarried. Was Wink afraid his first wife would scuttle his marriage to Lea if he didn't give her what she wanted? Had the first Mrs. Wink used his abuse to blackmail him into higher payments? And once the abuse became public knowledge, did Wink no longer have a reason to honor this commitment?

Tess checked Wink's name in the criminal system. He had no record for assault, but that wasn't a surprise. Prosecutors had only recently started pursuing cases where wives wouldn't testify against abusive husbands. The city police department hadn't even kept separate statistics on domestic violence until 1994. During Wink's first marriage, it was likely that the cops who'd answered calls to the house hadn't considered domestic violence a crime. They had probably taken Mrs. Wink's statement, then taken a beer from Wink, laughing with him. *Dames. Broads. Bet she was on her period.*

What had really happened between Wink and his first wife? Kitty, who had been married for exactly six weeks in her twenties and seldom spoke of it unless she had too much to drink, liked to say there were only two people who knew the truth about any marriage.

In Wink's case, there was now only one.

Chapter 18

〰〰〰

There were only two Wynkowskis listed in the Baltimore phone book and Tess had already made the acquaintance of the first. The second, Linda Stolley Wynkowski, lived in Cross Keys, one of the city's first gated communities. An understated cluster of townhouses and high-rise condos on the city's north side, Cross Keys over the years had attracted such disparate individuals as John Dos Passos, one-time NAACP director Ben Chavis, and—most impressive to Tess—the original *Romper Room* teacher, Miss Nancy. Tess still had a soft spot for *Romper Room*, despite the fact that the Magic Mirror never saw a Tess, or even a Theresa, in all the years she watched.

She had not called ahead. It was so much harder to say no to a face than it was to a voice, especially someone who looked as harmless as Tess. Her mother might have despaired of her hair and clothes, but mild dishevelment worked for Tess. She looked like a jock, or jockette, and people equated jocks with stupidity, or at least a certain rah-rah thickness. It wasn't flattering for people to assume you were dumb, but it was often an advantage.

Sure enough, the building's front desk clerk—Karl the concierge, according to his name tag—was positively chummy when Tess asked him to ring Mrs. Wynkowski's apartment.

"I should have made an appointment, but I happened to

be in the area and it is terribly urgent," she said, then lowered her voice. "It's about her ex-husband's will."

As she had hoped, the concierge was the type of young man who loved being taken into one's confidence.

"You just missed her," he said in an affected, campy voice, his eyebrows twitching in a way that suggested his every utterance arrived with an overcoat of irony. "Wednesday is Octavia day."

"Excuse me?"

"At least, I think it's Octavia day. Or is it Ruth Shaw day? I do have trouble keeping them straight."

"She alternates Octavia and Ruth Shaw," said the doorman, who was leaning against the front desk, seeking refuge from the day's sleety rains. "Octavia or Ruth Shaw on Wednesday, Jones & Jones Thursday, the shoe store on Friday, Betty Cooke jewelry from the Store, Ltd., on Saturday. I know because she always has the packages dropped off later, and I have to carry 'em up to her apartment."

"And on the seventh day, she rests," Karl said. "But only because the stores in Cross Keys are closed on Sunday."

"The malls are open," Tess said. "If she's such a shopaholic, she could go find plenty of other places to go."

"True, in theory," Karl the concierge said. "But in practice, Miz Rhymes-with-Witch never leaves Cross Keys. Hasn't been off the reservation in years, to my knowledge. Says everything one needs can be found right here—shops, restaurants, the tennis barn. Doesn't need a gas station because she never takes her car out of the garage. And she may be the only person in America who doesn't own a VCR, because you can't rent videotapes in Cross Keys. Thank God for cable and pay-per-view, or she wouldn't even know who Brad Pitt is, and that would be truly tragic."

Tess glanced at a framed Christmas photograph of Karl, a heavy-set woman, and five children who favored him, with their lean builds and mean little mouths.

"I'm getting the impression you don't like Mrs. Wynkowski very much," she said.

"*Moi?* Dislike anyone? Why, I adore the woman, especially at Christmastime, when she gives me *ten whole dollars* for all the little extra services she expects through the year. You trot over to Octavia and I'm sure you'll see just how charming Miz Rhymes-With–Hunt Cup can be."

The shopping center at the heart of Cross Keys was small and set on an open plaza, an arrangement that seemed quaint and dated in this age of malls. Tess did not see how its dozen or so shops could keep one busy for a single day, much less fill six days a week.

There were no customers in Octavia and the sales clerks were too dispirited by the gloomy day to force themselves on Tess. She held a plain black dress in front of her, glancing at its price tag. Too rich for her blood, but then, she wasn't guaranteed $20,000 a month for life. As she returned the dress to the rack, a frosted, frosty blonde stalked out of the dressing room in a bright turquoise suit and stocking feet.

"Marianna," the blonde whined. "Marianna, this doesn't hang right. The jacket should be more fitted through the waist, don't you think?"

"Would you like to have it altered, Mrs. Wynkowski? You know we're always glad to have alterations done for you."

"I don't know. I'm not sure the color is right, either. And it feels awfully heavy for a summer-weight wool." Glumly, she walked over to a rack of suits and began shoving the clothes back and forth as if she wanted to punish them for not being exactly what she wanted.

Studying her, Tess again was struck with the sense that Wink had gotten his wives in the wrong order. Here was what one expected in a second wife—a bottle blonde, pampered and reconfigured. If something could be painted, tugged upward, or filled with plastic, Linda Wynkowski had tended to it. And unlike Lea, her eyes were not red and underscored by black circles. She hadn't been losing sleep lately.

"None of these is right," the first Mrs. Wink muttered to herself. "I hate all these Easter egg colors they're showing this year."

"What about this?" Tess held out the black dress, whose only real distinction was its price. "This would look great on you."

The first Mrs. Wink snatched the dress from Tess's hands. "Not bad," she agreed. "But I probably have fifteen black dresses. I'm not sure I need another one."

Fifteen black dresses, yet she never left Cross Keys? Why did she need even one?

"You're Linda Wynkowski, right?" Tess asked. "Actually, I came here looking for you. We need to speak."

Linda frowned slightly, then willed her face back into blankness, as if conscious of the wrinkles caused by too much animation.

"About what?"

"The annuity, which guarantees your alimony, now that Wink is dead."

"Are you from the insurance company? You should be talking to my lawyer, not me. He'll explain how it works. No matter what else Wink owes, I still get my money. That was the point."

Tess allowed the misunderstanding to stand. "His wife says—"

"The little breeder? She's nuts. You'd think I'd stolen her husband instead of the other way around, that girl is so jealous of me." Without a trace of self-consciousness, Linda began disrobing in the store, unbuttoning the turquoise jacket and exposing a royal blue slip with lace inserts. "Look, if you wanna keep talking about this, you better come into the dressing room with me."

Tess followed Linda to a curtained cubicle with a chintz-covered chair and at least a dozen outfits, most of them wadded up and left on the floor.

"What's your problem with Lea?" Tess asked, as Linda

quickly stripped down to her camisole and pantyhose. Although thin and surgically improved, her body had the soft, oily sheen and consistency of Brie at room temperature. "Your marriage to Wink was long over before she showed up."

"I don't have a problem with her. She has a problem with *me*." Linda looked Tess up and down. "Are you one of her lawyers, trying to figure out how to break the annuity? Don't waste your time. It's air-tight. Besides, it's not my fault Wink offed himself and she won't get anything from the life insurance. Maybe she should have made him happier, you know what I mean, and then he wouldn't have been so quick to take a one-way trip in his Mustang."

Tess decided trying to fake an identity would be too complicated. "I'm not a lawyer, and I'm not from an insurance company. I work for the *Beacon-Light,* where I was . . . double-checking some of the files on your husband today. I saw your alimony had been increased several years after the original divorce decree. That's a pretty unusual arrangement, and I thought there might be some explanation."

Linda slipped a cashmere turtleneck over her head, then stepped into a knee-length plaid skirt, apparently her own. "Let's just say Wink finally did the right thing by me. About five years ago, I was diagnosed as an agoraphobic and couldn't work anymore. He came through for me. I asked him to set up the trust because I always had a hunch Wink would die before I did. I didn't expect it to happen this soon."

"Lea told me she and Wink were really strapped. She thought you might have coerced him into signing that agreement."

"Lea shouldn't try and think," Linda said. "She'll get dents in her adorable young forehead."

"Did Wink threaten to cut you off after the story came out and the secrets of your marriage were exposed? Did he tell you all bets were off?"

Linda Wynkowski smiled strangely. "If anything, the

stakes were higher than ever after the story came out.''

''Did you talk to the *Beacon-Light*? Were you the source?''

Linda's eyes remained fixed on her image in the mirror. ''Wink and I had an agreement to never discuss our marriage with anyone. I kept *my* part of it. I told that other girl from the *Beacon-Light* that I wouldn't comment at all.''

''The article said you didn't deny the charges.''

''Well, it was half right. I told her I wouldn't confirm or deny anything she asked me about my time with Wink. Funny, how much it changes the meaning, losing a word here and there. I called Miss Ruiz to complain and she told me the error had been edited into the story and she would ask for a correction. I'm not holding my breath. I've lived in Baltimore all my life, I know how arrogant the *Beacon-Light* is.''

One of the sales clerks opened the curtains and gave an involuntary cry when she saw Linda and Tess ankle-deep in hundreds of dollars of clothes. ''Oh, Mrs. Wynkowski, couldn't you at least put the dresses over the chair? You know I'm glad to hang them for you when you're done, but we can't have them on the floor.''

To Tess's amazement, Linda shoved roughly past the young woman, knocking her into the wall, then stepping down hard on her foot.

''The customer is always right,'' she called over her shoulder, as tears came to the clerk's eyes. ''Didn't anyone ever tell you that?''

On the way back to the *Blight,* Tess puzzled over what Linda Wynkowski had told her. Despite her antipathy toward Rosita, she knew editors did insert errors into stories. And people often complained of being misquoted when what they really had was a bad case of interviewee's remorse. Possibly Rosita had confused Linda with a jumble of reporting jargon: *on background, off the record, not for attribution.* Given that most reporters couldn't agree on the meaning of those terms, it was impossible for a civilian to understand. But Linda had seemed quite definite that she had told Rosita she would neither confirm nor deny. She was right: dropping one word made a lot of difference in that quote. She had offered a no comment; Rosita had twisted it into serving her needs.

As Tess got off the elevator on the third floor, Feeney got on, barely glancing at her. She darted back in at the last second, the elevator doors bouncing off her shoulders.

"It's funny, Feeney. You're one of two people I know in this whole building and you're the one person I never see or hear from. Whitney at least sends me electronic greetings and drops in."

Feeney studied his shoes. Penniless penny loafers, as usual. Worn with no socks, as usual. "This basketball story has taken over my life. It's like a greased boa constrictor. It twists, it turns, and just when I think I've got it pinned down, it turns out the snake's about to swallow *me*."

"Does Baltimore still have a chance to get a team?"

"Maybe. The deal has lost a lot of momentum since Wink's death, although there's actually more real money connected to it, now that the Tucci family has decided to put its full weight behind it. With Paul as the majority partner, the family is willing to put up a lot more than before. But money isn't everything. Wink may not have brought that much money to the table, but he did have cunning and charisma, something Paul Tucci can't fake. Tucci's not exactly the brightest light on the Christmas tree. Why do you think he's still not a full partner in his father's business?"

The elevator had reached the first floor. Tess walked outside with Feeney, determined to prolong their conversation. She wanted to bring him around to his phony alibi, the lie that had her wrestling with her own greased boa constrictor, but she knew better than to be too direct or confrontational.

"What a difference a week makes. Last time we talked, you were delivering the eulogy for your own career. Remember?" *The night you lied about your whereabouts, and dragged me into this whole mess.*

Feeney made a strangled noise, half-grunt, half-laugh.

"Then comes what your publisher likes to call the 'unscheduled publication' and—*bam*—everything starts falling into place. The first story leads to the tip from the guy in Georgia and you suddenly have the story of your career."

"And Wink is dead."

"How did you get there so fast the night Wink died, then get the story in the paper? It must have happened right on deadline."

"I dictated from a pay phone outside a Royal Farm on Reisterstown Road."

"But the story said the cops didn't arrive until ten-thirty, so you had to be right behind them. Who tipped you off? County police? The medical examiner? An ambulance driver?"

"I didn't get there right behind the cops, Tess. I got there right before them."

Tess stopped at the bottom of the long, low steps in front of the *Blight* and grabbed Feeney's arm, forcing him to stop and look at her.

"Wink? Wink called you?"

"He called my beeper and left his phone number. I recognized the number—I'd been dialing it almost every day, if only to get a 'no comment' from him or a 'drop dead' from his wife. I called back, no answer. I figured if Wink was ready to talk to me, I shouldn't let the mood pass, and I drove out there. The garage was closed and locked, but the front door was unlocked, as if he had been waiting for me all along. And I guess he was, in a way. Wink always did do things with flair."

"What did you do?"

"I called the cops from his house. And then I got out my notebook, took down all the information, and filed my story, like a good boy."

"The story said the cops found the body."

"No, we neatly sidestepped that detail. I wanted to put it in—I thought it made for a nice ironic touch. You know how the editors like those phrases 'The *Beacon-Light* has learned,' or 'As the *Beacon-Light* first reported.' I dictated: 'The *Beacon-Light* last night discovered the body of Wink Wynkowski, an apparent suicide.' Colleen and Jack overruled me.''

''It *is* a little melodramatic.''

''Have *you* ever seen a dead body?'' Feeney asked, then blushed, remembering Tess had seen her share. He jammed his hands in his pocket and began walking north along Eutaw. She fell in step beside him, too intent on their conversation to be put off by his rudeness.

''You shouldn't feel guilty, Feeney. I bet Rosita doesn't have any guilt pangs, and she's as responsible as you are.''

''Rosita's young. She's probably mad he didn't beep *her*. Rosita always thought she could crack the story wide open if she had a few minutes with Wink. She does get people to open up to her, I'll give her that. I don't know how she does it.''

I do. She doesn't let their quotes get in the way of the story.

''How much reporting did she contribute to the first story? Without any help from you, I mean.''

''Most of the personal stuff about Wink, the details about his marriage and his childhood. And she was the one who got the call from the guy who knew him at Montrose. She wanted to do that interview by herself, but Sterling was skeptical about the guy, wanted to good-cop/bad-cop him, make sure he wasn't some petty psycho. Rosita went in all empathetic, while I was the hard-ass. The guy was solid, though, and my courthouse source backed him up.''

''Did the courthouse source help you out on the first story? Was he one of the people you didn't want to identify?''

''Yeah, he's given us lots of stuff over the years, it would be crazy to burn him. But the key was the financial source, someone who—well, let's just say he was a former business associate whose creative accounting tricks for Wink could have resulted in jail time. Now he's born-again, the father of three little girls, soccer coach, PTA president. I was so careful to protect his identity I never even wrote his name in my notebook. He was just U.C.—the Unknown Citizen.''

In her memory, Tess tasted gin, heard the congenial buzz of the Brass Elephant, saw Feeney's red face as he slurringly declaimed a few lines of poetry.

''That's *what* you recited to me in the bar, the allusion I couldn't place. Auden's 'The Unknown Citizen.' '*Am I happy? Am I free?*' ''

''Did I?'' Feeney asked unhappily. ''I don't remember.''

''It was your exit line,'' Tess reminded him. ''When you stormed out at eight o'clock and left me alone with your tab.'' He squirmed a little, as she had expected he would, as she wanted him to. Good: now they had acknowledged the lie between them, the way he had used her.

''Well, obviously he was on my mind,'' Feeney offered. ''I'm surprised I didn't blurt out his name, in the state I was in.''

''Go ahead and blurt it out now. I'm an old friend, you can trust me.'' Tess's mind was racing ahead: if Rosita had conducted any of the interviews with the Unknown Citizen, perhaps she had twisted his words the way she'd twisted Linda's. It was worth checking out.

Feeney's face was pensive, the way he sometimes looked before a poetry jag, although he was obviously stone-cold sober now.

''Tess, as long as you work for management, you're not my friend and I don't trust you. And if you want to continue this conversation, I suggest we find my union rep.''

He turned and began walking quickly toward the Shrine of St. Jude. Tess stood on the corner, as breathless as if he had just punched her in the stomach. How had Feeney gotten things so twisted? She was here because of his deceit, because he had used her as his alibi, and if she didn't make the case that Rosita had sneaked the story into the paper out of unalloyed ambition, Feeney might take the fall. Typical Feeney, going on the offensive when he should be offering profuse apologies.

"Fuck you, Kevin Feeney," she called after him, although he was already too far away to hear her. "You can take care of yourself from now on."

The sleet had finally stopped, but the wind had picked up, stinging and bitter. *That's the only reason my eyes are tearing,* Tess told herself as she walked back inside. *Because of the wind.*

Chapter 19

A dispirited Tess left the *Beacon-Light* at 4:30, sick of the media, only to arrive home in time for the tail-end of a press conference at Women and Children First. All four local television stations were crowded into Kitty's bookstore, along with the reporter from the *East Baltimore Guide,* a neighborhood paper, and someone from the city's alternative weekly. The object of their attention was a quivering Esskay, whom Kitty had brushed to a high shine and beautified by intertwining a green velvet ribbon through her collar. It was a toss-up who was going to lose control of her bladder first—Esskay, or Tess, who couldn't believe Kitty was pulling a stunt like this.

"Yes, this dog was an outstanding racer," Kitty was saying, in response to someone's question. "The top earner at her track in Juarez last year. But her owner decided to let her retire at the top of her game and become the official mascot of Women and Children First. Esskay—that's her nickname, her full name is Sylvia Quérida—will also serve as a model for a children's book I plan to write and illustrate about the greyhound rescue movement."

Illustrate a book? News to Tess. Kitty couldn't draw a stick figure with a ruler.

"How's a high-energy dog like that going to get all the exercise it needs when you don't have a real yard?" asked one reporter, a hard-nosed skeptic by television's standards.

"As some of you know, residents near Patterson Park take their dogs on patrol every night, in an attempt to discourage prostitution and drug-related crimes. We'll walk Esskay as part of the patrol at night. As for her morning walks, some old friends of mine have volunteered to take her out."

Kitty waggled her fingers at two muscular men in Spandex leggings and tight T-shirts. "These police officers plan to jog with Esskay as part of their conditioning program. But if this wintry weather doesn't go away, we'll have to get Esskay a sweater—she doesn't have any body fat to protect her. Then again, neither do the officers."

The reporters laughed as the officers blushed a bright, happy red. Kitty then fished a dog biscuit out of a box propped next to the cash register, climbed to the top of the counter, and held the treat straight out from her shoulder, about eight feet above the floor. In one graceful movement, Esskay leaped up and snatched the bone from Kitty's hand.

"Beautiful visual," Tess muttered to herself. "That's going to be on every channel tonight."

So it was. But the stations cut away from the next shot: Esskay, crouched over her treat, looking up to see four television cameras approaching her. The overwhelmed dog made a strange yodeling noise deep in her throat, lost control just as Tess had thought she might and, profoundly humiliated, bolted from the room at top speed.

"That which you cannot hide, proclaim," Kitty expounded to Tess and Crow that night, after a dinner designed to chase away the winter blues while it packed on pounds: corn chowder with sherry, a chicken-and-rice casserole, Crow's home-made rolls, and gingerbread with a heated caramel sauce *and* fresh-whipped cream. Stuffed and contented, they sat in Kitty's kitchen, listening to the wind whipping around the building as if looking for someone it had a long-standing grudge against. Kitty and Tess sipped coffee with healthy slugs of Kahlua, while Crow settled for straight-up caffeine. He still had to take Esskay out for her first jaunt with the Patterson Park patrol.

"Okay, so we've proclaimed Esskay," Tess said. "But we've also taken out an advertisement for our friends in the shit-and-salmon car. *Hey guys! Come and get her. The dog you're looking for is at the corner of Bond and Shakespeare Street.*"

"They would have found you eventually, if they haven't already," Kitty said. "Now that Esskay is famous, those men who have been dogging you—if you'll pardon the expression—will have to be much more careful. They won't go after two police officers jogging with a dog. And they're not going to wade into that pack of dogs who roam Patterson Park with their civic-minded owners."

"What about the stuff you made up, like her racing record?" Crow asked. "What if the reporters check?"

"Even if they do think to call a dog track in Juarez, I think there's going to be a slight language problem."

Crow laughed, but Tess sighed. "Still, I wish you hadn't brought the cops into it. Remember, we don't know how Spike came to have this dog, or what he has to do with her altered tattoo. The less the cops know, the better."

"I thought of that, too," Kitty said, her voice a smug purr. "The 'officers' are actually bartender friends of Steve's. The reporters think they're police officers because I told them they were. Perception is more important than reality."

"My, you're just full of aphorisms tonight. When do we get to hear the one about the penny saved? Or how about the early bird, Aunt Kitty? Will you tell us that one, pretty please?"

Kitty bounced a leftover roll off Tess's head, which Esskay caught neatly on the rebound and devoured. "I was thinking more of gift horses and the bodily cavities you're not supposed to inspect, a train of thought that leads me directly to your uncanny impersonation of another part of the horse's anatomy."

"Ladies, ladies." Crow still didn't know what to make of the way Tess and Kitty bickered with one another, even if it was all in good fun. His parents, onetime Bostonians who had fled the winters and settled in Charlottesville, Virginia, were almost painfully civilized in their affection for one another. Esskay, however, liked the mock yelling and rushed to the fray, eager to see if more food bits might fly.

Crow snapped a leash to the excited dog's collar. "I hate to leave this warm kitchen, but we might as well get this over with, girl. Maybe you'll make friends with the other pooches."

"Don't talk to strangers," Tess advised, half-serious.

"We won't. And we won't take any dog biscuits from strangers, either."

Almost an hour later, Tess was stretching on the bedroom floor when she heard Crow and Esskay clattering up the stairs. Her muscles were tight—she hadn't been cooling down after her workouts and the lapse was catching up to her, a sure sign of age. Only twenty-nine, and yet twenty-nine was old in some ways. By twenty-nine, for example, it was too late to improve one's bone density; all you could do was protect what you had with high calcium food, exercise, and daily doses of Tums. By twenty-nine, baby-oil sunbaths from high school had already damaged your skin irreparably. And by twenty-nine, it was too late to have a baby to reduce one's risk of breast cancer. Tess imagined she could feel the engine of her body slowing down, burning fewer calories every day. Eventually, she would have to work out more or eat less. The first option seemed impossible, the second highly undesirable. She calculated quickly: running one extra mile a day burned an additional 100 calories, which could offset a weight gain of ten pounds over a single year. One mile, not even ten minutes. She could probably squeeze it in.

Esskay, fur cold, nose colder, pounced on Tess, ending her aerobic reverie. Tess wrapped herself into a tight ball and the dog took her braid in her mouth as if it were a toy, shaking it with surprising vigor.

"Boy, she's revved up," Tess said, rescuing her hair as

Crow flopped on the bed with a groan. "She must have had a good time."

"Too good a time. I never noticed how aggressive she is with other dogs. She tried to pick a fight with a Rottweiler, for God's sake. He snapped at her and she backed down, but I still had to choke up on her leash."

"Did you see any prostitutes working the park?"

"A few brave ones, but they weren't doing any business. I don't think the Pooch Patrol can claim credit, though. You take anything out of your pants tonight and it's going to snap off."

Crow, who didn't own a real winter coat, had dressed in several ratty layers—a leather jacket and wool muffler over three sweaters and a thermal undershirt. Now, as he stripped down to the undershirt, he reached inside the leather jacket and pulled out a long manila envelope from its breast pocket. "I almost forgot. This was on your car when we got back. I thought it was a ticket at first."

"Probably some new advertising gimmick dreamed up by one of the megabars," Tess said, opening it. Photocopies spilled out, along with two pieces of cream-colored stationery, a stark black name emblazoned across the top.

Rosita Ruiz.

"What is it?" Crow asked

"Rosita's résumé." Tess was bewildered. "And her cover letter, as well as copies of stories she wrote for the San Antonio newspaper, and her evaluation at the *Blight*. It's her whole personnel file, a highly confidential thing. Crow, did you see who left this on my car, by any chance?"

He shook his head. "All I saw was the envelope beneath your windshield wiper."

Tess turned the envelope inside out and shuffled all the papers. "No note. Well, it's obviously not Colleen, and Sterling would just hand it to me. It must be one of her underlings, Hailey or Whitman. But what's the point? I don't see any smoking gun here."

"Editors as anonymous sources? This job is getting stranger and stranger, Tess."

Tess, still thinking about those extra calories that her thirties would demand, decided she better go back to two-a-days at the gym until it was warm enough to row. She stopped by Durban's the next morning, resigned to a long session with the weight machines.

Weights require unrushed discipline, perfect form, concentration—not Tess's strengths, especially when she worked on her lower body, whose creaky joints protested that running, cycling, and rowing should be quite enough, thank you. Sweating lightly in the overheated room, she lay on her stomach on the Keiser hamstring machine and jerked her heels toward her butt, feet hooked beneath padded bars. Right side, then left side. Up on a two count, release on a four. What could be more boring? At least mornings were quiet at Durban's, a bored attendant the only other person in the room.

She zipped through a second set, then pumped the button for more resistance. As usual, she felt invincible on the first three reps, increasingly mortal on the next five, painfully decrepit by the last two. Rushing the last rep just a little, she sensed more than saw a movement in the room, someone lumbering toward her. Before she could push her upper body away from the bench, a man's large bulk flattened her into the vinyl. She wrenched her face to the side, assuming she would see one of the men from the shit-and-salmon car.

"So how's the jewelry business?" asked Paul Tucci.

"A little slow right now." Tess tried to raise her head, but Tucci pressed his palm against her ear, pinning her head until she heard the ocean. He was such a dead weight across her back she couldn't even ease her feet from under the pads without wrenching a knee. Weight-training equipment that doubled as a torture device—now *that* was cross-training. Where was Durban's attendant?

Tucci didn't move his hand, but he shifted his bulk until

he rested more comfortably on Tess's fleshier parts.

"It took me awhile to remember exactly where I had seen you," he said. "Once I did, I knew how to find you. What were you doing, sneaking into see Lea with that stupid bracelet story? And you went to see Linda, too. What lie did you tell her?"

"Someone I know was worried about Lea." A truth, more or less. "A lot of people are worried about her. You'd have to have a heart of stone not to be worried about a widow with three kids under the age of five. Linda was an . . . afterthought. She lost someone, too."

"Look, if you're from one of Wink's creditors, you're gonna have to get in line. And if you work for some shyster lawyer, you can forget about it."

"Lawyer?" she asked, in what she hoped was an innocent voice, but there was something about a palm pressing against one's ear that made every utterance come out whiny and defensive.

"Every personal injury shark in town has sent someone to Lea's door, although the rest weren't as clever as you. They think there's gotta be some deep pocket to sue. A psychiatrist who didn't realize Wink was suicidal? Wink didn't have a psychiatrist. Malfunctioning garage door opener? It's not like he tried to open it at the last minute and it failed. He didn't want it to open. Booze and drugs? Hey, it says right on the label not to mix them. And not to operate heavy machinery, which takes us back to the car. What are you going to do, sue Ford Motor Company because the '67 Mustang didn't have an automatic shut-off to stop someone intent on killing himself?"

"How do you know he had drugs in his system?" Tess asked. Tucci had loosened his grip slightly, but she could still feel the blood pounding in her ear. "The tox screens aren't back yet and there hasn't been anything in the papers about the cops finding drugs at the scene. All they tested for that night was alcohol."

Tucci grabbed her braid with two hands, pulling her head back the way Esskay had the night before, only not as playfully. "I know Wink. He wouldn't have been able to go through with it unless he was knocked out. He would have lost his nerve, bailed at the last minute. He was kind of a wuss, when you get down to it. The cops told Lea he broke open a new bottle of Jack Daniels that night, had two, three glasses at the most. His blood alcohol wasn't even .10, he was legal to drive. That *was* in the paper. So I figure he took some over-the-counter shit to speed things up. Makes sense, doesn't it?"

"Sure." She was inclined to agree with anything Tucci said, as long as he had a hold on her. But why was it so important to him that she agree? Why did it sound as if he were rehearsing a story he might want to tell again?

"Good. Now-why-don't-you-tell-me-what-you-were-doing-hanging-around-Lea-and-Linda?"

With each word, he bounced for emphasis. Tess was thankful she had no breakfast to throw up.

"You've really packed on the pounds since your lacrosse days," she said. "How much weight have you gained? Twenty pounds? Thirty? And all in the butt and the gut, from what it feels like."

Tucci stood up, sucking in his belly as he smoothed down his shirt front and confronted his profile in the mirrored wall. "Nothing a few sit-ups wouldn't cure," he said, which gave Tess the opportunity she needed to free her legs, roll over, and take aim. Was it the right knee the doctors had just replaced? It was. Tucci screamed and fell to the floor, writhing in pain.

"You fucking *cunt*," he gasped out. "I'm probably going to be back on a cane because of you."

Tess didn't wait to hear the rest of Tucci's self-diagnosis. She ran down the stairs and into the street, where she found Durban's attendant smoking a cigarette. At least he had the decency to look furtive and embarrassed when he saw her.

"He said he just wanted to talk to you, private-like," the attendant said sheepishly, knowing this was no excuse, not at Durban's, where Spike's niece was to be shielded against all male interest. "He gave me twenty bucks to take a long smoke break. I didn't see the harm in it."

"Well, maybe he'll slip you another twenty to call a doctor. He blew out his knee, he's in a lot of pain."

"How'd he do that?"

"Um, I forgot to spot him on the hamstring machine."

"You don't spot on hamstrings," the attendant pointed out.

"Maybe that was the problem."

It took him a second. "Jesus, Tess, what do you think you're doing? Your Uncle Spike hung out with some rough people, but even *he* had the good sense not to fuck with the Tuccis. Do you have any idea what you're doing?"

"Not really."

Chapter 20

Rosita Ruiz.

The name glared at Tess from the top of buff-colored paper—heavy-weight, expensive stuff. It was in 24-point type, maybe 36, as black and intense as Rosita's eyes. Tess stared back, still trying to figure out what her mystery guest wanted her to find in a collection of clips, mostly sports stories, and this skimpy work history. Rosita's professional life to date could be summed up by grade school in Roxbury, college at Boston University (history major, cum laude), one summer internship at a small Massachusetts paper, another internship at the *San Antonio Eagle*, and one award, a second-place in the Society of South Texas Journalists. How had this slender résumé landed Rosita a job at one of the country's top twenty newspapers? Tess had had five years when the *Star* had folded, and she hadn't made the first cut at the *Blight*.

Well, Ruiz, Tess thought ungenerously. And a female covering sports, to boot. A two-fer in the wonderful world of newspaper affirmative action hires. Not that equally unqualified white guys didn't get jobs all the time. For every underqualified minority or woman, there were at least three white men who were equally inept: that was the true legacy of affirmative action, lowering the standards for everyone. Besides, Rosita's academic credentials were impeccable—assuming they were true.

The registrar at Boston University confirmed Rosita's graduation date and major—once Tess claimed to be a *Blight* employee fact-checking a résumé. Well, she was, wasn't she?

"One small thing," the woman in the registrar's office said. "She actually was *magna* cum laude. We don't usually see students make that kind of mistake, but possibly 'magna' was inadvertently dropped from her résumé."

"Possibly," echoed Tess, unconvinced. It didn't seem in character for Rosita to underreport her accomplishments.

She spread the contents of the envelope across her desk, so she could see everything at once. Perhaps the pieces formed a whole. Was there anything of value here, was there a pattern to what she had been given? No, it appeared someone had grabbed whatever was available, shoved it in this envelope, and stuck it under the windshield wiper on her car. It was up to her to figure out where to go from here. Was she being challenged by someone who, like Whitney and Tyner, was trying to push her forward? That would suggest Jack Sterling. Or was the envelope from someone lazy and desperate, who hoped Tess could find something where they could not? Any of the other editors might fit that description.

She read Rosita's clips for the second time. One mystery was solved: here was the breathless hyperbole, the creaky clichés that had invaded Feeney's work once the two were paired. Funny, she had been paired in San Antonio, too, and had included one of those clippings. By Rosita Ruiz and Alann J. Shepard. It was the only Page One clipping in the batch, one of those blow-by-blow Sunday stories that told you more than you ever wanted to know about a recent controversy, but didn't really tell you anything new. A pro baseball player who had gone straight from the San Antonio barrio to the Texas Rangers had propositioned an undercover policewoman posing as a prostitute on one of his trips home. "How about a little half-and-half?" he had asked her. If only he had stopped there, he could have argued persuasively he really was looking for cream in his coffee.

Alas, the police wire tap had preserved his next statement as well. "I'll pay you forty bucks." Not even convenience stores charged that much for half-and-half.

Still, it was a petty offense, the kind of rap a popular athlete or actor routinely survived after the ritual round of media mea culpas. But the officer was white and the baseball player Latino, and that had changed the dynamic. The department had been accused of a racist conspiracy against the ball player, of trying to entrap him specifically in order to tear him down. Yet the baseball player's own mother seemed to believe the cops' version of events. "Men!" she had told the reporters in Spanish. "What do you expect? They can't keep it in their pants. He plays better when he's happy, that's a fact."

An interview in Spanish? Rosita had probably conducted it. On a hunch, Tess dialed the *San Antonio Eagle* again, and was transferred only twice before she reached Rosita's erstwhile partner.

"A. J. here."

"As in Alann Shepard?"

"No astronaut jokes, okay? I've heard them all in my time."

"I'm Tess Monaghan at the Baltimore *Beacon-Light* and I'm doing a background check on Rosita Ruiz."

If his face matched his voice, it must have the world's largest smirk on it. "What has she stepped into now?"

The Lone Star version of Feeney. Tess found herself warming to him, then remembered she was on less than wonderful terms with the real thing.

"Nothing that I know of. This is purely routine. I'm curious about your experience working with her."

"A 'purely routine' background check six months after she arrives at the paper and less than two weeks after she has her first big story? I'll buy that. If history repeats itself, she'll use that story to jump to yet another paper, and leave the *Beacon-Light* to clean up behind her. Let's hope the *Boston Globe* or the *Washington Post* is smart enough to ask these questions before she signs on the dotted line."

"I talked to Ed Saldivar, but he wouldn't do anything other than confirm her dates of employment."

"Boy, you guys up there really are resourceful. You get a no comment and you stop digging. To think I was envious when Rosita moved on."

"I'm talking to you now," Tess said pointedly. "Obviously I haven't stopped digging. And you obviously have something you're longing to tell me, so why not get to it?"

There was a long pause. When he spoke again, the smarmy tone was gone and his voice was quieter, sadder.

"There's a lot I want to tell you. I want to tell you about invasion-of-privacy lawsuits, which can be as troublesome as libel suits any day. I want to tell you about big-eyed little girls who go up to barely literate Mexican women and say, 'Oh, I know you're not talking to reporters, but may I come in for a glass of iced tea? It's such a hot day.' I want to tell you the way gossip works in the newspaper world— no one in Texas will touch Rosita, but some Eastern newspapers don't have any contacts here, so they don't know the whole story. I want to tell you that when a newspaper pays someone off for the crimes that appear under a double byline, the blameless partner never gets exonerated. I want to tell you all these things, but the out-of-court settlement came with a gag order, and I could lose my job for what I've already *not* said."

"Can't you tell me anything more? A few details, or some names?"

"Look, re-report the stories she's done for you. Talk to the people she interviewed, look at any document she used, trace her steps. My hunch is you'll find so much up in Baltimore, you won't need to worry about what happened here." A slight pause. "It's old news, anyway."

Tess heard a voice screaming at him in the background. "Hey, Earth to A. J. You got another call, can you take it, or should I have him orbit until you re-enter?"

"I'm getting off," A. J. said wearily.

"May I call you back?" Tess asked.

"Call me back? Lady, I've never heard of you."

*   *   *

Re-report Rosita's story. Without intending to, Tess had been doing that all along. She had spoken to the two Mrs. Winks, quizzed Feeney on what Rosita had contributed to the original story. She had studied the case files on the Wynkowski divorce, looked for police records that would confirm the domestic violence. In her bragging, Rosita had even provided a handy checklist of everything she had done, and Feeney had backed her up. *Feeney got the financial stuff, but I got the stuff about his marriage and his gambling problem. If you listen to what people are talking about around town, it's my part of the story.*

Tess drew a line down the center of a legal pad and created two categories—matrimony and betting. Lea had sworn Wink wasn't a gambler, but wives didn't know everything. She then called up the archived electronic copy of that notorious first story, preparing to jot down the names of Rosita's sources and call them back.

No wonder Jack and Lionel had been troubled: there wasn't a single person speaking for attribution in the entire piece, unless the information was so innocuous as to be meaningless. ('' 'Everybody loves Wink,' said longtime friend Paul ''Tooch'' Tucci. 'Even when they lose to him, they love him.' '') At least Feeney had a trail of court papers to buttress his claim Wink wasn't liquid; Rosita had *a friend close to Wink, or someone close to the couple.* It would be impossible to double-check any of this. Which was probably the point. Rosita had learned at least one thing since leaving San Antonio: how to cover her tracks.

She read the story again, hoping for a lead to follow, anything. Here was the detail about Wink and Linda's bungalow in Violetville, the neighborhood that Jack Sterling had found such an incongruous place for a tough guy. ''The wood-frame bungalow on MacTavish looked like the archetypal honeymooners' cottage from the outside, with its new plantings and fresh paint. But a source close to the couple said the honeymoon was over from almost the day the two crossed the threshold, as Wynkowski repeatedly battered his new bride.''

The *Blight* had thoughtfully provided Tess with a city crisscross. Finally, a break. Half the residents on Mac-Tavish, barely two blocks in length, had lived there when Wink and Linda were keeping house, according to the listings. The neighbors probably knew as much about the couple's marriage as anyone, Tess figured. Wood-frame bungalows, with their thin walls, were notoriously bad at keeping secrets.

Chapter 21

〜〜〜〜

Had violets ever bloomed in Violetville? It was hard to imagine now. The neighborhood was in the city's industrial southwest corner, barely within the city limits, an important distinction, for Baltimore is the rare municipality that lies within no county. It stood alone when it was rich, and now it stood alone in its poverty, a civic pariah. Violetville was one of those strange islands one found along the edges.

Still, it was holding on to middle-class status by the skin of its teeth. Streets with names like MacTavish, Sharon-Leigh, Benson, Clarenell, Haverhill—names with no connection Tess could discern—looked like John Waters, circa *Pink Flamingos*. Modest houses, green corrugated awnings, metal porch chairs, kitschy yard art that didn't know it was kitschy. Even the lighting was the same as Waters' early work—washed out, harsh, wintry. The old Wynkowski house—the "honeymooners' cottage"—was the seediest on MacTavish, as if Wink and Linda had left all their bad karma behind when they'd moved on.

Tess canvassed the block, working a loop that took her north, then across the street and south along the brick row-houses, then north again, until she had arrived at the Wynkowskis' neighbor. Along her circular path, a few residents had remembered the telltale signs of a tempestuous marriage: bursts of noise, especially in the summer, when windows were open and voices carried. But nothing more.

Everyone was happy to talk to her—Tess had the sense she was the most exciting thing to happen on MacTavish in quite some time—but their memories were blurred, or vague, and they had nothing but praise for Rosita. *"Such a polite young woman."* By the time Tess reached the last house, she was bored and anxious to move on. She almost hoped no one would answer.

A wizened figure in a faded blue bathrobe answered the door while her knock still echoed. Tess stared down at a pink scalp and wispy white hair, which contrasted nicely with the baby blue robe and matching slippers. From this perspective, it was impossible to tell if the person staring at her sternum was male or female. The hair, while thin, was longish and untidy. A man overdue for a haircut? Or a woman who no longer took pains with her appearance?

"What can I do you?" Even the voice did not give away the gender. It was a smoker's rasp, neither high nor low.

"I'm a fact-checker at the *Beacon-Light*." This was one of several stories Tess had told as she had gone door to door, varying it in order to keep herself interested. "It's part of our new 'Aim for Accuracy Always' program. The Triple A. We want the community to know we're committed to getting things right."

The gnome squinted up at Tess's face. The gender was still a toss-up. The hair had a mannish style about it, but there were a few chin hairs, which seemed more appropriate to an elderly woman with bad eyesight.

"It's a bit backwards, innit, checking the facts *after* you print 'em?"

"Oh, we check beforehand, too. This is the double-check, I guess you could say, in case something erroneous slipped through despite our best efforts. Mi-mi—I'm sorry, I didn't catch your name."

"Athol. Bertie Athol." Great. Even the name was asexual.

Bearded Bertie led Tess into a dark living room, which did not appear to have been dusted since the Iran hostage crisis. *A man,* Tess thought. *Only a man could be such a careless housekeeper.*

Or a near-sighted woman, she amended, as Bertie bumped into the water-stained oak table next to his/her chair, a stuffed chair whose faded gold damask bore the faint outline of Bertie's lumpy body, like a watermark.

"So what do you want to ask me about? I tell you, I hate them new stock tables. Print's too small, I can't follow my mutuals. Box scores, too. Everything's too small. You skimpin' on paper down there?"

"Actually, I'm not here to talk about the stocks or the scores, although I will make a note of your concerns. We're interested today in your impression of the stories about Wink Wynkowski."

"The Wynkowski boy? Why, he used to live right next door. Has he been up to something again?"

"Um, he's dead."

"You don't say." Bertie began to laugh, a dry cackle. "I'm just having fun with you. Of course I knowed what happen to Wink. I talked to that little girl when she was here. We spent quite a bit of time together."

"Did she use anything you told her?"

"Why, I'm the source close to the family! You know, where it says—" and Bertie paused, taking the time to gather up the right words from memory. "Where it says, 'But a source close to the couple said the honeymoon was over from almost the day the two crossed the threshold, as Wynkowski repeatedly battered his new bride.' Very elly-gant, the way she put it. I'da never thought to say it so good."

Tess stared at the old man/woman skeptically. "You're the source? Were you really close to Wink and Linda?"

Bertie jerked his/her chin in the direction of the Wyn-kowski's onetime home. "I don't know how you could be closer. Not even ten feet from my kitchen winder to their bedroom winder. In the summers, when I was warshing the dishes in the zinc, I could hear 'em going at it many a night."

Warshing the dishes in the zinc. Bertie could give lessons on Bawlamerese. Whatever the gender, the speech had all the touchstones. Probably listened to the Erioles, thought a far was something you toasted marshmallows over, and went downy eauchin in August, to a rented condo on the boardwalk.

"Is that what you told Rosita Ruiz?"

"Yeah, the girl from the paper, Rosie. I got her card around here somewhere still." Bertie began patting the bathrobe's pockets, as if the card might materialize, but only a few used tissues turned up.

"Did you know for a fact that there was violence involved, Bertie? A lot of people get loud."

"Yeah, but they don't start throwing furniture at one another. And they don't call amb'lances."

This was new. "An ambulance?"

"Uh-huh. At night. It's easy to see an amb'lance at night. And, of course, Mr. Athol was alive then, and I remember we talked about it, how sad it was for a young couple to be so unhappy all the time."

At least she had solved the mystery of Bertie's gender. "Yes. Yes it is. Can you remember anything else about those fights? When the amb'lance came—" Jesus, Bertie's inflections were catching. "When the *ambulance* came, did they have to take Mrs. Wynkowski out on a stretcher, or did she walk out on her own? Could you tell how badly she was hurt? Was it the kind of injury that might have happened accidentally?"

Bertie closed her eyes and leaned back as if reliving a particularly vivid dream. It was very dramatic, but not particularly effective.

"I don't recall," she said, after several seconds. "All I remember is the lights. It's not like I stood there all night, peeking through the curtains."

I bet you stayed until the show was over, though. "Thank you, Mrs. Athol. We're glad to know we got your part of the story right. You were very helpful."

"So how much money do I get?"

Tess was confused. "Newspapers don't pay for information, Mrs. Athol. It's unethical."

"The other girl did. You see, at first I just remembered it being the one time the amb'lance came. She asked me if I could be wrong, if maybe it came three times instead of the oncet, or at least twice, if there was a pattern. That was the word she used, pattern. She gave me fifty dollars, and I remembered it was more like three times."

Tess felt a strange flip in her stomach, at once hopeful and unhappy. A. J. Shepard had told her this would be easy, but she couldn't believe Rosita would be this stupid. "Are you sure?"

"Course I'm sure. You think someone hands me fifty dollars, I'm gonna forget? Now, today, today is more of a twenny-dollar interview, doncha think?"

"You want money?"

"Only twenny dollars," Bertie wheedled.

"I'm not authorized to do that."

"How about a discount on my subscription?"

"No, Bertie. Not even the reporters get a discount."

Bertie pushed her lower lip out in a pout, a mannerism that was probably downright adorable as recently as thirty years ago. Now, with jowls hanging loosely and her neck as wrinkled as the corrugated awnings along MacTavish Avenue, she looked more like a bulldog.

"Why do the reporters need a discount? They already know what's in the paper."

An only child, Tess had had relatively little experience with the lurid charms of tattling. Should she tell Sterling what she knew about the pay-off to Bertie Athol? Should she keep going, see if there was more damning information to be uncovered about Rosita's reporting methods? At least the leopard had changed her spots. Now she paid people up front and didn't use their names.

Sterling would want to know, she was sure of it. Checkbook journalism was so low that some of the tabloid television shows had forsaken it. But Tess was uncomfortably aware she longed to speak to Sterling for other, less self-righteous reasons. She wanted his approval, wanted him to smile at her and say, "Great work!" A crush. She was in the throes of a damn schoolgirl crush.

Well, at least Violetville was convenient to St. Agnes. She might as well check in on Spike, give her mind and hormones a chance to cool.

She was glad to see one of Durban's boxers waiting unobtrusively in the hall. At least something was going as planned. When Tess walked in, Tommy was already there, a chair pulled up by Spike's bed. It was true, only family was allowed to see Spike, but the hospital, apparently under the misapprehension that Tommy was Spike's life partner, as opposed to his business partner, had thoughtfully included him in this group. He held a box of chocolates on his lap, a strange get-well gift for a man in a coma. Tommy had probably selected it because he knew he would be free to plunder his own offering. He held the box out grudgingly to Tess, but he had picked out all the nutty ones, so she passed.

"Hi, Uncle Spike." He was so still. What had she expected—someone sleeping like a man in a cartoon, or like one of the Three Stooges, his chest rising and falling with an exaggerated movement, a faint whistling noise escaping around the various tubes. Tess thought she saw his eyelids flicker, his mouth twitch. Wishful thinking.

"What's the doctor say?"

"Nothin' to me," Tommy said sullenly, his bad mood erasing the usual question marks. It would be a while before he forgave Tess their last meeting. Had it really been just yesterday morning?

"My folks been here?"

He snorted, then trilled. *"It's not that we don't love him as much as you do, Tommy. It's just that we have jobs."*

Tess laughed. His imitation of Judith was uncanny.

"I miss him," he added in his own voice.

"We all do."

"No, you don't, not the way I do," he said, his voice

so fierce and loud that Durban's bodyguard poked his head in to make sure everything was all right.

Tommy dropped the volume, but his body quivered with emotion. "If he died, you'd be sad, but you wouldn't miss him every day, every minute, like I do. You'd miss him when you wanted to stop off at The Point with your friends, giggling at how ugly it is. Or you'd miss him at fambly gatherings. But you wouldn't miss him every day, any more than you miss the City Fair."

"Tommy, there hasn't been a City Fair for years."

"Exactly. And when was the last time you thought about it?" He stood, putting the candy box on his chair, and stalked from the room.

Tess couldn't decide if Tommy was right, or merely annoying. Or annoying *because* he was right. She walked to the window, with its view of the parking lot and the driveway in front of the emergency room. Her parents had roared up that drive so many times in her youth, Tess bleeding in the backseat from yet another accident. A dropped jar of fireflies, one shard of glass ricocheting up and carving out a sliver of Tess's calf. A broken ankle when she had jumped out of her bedroom window, playing Goldilocks. A long, thin cut, hidden now in the curve of her eyebrow, where a neighbor boy's lacrosse stick had knighted her. And then there was the bloodless night in high school when Ipecac had done its job too well. She had vomited and vomited until she was dangerously dehydrated, her body still intent on emptying itself long after it had purged the sixteen-inch pizza and half-gallon of mint chocolate chip. Her parents, frightened out of their senses, bought the story that she had taken the Ipecac by mistake, thinking it was a cold remedy. Back then, they didn't know she binged, so how could they suspect she purged?

She had never needed an ambulance, though, just a washcloth to press against the mess of the day as her father did his best Mario Andretti down Wilkens Avenue. The ambulances carried people with graver injuries, people who needed oxygen or CPR. Tess had never lost consciousness, not after vomiting all night, not even when she had fallen on a broken bottle in some underbrush and emerged with a most unexpected view of the inside of her knee, straight to the bone, like some illustration in a textbook.

She watched a young man help a woman out of a battered old Dodge. He could have been the same man she had met at the courthouse, the one who was so pathetically proud of his legitimate marriage and his almost legitimate child. This woman held her arm awkwardly in front of her, as if it were an interesting piece of driftwood she had found on the beach. The man—really more of a boy-man—circled her shoulders with his arms as if she were made of porcelain. *So why did you break her*, Tess wanted to ask, for she had no doubt he was the one who had brought her here in every sense of the word. Of course, she had domestic violence on her mind just now.

Only two people know the truth of a marriage, Kitty's voice chided her again. No one really knew what had happened in Violetville. Wink was dead and Linda wasn't talking. But Bertie had seen the ambulance, even if she had seen it only once. It was wrong of Rosita to pay for that information, and the money had probably encouraged Bertie to exaggerate, but Tess didn't doubt it was basically true. Hit your wife once, you're a wife beater. And almost no man ever hit just once. If he got help, perhaps, saw a therapist—but it was impossible to imagine Wink seeking help to control his violent temper, the same temper that had made him beat the old shopkeeper so badly. Montrose had only taught him how to hide his temper, how to pick better victims. Wink was too busy building an empire—from A to Z, as Feeney had said—to worry about his karma. Rosita might have gotten the facts wrong, but she had nailed down the truth.

No, if Tess was going to retrace Rosita's reporting, she probably should concentrate on the gambling angle. Alas, her best source for that line of inquiry was right here, but he wasn't going to be able to help her anytime soon. If he ever did regain consciousness, she had more pressing questions. *Why would someone try to kill you for a greyhound, even one with altered tattoos?* She studied his dear, pointy head, wishing she could climb inside and wander through his memory. As that was impossible, she left.

An ambulance almost wiped her out as she crossed the driveway. That would make an interesting lawsuit. Her own memory came to life, like a pinball machine with all the lights flashing. It wasn't Wink's empire that ran the gamut from A to Z. It was the *lawsuits*, the bills he never paid, from ambulances to zippers. "Amb'lances," as Bertie would say. Word of the day. Call it whatever you like, but if you called an ambulance and didn't pay for its services, there would be paperwork, which might detail what had happened to whom. And if someone had that paperwork, they could hold it over someone's head, unsavory proof of what a less-than-nice guy he was. Why hadn't Feeney thought of that? Why hadn't Rosita, flinging fifties along the length of MacTavish Avenue, taken time to track down proof far stronger than some geezerette's faulty memory?

Tess glanced at her watch and tried to remember the shopping itinerary chanted by the doorman at Linda Stolley Wynkowski's apartment building. If memory served, Thursday was Jones & Jones day. Or was it Ruth Shaw?

Chapter 22

Linda Wynkowski stood in front of a full-length mirror, arrayed in a royal blue dress with an organza skirt, its hem so haphazard and ragged it couldn't cost less than $500. Seen from a distance, through the windows of Jones & Jones, she was lovely, the blue dress setting off her white body and blue eyes, while playing down the fact the former was too soft, the latter too hard. Tess would have liked to remain at a distance, but this was not an option.

"You again," Linda sighed.

"I just came from MacTavish Avenue."

"Lovely, isn't it?"

Tess wasn't sure if she meant MacTavish or the dress. "It's not so bad," she said, feeling the answer was appropriate to both.

"No, unless you expected more. Unless you'd been led to expect more. Wink talked so big, I thought we were going to be living in a nice new house out in Owings Mills. You know, like the one he and his second wife have. But that kind of money didn't come in until after we had separated. We fought about money all the time back then. If I spent fifteen dollars on a dress at Hoschild's, he'd go crazy."

"Is that how the arguments began? Over money?"

Linda rose on her tiptoes and did a full turn in her gown, looking at her own reflection. "I told you, Wink and I had an agreement not to talk about our marriage. Whatever happened between us is private.''

"Wink dead. Unless you promised to take his secrets to *your* grave, you don't owe him anything.''

"Do you have any earrings to go with this, Tara?'' Linda called over her shoulder to the salesgirl, a pretty young coed who had cultivated a chic European look not many Baltimoreans could pull off. Tara rushed forward with crystal balls strung on sterling silver strings of varying lengths, chunky flies caught in a spider's fine web.

"Those aren't right at all,'' Linda said, throwing them back at the girl. "This dress needs something bigger—you know, more dramatic.'' Tara scurried away.

"I talked to your neighbor on MacTavish,'' Tess said. "Bertie Athol.''

"Bertie the busybody.''

Tess lowered her voice, aware Tara was probably eavesdropping keenly from her post behind the display case, where she and an older saleswoman had fallen conspicuously silent. "Bertie told me she heard the fights, and that she saw an ambulance in the night. She's the only one who really knows, isn't she, even if she doesn't know anything? Bertie, the doctors. And you.''

Linda Wynkowski gathered her blond hair in her hands and piled it on top of her head. It did look better up, but what was the point of fiddling with hairstyles and accessories for a dress she would never wear, for a dress that would never go anywhere but her walk-in closet? She was ruined, and $20,000 a month suddenly didn't seem a lot to pay for turning someone into a doll, scared to leave her dollhouse village.

"You know, he always cried.'' Her tone was matter-of-fact, as if describing her former husband's preference for string beans. "After, I mean. He cried and said he still loved me. When we separated, he was the one who never wanted to make it official, because he loved me so much he didn't want to get a divorce. At least, he loved me until he met her, and then he didn't care about me anymore.''

"But you had something on him, something concrete," Tess prompted. "Ambulance bills he didn't pay, or insurance papers detailing exactly what had happened. You kept them, and when he decided he wanted to remarry, you used them to get the support order increased."

"Yes. Yes I did." Linda almost seemed to be in a trance before the mirror, eyes locked on her own reflection.

"May I see them? Could I see what you used to"—she didn't want to use the term blackmail—"to convince Wink?"

"So Bertie knew all along, huh? She tell anybody else?"

"With Wink dead, I don't think anyone will be coming around to ask her."

Linda gathered up the long, shaggy skirt of her ballgown and swept out of Jones & Jones in her stocking feet. Tara the salesgirl, wiser than Marianna at Octavia, simply watched her leave, allowing a tiny whistle of a sigh to escape.

"If she doesn't come back in twenty minutes," the older saleswoman said, "we'll wrap up what she left and send it to the apartment, along with a bill for the dress. It won't be the first time."

Tess followed Linda out of the store, assuming she was headed for her apartment, just straight ahead, not even 100 yards away. Instead, she turned right and led Tess to the branch bank in the shopping center.

"I keep all my important papers in a safe deposit box at the bank here in Cross Keys." Linda was strangely manic, as if she had wanted to tell someone this story long ago but had never dared—first because she was scared, then because she was paid. "That's the wonderful thing about Cross Keys, everything is right here. It's so convenient."

Linda pushed through the bank's double set of glass doors. No one raised an eyebrow at her ballgown and stocking feet; the bank employees must know her as well as the salesgirls. Soon, she was unlocking her safe deposit box on the counter just beyond the security gate, Tess at her side.

"You know, for a long time, it didn't even occur to me

I had anything to tell,'' she said, as Tess's hands closed greedily on the photocopies, folded into careful fourths so long ago that the creases had turned gray. ''Then, when that stupid story came out, I hated everyone thinking—but $20,000 a month. Well, it makes up for a lot.''

Tess skimmed the hospital forms, with their coded comments on the various injuries treated. A broken collarbone. Lacerations. A concussion. A broken nose. Oh, Jesus, this must have been the night the ambulance was called. First-degree burns from hot grease, and the spleen so badly injured the doctors had almost removed it. And yet the hospital didn't even have the decency to grant Linda her own name on the forms. They just listed her as Gerard S. Wynkowski. His property. His chattel. His to do with as he pleased. *Gerard S. Wynkowski.* Not even a ''Mrs.'' You would think Wink had been the patient.

''I can't believe they kept getting the name wrong, as many times as you went in there.''

''Hell, no one can spell Wynkowski. Took me years.'' Linda looked over Tess's shoulder. ''No, no, that's right. Gerard S. Wynkowski. The S is for Stanislaus. He hated it, how the hospital would call him Gerard instead of Wink, and use his middle name. He said that was the worst part of going, hearing them call out his full name in the emergency room.''

''Call out his name? Why would they call out *his* name?''

''When the doctor was ready to see him. Haven't you ever been in an emergency room?''

''But they call out the patient's name—'' And finally Tess understood.

''But you said you knew,'' whined Linda Stolley Wynkowski, pushing Tess against the bank of metal boxes. It was a child's petulant, impetuous shove, the opening salvo in a full-fledged tantrum. But unlike a child's shove, it was really hard: Tess's shoulders smacked the wall with enough force to leave a bruise, and she remembered the frightened salesgirl at Octavia, how Linda had ground her heel into her foot. "You said Bertie told. Bertie *told!*"

Tess sat in the parking lot of Eddie's on Charles Street, eating her way through a half-pound of Eddie's peanut clusters, her lunch for the day. She had been yearning for chocolate-covered nuts since Tommy had held his picked-over box of candy out to her, and she was a great believer in yielding to temptation. To her way of thinking, the one part of her body that actually knew what it wanted deserved to get it.

After leaving Linda Wynkowski, she had driven straight to the gourmet grocery store, her car homing in on the nearest source of peanut clusters as if it had a microchip designed just for that purpose. Eight ounces gave you about a dozen pieces. Between bites, she took huge draughts from a twenty-ounce Coca-Cola. But all the sweetness she forced down her throat couldn't wash away the sour taste of the story Linda Wynkowski had told when her fury had passed. It had passed pretty quickly, too, for Tess had done the one thing Wink apparently had never dared—slapped Linda square across the face and grabbed her shoulders, shaking her until she calmed down.

The first time, we had been married about six weeks and he went out drinking with his buddies, that greaseball Paul Tucci. And he didn't get home until four A.M., *and he didn't call, and I was hysterical, asking where had he been, why hadn't he called. I was scared to go out by myself, and I was scared to be there alone. He just shrugged, you know, the way men do when they're saying you're just some little bug they can't be troubled listening to, so I picked up this ashtray— we smoked then, both of us—and threw it at him. My aim wasn't very good, but it caught part of his cheek and left a good bruise.*

Put it to music and it could have been a country song. Substitute Wil E. Coyote and the Road Runner for Wink and Linda, you had a Warner Brothers cartoon. Rig up a puppet show and it was Punch 'n' Judy time.

Wink just wouldn't hit back. I don't know why. Maybe because I was a woman, maybe because he couldn't ever forget what had happened to that old guy. He wouldn't even run away, just go limp. It made me so mad, the way he wouldn't fight; I'd go wild, I'd hurt him more and more, trying to get some reaction out of him, but I never could. Finally, he said we had to live apart, he thought I might kill him the next time. He paid me support and I really couldn't complain. But then he got rich and he wanted to marry again. So I told him: you give me what I want financially, or I'll tell everybody Wink Wynkowski, Mr. Tough Guy, is a little wimp who let his wife beat up on him. He gave me what I wanted then, and I moved here. Nothing goes wrong here.

How surreal it had been, standing in the alcove of safe deposit boxes with prom queen Linda as she'd told her story. A story, not incidentally, that happened to be the complete opposite of what the *Beacon-Light* had reported. *When did you stop beating your wife, Mr. Wynkowski? Actually, she beat me. Oh sure, Mr. Wynkowski.* Even the bit about Linda's agoraphobia had been made up. The only reason she never left Cross Keys was because she was a lazy eccentric without any friends.

As a dead man, Wink couldn't be libeled, not in this state. Yet he hadn't been dead when the story had first run. Maybe the widow Wynkowski had a wrongful death suit on those grounds. Unfortunately, Tess did not work for the widow Wynkowski, she worked for the *Beacon-Light*, and all her information belonged to them, even information that had nothing to do with how a certain story got into the paper, and everything to do with how screwed up it was once it got there.

Rosita's use of checkbook journalism had been a toss-up, slimy but not illegal. Paying and getting the story ass-backwards—Tess couldn't keep this to herself. Gee, if only Bertie had known the real story, she could have made so much more. Not as much as $20,000 a month, perhaps, but definitely more than fifty bucks. But Bertie, peering through the curtains in the darkness, had seen what she'd expected to see, and Rosita had found what she'd expected to find.

She finished off the dregs of her Coke, then put her car in gear. Despite having consumed almost 100 grams of simple sugars, she felt sluggish and still had a brackish taste at the back of her throat that the Coke couldn't wash away. Strange, she had thought victory was suppose to taste sweet.

Tess found Jack Sterling in the *Blight*'s basement level canteen. The room's vending machines, the only source of sustenance in-house, gave new meaning to the phrase "strictly from hunger." Olive loaf sandwiches, tins of stew, lots of pork rinds, rock-hard Gummi Bears. And according to the lights on the soda machine, the only drink selections were practically fluorescent—orange, grape, and diet lime.

Sterling stared longingly at some of the dusty chocolate bars in the candy machine's metal coils, sighed, and resignedly settled on a bag of honey-mustard pretzels. Ever the gentleman, he offered the bag to Tess first, but she shook her head.

"I just had lunch," she said.

"I hope it was something elegant and fattening. A metabolism like yours is a terrible thing to waste."

"Well, it was from Eddie's," she said. "Look, remember when you asked me to talk to Wynkowski's wife?"

"Of course I do, Tess. I told you how much I appreciated that, what a relief it was to know she didn't think we were culpable. Perhaps I didn't stress my gratitude enough—"

"No, no, I'm not digging for a compliment. It's just—well, I didn't stop there. Some things she said made me curious, and I decided to look at Wink's divorce papers. And I noticed something odd in the file, so I went to talk to the first Mrs. Wynkowski." She decided to skip over the detail about Rosita's personnel file ending up on her windshield. That would only confuse things. "The next thing I knew, I was canvassing MacTavish Avenue in Violetville, trying to figure out who could have told Rosita about the domestic abuse, because it sure wasn't the first Mrs. Wynkowski.''

Sterling tried to keep his voice even and calm, but Tess could tell he was annoyed. "I arranged for you to be able to come and go as you pleased so you could look into your uncle's beating, not so you could meddle in a story that the *Beacon-Light* is still pursuing. What in hell were you thinking? You could have compromised our coverage, or worse yet, inadvertently let it slip that the first story was published by accident.''

Tess folded her arms across her chest, chastened and defensive. So much for the pat on the head she thought was her due. "Rosita had some problems in San Antonio. Someone down there suggested if I followed in her footsteps, I would find the same pattern here. I did, and I did. Wink never hit his wife, Jack, she hit *him*. Rosita paid someone for her information, and she didn't begin to try to check it out. I mean, she got a no comment, but she even twisted that to make it sound as if Linda Wynkowski was scared to confirm the story—''

Sterling held up a hand. "Slow down, Tess. Take a deep breath, start over, and tell me everything in straight chronological order, okay?''

And so Tess did—almost. She still held back the detail about the envelope she'd found on her car. Perhaps because it seemed a little sleazy, as if she'd been manipulated by an unknown source whose agenda was still unclear.

"I know I wasn't asked to do any of this,'' she finished. "But sometimes my curiosity gets the better of me. You were the one who asked me what I thought about that story, on a gut level, and I really didn't have an answer at the time. Now I think it was the combination of solid reporting and sordid gossip that made it seem slightly off. Rosita's work undermined Feeney's at every turn.''

"Feeney is a friend of yours, isn't he, Tess?''

Uh-oh. "Baltimore is a small town of 650,000 people. Everyone knows everyone here.''

"Do you know him the same way you knew Jonathan Ross?"

"No!" Shit, she was blushing. "I mean, we're friends. We have a drink from time to time, that's all."

"Don't you think it was an ethical breach for you to take this job, given your relationship with him?"

"Well, yes." Something in Sterling's gentle manner tempted her to tell the truth—it would feel so good to get some of those lies off her ledger. Besides, she no longer felt a need to protect Feeney, not after his behavior yesterday. Still, if she veered from the official version, things would get tricky.

"I was told he had an ironclad alibi for the night, so it wasn't an issue."

"*You were told.* Nice little wiggle phrase, there."

"What does it matter now?" she said, feeling a little desperate under Sterling's questions. She suddenly realized what a good reporter he must have been in his day. "Doesn't what I've learned today make it pretty obvious Rosita slipped the story into the paper? She's ruthless as hell."

Sterling stood up, crumpled his pretzel bag in his hand, and flicked it at the trash can for a clean two-pointer. "Your information doesn't suggest or confirm anything about the original incident. But I want you to come with me now and talk to Lionel about it."

"Why?"

"Because I think Rosita Ruiz's days at the *Beacon-Light* are coming to an end."

Chapter 23

⸘⸘⸘

It snowed on Friday morning, a heavy, wet snow with fat flakes that stuck only to the grass, but it was enough to throw the morning commute into complete chaos, as cars spun out in anticipation of spinning out and the local schools announced they would start one hour late, two hours late, then not at all. Tess had tried to take the bus to the *Beacon-Light*, thinking it might be marginally faster, but the bus had been sideswiped, which was seen as a kind of open lottery in most city neighborhoods, and pedestrians began climbing on until it was standing-room only. Finally, a young security guard got on and held the doors shut, as thwarted plaintiffs surrounded the bus and pounded on its sides. Tess squeezed out the back door, letting a few more potential plaintiffs on in the process, and hailed a taxi. In fact, her neck and shoulders were sore, but she had a hunch it was the *Blight,* not the transit sysem, that was at fault.

Although she was twenty minutes late, the meeting in the publisher's conference room had yet to start. Five-Four and Lionel Mabry, who lived far out in the suburbs, were still en route, and Sterling was sequestered with Rosita. Colleen Reganhart sat glumly at the table with Guy Whitman, whose face brightened when Tess walked in.

"Snow, and this weekend is Palm Sunday. It's certainly been a strange winter," Whitman said, making conversation. "Now, is Friday the good day for firing, or the bad day? Or is it neither? I always get confused. What do you think, Tess?''

Tess, who had been laid off on a Wednesday, thought every day was a bad day to lose one's job. How unexpected it had been, how ill prepared they all had been, when the *Star*'s publisher had asked the staff to gather in the newsroom soon after their afternoon paper had gone to bed. As a coup de grâce, the *Star*'s corporate owners had not even allowed its workers the catharsis of putting out a final edition about their paper's demise. Tess's last piece of journalism had been a four-paragraph story about a water main break downtown.

Whitman answered his own question. ''Actually, there are several schools of thought about terminating employees. If you worry that an employee is prone to, uh, severe emotional responses, a Friday might be ill advised, as the employee could harm himself over the weekend. Others hold that Monday is the best day for firing from the management point of view; otherwise, the task would hang over the manager's head throughout the week, providing an unwarranted distraction. Violence cannot be discounted as a possibility. When the *Los Angeles Times* had to down-size by reducing its staff by more than a hundred people in a single afternoon, the company issued a directive stating—''

''Oh, shut the fuck up, Guy,'' snapped Colleen, who had gotten up and started pacing the room with a lighted cigarette.

''You know, you're not suppose to smoke in here,'' he countered.

''For now, I outrank everyone in here.''

''For *now*.''

It all began here, Tess thought, *and now it's going to end here.* Sterling had promised her the *Blight* would buy out the rest of her contract, as long as she agreed to appear here today, and, if necessary, present her notes about Rosita's reporting methods. Although they couldn't prove Rosita had slipped her story into the paper, Lionel and

Five-Four were convinced she was the culprit. But she would go down for paying Bertie. It seemed highly unorthodox, perhaps even illegal, but Tess was so anxious to be free of the *Beacon-Light* at this point, she would have agreed to almost anything.

Five-Four's secretary opened the door and announced: "They're on their way." Colleen sucked down every drop of nicotine she could extract from the butt-end of her cigarette, then opened the window and tossed it to the street below. She had just slammed the window shut when Five-Four arrived, trailed by a chipper Lionel Mabry, absent-mindedly whistling a pretty tune. It took Tess a few bars to identify it: "There Is a Rose in Spanish Harlem." Now, that seemed in dubious taste. He seemed to realize this, too, and the song stopped abruptly as Sterling and Rosita entered.

"Have a seat, Rosita." Sterling's voice was disarmingly gentle, but Tess suspected he was probably the angriest of all those assembled. Rosita took the chair at the far end of the table, opposite from Five-Four. The big chair seemed to swallow her and Tess was moved to something almost like pity—until she saw Rosita's hard, defiant face. The little reporter had waived her right to bring a union representative to the meeting. She had, in fact, forbidden the shop steward from accompanying her. She was so sure she didn't need anyone. She didn't think she needed Feeney to get the story, she didn't think she needed the union to keep her job.

Sterling looked down at a blank legal pad as he spoke. "I briefed you earlier on the evidence Tess Monaghan has gathered about your, uh, methods. We also have a signed statement from Bertie Athol that she was paid for information on the Wynkowski story, information that turned out to be exaggerated and false. And we can get photocopies of the papers Tess saw yesterday, the ones that establish Wink Wynkowski was the victim in his marriage, not the aggressor. We believe the cumulative result of these findings warrants your immediate dismissal. However, we are prepared to give you six months' severance—you'd only be entitled to two, normally—and assistance in finding another job. Some of us feel—I feel—we failed you here. Perhaps at a smaller paper, where the pressures to perform would not be so great, you could concentrate on some of the basics you appear to have skipped over in your career to date.''

Rosita wasn't mollified by this offer of help, nor cowed by Sterling's talk of a generous severance package. ''Those papers, assuming they're not forged, may prove Wink suffered injuries, but you can't prove he never hit Linda,'' she said coolly. ''For all we know, there are other hospital records, and she chose not to show them to Tess. I stand by my story.''

''Can the shit, Rosita.'' Colleen shook a cigarette from her pack, began to light it, then crumpled it in her shaking fingers, as if she hoped to absorb the nicotine through her sweaty palms. Tess couldn't figure out why she was so upset. *Because she had been Rosita's champion, because Rosita was a woman? Or was it because Colleen would have to take the fall for Rosita's failings?*

''This isn't some fucking high school debating society, you're not going to win any points here with this goddamn nitpicking. You made shit up. For your own glory, yet, because the story was good enough as it was. You just wanted a piece of it. Were you scared we wouldn't put your name on it if you came up dry? Or did you need a sexy clip for your next job?''

''I made an honest mistake,'' Rosita insisted.

Tess couldn't help being impressed at her self-assurance. Then again, if Rosita really was a pathological liar, she had been doing this all her life.

''Yes, I gave Bertie Athol fifty dollars—she's on a fixed income, she could use a little money. But I did it after the fact, to pay her for her time, not to encourage her to exaggerate. How is that any different from taking a source to Tio Pepe's or the Maryland Inn? We do that all the time and no one squawks. What I didn't do is tell Mrs. Athol to

lie, to pretend to know more than she did. She told me the
Wynkowskis fought tooth and nail, that Linda had been
taken away in an ambulance on several occasions. Okay, I
made a mistake, but not a huge one. This is a lynching
party. You're using this to get rid of me because I'm close
to my biggest break yet on the story, something much bigger than anything that's happened so far, and you want to
hand it off to another reporter. Well, if I go, I'm taking my
story and my sources with me.''

Sterling's curiosity got the better of him. ''What are you
talking about, Rosita? Do you know something you haven't
told us? There's nothing on the budget line about a new
development.''

''I don't tell you everything,'' Rosita taunted him. ''But
yes, I have it on good authority that Wink didn't commit
suicide. He was murdered, probably by someone who had
even more to lose than Wink did if the basketball deal
didn't go through.''

''Who's your source?'' Whitman broke in impatiently.
''The autopsy isn't official yet, and no one at the cops or
the M.E. have indicated they think it was anything but suicide.''

''She's still making shit up.'' Colleen's voice was shrill,
almost hysterical in its fury. ''Wink's death hurt the prospects of landing a basketball team, so why would someone
kill him over it? I wouldn't believe anything she said now
unless it was on fucking videotape. Even then I'm not sure
I'd believe it.''

Rosita just shook her head back and forth, like a head-
strong two-year-old. ''I'm not saying anything else unless
you guarantee my job. That's the deal. Let me stay—I'll
take probation, I'll even go home for a few days without
pay—and you get the story. I go, and the story goes with
me.''

Everyone, even Five-Four, turned to Lionel then. The
decision would be his to make. He looked at Rosita with
large, sorrowful eyes, then stood, unfolding slowly. It was
if someone new had entered the room, replacing the sham-

bling Lionel Tess knew, the Lionel who seemed so stooped and blurry, his bones a collection of bent wire hangers holding up his clothes. Now he stood straight and tall, head thrown back. *So this was the Lion King.*

"You are not in a position to make demands, Miss Ruiz," Mabry said, his voice stern yet regretful, as if she were a daughter who had disappointed him. "At every turn, you have demonstrated a complete absence of ethics, judgment, and professionalism. It is one thing to risk your credibility, but you risked my paper's credibility as well. Don't you understand that Rosita Ruiz, by herself, is insignificant? It is Rosita Ruiz, *Beacon-Light* reporter, who gets officials on the phone, who convinces private citizens to share their confidences. You care nothing for this institution, you care only for yourself, but you are nothing without the institution. You used your computer skills to slide your story into the paper because you knew it could never withstand the scrutiny that Jack Sterling and I had brought to the process. In your conceit and your egotism, you embody everything wrong with journalism today."

"I'm what's wrong with journalism?" Rosita jumped to her feet, and although it wasn't quite as dramatic as Mabry's performance, she did manage a stumpy kind of dignity. "What about you, you relic, you dinosaur? What was the last story you ever reported, the influenza epidemic of 1908? All you do is sit in your corner office and tell your war stories and hope the paper lurches into a Pulitzer by sheer luck. Well, when I walk out this door, I'm not only going to take my prize-winning story with me, I'm going to take some other stories as well. Stories about this godforsaken place, with its sexual harassment, rampant mismanagement, blatant conflicts of interest, editors who sleep with reporters—"

"Whitman, you crotch-sniffing dog!" Colleen turned on him and he shrank back as if he thought she might strike him. "Couldn't you keep it fucking zipped for once in your life?"

"I swear, I don't know what she's talking about," he

whimpered unconvincingly. "Haven't a clue."

Lionel did not allow this ancillary drama to distract him. "Tell me, Miss Ruiz, where will this story of yours appear? What responsible news organization will listen to a dismissed employee without calling to check your allegations? It's my fervent hope there aren't too many reporters whose morals and standards are as lax as your own."

Before Rosita could retort, two security guards entered the room, one carrying a cardboard box filled with notebooks, files, dictionary, AP style book, and one not-quite-clean coffee mug. The detritus of a reporter's desk, Tess realized. But did they really need two beefy men to escort one small woman from the premises, even one as angry as Rosita?

"We've taken the liberty of cleaning out your work space while you were in here, Miss Ruiz," Mabry said. "We have decided to let you keep all your notes and files, although we could claim them as the paper's property. I hope your big story is in one of those notebooks. Alas, I suspect it's mainly in your imagination."

Tess had to admire Rosita for not bursting into tears, begging for one more chance, or groveling to regain Sterling's offer of help in finding another job. Instead, she grabbed the box from one of the security guards and left the room so quickly the guards had to break into a trot to keep up with her.

No, it was Colleen who had tears in her eyes, while Whitman continued to stammer general denials. Sterling stared at the long table, his face ashen, and even Five-Four seemed discomfited. Only Lionel was flush with victory, his piss-yellow locks flying around his head, his yellowish teeth bright in his face.

"Back to work," he said. "We still have a paper to put out. Jack, please find Feeney and tell him about Miss Ruiz's babblings, on the remote chance there's even a grain of truth in them. Whitman, call human resources and tell them to prepare a final check for Miss Ruiz. And Colleen, I'd like to see you in my office *now*, to discuss your taste in protégés.''

Whitman almost bowed as he ran from the room, grateful for the chance to live another day in abject fear. Colleen was composed but deathly pale as she stalked out behind him, while Five-Four tried to give Mabry a manly pat on the shoulder which ended up closer to the small of his back. Only Sterling was left behind, still staring at the blank legal pad in front of him.

''I wonder what she'll do,'' he said.

''Find a new job, start over. What else can she do?''

''She could still fight it, if she was smart. File an EEOC complaint, say she was railroaded out because she's a minority and a woman.''

''I don't think the facts of Rosita's firing make her an ideal candidate for any kind of job action.''

''But it was so ugly, so vicious,'' Sterling said. ''I've never seen anything like it, not in all my years in the business. I tried to prepare her for it, but I don't think she understood the severity of her circumstances. She thought I could save her, but I couldn't, I really couldn't.''

''No one could. Besides, it was Lionel's decision in the end, not yours.''

''I was part of it, though. We were all part of it. If Rosita is a monster, we're Dr. Frankenstein.''

Tess wanted desperately to comfort him, to remind him he was a good person, albeit one in a rotten business. She tried to put her arm around his shoulders, but it was awkward, reaching around the padded leather chair, and she ended up pressing her cheek next to his. She couldn't believe how hot his face was, how hard the pulse beat in his temple.

Sterling was the one who pulled away. ''So you're free of us now.''

''I guess I am. Won't take a security guard, or even a box to clean out my desk. I never settled in.''

''It will probably be weeks and weeks before you get

paid. We're not very timely in sending checks out to our independent contractors.''

So that's what she was to him. An independent contractor.

"No problem." She grabbed the straps of her knapsack, ready to flee. She didn't have a reason to see him anymore, she realized. That also was part of the bargain she had struck.

Sterling's voice stopped her before she reached the door. "Tess—what's Tess short for, anyway?"

"Theresa."

"Whitney refers to you as Tesser, sometimes."

"Do you and Whitney talk about me?" She didn't know whether to be flattered or troubled.

"Before you were hired, she briefed me on you. Remember my little instant thumbnail description of you? Whitney fed me most of my information."

"She was a double-agent, then. She did the same for me. Anyway, Tesser is the way I said my full name, Theresa Esther, when I was a kid.''

He had seemed to be cheering up, but his low spirits suddenly overtook him again. "Everybody was a kid once, pure and hopeful. You. Rosita. Wink. No one plans to fuck up, do they?"

"I don't plan on it, but I *do* count on it."

Good, she had made him laugh, and his bad mood lifted for good this time. Strange, his ambivalence over Rosita only made him more attractive to her. He was the only person here today—Rosita included—who seemed to understand that there would probably be no second chances for Rosita, no hope of starting over. She was damaged goods at twenty-four. Well, she could go to law school, or find some other profession where a situational approach to the truth was less of a detriment. But she'd probably never work as a reporter again.

Sterling stood up to leave. "Good-bye, Tess. Good luck. Everything I've seen suggests you're going to be a hell of an investigator. I bet you were a pretty good reporter, too."

"Thanks. I'd say it's been fun, but—"

"I know. It hasn't." He jingled the change in his pocket, suddenly self-conscious. "Look, I don't want you to think I'm another Whitman—for one thing, I don't have a wife and five kids at home—but would you like to have dinner sometime?"

"Sure." She waited to see if he was going to make the invitation concrete, or if he was merely being polite.

"Saturday night?"

"I'm free."

And having said that, she had to make it true.

Tess found a lot of reasons not to go home that afternoon. She puttered around Tyner's office, then went to Durban's, where she set out to run five miles on the treadmill, then found herself doing seven. Finally, there was no place else to go.

When she arrived at the apartment, Crow was puttering on the terrace, almost ridiculous in his perfection: the postmodern boyfriend, potting pansies and singing softly to man's best friend. Esskay was under his elbow, nosing through the mulch and topsoil and demanding attention even as he worked. It was staying light longer now and the purple dusk picked up the new violet strands in his hair. *He looks like a little boy playing with mud pies*, Tess thought, *or Martha Stewart as a punk rocker. I'm surprised you can't order him from the Smith & Hawken catalog.* The truth was, he looked like what he was, what he had always been—a kind, considerate man-child. The kind of guy she had longed for when she was in college. He was only seven years too late.

"It's too early, even for pansies," she said, a little too harshly. "It snowed this morning, remember? We'll probably have two or three more freezes into April."

"I'm going to bring them in and keep them next to the French doors. They'll get good light there. I was thinking, this would be a great spot to grow tomatoes this summer, with all the sun. I also want to put in a little herb garden.

Parsley, sage, rosemary, and thyme.'' He sang the last. ''And basil, so we can have *linguine alla cecca* all summer long. That's pasta with chopped tomatoes, fresh basil, olive oil, and cayenne pepper. It's the best thing you'll ever eat.''

Tess grunted noncommittally. She didn't want to plan her summer menus in March. She didn't want to plan anything with Crow right now. Lost in his dreams of Early Girls and Beefmasters, he sprinkled a handful of mulch across the topsoil, then patted it tenderly in place. Everything he touched, he touched with this indiscriminate love and care. For a moment, Tess tried to frame an objection to him on this basis, but not even she could be that contrary. Crow loved her, he was good to her, he was a good person. The sad fact was, none of those things obligated her to love him back.

''Do you know the significance of April?'' he asked.

''Opening Day? The cruelest month? The Mary Sue Easter egg jingle on the radio twenty-four hours a day, driving one slowly insane?''

''Our six-month anniversary comes in April. April twenty-third. Know where I'd like to go to celebrate?''

''Lourdes?''

He was too happily absorbed in his plans to really hear her. ''The community health clinic for HIV tests. Then, when we get our results, we could make a commitment to one another.'' He put down his shovel and came over to hug her, smelling of dirt and mulch. ''Nothing official. It would be just a way of formalizing what we're already doing.''

''I want to say yes,'' Tess muttered into his collarbone. ''I want to *want* to say yes.''

Crow pulled away from her. ''What are you saying, Tess?''

''It's what I'm *not* saying, Crow. I'm not saying yes. I'm not saying I'm ready for a committed relationship. Sometimes I think we jumped into this a little too quickly. So much was going on last fall. So much is going on now. And when you talk about summer and tomatoes and linguine and AIDS tests—Crow, I'm going to be thirty this summer.''

''What does your age have to do with anything?''

''Everything—when you throw in your age as well.''

''As time goes by, the difference in our ages will seem smaller and smaller.''

''Maybe. But I have a feeling it's going to get larger before it gets smaller.''

Crow gave her a long, puzzled look, then went into the apartment. She heard drawers opening, the sound of plastic CD boxes smacking together as he sorted through their commingled music. Heavy footsteps on the stairs, three trips in all, as he carried things to his car. Esskay watched anxiously from the French doors, confused as always by anything remotely out of the ordinary. Crow gave the dog a long, lingering pat as he came back out on the terrace. His expression was as troubled and perplexed as the greyhound's.

''I'll probably end up giving Kitty my notice. I was planning to, anyway, things are heating up with the band.''

''That's okay. She's used to people coming and going.''

''And you? Are you used to it, Tess?''

She had no answer for that.

''I loved you.'' Not a question, not an attempt to change her mind, just a statement of the facts. Again, Tess had no reply, other than ''I know''—and that would be too cruel.

''You're a good person,'' she said at last. ''You're one of the nicest people I've ever known.''

''There are steamed vegetables for Esskay's dinner.'' And he was gone.

It was dark now, and getting cold on the terrace, just as Tess had prophesied. She dragged the heavy planters of pansies into the apartment, found Esskay's length of chain—Crow still hadn't gotten around to buying her a proper leash, *there*, that was something he had screwed up—and took her out, largely for something to do. They walked to the pier at the foot of Broadway, so Tess could watch the water and Esskay could lunge at pigeons and seagulls.

She thought she would feel exhilarated—break-ups were usually enormously liberating if one initiated them. And if the other person broke things off, well, that was usually good for taking off a quick ten pounds. Tonight, she still had her appetite, but was she happy, was she free? As Feeney's friend Auden had said, the question was absurd. She was depressed, hungry, and strangely sad.

Esskay rested her head on Tess's knee, gazing into her eyes in the soulful way that meant ''Pet me,'' unless there was food handy, in which case it translated to ''Feed me.'' Tess scratched beneath her chin and along her nose, picking a few flecks of mulch from the dog's long snout. The slightly acrid, tangy smell made her think longingly of the daffodils and tulips that would soon appear throughout the city. And her mother's flower beds, with their red, white, and blue flowers in perfect rectangles along the house. She smiled at the image of Uncle Spike, showing up with her mother's winter mulch, ten whole bags of it, just as spring was beginning. Judith didn't use that much mulch in a decade. What had Spike been thinking?

What had *she* been thinking? No, the problem was, she hadn't been thinking at all. Neither had her mother, nor her father. The reason for Spike's beating had been with them all along.

Chapter 24

∽∾∽∾∽

Tess was too anxious to take the time necessary to wrestle Esskay up three flights of stairs and settle her down with water, supper, and a post-walk treat. Friday was grocery shopping night in the Monaghan household, a time-consuming ritual in which Judith and Patrick worked the aisles at the Giant side by side, picking fights over virtually every item. *Creamed corn, pro or con? Was there really a difference between name brand toilet paper and the generic store brand?* But now it was almost eight, which meant Tess had less than an hour until they returned. It would be better to find whatever Spike had hidden, take it, and leave, allowing her parents to remain in blissful ignorance.

She parked on the street and walked up the driveway, Esskay trotting happily alongside her, just pleased to be in on this adventure. The garage was padlocked, but the side entrance, where her mother kept her potting bench and gardening tools, was always open.

Inside, the naked sixty-watt bulb wasn't a match for anything past dusk, and the corners of the shed were lost in gray shadows that made every shape sinister and suspect. Ten plastic garbage bags sat in the back like huge toadstools, fat and poisonous. She opened one, sniffing. The fragrance was sharper than whatever Crow had been using, but this was definitely mulch. Now what?

She plunged her arm into the elbow, then to the shoulder,

fingers wiggling in search of anything that was not mulch. It might be hard or soft, as big as a gold brick, as small as a diamond ring. Again and again, eight times in all, she repeated the exercise, coming up with nothing more than a sleeve loamy with traces of tree bark. But on the ninth bag, the mulch was only a soft, shallow cover for something harder. A handful of little triangles, dried and stiff, like misshapen tortilla chips.

Curious, she pulled a few out. Esskay sniffed experimentally, then backed away, whimpering strangely. Tess held the triangles closer to the light. No, they weren't chips, and they weren't edible, not unless a dog was a cannibal. The triangles were made of flesh and hair, and although they had shrunk when they dried, the tattooed numbers were still visible.

The ears. The *ears*. That's what Spike had seen, not the years.

Tess dropped them on the floor, recoiling at the light clattering sound on the concrete floor. Her first instinct was to run, as if by fleeing she could put some distance between herself and a world where someone methodically sliced the ears from greyhound corpses, ensuring they could never be traced, then beaten her uncle so he couldn't tell what he had seen, or share what he had found.

But she couldn't just run away. She had to gather up the evidence, gruesome as it was, and take it to someone. The police? The Humane Society? She'd figure it out later. Grabbing her mother's rake, she pushed the scattered ears into a pile, then dropped to her knees to put them back in their bed of mulch. Esskay's whimpering escalated into a high-pitched wail, a dirge for her fallen comrades. *Ru-ru-ru-ru.*

Perhaps it was this plaintive sound that masked the footsteps in the driveway. At any rate, it was only when the door creaked behind her that Tess stood and turned, but before she could make a sound, her face was smothered in a man's leather jacket—the leather jacket of someone broad-shouldered and at least 6' 6".

"Finally," a familiar gravelly voice said from somewhere behind the man, who held the back of her neck just hard enough to let her know he could crack her spine if he wanted to.

"Is it just the one bag?" her captor asked.

"Looks that way, but we better take 'em all, just in case. Maybe we'll get lucky and find the other thing, too."

"We could look around. It could be somewhere else in here."

"No time. But we'll take her, see if she has any ideas."

Leather Jacket released the pressure on Tess's neck slightly and shoved a handkerchief into her mouth. His callused hand smelled of onions and motor oil. She thought of biting the hand that gagged her, but it seemed futile and most unsanitary. From behind her, another hand fished through her pockets for her car keys.

"Let's go," Gravel Voice said. The two men linked arms on either side of her, as if she were Dorothy, ready to gambol down the Yellow Brick Road with Tin Man and Scarecrow. When she tried to go limp, forcing them to drag her away, one poked a hard object in her ribs—presumably a gun; she didn't have the heart to find out for sure by struggling. *Where was the Ten Hills neighborhood watch when you really needed them? Why wasn't one of her mother's nosy friends peeking out her window now, taking in this scene?* Esskay jogged beside them, determined not to be left out.

"Like the new car?" Gravel Voice asked, as they pushed her into the backseat of a black Oldsmobile, a far more discreet car than either of their previous vehicles. Esskay hopped in beside her. There, yet another man in a leather jacket forced her head down below the seats, using his armpit like a vise, a leathery, sweaty vise. "We realized the other one was a little too recognizable, so we traded up."

Tess's muffled voice almost managed to sound confident. "My parents are going to come home soon and when they see my car at the curb, they'll have the cops out looking for me immediately."

"Why do you think we took your keys?" Gravel Voice asked from the front seat. "Our friend's going to follow us in it. There's not going to be any car at the curb when your parents come home, or any bags, or any dog. They'll never know you were here, and I don't think the cops are going to put out an all-points-bulletin for a bunch of dirt."

"Jesus fuckin' Christ!" The man who had been holding Tess loosened his grip, letting her up for air, just in time to smell something even less appealing than the poorly aged leather of his jacket. Esskay, overwhelmed by the evening's events, had emptied her bladder on the floor of the car. The armpit returned, dragging Tess back into its rancid world.

She muttered into the crook of his elbow: "If I promise to keep my head down in my own lap, would that be okay?"

No verbal reply, but the arm released her and she pressed her face into her thighs. Her black wool trousers carried a faint whiff of mothballs. Mothballs, and it was almost time to put them back in storage. It depressed her, yet another sign of incompetence on her part.

Beneath her, she felt the car make two right turns and a left, then head down a long straight-away marked by frequent intersections, judging by the stops every 100 feet or so, and more frequent potholes. This was probably meaningful information, but Tess had no idea what to do with it. The Oldsmobile also had bad shocks and a few empty cans of Miller Lite rolling around on the floor. Esskay whined at each jolt.

"Look, you've got the ears," she said. "Once you take them, there's nothing anyone can do to you. What else are you looking for? What do you want with my dog?"

Gravel Voice said, "The last thing we need is another fuckin' dog."

The man next to her shook with suppressed laughter; Tess felt the vibrations where their hips touched. Then the car was quiet, rolling to a stop in what appeared to be a long driveway.

It took a few seconds to stand straight again, once she

was out of the car. Tess pretended to be stiffer than she was, which allowed her to steal a glance at the neighborhood as she stretched and stamped her feet as if they had fallen asleep. Large Victorians, set far back from the street, big lawns. Suburban, but not overly so. A block away, she could see the haze of streetlights along a fairly busy street. The traffic sound was constant, and they couldn't have driven more than twenty minutes. Catonsville, only a few miles due west of her parents' house. Either these guys didn't care if Tess knew where she was, or they didn't think she was going to have a chance to tell anyone.

They dragged her into a once-grand house, seedy after what appeared to be many months of vacancy. In the living room, with its high ceilings and old-fashioned chandelier, a man sat in a slightly ramshackle Morris chair, the only furniture in the room, holding a small dog in his lap. Tess didn't recognize the man, but she remembered the yapping dog from their encounter on South Street. Charlton? Carleton? Something like that. The dog had silky red-gold hair and an ugly rat face. The man had plain brown hair and an ugly rat face.

"We tried to tell you your uncle had things that didn't belong to him," the man in the Morris chair said. "I don't know why you couldn't help us recover our property sooner."

"I didn't know what you wanted. I only found the— them—on a hunch." She didn't want to say out loud what she had seen, what she had touched.

"But there is something else he has stolen from our employer, and it is urgent we find that as well."

"It might help if you told me what you were looking for. All this time, I thought you wanted my greyhound."

Morris Chair shook his head. His face was long and thin, with deep hollows in his cheeks that gave him a wasted look.

"This dog was part of an earlier program that proved to be too, uh, labor-intensive. It's of no interest to us, and frankly, neither are you. But I guess you're going to be our guest for a while. Perhaps your uncle's friend, the little dishwasher, will suddenly remember where our property is, if he has some incentive.''

''Tommy doesn't know anything.'' Tess felt desperate, thinking of her fate in Tommy's hands, imagining Tommy opening up a box with, say, her index finger in it. He'd probably deep-fry it and serve it during Happy Hour. ''You know, when I went out tonight, I told my aunt to call the police if I didn't return within the hour.''

All the men laughed at that. Tess wasn't sure if they didn't believe her or were simply confident it didn't matter. Nonplused, she gave Esskay a little slack on her leash, hoping the dog might pee on someone's leg. But the greyhound simply stared with bright eyes at Morris Chair, her brain's signals almost audible. *Dinner, dinner, dinner.* Tess would have been hungry, too, if her stomach wasn't so tight with fear.

''You won't be returning within the hour,'' Morris Chair advised her. ''You won't be returning at all until your uncle's friend cooperates.''

His lap dog jumped to the floor and sniffed her owner's shoes. Shiny slip-ons, sort of like patent leather bedroom slippers. And he wore a leather blazer, fingertip length, over a navy blue polyester sports shirt. All the men were dressed the same, more or less. Leather jackets or blazers, knit shirts, polyester pants, and shiny, soft loafers. Despite herself, Tess wondered where they shopped.

''Now, are you sure you don't have any ideas about where else your uncle might have hidden something?''

The little dog saw something move near the fireplace— a roach, a rat, a shadow—and gave chase, yapping excitedly. Tess felt a strange burning sensation against her palm as Esskay's metal chain jerked through her fingers before she could grab it. The greyhound had joined the hunt. But Esskay didn't want the small dog's prey. She wanted the small dog, whom she quickly trapped in the corner.

''Charlton!'' Morris Chair screamed, rising from his chair. Too late. Esskay sank her teeth into the dog's soft belly, shaking it ferociously from side to side. The race was won! And Esskay had *caught* the rabbit, something no other dog at the track had ever done. She was almost delirious with joy, prancing around the room like a majorette.

Morris Chair made a horrible keening sound. The three other men rushed into the fray, then backed away, unsure what to do. Esskay kept her jaws clamped on the smaller dog, shaking it as if it were a small dust mop. Tess began edging toward the door, but stopped when she saw one of the men, the tall one who had first grabbed her, reach into his jacket and pull out a gun.

"Are you crazy?" she screamed, pushing past him and seizing Esskay by the snout, forcing her jaws open easily. After all, this wasn't a pit bull, or a Rottweiler. There was no strength here, no danger, nothing to fear except halitosis. The smaller dog writhed on the floor, possibly in shock, but the only visible damage were two small puncture wounds to its abdomen.

"Charlton," Morris Chair whimpered, when she picked up the little dog and handed it to him.

"There's a twenty-four-hour vet not far from here," Tess offered, surprised that she could feel some empathy for the man and his hideous little dog. "Out Route 40." Her three captors just stared blankly at her, as Morris Chair cradled Charlton in his arms.

"It's probably the road you brought me here on," she explained. "At least, I think that's the route, unless we came out Frederick Road. Route 40 runs off the Beltway, parallel to Frederick, you can't miss it. The vet is opposite the Toys R Us."

"You stay here with her," Morris Chair told Leather Jacket number 1, the tall one who had grabbed Tess in her parents' garage, as he rushed out, followed by Gravel Voice and Leather Jacket number 2.

"He loves that dog," her remaining captor said, putting his gun on the mantel, as if to remind Tess it was still at hand. "Anything happens to it, your dog's dead. Probably oughta be put down anyway, vicious as it is."

He spoke without irony, this thug who had kidnapped her, beaten her her uncle, and tried to shoot Esskay.

"I think Charlton'll be okay. It was only a puncture wound." She sank into the vacated Morris chair, her knees a little wobbly. Esskay tucked her nose under her elbow, looking for the treat she was sure she deserved.

"Wish we had a TV here," he said. "NCAA basketball is on."

Not a Baltimore accent, but close. Obviously not familiar with the city at all, if they needed directions to Route 40. Philadelphia? Wilmington? Spike had claimed to be coming from the Delaware racetracks when he'd left the mulch for her mother. And Spike didn't go in for elaborate lies, preferring simple sins of omission when he couldn't tell the truth. What was the other thing they wanted? How could she find out?

"I know a good way to pass the time. Do you know how to play Botticelli?"

"Is that Italian for 'Spin the Bottle'?"

"No, it's like twenty questions. You see, you pick a letter—say, S—and I ask you a question about a person whose name begins with S. For example, say your person was Mike Schmidt—"

"Greatest third baseman to ever play the game."

Definitely from Philadelphia, Tess decided. *A local would pick Brooks Robinson every time.* "Whatever. Anyway, if your letter is S, I might ask, 'Are you a classical composer?' If you can't think of an answer—say, Stravinsky—I get to ask a yes-no question about your person, until I have enough clues to finally guess the identity. Get it?"

Long pause. "Yeah."

"Good. Now to make it really interesting, why don't you tell me the letter of what you're looking for, and we can play for that."

"I dunno—"

"Oh, c'mon. What are the odds I'll actually guess?"

Another round of deep thought, as if he were actually calculating her chances. "You got a point."

"Good. Now what's your letter?"

"I guess it's V. Could be C—no, it's V, definitely V."

"Okay. Are you a twentieth-century writer with a cult following?"

"You gotta be fucking kidding me."

Tess imitated the sound of a game show buzzer's rude call. "You're not Kurt Vonnegut. Now I get to ask a yes-no. Are you—the item you're looking for—related to betting?"

"Can I say kinda?"

"Usually not."

"Well, I'm gonna say kinda. It's kinda about betting, but not really. Tangential, you might say."

"Fair enough. Next question. Are you Lolita's creator?" The real rules were clear that only last names could be used, but Tess had been deliberately vague in explaining the rules.

"I am not . . . I am not . . . I am not Valentine? Volare? Some Greek god, right?"

"Good try. Vladimir Nabokov. Do you have a monetary value?"

"No. I mean, it could, but only to a few people. You couldn't sell it from the back of a truck, but some people might pay you big money for it."

"Okay. Are you the Pope's residence?"

Her competitor looked insulted. "I'm not the Vatican." He crossed himself.

"Good. Very good." A right answer would soften him up, she decided, although she hadn't intended to ask him anything he knew. "Are you a UN official with a Nazi past?"

A blank look.

"Kurt Waldheim," she said, giving it the German pronunciation. He wouldn't know how it was spelled. "Was this thing ever alive? Or part of something alive?"

"That's two questions. But no to both of them."

"Well, I guess that's a good sign." Esskay stuck her snout in her lap, insistent on affection. Tess rubbed the dog under the neck, trying to think of her next question. *Botticelli was harder with an it than with a person.* Esskay's fur was matted and chafed beneath her collar. *She could ask him a question about Voltaire, or Venus.* The greyhound books said you were suppose to use a nylon leash, but there had never been time to replace this length of chain, Spike's improvisation. *Sid Vicious? Dick Van Dyke?* She played with the catch, clicking it open and closed, holding the dog close to her all the while.

"C'mon, ask me another question. This is kind of fun."

"Are you a moron?" Tess asked.

"Wait, I know this one. Some comedian, right? The guy who plays retards in all his movies. I am not . . . I am not . . ."

Tess leaped from the chair and lashed out at him with the chain, catching him across the face. He wasn't quick enough to grab the lethal leash, and he wasn't close enough to grab her. Tess backed away from him, moving toward the door and away from the fireplace, where his gun still sat on the mantel. He kept advancing, so intent on taking the chain away from her that he didn't think to retreat and grab his gun.

"Stupid bitch," he panted. "I am going to"—another futile grab—"make you so sorry." He caught her left wrist just then, but Esskay interceded, sinking her teeth into his hand. Not much of a grip, but she could do some damage. He yelled and fell back, then scrambled for the other side of the room, where his gun waited. But Tess and Esskay were at the door by then and Tess wrenched it open, letting Esskay go first and set the pace, praying the dog would have the good sense to run toward the streetlights, not into the alleys, where they were less likely to be seen. Her keeper might have enough power to overcome her in a sprint, but she was sure she could outlast him over anything more than a few blocks. And she was pretty sure he wouldn't want to fire his gun on this quiet suburban street.

Esskay ran, easy and happy, kicking up her back legs in the now-familiar kangaroo style. Tess followed breathlessly behind. By the time they stopped, they were at a Royal Farm a quarter-mile up Frederick Road and their captor was long behind them, if he had tried to chase them at all. Tess had never looked back. She called the police from the pay phone, then convinced the clerk to let her and Esskay wait in the back, where the greyhound finally received her long-awaited treat—two slices of bologna and three of her own namesake hot dogs. *Taste the difference ka-wality makes*, indeed.

Chapter 25

∽∾∽∾∽

"Did you really hit him with a dog chain?"

"Don't you believe everything you read in your own paper?"

"The story won't be in 'my' paper until tomorrow. Remember, we didn't find out about your little adventure last night in time for today's editions. It's a good read, too, but I can't help being nervous, dining with a woman known to lash men with dog chains."

For once, it was Tess who blushed, while Sterling smiled at her discomfort.

They were in the Joy America Cafe, the restaurant on the top floor of the American Visionary Art Museum. The food at the Joy America, as visionary and unusual as the museum's world-class collection of outsider art, was a little determinedly creative for Tess's taste. Citrus and pumpkin-seed seared antelope with Virginia ham and butternut squash succotash. Food miscegenation, Whitney called such cuisine. Tess thought of appropriating the line as her own, then worried Sterling would be offended. He could be a little on the earnest side.

"Have you noticed people still call this the *new* Visionary Museum, although it's been open for almost two years?" she asked instead, falling back on the reliable conversational gambit of mocking her hometown.

"There are people here who still think of the Inner

Harbor as new, and it was redeveloped almost two decades ago. I'm resigned to being called the new guy for the rest of my career at the *Beacon-Light*.'' Sterling took a tentative sip from the soup before him, a deep terra cotta color with a slash of avocado green through it, like the mark of Zorro. ''Chili powder and cilantro in mango soup. Not bad, but I detect some cream in here, despite the waiter's assurances.''

Tess tried not to make a face. She was eating field greens dressed in raspberry vinaigrette, a prosaic choice by Joy America standards. The waiter had *not* approved. That was fine, she had not approved of the waiter. While her brain understood this was one of the city's best restaurants, her palate secretly yearned for less determinedly fashionable places. Antelope was a poor substitute for Hausnner's potato pancakes, or a plate of tortellini from the Brass Elephant. But you couldn't veto your host's choice and Joy America did have a spectacular view of the harbor—the National Aquarium and the Columbus Center, the rowhouses and churches of Little Italy beyond them. She could even see the Fells Point waterfront, lights blazing on a Saturday night.

''If it were daytime, you might be able to see my terrace,'' she said, waving her fork toward the windows.

''Sounds quite grand.''

''Only if you consider living over a store grand. But it's a nice place and Aunt Kitty gives me a break on the rent.''

''Kitty?'' Sterling looked up from his soup. ''Wasn't she in the photograph, the one that's running with your story?''

''Um, yes.'' Upstaged by her aunt again, whom the *Blight* photographer had insisted on getting in the shot.

''Tell me—'' Here it came. He was going to ask for Kitty's number, try to find out if she was available. ''Aren't you worried those guys are going to come back for you?''

She almost laughed in her relief. ''Only one got away. The cops picked up the other three while they were still in the vet's waiting room. The fourth one drove my car to the Maryland House rest stop on I-95, helped himself to another car, then dropped that outside Philadelphia. The cops think he'll be more concerned with staying out of the state, now that he's wanted for felony kidnapping.''

"Still, it sounds as if these guys were working for someone else. What's to keep them from sending new recruits to find whatever it is they want?"

"I don't know. The man who got away did have the presence of mind to take the ears with him. They won't be able to trace the dogs who were killed.''

"Presumably killed." Sterling's correction was automatic, an editor's tic.

"Well, I guess there could be some earless greyhounds running around somewhere, but what would be the point?''

The waiter cleared away their dishes. The mango soup had proved too rich for Sterling, who had abandoned it after only a few spoonfuls.

"At any rate, you've fulfilled Warhol's prophecy. Sorry you won't get better play. I thought the story merited the local section front, but I decided to recuse myself from that decision, as I have a conflict of interest here." He paused. "That is, I hope I'm going to."

Tess felt as if she were right at the edge of the kind of happy normalcy that had eluded her for so many years. Dinner on a Saturday night. A nice man, with a real job instead of a band. Everything was perfect. Then something began ringing in Sterling's jacket pocket.

"Sorry," he said, pulling out a cell phone. "I always have to stay in touch with the desk.''

The connection must have been bad, he almost had to shout to be heard, and the other diners stared in pointed disapproval. "Who? What? Where are you?''

"Don't forget when and why," Tess teased, even as Sterling handed her the phone.

"It's Whitney. Says it's some kind of emergency.''

Whitney sounded as if she were shouting from inside a wind tunnel, a wind tunnel with loud music and hoarse laughter in the background. "There's a situation here I really need your help with,'' she said without preamble. ''I'm at the Working Man's Bar and Grille.''

''Feeney?''

''Close. Colleen Reganhart is here and she's about sixty seconds away from leaving in a cop car, but she says she wants to talk to you before she goes anywhere.'' Whitney paused. ''Look, I know my timing sucks. But there will be other dates, right?''

''How did you know about—'' She didn't want to say Sterling's name in front of him, or repeat the word ''date,'' so teen-agerish and vapid. ''How did you know where to find me?''

''Newsrooms can't keep secrets, Tess. Don't you know that by now?''

The Working Man's Bar and Grille was the most notorious of Fells Point's megabars, a sprawling warehouse on the waterfront. Its deck, strung with Japanese lanterns, had been part of the pretty lights that made the view from the Joy America so charming. Close up, the charm quickly dissipated. The bar's ersatz Marxist decor—machine parts from its paper-recycling past, the '30s-style posters of brawny working men and the real picket signs from famous Baltimore strikes—was incongruous, almost offensive, alongside five-dollar microbrews and margaritas at seven-fifty. And its college-kid patrons thought working with one's hands déclassé, although urinating in public and walking on top of the parked cars of Fells Point was apparently just another Saturday night.

Whitney was at the rubber-topped bar, designed to look like a conveyor belt. Colleen Reganhart was more or less *on* the bar, facedown, arms spread in a crucifixion pose, black hair fanning out into the dipping sauce from a half-eaten plate of Buffalo wings.

''She looks pretty docile,'' Tess said.

''Watch this.'' Whitney patted her arm. ''Colleen, don't you think we ought to be running along now?''

Colleen raised her head a few inches, looked at Whitney

with bleary eyes and said, "Fuck you, Talbot. You're the last person I want to see tonight."

"Tess is here. Didn't you say you wanted to talk to her?"

Colleen managed to pull her entire upper body from the bar and turned toward Tess. "Did I? Well, fuck you, too."

The bartender came over. It was Steve, Kitty's most recent dalliance. But Kitty had already dropped him, so he saw no percentage in being helpful to her niece.

"Look, Tess, I cut her off half an hour ago, but she won't leave and our crowd is starting to pick up. I can't have this broad taking up prime real estate and mouthing off at anyone who brushes against her. Blondie here said you'd take care of it."

Whitney raised an eyebrow. She didn't feel a bit guilty, Tess could tell. She might even be relishing the way she had interrupted her dinner with Sterling.

"My car's out front," she said blandly. "I need your help to carry her, then we'll drop her off at her apartment and put her to bed."

"How did you become the chaperone?" Tess said, tucking a hand beneath Colleen's armpit, as Whitney propped her up on the other side. Colleen didn't put up much of a fight, simply muttered a cursory list of curses as they propelled her to the door.

"Another favor for Lionel Mabry. He'd prefer his top people not to get arrested for public intoxication. She called him from a pay phone here an hour ago, threatening to quit one minute, then just threatening *him*. He convinced her to tell him where she was, then he called me and asked that I take care of it."

"With my assistance."

"I couldn't call anyone from the paper." Whitney glanced at Tess, taking in the good winter coat, the sheer hose and high heels, the upswept hair. "Although Sterling was welcome to come along. How was dinner, by the way? Did you make it to dessert? Did you have that whirligig thing they serve, with chocolate and cinnamon?''

"Let's just get this over with, okay?''

Sometimes Tess wondered if there was a single warehouse left in Baltimore still doing an honest day's work. Colleen lived in Henderson's Wharf, which had started life as a storehouse for the B & O Railroad. It sat at the end of Fell Street, a short walk from the Working Man's Bar and Grille, assuming one could still walk. Colleen never would have made it in her heels—the cobblestones on Thames Street would have brought her down in only a few steps. She passed out during the five-minute drive, forcing Whitney and Tess to carry the editor into her building like so much dirty laundry.

"She's on the sixth floor," Whitney said. "Harbor side, naturally.''

"Naturally," Tess echoed.

Yet the duplex apartment they entered was simply a richer version of Rosita's spartan apartment, with almost no real furniture and not even one picture hung, although two rectangles wrapped in brown paper leaned against the exposed brick wall. Another woman on the move, Tess thought, so determined to get somewhere she never stopped and looked around at where she was.

"Should we try to put her to bed?''

"I don't want to carry her up the stairs," Whitney said. "Let's leave her on the sofa and help ourselves to her bourbon. I have a feeling that's one thing you can always find in Colleen's kitchen.''

Colleen didn't have any bourbon, but she did have good Scotch and an unopened bag of Mint Milanos. Whitney broke the seal on both with great glee, then selected two mismatched glasses from one of the kitchen cabinets.

"We've earned it," she said to Tess, as they sat in the carpeted area where the dining room table might have been, if Colleen had gotten around to buying one.

"I guess you can put it on your expense account. Another favor for Lionel." She turned the phrase over in her mind. It was suddenly rich with meaning. "What was the first favor, anyway?"

Whitney studied Tess. They knew each other so well. Tess could see her mind working, trying to calculate how much Tess had figured out, which would determine how much Whitney had to admit.

"Getting you to come work for him, of course."

"And the second? There was a second favor, too, right?"

Whitney didn't say anything.

"I'm guessing the second favor was leaving the envelope on my car, the one with Rosita's personnel file in it. Lionel wanted me to see it, but didn't want anyone to know where it came from. What did he want me to find, Whitney?"

"Something. Anything." Whitney went into the kitchen and came back with a steak knife, which she used to slice open a Milano as if she were shucking an oyster. She then licked the chocolate from the inside. "He didn't know you'd do as well as you did, though. He was quite pleased at how quickly you got the goods on her. Lionel always suspected Rosita was trouble." She put the licked-clean cookie aside, then opened another one and began reaming the chocolate out of it. "I told him you would do a good job."

"So this didn't have anything to do with Feeney's story, did it? That was just an excuse, a way to go after Rosita. Mabry wanted to be rid of her, wanted to do an end-run around the union, and he saw this as an opportunity. Nail her for the story, or something else equally egregious, and he could fire her, or scare her out."

"Rosita was trouble, Lionel figured that out early on. He tried to put her back on the copy desk, but she screamed racism and sexism and every other ism she could think of. So he let Colleen pair her with Feeney, figuring she couldn't get in too much trouble working with another reporter. But she managed to. You've heard of rogue cops? Rosita's a rogue reporter. She'd do anything for a Page One story. Lionel had to get her out, and he didn't have time for her dismissal to grind through the union process. It was only a matter of time before the *Beacon-Light* ended up with a major libel case on its hands. Jesus, it almost did, Tess. If Wink hadn't killed himself, he could have sued the paper over that first story."

"But he wouldn't have. Wink paid his ex-wife hundreds of thousands of dollars never to tell anyone what had happened. He was humiliated."

Whitney shrugged. "He might have been willing to come forward now, because it would have undermined everything else the paper said about him, even the true stuff. I'm surprised he didn't think about that before he killed himself."

"Rosita says he was murdered."

"If Rosita said nice day, I'd check it out. She lies all the time, about little things, just to stay in practice. I swear, I've caught her in the most idiotic inconsistencies. What she majored in, for example. What part of Boston she grew up in. Who lies about stuff like that? She's crazy."

"Crazy," Tess agreed, but she wasn't going to allow Whitney to distract her so easily. "So does being Lionel's favor buddy guarantee you Japan? Was that the deal?"

Whitney lifted her chin, which had a smear of chocolate on it. "It doesn't hurt. Look, I kept you pure in all this by not telling you everything. You did your job beautifully and you made good money doing it. What's your problem?"

"The problem is you told me some lies as well."

"Not really. I just left out a few details here and there."

"What about Feeney's alibi?"

Again, Whitney waited Tess out to see what she knew, or had guessed. She picked up a third Milano, but was rattled enough to eat it as a normal person would.

"Did Feeney really tell you that he was with me that night, or was that your way of ensuring I would take the job, because I'd be so worried about him I'd want to protect him?"

"I did ask Feeney where he was that night, and he did say he had been with you." But Whitney could no longer make eye contact. In fact, she couldn't even face Tess, shifting her body so it was a three-quarters turn away from her. "He didn't remember what time he left you. In fact, he doesn't remember much about that night at all. He more or less blacked out. I knew if you thought he needed you as an alibi, you'd be hooked. You've always had a soft spot for him."

Tess saw Feeney walking north on Eutaw after their last angry conversation. He had been furious with her, absolutely enraged.

"What did you tell him? I mean, you had to make sure that Feeney and I didn't compare notes, right? How did you arrange that?"

Whitney's voice was almost inaudible now. "I told him you were hard-up for cash and he should keep his distance from you, because you had denied knowing him to the bosses. I also told him you said you were keeping an open mind about who had done it, and you wouldn't cut him any slack if you thought he was the one. But he wasn't, so what was the big deal?" She finished off her Scotch. "I think my confession slate is clean now. Am I forgiven? Do you want to assign me some form of penance?"

Tess felt dizzy, the way a child feels after turning in endless circles, staring up at the sky. Bad enough to have been used and manipulated by Lionel. But Whitney had been his willing agent, playing friend against friend in order to get the Tokyo bureau. It was one thing to use the elevator technique, quite another to have taken everyone for a ride.

"Why did you call me tonight? You could have handled this alone."

"Maybe I figured it was my last window of opportunity between boyfriends. Or are you double-dipping now, keeping the little boy at home while you let Sterling take you out on the town?"

"You're jealous."

"Of Sterling? No, losing to him at squash was as far as I was willing to go to advance my career. Not that he ever asked. But don't worry, Tesser, I'm sure you'll have another date with him. You always have another date. Me, I have my job. If I'm lucky, I'm going to have a foreign assignment, then come back to an editing position. Very few women run newspapers. I plan to be one of them.''

"Why? So you can end up like Colleen in there, passed out on your sofa on a Saturday night, in an empty apartment, with no friends, no family?''

"Colleen is *sui generis*. The other editors have families, lives, outside interests.''

"The other editors are men. Look around you, Whitney. It's not just Colleen. It's you, it's Rosita. Work is all you have. Jesus, you're still living at your parents' place because you've never taken the time to find an apartment of your own. Most of your relationships last about two weeks, when the guy realizes Friday night is reserved for *Washington Week in Review*, while Sunday mornings belong to *Meet the Press*. What are you going to do if you want to have a baby—ask Tim Russert to be the sperm donor?''

Whitney stood up, dusting cookie crumbs from the lap of her tweed trousers. "Look, I have to go. Do you want a ride back to your place, or do you want to walk?''

"I'll walk.''

"Any more flaws of mine you want to enumerate, failings you want to catalog? I said I was sorry.''

"No, in fact that's the one thing you haven't said this evening.''

"Well, I'm saying it now. I'm sorry. Isn't there something you'd like to say in return?''

"Yes, yes, there is.'' Tess fluttered her fingers. "Sayonara, Whitney.''

Chapter 26

Tess ended up staying at Colleen Reganhart's until dawn broke. She had postponed leaving after Whitney's exit, stalling to make sure there would be no awkward encounters at the elevator, or on the street. Then, just when she thought it was safe to go, Colleen began retching. Her old college instincts kicked in; it was inhuman to leave someone alone in that condition. Fortunately, tending to Esskay had inured Tess to cleaning up after others. It was almost refreshing to deal with a mess that required nothing more than paper towels and some Lysol.

She sponged off the sofa and Colleen's face, then helped her upstairs, to a bedroom as barren as the rooms below—a bed, a nightstand, and several stacks of newspapers. At least the plain white sheets felt expensive, and the duvet was real goose down. She tucked Colleen in, positioning a plastic wastebasket next to the bed, then went downstairs and made a pot of coffee, resigned to a long night. Luckily, Old Mother Reganhart's cupboard was not quite bare—she had a pound of Jamaican Blue coffee and ten packs of Merits in the freezer, an almost empty carton of half-and-half in the refrigerator, and an economy-size box of microwave popcorn on the counter.

Tess passed on the popcorn, finishing off the Milanos while reading one of Colleen's books, a collection of Molly Ivins columns. The *Blight* had never run the tart Texan's work, their loss. *"Too funny and too smart about politics,"* Whitney had explained. *"Women pundits are supposed to be uterus-centric. Besides, the problem with funny women is that the next joke might be about penis size, and we just can't have that, can we?"*

She smiled in spite of herself, wondering how long Whitney's voice would live in her head, how many more times she would think of something funny or trenchant, then realize the observation belonged to Whitney. Maybe it was a good thing Whitney had sold her soul, throwing a couple others in for good measure, to get the Tokyo job. Baltimore was too small a town to hold two friends who couldn't be friends anymore.

"Any coffee for me?"

Colleen's voice had the rough-hewn rasp one would expect from someone who had been on both sides of a tequila bottle in the last twelve hours, but it was otherwise pleasant. Tess found a *Beacon-Light* mug in the sink, rinsed it out, and poured her a cup.

"I'm afraid I used the last of the half-and-half."

"That's okay, I take mine black." Cory gulped the coffee as if it were medicine she had to force down. "Where's Talbot? She contract this job out to you?"

"She left first and I was about to leave, but you—you weren't feeling very well. I thought someone should stay here, in case you did an Edgar Allan Poe. Although they say he died from rabies now, not in a drunken stupor."

"Kind of you," Colleen said, in a tone that made clear she didn't necessarily respect kindness. "But I don't remember much about last night, except for the quitting part. That was fun."

"Whitney said you threatened Lionel Mabry, too."

"Threatened him? All I did was rattle off a series of large, ungainly objects I wanted to insert into a particular orifice. I'm sure Lionel was shocked, but I doubt he actually feared for his life."

"You might be able to take your resignation back, under the circumstances."

"I don't want to. Better to leave now than wait until Lionel forces me out. The *Washington Post* has been flirting with me, maybe I can consummate the deal with them before word leaks out about my protégé's spectacular fall. I wouldn't be a managing editor, but I'd still be moving up, and on."

Colleen's face was streaked with make-up, her black hair still had traces of dipping sauce on the ends, and her red wool dress was so creased and stained that it was beyond the help of any dry cleaner. Yet she looked happy, as if giving up the fight for her job was a relief. She had been so lost inside protecting her position that she had lost sight of her other options. It was like watching a blind person recovering her sight.

"I guess I'll head on home."

"People are going to think you had a much more interesting night than you did," Colleen said, gesturing at Tess's Saturday night date garb. "Hey—did I say anything when I was out last night?"

"No, except for several exhortations for me to fuck myself."

"Did I . . . ask for anyone?"

"Whitney said you asked to speak to me, but you were beyond speaking when I showed up." Tess picked up the empty half-and-half container, shaking it in front of Colleen before pitching it into the trash. "But a black coffee drinker who keeps a carton of this around obviously has someone in her life."

"Could be for cooking," Colleen ventured.

"Sure, it makes a great sauce for microwave popcorn."

Colleen narrowed her eyes at Tess. "You are a pretty good little detective—even if you never did figure out who put that story in the newspaper."

"Everyone assumes Rosita did it."

"I *know* she didn't."

"How can you be so sure?"

Colleen opened the freezer and pulled out a fresh pack of cigarettes, bending over a burner on her gas stove to light one. A crack addict couldn't have looked much more blissed out at first puff.

"Because I did." Another drag, another little orgasmic sigh. But she obviously enjoyed Tess's dismay even more than she enjoyed the nicotine.

"You're the managing editor, why would you have to stoop to such a cheap trick? You call the shots down there."

"You'd think so, wouldn't you? But Five-Four wanted to kill the story, and Lionel was willing to do what was necessary to make Five-Four happy. They thought it was bad PR if we derailed the deal. Five-Four actually said as much to me. *'We don't want to be a bad corporate citizen.'* Total Chamber of Commerce mentality. And Sterling was no help, he was such a sanctimonious shit about the whole thing. *'Don't you believe in redemption, Colleen? Don't you believe men can change?'* As a matter of fact, I don't. Look, I'm sorry Wink offed himself, but we did the right thing. The people have—"

"Please don't say 'right to know,' or it might be my turn to vomit."

"Well, they do," Colleen said defensively. "The tax-payers were going to end up paying for this, they always do. Jesus, how many more sports teams is this town going to crawl into bed with? Doing the wave while Baltimore burns. As if four-dollar hot dogs sold by someone making three-fifty an hour could save the local economy."

Tess wasn't really listening to Colleen. Her mind was back at the *Blight,* at Dorie Starnes's elbow as she led Tess through the process, showing her how the trickery had been accomplished. *The story was overset, so the last five lines had to be cut.* And then there was Leslie Brainerd, complaining peevishly about his editor. "He cut it from the bottom."

Of course.

"I should have known it was an editor from the beginning. You bit the story from the bottom to make it fit. No reporter would do that to his own copy, not even Rosita.

And you kept trying to fire me because you were worried I might figure it out if I stayed around long enough.''

Colleen suddenly wasn't so chummy. ''That's a cute line of reasoning, but it won't prove anything, and I'll say you're a liar if you tell anyone. Besides, there's a confidentiality clause, remember?''

''That can't keep me from going to Sterling, or Lionel Mabry.''

''Lionel won't care—he just got two troublesome females off his staff for the price of one.'' Tess hadn't thought about that. Could Lionel be even more devious than she suspected? ''As for Sterling, he'll be too busy moving into my office to worry about how it happened.''

Colleen sipped her coffee, obviously quite pleased with herself. This had not been an accidental confession in a moment of weakness and vulnerability, Tess realized. Nor had it been a secret gnawing away at her. Colleen just wanted the last word, a final triumph over Tess.

''Don't you even feel guilty that your do-it-yourself Page One indirectly ended Rosita's career, while you'll be able to bounce back without a mark?''

Colleen laughed. ''If I had any talent for self-reflection, I would have quit this business long ago.''

There was one person who *would* care. Two, possibly— Tess felt close enough to Sterling to know he would be interested in the truth, even if he couldn't change anything that had happened. But it didn't seem particularly urgent that she tell him. He was a smart man. He probably knew how ruthless Colleen was, and how shrewd Lionel was, if not every specific detail of their various manipulations.

But there was someone else who really needed to know, or wanted to, someone she could tell without breaching the confidentiality clause. Tess allowed herself a catnap, then drove to the *Beacon-Light's* offices. Her pass was still good, although it didn't matter, as the security system was on the fritz again. The security guard had simply left the door propped open, then disappeared.

Even on a Sunday morning, system manager Dorie Starnes was in her office, tapping away.

"You want something?" she asked, refusing to look up from the monitor. "I thought your work was done here. I've already cleaned out your computer files."

"It wasn't Rosita who pulled off the computer stunt that got the Wink story in the paper. Colleen Reganhart did it. She told me so herself, then told me she'd never admit it to anyone else. She's planning to leave here for another job, so I guess she figures she doesn't have anything to lose."

"Really?" The tempo of Dorie's tapping changed. It was more frenzied now, more purposeful. "Oh dear. I just accidentally erased what appeared to be Colleen Reganhart's résumé from her personal directory. And there goes her computer rolodex. Dear me. I do hope she had back-ups, but I have a feeling she never heeded all my warnings about securing files. Aw, wouldn't you know? I printed out all her messages by mistake, including some from Guy Whitman. 'Doggie style?' I don't know what that could be about. Oh, and I printed their messages out on every darn printer in the building, too. They'll probably get mixed up in the daily budgets." She shook her head in mock disappointment. "Dorie, Dorie, Dorie, you are such a butterfingers."

So Whitman was Mr. Half-and-Half. "How long have they been having an affair?"

"Off and on since she came here. Every now and then, she catches him sniffing around someone else and they break up in a flurry of e-mail. But he always comes back. He has to—she's the boss."

"Was he sleeping with Rosita, too? She alluded to some impropriety when they fired her, and Colleen assumed it was Whitman."

"What do you think I do, spend my entire day spying on people?"

"Exactly. Especially if you suspect someone of messing

around with your precious system. I bet you turned Rosita's files inside out, looking for clues."

"Touché." Dorie's pronunciation was flawless this time. "But if Rosita was carrying on with Guy, she didn't leave a trail. She was pretty cagey all around, I admit. I erased her electronic files after they fired her Friday. They were indecipherable—no names, no phone numbers. I couldn't make heads or tails of 'em. And there's nothing to retrieve from the hard drive, not that I can find."

"I guess when you're making it up, it's better to keep things a little vague. Are there still copies of her notes in the system?"

"Our procedures clearly state that stuff goes to the trash. It's long gone. Why would you want to see them, anyway?"

"Curious, I guess. I'd like to know if she really did have any leads on Wink's death, or if she was backpedaling to save her job."

Dorie reached into the collar of her Ravens sweatshirt and pulled out a long chain with a small key on the end, which she used to unlock the bottom file cabinet. Tess glimpsed dozens of manila folders, bursting with documents. Dorie pulled one out, then slammed the drawer shut.

"I made printouts," she said. "Force of habit. If they ever come for me, I'll know how to keep my job."

"I didn't know they taught blackmail at Merganthaler Vo-Tech."

"Let's just say I acquired some real-life skills that I wouldn't trade for a Harvard MBA."

Tess handed Dorie one of her business cards. "Let's keep in touch. I have a feeling you might have skills that might come in handy."

Dorie scanned the card into her computer, then tore it into fourths and dropped it in the wastebasket.

"Paper is so dangerous," she explained.

Chapter 27

∾∾∾

Rosita's notes were virtually indecipherable. She had assigned numbers to people—Wink was obviously "#1," the rest a toss-up, although "#2" was someone close to him, someone who, judging from Rosita's notes, she suspected of killing him. And she had made a plausible case for homicide, arranging and rearranging the known facts of the case until a scenario emerged: Wink, drunk and then drugged by someone he knew, had been placed in the car when he passed out. The problem was, Rosita had made an even more plausible case for herself as a pathological liar. How could Tess trust anything she said, even in her private, coded notes?

"Garage door locked," Rosita had written. "But was door from garage to mud room locked? If number 2 had dragged number 1 to car from house, number 2 could have left through house. Ask cops about drag marks. Burglar alarm on? Ask number 3 who has keys to house. Ask the M.E. if it's possible to know whether number 1 was unconscious before carbon monoxide kicked in. Check enrollment records."

Enrollment records? Rosita had lost her completely. But perhaps Rosita was lost, too, for she hadn't been able to take these electronic files with her when she left. If Tess offered her the printouts, would she break the code in exchange? It was worth a try. If Rosita was working on something legitimate, it would be nice to pass the information along to Feeney as a peace offering, even if neither of them had started the war between them. Perhaps it was time for another surprise visit to Rosita's.

Cutting through downtown and heading uptown on Charles Street, she noticed people streaming out of churches, palm fronds in hand. How could it be Palm Sunday beneath these leaden skies? A lot of Easter hats and outfits were going to be wasted if the weather didn't improve markedly over the next week. No matter the weather, it was a torturous season for Tess. April meant the return of rowing, and it was always a struggle to readjust to a 5:30 A.M. alarm, especially after daylight savings stole yet another hour. Worse, this time of year meant putting in appearances at both the Monaghans' Easter Sunday dinner and the Weinsteins' Seder, with little time for recovery in between. April was the cruelest month.

At Rosita's apartment building, it was no trick to once again blend in with a group of residents, allowing them to carry her through the security door and into the elevator. On the eighteenth floor, she knocked—politely at first, then a sharp rap, and finally an out-and-out pounding. No response. Tess tried the door and it swung open. Wonderful. Maybe Rosita was down in the basement laundry room, or making a quick run for Sunday papers at the deli across the street. She'd just take a quick look around.

The apartment hadn't changed, with the exception of a pizza box and an empty Chardonnay bottle on the kitchen counter. Same impersonal air, same Kit-Kat Klock keeping time. Tess looked around, her gaze settling again on the pizza box. She couldn't help herself—she loved cold pizza and she hadn't eaten anything since the Mint Milanos at Colleen's apartment. She looked at the side of the box, trying to figure out which pizzeria it had come from, then flicked open the grease-spotted lid. Sausage, her favorite. She picked off one of the nubbly pieces, popped it in her mouth. Yech. Turkey sausage. What an aberration. What an oxymoron—healthful sausage, low-fat fat. You should do things full out, Tess always reasoned. Hedging, trying to have it both ways, was what got you into trouble. She'd have to share this bit of wisdom with Rosita.

The porridge segment of her Goldilocks impersonation concluded, she began prowling around the small apartment, looking for the box of files Rosita had carried home on Friday. Maybe the key to her notes was there. She checked the hall closet, looked beneath the sagging springs of the sofa, opened kitchen cabinets. The apartment was eerily quiet, the only sound coming from the swinging tail of the Kit-Kat Klock, moving back and forth in the same cadence as its wide eyes. Funny, Rosita didn't have a computer— that seemed unthinkable for someone of her age and profession. Perhaps she had set up an office in a corner of her bedroom.

A blast of cold air surprised Tess when she opened the bedroom door. The sliding door to the tiny balcony was open, its gauzy curtains blown parallel to the floor in the stiff wind. Tess walked over to shut the door, then stepped outside instead, an acrid taste in her mouth.

Some people experience dread as a sensation that their stomachs are falling twenty stories; others feel a humming-bird-fast pulse flapping high in their chests. For Tess, fear and anxiety always had the flavor of something bitter, like a shriveled peanut in a bag of fresh roasted ones. Or a piece of turkey sausage, when you were expecting the real thing.

She leaned over the balcony, not sure what she would see from this height, not sure what she was looking for. Everything was still so brown and lifeless, even the over-grown brush in the gully that ran behind the apartment house. The only color was from the hundreds of blue plastic grocery bags caught on the dried vines, like puffy wild-flowers. And a flash of white surrounded by beige, one shade lighter than the earth.

When the coroner pulled Rosita Ruiz from the gully, she was wearing bicycle shorts and the same mermaid T-shirt she had worn the last time Tess had visited her. *La Sirena.* Well, La Sirena had sung her last song.

*   *   *

Tess called Sterling from Rosita's apartment and he arrived while the two homicide detectives were still questioning her. The detectives were politely solicitous of Tess, who looked a little green at the edges, but she could tell they had no real interest in considering Rosita's death a homicide, not if it meant they had to consider Wink's death a homicide, too. That would involve admitting fault, prolonging a case the county cops were ready to close as soon as the tox screens came in. If there was an angry lover or ex-lover, someone with a personal grudge against Miss Ruiz—fine, they were all ears. But it was inconceivable to them that Rosita had been thrown off the balcony by Wink's killer, because it was inconceivable to them that Wink had a killer.

"That's kind of far-fetched, Miss Monaghan, especially when you consider Miss Ruiz was fired on Friday," said Detective Tull, a slight, short man with remarkably tiny feet and an acne-scarred face. The scars gave his handsome face a touching vulnerability. He must be used for the remorseful ones, Tess thought, the tearful women who yearned to confess.

"You see, Miss Monaghan, it makes more sense if she jumped—especially when you see the empty bottle of white wine. Alcohol is a depressant and she was probably plenty depressed, right? She drinks, she eats a little pizza, she thinks about her life, and she steps out on her balcony, then steps out into space. The medical examiner will look for signs of a struggle—skin beneath her fingernails, scratches on her body that might tell us more about how she fell. But everything here is saying suicide. A footstool is pushed up next to the balcony, so she could climb up to the railing. The open balcony door. No one reported hearing a scream last night or early this morning, and no one saw anyone going into her apartment last night."

"No one here ever sees anyone," Tess protested. "Besides, she was a writer, or thought of herself as one. She would have left a note."

"Notes are less common than you think. A whole bottle of wine is considerable when you're as small as she is and you haven't eaten very much—there are only two slices of pizza gone. My guess is the M.E. is going to find she was legally intoxicated." Tull turned to Sterling. "Do you know how to find the next of kin? We'll have to notify them."

"We should have a contact number down at the paper."

Tull stood to leave. His partner, a tall, graceful black man who looked like a dancer, had been standing all along, leaning against the kitchen counter as if he were just passing through.

"You know, normally we don't give the victim's name to the press until we've made that call," Tull said. "We can't keep you from printing what you know, but it would be better if you waited until we talk to her parents."

"Under these circumstances, there won't be a story. We don't write about suicides unless they're somehow public, or involve public figures."

"Well, for now, it's not officially a suicide." Tull looked at Tess, and she knew he was humoring her. "The M.E. will make the ruling on that. We're going to canvass the building, see if anyone heard anything or saw anything. You can sit here for a while, Miss Monaghan, if you don't feel up to driving just yet."

Tess smiled wanly at Tull. She did feel light-headed. Rosita's broken body had looked disturbingly peaceful and composed, sleeping on its bier of brambles and blue grocery bags. If there was an argument to be made for suicide, it was the strange serenity in her face, more relaxed in death than it had ever been in life.

As soon as the detectives left, Sterling got up and came back with a glass of water and two ibuprofen capsules from Rosita's medicine cabinet.

"I don't know what good these will do, but I can't help wanting to do something for you," he said. "You've had a pretty rough day."

To say nothing of a rough night. She thought of telling him about her conversation with Colleen Reganhart, but it didn't seem particularly important now. Her brain was stuck in a single gear, endlessly revving. She looked around the apartment—the strafing glance of the Kit-Kat Klock, the disappearing cowboy poster, the pizza box on the counter, the empty wine bottle, the piles of books and papers.

"Pizza!"

Sterling looked startled at her sudden interest in food. "Sure. We can go get pizza if you like."

"No, it's the pizza *box*. There's no delivery slip on it. When you order a pizza to be delivered, there a piece of paper on the box—trust me, this is one of my fields of expertise. Rosita was barefoot, in shorts and a T-shirt. Someone brought this pizza to her, Jack—used it to get in the door downstairs, so they wouldn't look suspicious."

"And then sat down, shared a couple of pieces with her and tossed her off the balcony?" Sterling shook his head. "I hate to side with the detectives on this, Tess, but that's nonsensical. She could have gone out and gotten the pizza, then changed."

"Okay, so where's the box, the box of notebooks and personal artifacts she carried home from work? It's not here, so someone must have taken it. And why would someone take it? Because her notes held the key to Wink's murder."

Sterling made the same walk-through of the apartment she had already made, opening drawers and closet doors, looking under the sofa's sagging springs. Then he picked up the pizza box, turning it slowly in his hands, as if the delivery slip still might show up.

"I'll go get Detective Tull," he said at last.

Sterling went back to the office to wait for Detective Tull's call. Tess went home and tried to sleep, but she was too restless and ended up at the Brass Elephant. Although anxious to hear what the police had found, she could never sit in the newsroom, where she knew the skeleton staff of Sunday reporters would be wandering around, stunned and bewildered. Journalists had no language for their own tragedies. When it was one of their own, they could not make grim jokes or callow rationalizations, or call up relatives with that age-old assurance: *it might be cathartic for them to speak of it.* And they could not reduce someone they had actually known to the series of meaningless catch-phrases used for strangers. *Smart but down-to-earth. Ambitious but caring. A quiet person who kept to himself*—no, that was the code reserved for demented loners. At any rate, by any measure, Rosita Ruiz was not a good death.

It was almost 8 o'clock when Feeney found Tess, an empty plate of tortellini in front of her. She had no memory of eating it. She could, however, remember martinis 1 and 2, and she was now on martini 3, using the discarded toothpicks to trace figures in the linen tablecloth. Curvy number 2s, which disappeared in a few moments, like the magnetic lines on those "magic" drawing boards you had as a kid.

"First things first," Feeney said. "Your uncle's awake."

"And?" Her heart sky-rocketed, then plummeted to earth. Feeney was playing good news–bad news with her.

"That's all I know. Kitty called the paper, looking for you. Said Spike's awake. His speech is a little slurry and his right side doesn't have much feeling, but he's awake. Keeps talking about the years, Kitty said."

"The ears," Tess corrected absently. "Now what about Rosita?"

"The box of notes was in the trunk of her car, and there's nothing in them, not of any importance. And there was pizza in Rosita's stomach."

"She was killed, Feeney, I know she was. By number two."

"Number two?"

"I saw files she had in the computer—don't ask me how, I won't tell you. But there was someone, someone she called number two. She thought this person killed Wink, although her notes didn't provide a motive."

"So who is number two?"

"I haven't a clue. It could be Lea—she's wife number

two, although the notes suggest she's number three. Or his first wife—if Wink is number one, there's no reason Linda couldn't be number two. If Wink had threatened to cut off her alimony because he needed to be more liquid . . . and there was something about enrollment records, and Wink and Linda were in school together after all—''

Feeney placed his hand over Tess's right hand, the one with the toothpick. Without realizing it, she had started drawing numbers again as she spoke.

''She killed herself, Tess. It's not your fault, but you'll probably always think it was.''

''I wouldn't say Rosita was murdered just because I feel guilty.''

''Why not? I sure wanted to think someone killed Wink. I was the one who encouraged Rosita to see if someone might have knocked him out with booze, then put him in the car. But how do you convince someone to drink himself into a coma, Tess? And if someone killed him, why would the murderer then call my pager and punch in Wink's number?''

''You interviewed all these people for the story, they all had your pager number. Besides, the tox screens aren't back yet. If someone slipped him some kind of drug—I've heard about this tranquilizer from Mexico, they call it the date-rape drug—the combination could have made him lose consciousness. Or any strong sedative. He wasn't a big guy, it wouldn't take much.''

Feeney's face was unbearably kind as he squeezed her hand.

''Tess, I know. I know what it's like to be an indirect agent in someone's death. I know what it's like to be the one to find him—or her. I also know all the conspiracy theories in the world aren't going to change anything. You're going to need help with this. Maybe professional help, but help from your friends as well. Don't make the mistake I did, pushing people away.''

''I don't have many people to push away right now. I

broke up with Crow, and now Whitney and I are kind of on the outs.''

"She told me. She called me today and made a clean breast of things. Whatever you said to her last night, it really hit home. But Whitney's not a bad person, she's just self-centered. She got lost inside her desire for something and she made a bad mistake, a mistake she's learned from.'' Feeney took a piece of bread from the basket on the table and swiped it through the rich sauce she had left behind. "Rosemary, that's for remembrance. You know, she's jealous of you.''

Tess meant to give a soft, derisive snort, but the martinis had robbed her of any modulation, and the noise she made sounded more like an old man blowing his nose. "Right.''

"You're a free spirit, while Whitney is weighed down by so many things. Her family's name, her money, everyone's expectations for her. She hasn't learned to live her life for herself yet. Maybe now she will.''

The bartender came over and Tess asked for a coffee. Feeney asked for a beer and helped himself to another piece of bread. "I don't know if I should tell you this, but there's a sad little coda to Rosita's story. She's *not* Rosita Ruiz.''

"Huh?''

"Part of the reason it took so long for Detective Tull to call back tonight is that the contact number in Rosita's file was for some family called Rodrigue in New Bedford, Mass. They kept insisting they had never heard of a Rosita Ruiz from Boston, although they did have a daughter named Rosemary, about the same age, working on the copy desk in Baltimore. She couldn't be a writer, they said, because she never had any stories to show them. I had to get on the computer to figure it out. The Social Security numbers matched—the one assigned to Rosemary Rodrigue had started showing up as Rosita Ruiz's number about two years ago, right after college graduation. But there was another Rosita Ruiz from Boston University—different Social Security number, now in a training program at some New York bank. Turns out Rosita—Rosemary—changed her name legally after graduation to match that of a former classmate, a Latina with stellar grades. Then, when employers checked her college record, it matched. That explains why she was inconsistent sometimes—she kept getting her two identities confused.''

A long-forgotten detail managed to come to the surface in Tess's martini-stewed brain. ''Like putting on her résumé that she was a cum laude, when the real Rosita—Rosemary—was a magna?''

''Yeah, that would fit.''

''So why do it? I mean, why steal a life that's essentially a lateral move?''

''Apparently, she wanted a little of that affirmative-action action. Without a journalism degree and no real newspaper experience, she thought transforming herself into a disadvantaged Latina from Roxbury was the only way to kick-start her career.''

''If Rosita—Rosemary—had been really smart, she would have had a sex change operation and appropriated the name and résumé of some Harvard boy. She'd have gotten ahead even faster as Roger Smith, Rhodes scholar.''

''Touché, Tess. Touché.''

Funny, how words echo, then change in their echoes. Dorie had said the same thing, only hours ago. Touché-Too-Shay-Tooch-Tooooooooooch. Two. The number 2 man on Wink's ownership team, his constant sidekick. She saw him limping into the Wynkowskis' home, the apparent possessor of his own key. She felt his heavy bulk on her back. ''I just figured he took some drug, because he's such a sissy.'' Wasn't he, in the end, the one who stood to gain the most from Wink's death? Linda's lot hadn't changed a whit, and Lea had lost so much ground she was almost back in Atlantic City. With three kids to raise, she would probably fall into the arms of the first man who promised to take care of her. And there was Paul Tucci, the man who had introduced her to Wink, the man who had always stood in Wink's shadow, suddenly at the forefront and in the limelight. The soon-to-be team owner.

"Drive me home?" Tess asked Feeney. "I'll take the bus back in the morning and get my car."

"Sure." He studied her face. "Peace will come, Tess. I don't know when—I'm still waiting for it myself—but you'll feel better sooner if you accept what's really happened."

"I'm feeling better already," she said truthfully.

Chapter 28

The first thing Tess noticed when Lea Wynkowski opened her front door the next morning was that damn gold bracelet on her wrist—even though Lea was still in her robe and nightgown at 11 A.M., her brown hair sticking up in tufts all over her head. She apparently had gone from the insomnia stage of grief to the sleep-all-the-time stage, a progression of sorts.

"Tooch said I should stop talking to people, people I don't really know," she said nervously, fiddling with the bracelet.

I bet he did. "This is important, Lea. I think your husband was murdered, but I need your help to figure out why, and who did it."

Lea twisted the bracelet around her slender wrist, staring at it as if it were a crystal ball that might reveal the right answers if you turned it often enough, in just the right way.

"I don't know," she sighed. "That newspaper reporter was over here on Saturday and she said the same thing, but I haven't heard back from her."

So she didn't know Rosita—Rosemary; Tess would never get use to Rosita's real, posthumous name—was dead. The television stations, like the newspaper, didn't report a private citizen's private suicide.

"What did she tell you Saturday?"

"Not much. She thought Wink was killed, but she

needed proof. So I gave her what she wanted and Tooch was so mad when I told him. You see, I thought it was a good thing if Wink was killed—well, not a good thing, but better, and not just because we'd get the insurance money then. It would have meant he didn't leave us, you know, me and his babies. But Tooch said the reporter was a liar who wanted to make more trouble for us, which is the only reason she wanted it in the first place.''

"Wanted *what*, Lea? What did you give Rosita?"

"The yearbook, the one I showed you.'' Lea lowered her voice as if there was someone who might overhear her, although there was no evidence of anyone else in the big house. ''I cut out that one page first, the one you saw. I was the one who wrote . . . that word on it. I know I shouldn't have done it, but I hated her so. She didn't deserve all that money. But the reporter might've thought Wink had done it, like you did—so I cut it out and put it down the garbage disposal.''

Check enrollment records. Rosita's memo to herself. Schools had closed Friday for spring break, making that difficult, so she had procured the yearbook instead, using it as a shortcut to something, or somebody. But the book hadn't been in Rosita's apartment, Tess was sure of that.

"Do you know if Tooch—Mr. Tucci—went to junior high with Wink?"

"Tooch? No, he went to parochial school before Loyola—calls it his sixteen-year stint in the Catholic penitentiary. The brothers at Mount St. Joe actually beat boys back then.'' Lea's eyes were wide at this story, which must have seemed as chronologically distant to her as the Industrial Revolution. ''Can you imagine, someone hitting little boys?''

Tess could. Worse still, she could imagine what little boys could do back.

Spike was asleep when Tess arrived at the hospital for afternoon visiting hours.

"You can sit with him if you don't pester him,'' the

nurse said. "And if he comes to, don't pester him with questions. The police just about wore him out."

"Fine with me," Tess said. "I don't think he has the answers I'm looking for, anyway."

She stared outside the window, wishing for a brainstorm like the one she had the last time she stood there, staring out over the parking lot and the ambulances. The brainstorm that had gotten Rosita fired. And now Rosita was dead, because of her own brainstorm. *Check enrollment records.* Tess had gone to the Pratt library, but the usually reliable Maryland Room did not carry junior high year-books. Meanwhile, the school administration offices on North Avenue had closed for spring break along with the schools. Tess was sure if she could only locate someone to ask, she would find that Paul Tucci, despite his proud pro-claimations about parochial school education, had attended Rock Glen Junior High through eighth grade with Wink, transferring to Catholic school about the same time Wink had ended up at Montrose—right after the robbery in which the shopkeeper had died. Too bad she didn't feel comfort-able confronting Linda Wynkowski so soon after their last meeting. She might know if Tucci were #2—the second boy in that long-ago assault, but one with a well-connected father who could keep him from serving the same sentence meted out to the fatherless Wink.

When Wink's past was revealed, he must have decided that Tucci should be humiliated as well. Or perhaps he thought Tucci was the source of the stories, that Tucci had set him up in order to force him from the ownership group. It would have been easy enough for Tucci to dose Wink's drink with Percodan, or whatever he took for his still ailing knee. Even lame, Tucci was big enough to carry a slight guy like Wink to his car, hoist him into the convertible, and wait for the carbon monoxide to work.

"There's my girl." Spike's brown eyes fluttered as he came to. His speech was slurry and soft, almost as if he had no teeth, but he was awake, he would live.

Remembering the nurse's injunction, she didn't try to ask

him anything other than "How do you feel?"

"Been better."

"I found the ears."

He looked troubled. "I didn't want you to."

"Yeah, well, when I'm allowed to interrogate you, I want to know more about that."

"I'll tell you everything I told the police."

"I'm guessing that's not much."

Spike smiled, closed his eyes, and drifted back to sleep.

"Good night, Uncle Spike, I gotta go see a man about a dog. One of the human variety."

"It's not a bad theory," Sterling said cautiously that evening, as Tess paced in his office, running through the scenarios she had concocted in Spike's hospital room. She could hear the skepticism in his voice, and it hurt. She had counted on him to be the one person who wouldn't think she was crazy.

"But not a good one, right?"

Sterling wasn't a great liar. Although he tried to smile encouragingly, his eyes made it clear he thought her idea half-baked at best. Tess turned away from him and looked through the glass windows of his office, toward the newsroom. Dusk had fallen and snow was in the forecast again, so deadlines had been moved up, stealing time from the production of the paper in order to ensure its delivery. Consequently, the reporters and editors on the city desk were frenzied, gripped in their own snowstorm panic attack. It didn't help that they were trying to report on something that hadn't actually happened yet.

"You think I'm spinning my wheels, trying to prove Rosita was killed so I can absolve myself in her death," she said flatly. "You think I should have stayed at the hospital with my Uncle Spike, rather than chasing down a junior high school yearbook."

"There's just not enough solid information to go to the police with your theory yet. You'll have to wait until schools open Monday to check your hunches. And I'm not sure enrollment records are public information."

"Oh, I'd get them somehow. I have an uncle in state government who could always call in a favor. I could have them by tomorrow if I really pushed."

Sterling played with a paper clip, twisting it into a straight line, then into a triangle. "There is a way we could make things move even faster, if you're willing to be a little devious."

"Always," Tess said. "What's your plan?"

"You told me Lea cut a page out of the yearbook before she gave it to Rosita. But if Tucci has the book, he doesn't necessarily know why the page is missing."

"So?"

"Think, Tess. What was Linda's maiden name?"

"What is this, the Socratic method? Linda's maiden name was Stolley."

"How many kids fell between Stolley and Tucci in the eighth grade at Rock Glen Junior High?"

Tess visualized the page. The photos had been small, in order to accommodate five across and eight down, forty in all. Linda had been in the middle of the page. Rock Glen was a big school, there were probably plenty of eighth-graders between ST and TU. Still it was possible—plausible, even.

"So if Tucci thinks that page is hidden somewhere . . ."

"He might be interested in getting it back. And even if we're wrong about his class photo falling on that page, if we're vague enough, he might think there's another page cut from the book, which does show his photograph, in some club or something."

Tess practically held her breath as Sterling picked up his phone, asked information for the number to the Tuccis' import-export business, then dialed.

"Paul Tucci, please," he said, after what must have been eight or nine rings. "I'm sure he'll want to take this call. Tell him it's . . . someone from the yearbook committee at his old school. His *real* old school."

Now, this is a man after my own heart, Tess thought happily.

"Mr. Tucci, I have the yearbook page I think you've been looking for. No, I'm sure you know exactly what I'm talking about. I'd like to make this available to you, for a price. Why don't we meet and discuss this, sooner rather than later? At the tennis courts in Leakin Park, in an hour. Come alone, Mr. Tucci. You may rest assured, however, that I won't be alone and I won't have the page with me, not tonight. It's in a safe place." He paused, let Tucci have his say. "Tonight, Mr. Tucci. No second chances."

He hung up the phone and Tess could tell he was pleased with himself.

"I'll have Lionel call Detective Tull and tell him what we're up to," he said. "But not until the last possible minute."

"And Feeney," Tess said. "You should alert him, so he can be in on the story from the first."

"No, I'm afraid the police would frown on that. Besides, how would you explain it to Tucci? Feeney will have plenty of time to follow the story. After all, I'm sure at least two of the primary sources will cooperate. Now let me go tell Lionel what we're up to, and give him Detective Tull's number."

"Sure," Tess said, studying her wrist the way Lea Wynkowski had, although she had no golden bracelet to twist. It didn't seem right for Feeney to miss out on this. As soon as Sterling was out of sight, she sat down at his computer, signed on, and sent Feeney a message:

This is Tess typing. Leakin Park in 30 minutes for the story of your life. SERIOUSLY!!!!!!!!

The message went through, indicating Feeney's computer at the courthouse was on, but he didn't reply. Maybe there was time to page him—

"Hacking again? I hope you're not sending messages out under my user name," Sterling said from the door. His voice was sharp, but he laughed when she jumped.

"N-no, no messages at all. I was checking the forecast, seeing how bad it's not going to be."

"Just teasing you. Look, Lionel thinks our plan is a little unorthodox, but he's going to back us up. Says he'll call the police at the appointed hour. Now, are you a McDonald's woman, or a Burger King loyalist?"

"Roy Rogers, pardner."

Only a few light flakes had started falling when they pulled into the gravel parking lot off Windsor Mill Road, but that hadn't kept other drivers from acting as if a full-scale blizzard was laying siege to the city. Roy Rogers had run out of buns—plenty of roast beef and ground beef patties, just no buns to put them on—and Tess had ended up making do with potato salad, while Sterling had settled for baked beans. It wasn't a half-bad dinner, but her stomach was doing nervous flip-flops, wondering how angry Sterling would be when Feeney showed up. *If* Feeney showed up—she couldn't be sure he had seen her message.

"Let's have our picnic in the snow," Tess said, getting out and then climbing up on the trunk of Sterling's car, a new-looking Honda Accord. She was conscious of testing him, checking to see if he was fussy about his car. She considered that a bad sign in a man.

Sterling rummaged through the glove compartment, then perched next to her on the trunk.

"Something to warm you up?" he asked, holding out a small bottle of amber-colored whiskey and a pewter Jefferson cup, the collapsible kind that came in fancy picnic baskets. She and Whitney had used them and a thermos to smuggle mint juleps into the Hunt Cup one year.

"You drive around with this in your car? I'm shocked, Mr. Sterling, shocked."

"You've heard of the old newspaper editor with a bottle in his desk? Well, I have bottles secreted *everywhere*. My nod to tradition."

Tess laughed, reaching for the bottle and cup, silver in

the moonlight. *Make new friends, but keep the old.* Sterling was rubbing his wrist the way he did because of his bouts with carpal tunnel. For some reason, it reminded her of Lea and the way she touched her bracelet, as if it were an amulet that could protect her from harm. *One is silver, but the other's gold. You're golden, Wink.* So Wink had been gold and Tucci was silver. Well, maybe silver plate. It was a stretch to see him as sterling.

Sterling. He was a good guy. She felt guilty now about ignoring his instructions. What would he say if Feeney did show up? "Look, about Feeney—"

Sterling tapped the cell phone he kept in his breast pocket, beneath his camel's hair coat. "Don't worry, I won't let him miss the big story. I always put the paper first."

Always? Abruptly, Tess dropped the cup and bottle, spilling the drink in her lap while the bottle skittered under the Honda, spilling out the rest of the bourbon before Sterling could retrieve it.

"Dammit," he said angrily, then softened his tone. "I'm sorry, it's just that I tore the knee of my pants leg crawling around on this gravel. And I admit, I was hoping for a little of this, too."

"I guess I'm a little nervous. My hands are shaking."

"Don't worry. I'll take care of you." He opened up his arms as if to embrace her.

"How do you mean that, exactly?"

Sterling looked at her strangely.

"Never mind." She glanced back at the road to see if there was any traffic—deserted, but there was an apartment complex on the other side, not even 100 yards away.

"You know, I bet he's not coming," she said. "If he's not here in fifteen minutes, let's bag this meeting and try it again tomorrow. What do you say?"

"You are a smart girl," Sterling said. He reached out and caressed her cheek with his gloved hand, then leaned closer, as if to kiss her.

"Look, Sterling—" she began. He punched her so hard

in the stomach she bent double and fell to the ground, the gravel tearing and scraping her palms.

"Jesus." She wasn't sure if she had spoken out loud, or only cried out in her mind. She tried to rise to all fours, but Sterling kicked her in the ribs, flattening her. On the proper foot, a Bass Weejun could feel like a blackjack.

"But—I—didn't—drink," she panted. And if you didn't drink the drug-laden drink, you didn't pass out, and if you didn't pass out, Jack Sterling couldn't put you in a running car or toss you from a balcony, then page his star reporter. She had figured that much out. So why was she down on the ground, feeling as if there were small fires burning all over her body—in her knees, on her palms, in her side, on her face?

"The Jack Daniels did have a little something in it, to slow you down, but three suicides would have been over-kill—if you'll forgive the expression," Sterling said, straddling her, digging his heels into her waist as if she were a horse he was trying to break.

"However, it *is* plausible you'd be found murdered, Tess. After all, you had that nasty run-in with those kidnappers. It was even written up in the paper, remember? I told you how worried I was that one might come back. I mentioned my fears to others, too—Feeney, Whitney, even Lionel. Lionel couldn't help noticing how fond I was becoming of you." He kicked her again in the ribs, then bent down and grabbed the collar of her coat, jerking her head back so hard she thought she might have whiplash.

Tess could not believe how quickly he moved, how expertly. Then she thought about the West Baltimore shopkeeper, his heart giving way after a boy, a boy who grew up to be this man, whipped a pistol back and forth across his face. *Wink could never hurt anyone,* Lea had cried. *He never hit me back,* Linda had sneered. No, Wink's great shame was that he couldn't hurt anyone, although he could stand by with the best of them and watch a man die.

"You were Wink's accomplice," she said. Her rib, cracked or broken, made it hard to talk. She felt as if she had tumbled down a long flight of stairs and was still falling. "*You're* the one on the yearbook page. If I had seen it again, I would have known you."

"Actually, I'm on the facing page. And Raymond Sterling was so fat, with such long hair hanging in his face, you probably wouldn't have recognized him. But I couldn't take that chance."

"Raymond?" If she hadn't been in so much pain, she might have laughed.

"Raymond John Sterling. I started using my middle name after my parents sent me to military school in Indiana. That was the deal my father cut with the judge—military school instead of Montrose. After all, I'd never been in trouble before. Wink was the bad boy. Wink was even bad at being bad—the only time I ever got caught was when I was with Wink. That's the real difference between bad boys and good boys, you see. Bad boys get caught."

She tried to rise again and he pushed her down by stomping on her back with his foot, then squatted over her. His mouth was close to her ear, his voice the soft, encouraging voice of the man she thought she knew. "I have to hit you a few times, Tess, to make it look realistic. Just a few more taps, then I'll shoot you, I promise. One quick, clean shot in the head, okay?"

He patted her cheek, then slapped her so hard that her teeth cut the inside of her mouth and blood began dribbling down her face. It was a strange sensation, wet, cold, and hot all mingled on her face.

"Silver and gold," she panted, spitting blood with each word. "Sterling and Wink."

"Yeah, that's me," he replied, not realizing she was still fitting the pieces together. The cell phone in his pocket, and the convenient call to Feeney the night of Wink's death, making sure the *Blight* got the story. The edge in his voice, when he'd found her at his computer tonight. He had spoken that roughly to her only once before—the day she'd confessed she had been to see Linda Wynkowski. Turkey sausage on Rosita's pizza, his constant quest for low-fat food. Little things, but they had come together in one moment of perfect clarity. If only she could have had that moment in a less deserted, better-lighted place.

Sterling brought a sleek, almost elegant gun out of the pocket of his coat. Even Tess, with her complete ignorance of firearms, knew it was exactly the sort of weapon the greyhound gang would have used on her. Sterling was careful, he thought things out.

"Rosita?" she asked. God help her, but she really wanted to know.

"She jumped," he said. "Honestly. We had been . . . together for a while, after I first came to the paper. Consenting adults, a no-fault break-up. But she tried to use that to get her job back, said she'd go to Lionel and complain I had harrassed her. Another blackmailer, like Wink. She crawled out on the balcony railing, said she would jump if I didn't get her reinstated. As if I could, after all she had done."

After all she *had done?*

"All I want to do is get on with my life," he said, almost as if he expected some sympathy. "That's all I've ever wanted."

High beams from an oncoming car swept across the parking lot and Sterling dropped his left hand to his side, so the gun was out of view. Feeney, Tess thought, at once hopeful and despairing. Sterling would simply kill him, too.

But the car that idled fifty feet away was an expensive utility vehicle, something Feeney wouldn't be caught dead driving. Tess heard its door open and slam, heard a key clicking in a lock, a trunk's springs yawning.

"Fancy meeting you two here." It was Whitney's voice, as clear and obnoxiously self-assured as if they'd met at some restaurant or museum.

"Gun," Tess said, or tried to say. Her nose was bleeding and her speech was getting gummy and thick. Sterling backed away until his car was between him and Whitney. Tess heard a shot, then a muffled sound of surprise. Jesus, he had killed her. She almost wished she could live long enough to see how Sterling was going to arrange this "accident." *College Roomies in Bizarre Murder-Suicide in Leakin Park/Longtime Relationship Suspected.* Both their mothers would die.

A second shot, much louder than the first. Tess still couldn't see anything—Whitney's lights must be on bright, they were so blinding. How had Sterling been able to aim? He hadn't. Sterling staggered forward, his right hand pressed to his shoulder, where a shiny mass, purple-black in the headlights, was spilling across his camel's hair coat. He dropped his gun and fell forward.

"That's the problem with hunting rifles," Whitney said, walking toward Sterling, who had joined Tess in the gravel. "They rip the shit out of things at this range. You probably won't have a tendon left in that shoulder, Sterling. No more squash for you."

Sterling didn't give up easily. He tried to crawl toward his weapon, reaching for it with his right hand. But he was left-handed, and his injury made him clumsy and slow.

"Oh, Sterling, give me a break." Whitney cracked the rifle hard against his injured arm, and he screamed again, a pathetic, high-pitched sound. For good measure, or perhaps for the sheer hell of it, Whitney took the butt of the rifle and brought it down hard on Sterling's nose, breaking it with a fearsome crack almost as loud as the gunshots.

"It's very important that you stay still now," she told him, as if he were a small child and she his babysitter. "I've had enough from you."

The passenger side door of Whitney's Jeep opened then. Tess, still at ground level, saw a pair of sockless ankles, red and chafed in the wintry night. It was the most beautiful sight she had ever seen.

"I called 911 on the car phone," Feeney said. "I told them we're going to need an ambulance."

"Feeney," Tess said. "Whitney?" She wondered if she was ever going to speak in complete sentences again, or even lift her arms over her head. But Feeney understood what she was trying to ask.

"When I got the message from you, I thought I could get Whitney to give me a ride in her four-wheel drive, maybe play peacemaker between the two of you and get my big story at the same time. It never occurred to me Whitney's hunting rifle would come in even handier than her Jeep Cherokee."

"You never know when you're going to need a little protection." Whitney raised an eyebrow at Tess, keeping her rifle trained on Sterling. "I believe I tried to tell you that once, back in the sub shop."

Feeney picked up Sterling's gun and held it in his palm a little tentatively, as if it might bite him. Then he pointed it at his boss, now almost unconscious from the loss of blood.

"I've waited my whole life to hold a gun on an editor," he said. "I thought it would feel better than this."

"Speak for yourself," Whitney said, but her voice was shaking.

Chapter 29

〜〜〜

On the first Friday in May, Spike left the hospital in a wheelchair. It wasn't altogether for show. Despite weeks of therapy, he still dragged his right leg, but his speech was clear now, or as clear as it had ever been, and his long-term memory no longer seemed like a piece of Alpine Swiss, the lacy stuff that was more holes than cheese. He could walk with a cane, but it was laborious and he didn't see any reason to pass up one last free ride. Especially, Tess suspected, when he saw the pretty young nurse who was to push him to the curb.

"You know, it was coincidental enough, you coming out of your coma just in time to get some action on the NCAA Final Four," she said, once they were settled in his car and heading to The Point. Tommy was driving Spike's rusting Lincoln coupe, so she could turn around in the passenger seat and study her uncle, regal and serene in the backseat. "But when your hospital discharge date happens to fall on the day before the Kentucky Derby, I *know* something's up."

"You saying I faked my coma 'til Tommy came and told me about how those guys who beat me so bad got themselves arrested, thanks to you?" Spike asked. "You think your old uncle could fool a whole staff of doctors and nurses, with their collitch educations? Then why would I stay so long, after I knew you was fine?"

275

"No, but . . . I mean—" Tess looked at Tommy, grinning as he perched precariously on the edge of the seat so he could reach the pedals with the toes of his zippered ankle boots. She looked back at Spike, studying the fast food joints and grimy stores along Caton Avenue as if they were the eighth wonders of the world. Perhaps they were to him. His recovery had bordered on the miraculous, doctors said, and Spike seemed to have a heightened appreciation of everything around him.

She was resigned to never knowing the whole story. Was Jimmy Parlez a real person, or some red herring Tommy had tossed out to distract her? Had Tommy been in on everything from the beginning, or had Spike, knowing how weak he was, made sure he was equally ignorant? Oh, well, some aspects of Spike's life had to remain mysterious, in part to protect the family from its seamier side, and in part because Spike liked being mysterious.

At The Point, Tommy pulled a small, brown-wrapped package out of the safe and handed it to Tess, while Spike settled on one of the vinyl padded chairs closest to the television.

"V is for videotape," Tess said, turning it over in her hands. "I guess my Botticelli buddy was playing fair and square, after all."

"Bottle of what?" Tommy asked.

"Never mind, it's too complicated to explain."

"Put it in the VCR under the bar TV," Spike said. Then, almost as an afterthought: "You eat breakfast today?"

"Of course."

"You'll wish you hadn't."

The video was of poor quality, a grainy black-and-white with the date and time in the lower right corner. But the images were clear enough—a large wooden fence in an oval shape, the suggestion of meadows on either side, stands of evergreens in the distance, all blurry as an Impressionist painting.

"What is this? What does it have to do with the ears?"

"It's a private 'hunting' club in Cecil County."

"I've never heard of such a thing."

Spike gave her a look, as if he expected more of her. "But you've heard of stocked ponds, for fishermen? Well, these are kinda the same thing. Rich guys come from all over the state—Washington and Philadelphia, even—hunt birds for sport. You ask me, ain't a sport if you can't bet on it, but they pay plenty for the privilege of bringing home a few mangled birdie bodies."

"Is it legal?"

"Yeah, if you're just shooting up ducks and pheasants. The legislature seen to that, year in and year out. But these guys take it a step further. Got a little gambling room on the side—poker, blackjack, roulette. I got no problem with them being enterprising. I've even played a few hands there myself, when I found myself in the neighborhood. But this year they added a new attraction. That's what you're about to see."

Tess studied the television. Even without the date, she would have known this video was shot in March—the scudding clouds, the muddy ground with patches of ice. It seemed so long ago.

"Fifteen seconds to post," Spike intoned. Tommy held his fist to his mouth, making a mock trumpet call with real spit. *"Dew-dew-do-do-do-do-do-do-do-do-do-deeeeeeeeew."*

A tiny object zipped across the railing and a blurry pack surged into the camera's view, trailing it. Tess needed a moment to realize they were greyhounds, not horses, and that the object of their frenzied desire was a mechanized rabbit.

"Illegal greyhound races? Why would anyone go to the trouble of setting those up?"

"Wait," Spike said grimly.

The dogs disappeared on the far side of the track, and Spike provided a fake call while they were off-screen. "And as they move past the second post, it's Down on His Luck in the lead, with Bum Steer hard on his flank. Down on His Luck. Bum Steer. Down on His Luck. Bum Steer.

Now Dead Last is making a move on the outside and *down* the stretch they come.''

The dogs swung back into view and Spike, using the VCR remote control, switched to slow-motion. The picture was a little clearer at this speed and Tess could see the dogs straining toward the finish, almost a frame at a time, like an animated cartoon reduced to its individual cels. The dogs looked as Esskay had when Tess first met her—too skinny, with raw patches on the fur—but their power was truly impressive. Tess unconsciously hunched her shoulders in rhythm with the dog in the lead, neck stretching forward until the cords were visible.

Then, just a few feet short of the finish line, the leader collapsed. A broken leg? The other dogs parted around the fallen dog, still intent on the rabbit. Another one fell, then another. In all, four dogs collapsed on the track well short of the finish, dark stains spreading beneath them.

''I—I don't understand,'' Tess said, fearing she did.

''They get retired racers from some sleazy trainers,'' Tommy said. ''Pay 'em twenny dollars a head, which is twenny dollars more'n most people would pay. Then these guys pay $200 to shoot 'em while they're running. Hit a dog, take home a set of ears. They haul the dead dogs off and bury 'em somewhere, somewhere secret. Don't matter if anyone finds them. Without the ears, there's no way to trace 'em.''

''But not all those dogs were killed. Two are still moving.'' She pointed to the dogs' limbs, twitching as Esskay's did in her sleep.

''They put down the maimed ones,'' Spike said. ''In some ways, it's the nicest thing they do. Now, hush a minute. The important part is coming up.''

Tess watched as a group of men streamed onto the track, waving their rifles over the heads and dancing around the bodies of the fallen dogs. They were quite pleased with themselves. It is difficult, after all, to hit a target moving almost forty miles an hour. One man leaned heavily on his gun as he grabbed the lifeless body of one dog, and Tess thought she could read his lips. "This is mine! This is mine!" The face was a little blurry, but awfully familiar. There was something in the walk, in the set of his shoulders.

"Is that—?"

"Shore is," Spike said. "Now you know why we're gonna do it the way we're gonna do it. Keep us all out of it, but still shut 'em down. Agreed?"

"Agreed," Tess said weakly. She had held onto her breakfast, but not by much. "How did you come to have this tape, Spike?"

"Guy who runs this place is a friend. *Was* a friend. Ran a decent joint, wasn't my business if people wanted to come shoot ducks. That was legal, after all. But when I stopped by last March and saw this—well, I couldn't stand by no longer. That night, when the action had moved to the house, I took the videotape out of a surveillance camera and grabbed the ears I found in the barn. I knew he'd send some guys after me. I just thought I'd have a bigger head start."

"If you hadn't taken Esskay, too, they might not have been able to link you to the missing ears and tape."

"But she smiled at me, when she saw me in the barn," Spike said, smiling himself. "How could I leave her behind?"

"I guess it's as good a time as any for me to give you something," Tess told her uncle. She walked over to the store room and opened the door Tommy had opened almost two months ago. But the dog who bounded out was a different creature—glossy fur, bright eyes, the compleat hedonist. Esskay pranced around Spike, rooting under his armpits in search of treats. *Just like she had with Crow.*

"See, she's glad to be back with you," she said. Her voice didn't catch so much as it slipped.

"Aw, she likes me because I got the keys to the pantry. That's not real likin'. Anyway, how'm I gonna walk a dog, with my bum leg?" he asked, slapping the leg in question. "You do your old Uncle Spike a big favor and keep this mutt for now, okay?"

Tess smiled tremulously: Esskay was hers. She hadn't dared to hope for it. She hadn't even admitted to herself that she really wanted the dog. As she bent down to fasten the leash to Esskay's collar—a proper nylon one, no need for a heavy chain any more, not since she had broken down and purchased her first gun two weeks ago—she asked Spike a question that had nagged her for some time.

"Where was the tape all this time?"

"In the safe deposit box Tommy and I share. Whaddaya think I am, stupid or something?"

Tess laughed then, although laughing still hurt her ribs. Sterling's kicks had cracked two of them, keeping her off the water for much of this spring and limiting her other workouts. A fitting revenge for the former fat boy, always so covetous of her metabolism. Until she healed, she actually had to watch what she ate. She wondered if this would be much of a consolation to Sterling as he sat in the city jail, charged with Wink's murder and her attempted murder.

The police had found his fingerprints on the door to Wink's Mustang; the tox screens had turned up a prescription drug that matched the painkiller Sterling had been given for his on-again, off-again carpal tunnel problems. THE EDITOR WAS A KILLER. Juicy stuff, but the *Beacon-Light* wasn't giving the story much play, preferring to concentrate on Paul Tucci and his increasingly desperate attempts to land a basketball team. The *Blight* had left it to the *Washington Post*'s media critic to chronicle Sterling's rise and fall. It hadn't been a particularly difficult story to report, despite the former editor's refusal to be interviewed. Raymond John Sterling had left a trail as bright and as slimy as a slug in the moonlight.

"No, Uncle Spike, I know you're not stupid," Tess assured him, holding her aching sides. "After all, you're the one who is going to tell me how to shut down this place without going to the police."

"I've just never felt the police really *understand* me,"
Spike said.

"They're such strictlers for detail?" Tommy added.

Tess hadn't planned on having Esskay with her when
she'd made the 11 A.M. appointment with Lionel Mabry
earlier that week, but there wasn't time to take the dog
home. Maybe it was for the best. Mabry might have kept
her waiting even longer, if it weren't for the snorting canine
companion with the impulsive bladder.

"Miss Monaghan," Mabry said, entering the conference
room. Not the grand one off the publisher's office—she no
longer rated that; but a ratty one in the news room, the site
of the endless editors' meetings.

"How you doing, Lionel?"

He seemed a little taken aback to hear her use his first
name. "I am sorry it took so long for accounting to prepare
your check—they raised a stink about some of the expenses
you submitted. Something about a bill for a bracelet? But
if you hadn't *insisted* on picking it up in person, you could
have had it days ago through the mail. You didn't need to
come down here again."

"The thing is, I have something for you," she said, holding out the tape, along with a letter explaining its contents,
the circumstances by which it had been obtained, and a list
of those people Spike knew frequented the hunting club.
Lionel scanned it quickly. He was a quick study, Tess realized. A shrewd man, shrewd enough to let others think
he was soft and unfocused. An act not unlike the dumb
jock one she liked to pull.

"It's a good story," he said. "A very good story indeed.
Generous of you to bring it to us. I know your experiences
with the paper have not been exactly, uh, copacetic."

"You should know that Paul Tucci is one of the men on
the tape. In fact, he'd probably be doing a victory dance if
it weren't for his bad knee. Is that going to be a problem?"

Mabry looked puzzled. "What a strange question. If anything, it heightens our interest."

"But you didn't want to run the original Wink story, the one with all the unsavory information about *him*, because you didn't want to kill the city's chance for a basketball team. What's the difference?"

"Miss Monaghan, you shouldn't believe everything a reporter says, even when the reporter is one of your friends." She squirmed a little under Mabry's knowing smile. "Our publisher did have some concerns along that line, but I was uncomfortable with the Wink story simply because I didn't see the point of dredging up pieces of his past when that had nothing to do with his fitness to own a sports franchise. Jack Sterling understood my feelings and he played on them. Of course, now I know Jack had his own agenda and that his articulate speeches about letting people reinvent themselves were neither dispassionate nor disinterested. But I still stand by my decision that Wink was entitled to know the names of his critics."

"You knew Sterling better than anyone here." *Anyone living*, Tess amended in her mind, thinking of Rosita. "Why did he follow you here, knowing someone might recognize him?"

"I think he wanted the job so badly he convinced himself no one would remember a fat boy named Raymond from thirty years ago. Then Wink came to an editorial board meeting and Jack was discovered. He still could have confessed—I wouldn't have fired him, although I would have made damn sure he had nothing more to do with the Wynkowski story. Instead, Jack promised to kill the story in return for his old friend's silence." Mabry paused. "Funny, how in the end it was Colleen who set Jack's downfall in motion. If she hadn't put the first story in the paper, there would never have been a second one, the one that so enraged Wink. And Jack might have figured out a less dire way to ensure Wynkowski's silence."

Tess made a polite, noncommittal sound. Lionel Mabry wasn't a bad person at heart, and that was a limitation. He could never imagine the Jack Sterling she had faced in Leakin Park. Yes, Sterling was trying to protect himself and the life he had created. But the man who had struck her had also been having a suspiciously good time. It was as if he had waited all these years to indulge those instincts again. "Bad boys get caught." Well, he was a bad boy now.

She stood to leave. "One more thing about the track story—I want Kevin Feeney to write it."

"Miss Monaghan, I do not let outsiders dictate internal decisions." Mabry was the Lion King again, tossing his hair back indignantly, growling and posturing as if she were an employee he could tyrannize.

"I understand that in theory. In practice, if you don't give the story to Feeney, I'm going to distribute copies of these videotapes to every television station in town, as well as the *New York Times*, the *Philadelphia Inquirer*, and the *Washington Post*. Be awfully embarrassing to be scooped on a story in your own backyard."

Mabry hesitated. Tess could tell he was torn between wanting to make a point and wanting exclusive title to the story. You could almost hear the point-counterpoint echoing in his brain. *Principle or potential Pulitzer? Principle or Pulitzer? Principle-Pulitzer? Principle-Pulitzer?*

Pulitzer won. She had thought it would. "I don't appreciate your tactics, but Feeney is an excellent reporter. I'm sure he'll do well on the story. Is it all right with you —" Mabry couldn't resist a small spin of sarcasm "—if I assign another reporter to work with him?"

"Sure, as long as it's someone who doesn't buy information or twist people's quotes." She regretted the words as soon as she said them. Rosita's crimes seemed so small now, certainly too small to die for.

"Do you ever think about going back into reporting?" Mabry asked, walking her to the door, always the gentleman. "We still haven't filled some of the vacancies caused by, uh, this spring's events. You obviously have potential as an investigative reporter."

The question was only two years too late. Still, it was nice to hear. Nicer still to say: "No thanks, Lionel. I have a job, a job I think I'm getting pretty good at.''

One of her ribs sent up a little shoot of pain just then, as if to remind her not to be too cocky.

Funny, to think of the injustices to which Tess had been blind before Esskay had come into her life. For example: why was it so difficult to find a restaurant in Baltimore where dogs were allowed? The bars in Fells Point welcomed them, but Baltimore had few of the sidewalk-type restaurants that made it possible for a dog to enjoy a good meal. How species-ist.

She and Feeney settled on Donna's, a local chain of coffee bars with pretty good food, once you got past its New York aspirations. And while Mount Vernon was a little grimy for outdoor dining, the day was too beautiful to waste: a cloudless sky, a light breeze that kept the sun from being too hot. Baltimore springs had the life span of a fruit fly, so it was important to cherish each fair day. Summer would be here soon enough.

Tess ordered wine, and after a brief inner struggle, decided on the mozzarella sandwich with pesto, on olive-oil-rich focaccia. She'd be back at full strength soon enough, she'd work those calories off. Feeney had the turkey sandwich with tapenade, on sourdough, while Esskay had the roast beef and provolone, hold the bread.

"This is a great story, almost makes up for me not being able to write about Sterling," Feeney said, studying her notes. "Sure it's mine?"

"As sure as I can be. There's a reason he's called the Lyin' King."

"Yeah, but he's competitive. He'll put the paper first. He always does in the end."

"So did Jack Sterling. I wonder how he would have arranged for the *Blight* to get the exclusive on *my* death?"

Esskay, who had downed her lunch in seconds, was straining at her leash, desperate to chase the dogs she saw in the park across the street. Then her quicksilver attention turned to the trash blowing past in the breeze. A white hot dog wrapper caught an eddy of air, floated upward, then reversed direction and plummeted to earth. Had Rosita fallen like that? Had she known she was falling? Had she been knocked out, like Wink, or just woozy enough for Sterling—her former boss, her former lover—to pick her up in his arms for one last embrace, then toss her over the balcony before she realized what was happening? But maybe she had jumped, as Sterling still maintained.

"Detective Tull told me they'll probably never be able to charge Sterling with Rosita's death. If she had painkillers in her blood, like Wink, it would be different. But all they found was alcohol. And it made sense for his fingerprints to be all over the apartment. He searched it, remember?"

"The yearbook never turned up, did it?"

"No, Sterling tossed it in a land fill. Lea Wynkowski has gotten it into her head that it's my fault somehow. I made it possible for her to collect the life insurance and kept her out of Paul Tucci's clutches, and she's pissed at me over a yearbook. Isn't that rich?"

"A grateful mind / By owing owes not." Feeney smirked at her blank look. "Milton. *Paradise Lost.*"

"Well, aren't you branching out?" Her voice was harsher than it meant to be, her mind unable to turn off the image of Rosita falling through space.

"Don't mind me," she added contritely. "It's just that I should have known. From the moment I saw that pizza, I should have known it was Sterling."

"How?"

"Turkey sausage. You have to be a psycho to eat that stuff."

Feeney pointed up the street. "Speaking of psychos, look at Whitney, trotting to keep up with Tyner's wheelchair on the downhill grade. I didn't know they were coming along today."

"Whitney said she had something big to tell us. I assume she finally got Tokyo."

They arrived a few seconds later, Whitney breathless from keeping pace, but still able to bark out an order for hot tea. Tyner motioned the waitress away impatiently, as if surprised that someone expected him to place an order at a restaurant.

"*Hot tea?*" Tess asked Whitney. "We know you're going to Tokyo, you don't need accessories to break the news."

"I am going to Tokyo," she said, "but not for the *Beacon-Light*. I resigned today."

Tess looked at Feeney, but he was as baffled and surprised as she was. Whitney speared a sweet potato off Tess's plate.

"It's true," Tyner confirmed. "She was in my office, going over the terms of her trust, making sure it could support her at the current yen-to-dollar exchange rate."

"Tokyo on a trust fund," Feeney said. "Very brave of you."

Tess threw a piece of focaccia at his head, missing on purpose so Esskay could have a little more food. "Hey, it *is* brave. Whitney's finally doing something for herself, instead of fulfilling everyone's expecations of her. It may be the bravest thing she's ever done."

"I'm here," Whitney said with uncharacteristic quiet. "I can speak for myself. The fact is, things aren't going so well for me at the *Beacon-Light*. As it turns out, shooting an editor in the shoulder wasn't the best career move."

"You saved my life," Tess said. "Isn't that a mitigating circumstance?

"Only to the police and grand jury. At work, I make the other editors nervous now. Especially all the new ones they keep hiring. They point and whisper behind my back. 'Shot a man in Leakin Park, just to watch him die.' I had a disagreement with my boss over punctuation recently, and he called security." Whitney sighed, then took a sip of Tess's wine, ate another of her sweet potatoes. They were back in synch again. How could Whitney move to the other side of the world?

"It's not forever," Whitney said. "Six months, maybe a year."

"But you'll be on the other side of the international date line. You'll know what's happening before I do."

"Tess—" Whitney's smile would put a Chesire cat to shame. "I always did."

Epilogue

～～～

Two weeks later, a package arrived from Tokyo. While Esskay watched, Tess pulled out a birdcage in the shape of a pagoda. The accompanying letter, on hotel stationery, said only: "Is it true the crow always flies in a straight line? I'm not so sure. Birds, like all of us, might need directions and encouragement."

Certainly, it was all the encouragement Tess needed. As she dialed the phone, she realized she had been waiting all along for someone to nudge her into action. As usual, that person was Whitney, even if she was 5,000 miles away.

"Maisie? Tess Monaghan. Where's the Floating Opera landing tonight?"

It was a new site, at least to Tess, an old cannery in West Baltimore on the same block as Bon Secours Hospital and several methadone clinics. Convenient for this crowd. She waited until 3 A.M. to show up, hoping Crow would already be on stage. He was, but without his band, or any instruments. He sat on a stool, microphone in hand, his black hair down his back in a long glossy braid without any of the not-in-nature highlights Tess remembered. He began to sing, a cappella.

The song wasn't recognizable at first, not in this dirgelike incarnation. "Thunder Road." Tess actually heard a few hisses in the audience, which apparently considered itself too avant-garde for Springsteen, Wink's beloved Boss. But something about Crow's face, and the unadorned beauty of his voice, snuffed out the crowd's initial hostility.

Did Crow remember this was the song that had been playing on Wink's stereo the night he died? He had been so taken with the detail at the time, intent on discussing various suicide-suitable songs. Now everyone knew it hadn't been Wink's choice at all, but Jack Sterling's. A town full of losers, indeed. Baltimore did have a knack for memorable losses—the '69 Orioles, the '84 Colts, 1996's American League Championship series, stolen by a twelve-year-old Yankee fan with a big glove—but it made for a gracious city. Anyone could win with élan. Baltimore knew how to lose, and how to go on, still strangely hopeful.

His song done, Crow tried to leave the stage, but the audience insisted on an encore, stamping their feet until he returned.

"It never entered my mind," he said. At first, Tess thought he was acknowledging the crowd's enthusiasm, but then he began to sing and she realized he had simply been announcing the song's title, one of her favorite Rodgers and Hart ballads. Men seldom sang it, given that it was impossible to make the kind of rhyming cheats necessary to change the gender of the song's forlorn lover, who worried about mudpacks and face powder.

> *Once, you warned me, that if you scorned me*
> *I'd sing the maiden's prayer again*
> *And wish that you were there again*
> *To get into my hair again*
> *It never entered my mind.*

Crow shook his head until the long braid unraveled and his black hair fanned out around his shoulders. *He looks like someone I know,* Tess thought. *Willie Nelson? No, it's* me. *That's* me *up there, singing about the mistake I made when I let him go. Does he know I feel that way? Or does he simply hope I feel that way? Or do I hope he hopes I feel that way?*

The set over, she worked her way down front, not caring if she was just one of several women working their way toward Crow at this precise moment. Lovely young things crowded around him, falling back when they saw her. Apparently Maisie and Lorna hadn't gotten the news out that Tess no longer had any claim on Crow.

"Rodgers and Hart," she said.

"It sank in."

"I guess anything will, if you wait long enough."

He shrugged noncommittally. This cool, taciturn Crow made her nervous, and she began babbling: "I still have Esskay. Spike got out of the hospital, and he's okay—well, his leg bothers him, but he goes to therapy—but he let me keep her. Then Whitney sent me this birdhouse from Japan and it made me think—"

Crow stared at her. She had wanted him to be older, more mature. Now he was, thanks to her. She had hurt him into adulthood.

"I'm graduating," he said at last. "My parents are so thrilled, they've given me the money they put aside for next year's tuition. We—the band and I—are going to Texas. To Austin."

"To Austin," she repeated stupidly.

"I know, it's kind of a cliché, but at least people there still get excited about music."

"For how long? I mean, how long will you be there?"

"I don't know." He hesitated—Crow, who never thought about what he was going to say next, or how to say it, or how it might sound when he did say it. "I might not like it, anyway."

"Then where will you go?"

"I don't know."

She cast around for something more to say, something that might shatter this stranger's mask and reveal the man she had known, the man she had loved without knowing she loved him, without knowing he was more of a man than the illusion of one she had desired.

"Crow—I made a mistake."

Again, he thought before he said anything. "Yes, you did."

Tess wandered outside, where she briefly considered some Scarlett O'Hara histrionics: throwing herself to the ground with wracking sobs, then lifting a luminous tear-streaked face to the heavens, vowing to get him back tomorrow. But in this neighborhood, hurling one's body about in such a heedless fashion would only result in contact with a discarded needle or a broken bottle of Pabst Blue Ribbon. She sat down gingerly on the curb, wishing she had a drink or some chocolate. But there was nothing close at hand. Even the methadone was locked up securely for the night. Methadone, now there was a concept: a drug for life that blocked the effects of the drug you really yearned for. Were there such remedies for one's heart?

Now, if Feeney were here, he would have quoted poetry, pointing out there would be world enough and time, or that we must love one another or die. But Feeney was at home, sleeping the contented sleep of a reporter with a great story. Besides, as his good buddy Auden liked to say, poetry never made anything *happen.*

Kitty would have said something at once maddeningly wise and banal, the lover *de nuit* bobbing his head in dreamy agreement. Tyner would have recommended stepping up her workouts: no time for your heart to hurt while your muscles were sore. Spike would advise playing the odds.

And inscrutable Whitney was in scrutable Japan, where it was already tomorrow. Perhaps Tess should call her and find out what the next day held. No—she'd much rather be surprised.

Permissions

"Adopting the Racing Greyhound" reprinted with permission of Macmillan Publishing USA, a Simon & Schuster Company, from ADOPTING THE RACING GREYHOUND by Cynthia A. Branigan. A Howell Book House publication © 1992 by Cynthia A. Branigan.

Lines from "September 1, 1939" from W.H. AUDEN COLLECTED POEMS by W.H. Auden, edited by Edward Mendelsohn, copyright 1940 and renewed 1968 by W.H. Auden. Reprinted by permission of Random House, Inc.

"IT NEVER ENTERED MY MIND" by Richard Rodgers and Lorenz Hart © 1940 Chappell & Co. Copyright Renewed. Rights for the Extended Renewal Term in the United States Controlled by THE ESTATE OF LORENZ HART (Administered by WB Music Corp.) and FAMILY TRUST U/W RICHARD RODGERS AND FAMILY TRUST U/W DOROTHY F. RODGERS (Administered by Williamson Music) All Rights Reserved. Used by Permission.

New York Times Notable Author

LAURA LIPPMAN

NO GOOD DEEDS

978-0-06-057073-6/$7.99/$10.99 Can

When her well-meaning boyfriend brings a street kid into their lives, p.i. Tess Monaghan doesn't know that the boy holds an important key to the unsolved slaying of a young federal prosecutor.

TO THE POWER OF THREE

978-0-06-050673-5/$7.99/$10.99 Can

Three high school friends are found shot in the girls' bathroom. Two are wounded—one critically—and the third girl is dead.

BY A SPIDER'S THREAD

978-0-06-050671-1/$7.99/$10.99 Can

When his wife and children vanish, a successful furrier turns to p.i. Tess Monaghan for help.

And in hardcover

WHAT THE DEAD KNOW

978-0-06-112885-1/$24.95/$31.50 Can

Visit www.AuthorTracker.com for exclusive information on your favorite HarperCollins authors.

Available wherever books are sold or please call 1-800-331-3761 to order.

LL1 1206